Latin American
Popular Theatre

Judith A. Weiss

with

Leslie Damasceno

Donald Frischmann

Claudia Kaiser-Lenoir

Marina Pianca

Beatriz J. Rizk

Latin American Popular Theatre

The First Five Centuries

University of New Mexico Press

Albuquerque

FIRST EDITION

Library of Congress Cataloging–in–Publication Data
Weiss, Judith A.
Latin American popular theatre : the first five centuries / Judith A. Weiss with Leslie Damasceno . . . [et al.]. — 1st ed.
p. cm.
Includes bibliographical references and index.
ISBN 0-8263-1401-5 (cl). —
ISBN 0-8263-1402-3 (pap)
1. Theater—Latin America—History. 2. Theater and society—Latin America. 3. Latin America—Popular culture. I. Title.
PN2309.W45 1993
792'.098—dc20 92–19063
CIP

Contents

Preface

This history of Latin American popular theatre is the first full-length cooperative study published by the ATINT Research Collective. The collective, which is made up of the six members of the Executive (1985–92) of the Association of New Theatre Workers and Researchers (Asociación de Trabajadores e Investigadores del Nuevo Teatro), was constituted in 1986 to join the theatre history already undertaken by the project director on a research grant from the Social Sciences and Humanities Research Council of Canada. It is a groundbreaking project in several respects. The collective nature of the research, the planning, and the writing make it, as far as we know, the first project of its kind to embrace the humanities and the social sciences. Moreover it has come to reflect both the philosophy and the methods most commonly found in our main subject, the New Popular Theatre, in which a common value system serves to unify a diversity of currents of thought and practice. The object of the collective effort is not only the final product, but the very process of exploration, creation, and intellectual growth.

The geographic parameters of our subject caused some debate within the group. We all recognize that Latin America as a geopolitical entity encompasses more than just the immediate past colonies of Spain and Portugal, which are known more precisely as Ibero-America. Haiti, Guadeloupe and Martinique, and the English-speaking West Indies and

Guyana are all partners in the Caribbean basin, as are the English-speaking communities of the Atlantic Coast of Central America, and they share a common history with the regions that we cover in our study. While we would have wished to include them, the scope of our undertaking was sufficiently ambitious, and we were unable to do so. Yet with this book we are also proposing an operational model for a social history of the theatre that can be extended to the French- and English-speaking Caribbean.

Even within the geographic confines covered in our work, there were complex questions concerning the history of theatre itself and its broader context with which we did attempt to deal. Although it was clearly impossible to study the roots of the New Theatre movement of the past thirty years without an understanding of the political theories and forces that affected popular culture, we were not seeking simple deterministic patterns. We realized, of course, that we would not be able to integrate all the possible approaches and methodologies that seemed to be called into play by the subject, but we were compelled nonetheless to look more carefully at the ideological currents that have influenced Latin American societies and their arts.

None of us thought, when we undertook this project, that it would be easy to navigate through the many, sometimes blurred or conflicting definitions of popular theatre and popular culture, or through the uneven development of the societies that generated, nurtured, and sometimes destroyed the types of cultural creation that we undertook to study. Our individual work on different geographic areas of Latin America and on common problems of the contemporary theatres of the hemisphere had already demonstrated to us the complexity of the problem, and our common work on the *Nuevo Teatro Popular* (New Popular Theatre) of the 1960s and 1970s in numerous academic conferences and finally in this project, enabled us to define the problem more sharply.

It became clear that multiple approaches would be beneficial for dealing with the diverse factors (social, historical, artistic, and ideological) that determined the Nuevo Teatro Popular, and so we sought to balance Latin American and non–Latin American approaches to our subject. In our introduction we summarize some of the key elements of those readings that either coincided with (or substantiated) our position or offered an interesting new underpinning for our study. Together they approximate the interdisciplinary approach that we intended. We have not omitted any valuable source intentionally, nor have we attempted to consider every major source from outside Latin America, because we chose to concentrate on the most significant Latin American contributions in the field of popular culture and Nuevo Teatro Popular.

In part I we turn to the origins of theatre in the Americas, with an emphasis on traditional drama and nonliterate cultures, comparing the theatrical forms of three principal cultural currents that formed post-conquest America. Part II emphasizes the broad categories of urban theatre, including the organization of institutions and space, the genres that reflect a syncretic culture, the growth of nationhood, and issues of race and class.

A double current persists over the past two hundred years: the submerging or marginalization of popular expression and the appropriation of popular elements by a commercial theatre that comes to be considered popular theatre. In part III, an overview of the New Popular Theatre, we were therefore interested primarily in establishing points of contact for our intertextual study, both among similar theatrical phenomena in different regions and between earlier forms of production and those of the popular theatre. We survey the principal currents of this broad movement, and we describe the commonalities and differences between theatre produced primarily as art and the more instrumental theatre of education and development.

One object in writing this book was to highlight the relationship between popular and populist, between the marginal/peripheral and the dominant/central, and ultimately, between a theatre that serves existing hegemonic interests in a variety of ways and one that could pave the way for the formation of a counter-hegemonic culture.

Introduction: Charting Our Course

Ideology and the Problematization of Culture

The social history of popular theatre (that most collective form of cultural creation) cannot be divorced from a unifying approach to history; most of our readings generally follow the lines proposed by Antonio Gramsci (1957, 1971, 1977) and Lucien Goldmann (1976). Our study takes into account the social history of the Americas, with their particularities of class and ethnicity, and the history of the theatre, particularly the popular theatre, which we shall be examining in the context of Latin American society.

The Nuevo Teatro Popular (New Popular Theatre) of the past three to four decades is itself a product of artists and writers whose methodology and philosophical orientation were influenced by some of the same authors. This international movement, which reached its peak of activity between 1965 and 1975, originated in university and workers' theatre and in Brechtian art theatre. It consciously integrated the more appealing elements of commercial popular theatre (e.g., vaudeville and musical comedy) and street theatre (buskers) and explored folk drama as a source and a viable medium. Because the determinants of the New Popular Theatre were both artistic and social, our initial studies of this cultural movement led us to search for its roots in the social history of the theatre—particularly those forms of theatre or dramatic performance that can best be termed popular (Williams 1988).

The work of Raymond Williams emerged as the most directly significant in the Gramscian school. Armando Mattelart, Néstor García Canclini, Jesús Martín Barbero, Guillermo Bonfill Batalla, and Roger Bartra all apply derivations of Gramsci's models to their studies of popular culture, cultural politics, and mass communications, specifically in Latin America. Bartra (1989) is of particular interest in our approach to historical contexts because he identifies "prototypical dramatic characters" as myths of cultural identity that were instrumental in creating the consensus to legitimate the modern state.

In the area of Latin American intellectual history and the social history of cultural creation, Hernán Vidal and scholars of the Minnesota school, and Jean Franco and scholars working mainly out of New York and the West Coast (e.g., Yudice and Masiello) have pioneered the North American scholarly study of marginal literatures (particularly by women). Most of these studies, undertaken since the late 1970s, broaden the scope of a field that owes a great deal to the contributions of Angel Rama and Alejandro Losada in the 1960s and 1970s.[1]

For dramatic theory and its connection to cultural production and cultural politics, we draw most directly on the works of Enrique Buenaventura and Augusto Boal. They coincide in ranking the problem of hegemony (whether of class or of international relations) as a determining factor for the study of popular theatre, and of Latin American popular theatre in particular.

None of these scholars and critics avoids the critical and complex questions of class and historical bias. These are seen as a given, built into literary theory and into the study of cultural production. It is this vantage point that has allowed us to recognize the intermediary spaces and the contradictions, and to take into account the complicated relations of class, ethnicity, and historical development, as well as the flux of appropriated, traditional, and imposed elements. This is why, while acknowledging the ambiguities that plague both the interpretation and the determination of historical influence, we find a certain coherence emerging in Marxist and neo-Marxist scholarship, which has become increasingly unified in Gramscian approaches to the problem of cultural creation.

In the following sections we shall be referring to other sources that have helped to develop our conceptual approaches to the problems of this type of historical study. We encountered little difficulty in reconciling studies of specific fields (genres, performance, or organizations) with our own approach to popular theatre as historically bound and class determined.

With respect to geographic categories, the concept of regionalization proposed by Angel Rama (1974a, 1974b, 1984) has been useful for framing the vicissitudes of popular theatre in a shifting social and intellectual world. The more traditional approach to "national" literatures, which tends to be restricted to political boundaries, could not be ignored or entirely discarded, especially in discussing the period of approximately 150 years in which the nation states were formed and zealously consolidated. But even within the category of the "national" theatres of Latin America, we face the additional problem of narrow geographic and class definitions, not to mention the fact that *national theatre* has usually meant conventional, scripted drama.

Historical documentation on the dramatic product exists almost exclusively for performances in playhouses of the cities and larger towns of Latin America, which provided entertainment primarily for the more affluent or the emerging middle sectors. For the most part, then, documentation is scarcest in the area with which we are most concerned: the creations and collective expressions of and by the least-dominant sectors of Latin American society (with the possible exception of traditional popular forms, especially Native American drama). Much research and retrieval is currently being done by theatre workers and scholars in local and national archives, through oral history, and through the study of residual forms; they have been emerging in increasing numbers through small publications, research reviews, and conferences.

We were also looking for a more sensible approach to dealing with the three centuries prior to nationhood and with the decades of transnational cultural production that have followed the Cuban Revolution and that coincide with the global spread of a transnational economy of culture. Although national cultures remain important, there is now a growing reassessment of that importance because of the increased value assigned to residual and traditional cultures, which often follow regional patterns that defy the borders drawn in the formation of the nation states.

All these factors begged for an alternative to the standard, quasi-encyclopedic approaches to Latin American theatre and dramatic literature. For the purposes of this study, there was a more appropriate framework, offered by the social sciences: geo-socioeconomic features, which provide more consistent and coherent parameters for grouping literatures and cultural forms. The Americas are divided, accordingly, into cultural spheres that reflect demographic patterns and economic history. For example, Mesoamerican cultures would group sections of southern Mexico with parts of the Central American republics, and the Andean culture would group the interior of Ecuador, Colombia, Peru, and Bolivia with northern Chile and Argentina.

Another important factor to be taken into account is that of the differences between urban and rural cultures, despite the points of contact that may exist between urban and rural cultures. It is also important to recognize the existence, particularly in major cities like Havana, Buenos Aires, and Mexico, of stage activity directed toward lower economic sectors of the urban population.[2] While we wish to avoid the (mis)use of the term *popular* as a broad category to describe this successful commercial theatre, we do acknowledge its importance in the evolution of a historical line that leads directly to the Nuevo Teatro Popular.[3]

Historical Evolution of Latin American Popular Theatre

Just as regional approaches offer a more faithful reflection of the long-established cultural areas of the hemisphere, periodization proposes that literary studies be closely related to economic history, specifically to the encompassing periods of economic development that are in turn linked to geography and demographics.[4] Because this periodization assumes some degree of integration of cultural subjects and their products with the dominant economy, it can usually serve as no more than a general point of reference in the study of indigenous and peasant cultures.

Once indigenous cultures had been effectively destroyed or relegated to the periphery, what culture emerged over the first three centuries was predominantly an extension of the ideological apparatus of imperial Spain and Portugal. In addition there was a growing penetration by other influences (European, North American, Asian) into both the dominant and the popular cultures that developed in America. It would be imprecise, therefore, to accept uncritically the notion of syncretism as a determining dynamic of Latin American cultures, except where the population was predominantly non-European; even there, the dominant culture managed to remain relatively free of non-European elements.

There are some exceptions to the latter, namely in "borderline" areas. Examples are Caribbean and Brazilian society in areas heavily populated by Afro-Americans, or remote communities in the interior, where whites were often greatly outnumbered by Indians and where non-Hispanic culture influenced the elite through servants, nursemaids, street vendors, and concubines or occasional lovers from other social castes. Yet even in these cases, the non-Hispanic influence remained relegated to marginal or private frames of reference (an example of this being the knowledge of Guarani or Quechua by non-Indians, who will rarely, if ever, speak it among themselves), and it was often suppressed before adulthood as inferior or inconsequential.

Another important feature of the sociohistorical context in which we encounter Latin American theatre is the caste system that dominated the hemisphere and continues to be a determining element in social and cultural relations. Over a period of close to five hundred years, theatre has been both a diversion for the elites in which European upper-class models predominated and a form of popular entertainment more open to the cultural influence of marginal groups such as peasants, immigrants, artisans or even slaves as well as to non-European ethnicity and geographic disparity.

This diversity in the social history of the Americas is matched by the range of artistic influences that can be found here. In reviewing the medieval and early Renaissance currents of the theatre brought by the Europeans (both secular and liturgical/ritual forms), we paid particular attention to Spanish and Latin American studies of genres and types of theatre and performance, from the medieval *autos* and sixteenth-century *pasos* to the evangelical drama of the missionaries. We have also included an inquiry into indigenous and African theatres and have looked both at the entertainments offered at schools, universities, and viceregal courts and at the public pageants and festivals that fuse the elite and the popular, the European and the non-European.

We attempt to place them in the context of studies of European drama and of ritual, play and popular entertainment.[5]

The modern idea of "national" theatre or "national" culture can be clearly linked to the emergence of the nation states after the wars of independence and to programs of national consolidation whose key propagandists would almost invariably be the intellectuals and writers who belonged to the emerging ruling groups. This is one important reason why, by the mid-nineteenth century, we see popular cultures being definitively marginalized by the arbiters of taste or fragmented and assimilated in a decontextualized fashion by new forms of what we choose to term populist culture (which until recently have been widely labelled "popular").[6]

These forms served as "unifying" value systems for projecting and reinforcing dominant national and class ideologies.[7] Populist elements were cultivated so that the point of view of the popular or marginalized classes and their very dignity as subjects were often trampled or ridiculed in crass stereotypes. This was frequently done within the framework of apparent criticism that, upon closer analysis, seems to have been designed to defuse potential conflict rather than to analyze the issues—a product that one might call farce disguised as satire.

By the twentieth century, the dominant theatre ran to polar extremes: on one hand, serious drama and, later, experimental theatre that played to limited audiences; on the other hand, productions of mass appeal, such as variety shows, melodramas, and comedy, which often served as a medium and a training ground for some of the most talented composers, actors, and singers. Enter, shortly after mid-century, the Nuevo Teatro Popular, with its roots in workers' theatre and the Independent theatre of the 1930s, in circuses and tent shows, in Brecht and Piscator and their followers (Strehler's Piccolo Teatro di Milano, Mnouchkin's Théatre du Soleil, Vilar's T.N.P., and Peter Brook). This movement would offer an alternative to variety shows and musicals and to other dominant forms of professional theatre that appealed to small, select audiences, and it would validate often-forgotten forms that persisted in marginal areas of the cities and the countryside.

Popular Culture, Popular Theatre

The dichotomy between dominant theatre and the Nuevo Teatro Popular led us to examine the articulation of popular entertainment or popular culture vis-à-vis mass culture. We surveyed the evolution of the circus (which one hundred years ago provided the space for genuine popular theatre) and derived spaces, such as the Mexican tent shows (*carpas*), where whole families of actors and musicians learned and practiced their art.[8] We also surveyed the carnivals, which have never ceased to be an important space for expressions of popular theatre.[9]

Mass culture, a modern category that in some aspects coincides with commercial culture, has exercised an ever-growing influence on popular culture since the last century (with, for example, the mass production and distribution of sheet music); it has also been the single main competitor of popular culture. This is why it is important, in our opinion, to distinguish between mass culture and popular culture (see Adorno and Horkheimer 1984, Mattelart 1973).

Margulis and other Latin American social scientists (writing in Colombres 1983) provide a useful analysis of the antagonism between mass culture and popular culture. Although it is difficult to speak of uncontaminated exponents of either of these categories, the most fundamental distinctions can be traced through the examination of processes of gestation and control of cultural production (i.e., by whom and for whom culture is produced), or by analyzing the nature of the relationship established with the audience (as passive consumer vs. active participant).[10]

The influence of mass culture on the development of a working-class aesthetic is not to be underestimated, although some critics prefer to stress those aspects that supposedly reflect an autonomous workers' culture. In his work on the British theatre, John McGrath tackled the problem of middle-class vs. working-class taste in a way that reflects some of the categories outlined by Brecht (McGrath 1981, Brecht 1964). He does not enter into the influence of mass culture on working-class theatre, but he does identify elements of the preferred theatre of the working class. These, in turn, coincide to a great extent with those of Margulis et al. and dovetail with some positions of the leading practitioners of the Nuevo Teatro Popular. McGrath's categories, described under the general rubric of "taste," are similar to categories over which critics, scholars, and the audiences themselves continue to argue in the Latin American context, where the stress is on class identification or degrees of alienation.

In this regard Carlos Monsiváis (1985) offers an interesting counterpart to McGrath in his analysis of the impact of transnational culture on the Mexican urban working class through mass media and mass culture. Monsiváis takes a hard look at the alienation of urban workers from class identity and from traditional and national culture, focusing on this alienation rather than on the assimilation and recodification of elements of mass culture as seen in the work of many creators of an urban popular culture, from the carnival *murgas* (mummers) of the River Plate region to Mexican theatre workers like Los Chidos.

These critics are most pertinent, of course, to twentieth-century urban society, and both focus on a particular socioeconomic sector as consumer and recipient of cultural creation. But one might be able to extend to other periods in our study both Monsiváis's first-hand analysis of the impact of dominant, or hegemonic, culture on a weakened culture of a subordinate group and McGrath's emphasis on the continued differentiation of working-class values and preferences. The latter would be facilitated by an enquiry into the historical origins of those preferences, some of which could well be the products of imposed or assimilated values.

The Nuevo Teatro Popular, like its forerunners, can be appreciated for its multiplicity of approaches, of styles, of subjects, and of primary objectives. But while the intentions of the earlier manifestations of popular theatre were as diverse as their artistic expression and the groups in which they originated, the Nuevo Teatro Popular is all, in one way or another, part of an overarching project of radical social transformation. The contributions of its predecessors (with all their contradictions) emerged with a commonality of purpose in the Nuevo Teatro Popular. In describing these connections, then, we are also seeking to prove the depth of historical identification of this new popular theatre with regard to national culture, social problems, and art.

I

Roots of the Popular Theatre

1 • *Frames of Reference*

The beginnings of a Latin American theatre can be traced to the encounters of the cultures of three continents. Its development parallels the evolution of two primary sectors that made up that new society: the oral or nonliterate cultures, identified largely with the powerless and the marginal; and the literate culture of the elites, increasingly identified with power and authority, as the strength of the creole sector grew in relation to Spain or Portugal.[1]

If most theatre historians and literary scholars find it impossible to speak of the emergence of a specifically American theatre before the last years of the colonial period, in the late eighteenth century, it is mainly because their studies have covered primarily the study of dramatic literature and the evolution of the formal theatre in urban settings (moreover, most of this theatre is heavily derivative of European trends). Anthropologists, sociologists, and theatre historians who attach some importance to social history subscribe to a slightly different view, with a greater emphasis on acculturation or transculturation and syncretism, and the oral cultures and nonelite societies. Outside the realm of the literary studies there is a greater willingness to recognize traditional and folk drama and dramatic forms as theatre.[2]

Our approach to the theatre of Latin America since the conquest takes both tendencies into account. We do not dispute that some theatrical traditions of each of the three main strains (Iberian, Native American, and African) were preserved relatively intact because of the insulation (or isolation) of the classes or social groups from one another. On the other hand, this separation was not always impervious to external forces, and some of the most distinctive forms of theatre or dramatic traditions that can be classified as popular and identified with specific cultures include important elements from other cultures. In fact many derive from scripted texts, be these medieval miracle plays or nineteenth-century reconstructions of indigenous traditions.

Most postconquest Native American, African-American, and folk theatre must be understood in terms of syncretism. Oral and nonliterate cultures have contributed entire genres and important isolated elements to the development of an American theatre. At the same time, one cannot speak of purely oral or literate cultures, since powerless, marginal classes, for whom the written word carried prestige, were open to adopting scripts created by the more literate sectors; similarly, the cultural creations of the literate sectors in America, just as in Spain and Portugal, were never completely closed to popular influences.[3] We should therefore stress that here we shall be discussing types of theatrical expression that belong to, are rooted in, or have persisted primarily in the nonliterate sectors of Latin America. Any absolute categorization of theatre as purely oral or literate would, in our view, be quite arbitrary.

The first task is to identify key aspects of the dramatic traditions that met in America, and then to outline some of the most important traditions that became established during the colonial period and beyond, with reference to the three main bloodlines (America, Africa, and Europe). Our emphasis lies in (a) the traditional-popular, residual, and folk cultures, and (b) their points of contact, correspondence, crossover, or acculturation in the formation of a syncretic theatre.

The types of culture with which we are dealing have contributed theatrical forms or types of performance whose legitimacy as such is sometimes challenged. We decided to include in our study such forms as dance drama, ritual drama, and pretheatrical forms not only because they constitute the origins of popular theatre in the Americas, but also—and equally importantly—because many can in fact themselves be categorized as theatre. In his defense of Native American drama as theatre, Balmori (1955) listed a series of justifications that apply equally, in most cases, to European and African drama. We summarize these criteria as follows:

1. Use of specialized as well as general spaces (markets, public squares);
2. Movement, often with dance and music;
3. Dramatic structure (in many, if not all, works);
4. Dialogue, usually repetitive and formulaic (ritual/liturgical);
5. Religious nature, ranking it with early Mediterranean drama. It often uses mimesis (through sacrifices, personification of natural forces);
6. Cult of nature: nature plays, with nature's rhythms reflected in humans; fertility rituals;
7. Training and rehearsal of performers: in most advanced civilizations, schools for actors; high social position of official artists;
8. Stock characters, including spirits of the dead or of nature, animals, warriors, knaves, the sick and diseased, etc.

The criteria are amply met by most of the dramatic forms we have examined as well as by the process that led to their creation.

This broad coincidence of types of theatrical representation and of their roles in various cultures is one important reason for emphasizing the interconnections. Such an emphasis was not only unavoidable but deliberate; it is precisely this cultural quilt that interested us most when we first undertook this study. The patterns of transculturation were established relatively early in the history of the Latin American colonies, and they were the most deceptive to research, because what appeared to provide a wealth of information often left us with a number of unsolved puzzles, such as missing links that might prove influence or direct contacts between regions. In some isolated cases, what our most authoritative sources would define as one thing (e.g., a purely pre-Colombian or African provenance) might, with sources from alternative disciplines, be construed as something quite different.

Rather than simply ignore or evade subjects that offered more doubts than answers, it seemed appropriate to confront this question of conflicting interpretations and missing information. Just as it was not our intention to risk reproducing the tone or the scholasticism of colonial writing, neither would it behoove us to feign an impossibly pure attachment to the clarity and apparent directness of the oral tradition. As we walk the fine line between general overview and detailed chronicle, between straightforward attribution and cloudy or complicated relationships, we are trying in this part to capture the dialectics of dominant vs. marginal, of European vs. "other," of written vs. oral, of cultural growth and free expression vs. stagnation and intellectual or religious repression. These are the dialectics that set the stage during most of the past five centuries for the popular theatre of our time.

We must bear in mind several aspects of traditional and folk drama. Such drama usually originates with authority, e.g., the priest or native equivalent in the Church, such as the *cofradías* that sponsor the holiday performances, or a secular substitute such as a teacher or elected leaders, who present reenactments of historical events. It rarely, if ever, questions authority or challenges fundamental beliefs. It actually honors authority, either directly, in the person of the councillors, the government, or the priest; or symbolically, in its devotion to religious icons. It glorifies the same ritual repetition in the broader sense, as it perpetuates age-old traditions, usually with little structural modification. It also tends to perpetuate an asynchronic world view through such devices as telescoping and interchangeable roles identified with social status and religious meaning rather than with historical specificity.

We shall not enter in detail into the economic implications of the practice of folk drama, except to make two points that we consider important. First of all, although there may be similarities and even coincidences among the festivals and rituals of tribes, villages, or regions of the Americas, the quality and level of sophistication of the productions and the number of dramas, dances, etc., that they perform are contingent on several factors. These include: level of acculturation and relative degree of isolation of the community in question, which would determine the degree of "purity" of the provenance of the festival, drama, or ritual; historical changes in the sponsorship of the productions, including the intervention of government authorities or the decision by local political leaders to reduce spending on religious festivals, which has been known to bankrupt individuals and families; and the ethnic composition of the community and the level and type of political consciousness of its leaders, which would determine the will to continue or revive ancestral forms or to inject political concerns into the art.

Another point that bears emphasizing is the socioeconomic reality that determines the cultural creativity of Native Americans and peasants alike: over four centuries, a life of abject poverty or at best an existence controlled by the whims of nature, the government, or the nearest landowners. Communities that managed, at various times in their history, to escape the worst of such conditions have produced or maintained the most sophisticated dramatic forms; yet even the most impoverished cherish their cultural expression. Major catastrophes, such as earthquakes or massive forced displacements, may slow or interrupt the process of cultural creation, but it is only the ideological onslaughts of the sort that have been seen recently, after almost five hundred years of survival, that threaten to annihilate the culture of entire groups.

The reversal of the urban-rural ratio in Latin America in the last decades of this century (with 70 percent of the population now living around major cities) has marked an unparalleled shift from the traditional cultural bases (village and rural communities) to the atomizing alienation of megacity culture. But even where traditional demographic patterns might have remained, a variety of forces have militated against folk culture.

Weakened by a context of war, political repression, and economic collapse, communities have to deal simultaneously with a number of overwhelming forces. There is the influence of large numbers of local people returning from abroad with their values transformed, the breakup of the extended family or clan through shifts in the economic base, and the forced relocation by agribusiness or the state (and, in the case of Guatemala, the concentration of various *etnias*, or tribal groups, into the same "strategic hamlets," where their individual identities are diluted and where the "national," i.e., hegemonic, white man's language and culture are imposed).

Fundamentalist evangelical sects have invaded the entire continent (numbering over four hundred in Bolivia alone in 1990, according to government statistics); their missionaries, from Mexico to Paraguay, are forcing local people to abandon their "idolatrous" ceremonies. Finally, local air waves, theatres, and newspapers are dominated by a mass media that employs a "universal" (i.e., foreign, nonspecific) discourse and by foreign cultural products; the influence of local ownership and input—for good or for bad—has gradually been diminishing, and the infrastructure through which local forms might persist or evolve at their own pace is being lost. Not only does polyester displace local wool and plastic replace wood, but a driving, alienating consumerism and desperate attempts to survive are fast replacing traditional binding beliefs and rites of ecological significance. For "pure" entertainment, there are consumer-oriented game shows that reinforce atomization and soap operas that project elite, urban lifestyles: passive, individual viewing that is displacing participatory rituals. Against this dismal background, the popular theatre of the late twentieth century has been striving to draw new strength for its communities from traditional forms and themes.

The theatre that we describe below has, increasingly, an element of nostalgia about it, as people refer to a given form or style of performance as something they used to see before their village could no longer present it. The point of our account is, however, not to mourn, but to stress the resilience that has characterized folk drama and Native American forms through the centuries, and to point to those sources from which the contemporary popular theatre has drawn to fulfill its objectives (as we shall see in part III): the preservation of historical identity, the renewal of myths and legends as cultural models, and the rooting of the popular struggle in a broader perspective, such as that which myth and history can offer.[4]

The Historical Context

Two aspects of the conquest of the Western Hemisphere by Spain and Portugal are of particular importance to the history of the theatre: the stage of historical development of the European cultures at the time of the conquest, and the imposition of a culture based on the written word on societies where its equivalent was the oral tradition or forms of representation that were chiefly mnemonic devices for spoken, sung, or dramatized cultural forms. This holds true both for the aboriginal cultures and for the African cultures transplanted to the Americas by the slave trade.

The Europeans

The early stages of Iberian colonization were still connected to the culture of the late Middle Ages and the recently completed crusade to expel the Moslems from Spain. This task, which had occupied Iberian Christians for the better part of six hundred years, resulted in the establishment of Spain as a unified theocratic and secular nation and was a driving force in the project of empire launched with the fall of Granada, the expulsion of the Jews and confiscation of their property, and the first exploratory journeys of Christopher Columbus. At the same time, Portugal was engaged in consolidating new, alternative trade routes to the Orient that had been established as an early response to the closing of the Mediterranean routes by Venetians and Turks.

The transfer of medieval culture to the Americas, with the subsequent playing out in the new settlements of every successive stage of Spanish and Portuguese cultural development, has been an accepted focus of the historian. Its importance for our study lies in the fact that it was mainly a medieval European culture that took root in areas that would later become isolated from the dominant urban culture, with its ties to the evolving cultural production of Europe. By and large the themes, genres, and methods of production that became part of a residual popular culture in the Americas were those of the late Middle Ages and the early Renaissance.

The Africans

The Spanish and Portuguese were familiar with foreign civilizations before the conquest of America. Their complex, six-hundred-year relationship with the Muslim culture on Iberian soil, followed by the development of trade (including slave trade) with Africa, is emphasized in much of the literature as a factor that predisposed them to adapting with relative ease to a more intimate coexistence with Africans and Native Americans than the one enjoyed by the English or the French. The Muslims, known indiscriminately as Moors, were undeniably a part of Iberian culture at the time of the conquest, even though they usually embodied the spiritual and political Other, the dangerous Antagonist who had to be reduced and converted.

Africans, on the other hand, were not the Enemy, although their skin color, their languages, and their music were sometimes identified with the devil (Weber de Kurlat 1963:390–91). Eventually thousands of black Africans were brought to Spain and Portugal in the mid-1400s, to serve mainly as domestic slaves or servants; many were ultimately freed, to become servants, craftsmen, sailors, and other workers. One indication of their importance was the installation of a special "juez de negros," or judge for blacks, in Seville in the 1470s. Another sign of their presence in Iberian culture (albeit as foreigners) was the inclusion of African or black character types, with their speech patterns, dances, and music, in comedies of the early sixteenth century (Weber de Kurlat 1963:388). Blacks accompanied the earliest explorers of the Americas as crew members and craftsmen.

Africans and Iberians of African origin were first organized into *cabildos* and religious cofradías in Seville in the fourteenth century (Ortiz 1951:15). The first African slaves who came from Spain formed cabildos in every town or city of Cuba, according to their nation or tribe of origin. Members of both sexes met at rented houses or in their own homes to celebrate holidays, and they also set up mutual-aid societies with elected officers. The cabildo provided a space and a cultural context in which to continue their magic-religious practices, although their own fetishes were replaced by Christian icons. The cabildos decayed after the abolition of slavery, in 1886, and especially after 1888, when the civil government questioned the tradition and forced them to adhere to the laws of the colony; they then adopted the names of Christian saints, registered at the nearest churches, and agreed to transfer their assets to the Catholic church if they dissolved. This process apparently accelerated the syncretism of African and European cultures in Cuba and Puerto Rico, with a similar process taking place in certain regions of Brazil (Ortiz 1921).

The industrial model of the sugar and cotton plantations was not introduced into America until the mid- or late eighteenth century; the sugar plantations for which African labor was imported during almost three centuries after the first factories were established by the Portuguese on the West African coast and by the Spaniards in the Canary Islands, were small or medium-size enterprises. But in the sixteenth and seventeenth centuries, the Spaniards and their creole descendants did misuse African slaves on a grander scale, first in the mines of the Antilles, and then in the mines and farming estates of Mexico and the Andean region, where they were brought to replace the Native Americans, who were being driven to extinction.

We shall not enter into the theories espoused by Jan Carew (1988) and others, although some of the evidence that trade links had existed between Africa and America prior to the conquest is fairly convincing. The fact is that Native Americans as well as whites of the indentured servant and the artisan classes expressed relatively little prejudice against blacks as a group, while the individual black person, as Other, was often the target of what North Americans would consider to be racist comments and humor, a custom that has gone largely unchallenged until very recently. There was intermarriage between blacks and Native Americans, usually in the cities or in remote areas where runaway slaves set up their settlements, such as in the Guyanas and Venezuela.

Blacks in the Spanish and Portuguese colonies could buy their freedom with relatively few obstacles, and the crown established certain laws guaranteeing their basic rights. Black freedmen as well as many slaves worked most commonly as artisans and servants, or became identified with certain unusual occupations, such as the oarsmen of the Orinoco River and its tributaries. Thus African cultural influences (however diluted) extended beyond the sugar and cotton regions of Brazil and the Caribbean basin, into inland pockets (many of them urban) and into trades also held by whites, mulattoes, or mestizos. Slave rebellions—no less uncommon than uprisings by Native Americans—occurred throughout the colonies from before 1520 (in the Antilles).

The maroon (runaway slave) settlements probably played a significant role in the preservation of African cultures. Many of those settlements survived successfully for decades, some of them for centuries; their contribution to the wars of independence was particularly important in Cuba, where they also brought their traditional culture, including the dramatic art of the storytellers. Similar enclaves survived for varying periods of time in Brazil, Jamaica, and the Guyanas.

The Native Americans

The relationship between whites and Native Americans was marked by almost continual violence. The genocidal scale of the violence visited by Spaniards upon local peoples has been variously documented, and apologists of Spain notwithstanding, respectful and humane treatment of aboriginal people tended to be the exception rather than the rule. The aboriginal population of most of the Caribbean islands was exterminated; according to Todorov (1984) and other scholars, millions, rather than thousands, of aboriginal people on the mainland, chiefly in Mexico, Central America, and Peru, were wiped out by slave labor, which was often imposed under the guise of "tributary service" and justified as a continuation of Aztec or Inca laws, when it was not exacted as punishment in a "just war" (e.g., in response to rebellions or resistance).

The reality of the genocide cannot be disputed (Todorov 1984:133–34). Nor can the wholesale overturning of aboriginal cultures by the ideological advance guard of the empires, the priests and friars, whose chief objective was to convert local peoples into docile servants of the crown and its representatives. The fact that these religious men and women were also sincerely shocked by the practices that they encountered (human sacrifice, polygamy, idolatry, sodomy) explains the zeal and resourcefulness with which they used every mechanism at their disposal to change aboriginal customs and to substitute for polytheism and animism what they believed to be the only true and humane religion.

From the earliest expeditions, scholars like Fr. Raimundo Pané studied aboriginal cultures with an intense and genuine interest, at the same time as they documented the flora and the fauna (Pane 1974). Missionaries collected and codified or translated sacred texts and legends of local peoples, only to burn the originals along with the idols. After learning one or more aboriginal languages, some missionaries set about translating the New Testament or compiling dictionaries and texts of local languages. It would be difficult to decipher the true motivation of most of the missionaries, but there can be no doubt that many of those who chose to live under the most difficult conditions and to travel in hostile territory eventually came to share some of the world view of "their" aboriginals after decades of living among them.

If transculturation occurred anywhere, it would have been in the spaces carved out by the missionaries in rural areas, where the dedication of a small minority introduced European religion but could never entirely wipe out aboriginal beliefs. In urban centers aboriginal people and mestizos received a basic education in Catholic schools and provided their labor and artistic talent for the construction and decoration of churches and public buildings, while they also participated as a marginal and scorned minority in the life of the white elite. They were a dominant presence in the kitchens, the nurseries, and the marketplace, touching the white man's children subliminally with their language, their songs and stories, and their world view, much as the African Americans would in geographic areas where they constituted the majority of the servant class.

Identifying the "Popular" in Colonial Theatre

The term *popular* can be applied, according to one or another of its definitions, to much of colonial theatre, but particularly to what is commonly known as folk drama and to the remnants of European or indigenous forms that persisted primarily in rural areas. Few if any of these dramatic expressions are free of ideological contradictions, however; to some extent they can be seen as both hegemonic and counter-hegemonic exercises, however passive, neutral, or apolitical they may appear to be. It might therefore be helpful to review the applications of the term (as outlined in the introduction) to different expressions that have coexisted since the conquest.

Traditional cultures, which can be classified as popular insofar as they are expressions of an inclusive and participatory society, came together in the Americas for the most part through violent confrontations. After those initial confrontations, however, the struggle by the conquerors and the conquered, respectively, to impose and to preserve their national culture—however recent its formation—was waged through more subtle and intelligent strategies. One important cultural form of each of the three general groupings that made up Latin American societies (the Europeans, the Native Americans, and the Africans) embraced the performing arts (dance-drama, pantomime, pageantry, buffoonery or clowning, and storytelling and singing epic narratives, historically connected both to the dramatic monologue and to the epic drama).

In all the cultural regions of origin, these forms would often have been presented in the context of festivals. Falassi's classification (1987: 1–10) of the ritual acts or rites that make up festivals applies to European, African, and Native American cultures. The component rites include: framing (setting the festival into what Turner calls liminal time (Turner 1969), or "time out of time"), purification (expulsion of evil), passage, inversion (reversal of class, gender, space, etc.), conspicuous display, consumption, exchange, and competition (athletic contests or legendary battles, both of which, according to Falassi, evolved from the original symbolic contest between light and darkness, good and evil). Festivals often include ritual dramas (e.g., of creation), and they close with rites of devalorization, or a return to the normal.

Some of these dramatic forms have remained relatively pure over the centuries, while others have undergone varying degrees of transculturation. A number of manifestations of these forms documented by contemporary observers have remained to this day, others have disappeared, and still others have been revived by groups seeking to restore their connection to the traditional roots of their culture. This syncretic stage of traditional-popular theatre is what has been most commonly referred to in the twentieth century as folk drama.

The term *traditional* theatre implies a conservative intent and, as we shall see later, both its forms and its functions are quite similar throughout the cultures of the three continents that came together in America during the colonial era. Ritual or liturgical drama, ceremony or pageants, and festivals can all be categorized as traditional theatrical forms. The main function of these forms has been to reaffirm the unity of a community, from tribe or clan to region, nation, or empire; their message, whether implicit or explicit, is almost always an affirmation of established values and an uncritical reiteration of rituals or symbolic actions. These actions can provide moral reassurance; they may attack or defuse division, and they often reinforce connections to the legendary or mythical origins of the group. As we suggested in the introduction, the object of traditional-popular theatre and theatrical forms and even folk drama sometimes appears to contradict the aims of the New Popular Theatre, the twentieth-century movement that has consciously revived traditional forms. The central objective of this modern movement has been, after all, to dismantle or at least question the oppressive nature of established culture. However, insofar as one of the most important contributions of the New Popular Theatre has been the reaffirmation of the integrity of marginalized cultures and of significant cultural forms on the verge of extinction or assimilation, such revivals of the traditional/popular are not contradictory.

Whenever traditional forms are the main vehicle of expression of a tribal, regional, or national unit, and whenever they are participatory events, it is only fair to accept the term *popular*—particularly when they are the group's vehicles for affirming its identity vis-à-vis other competing groups, as was the case with Iberians, Native Americans, blacks, and eventually peasants and villagers. This has been the main reason why the New Popular Theatre has been so interested in reviving traditional theatrical forms, even though it is almost certain to present the content in a new, critical light.

A second category of "popular" theatre involves participatory events of a theatrical nature. Some of these also fall within the category of traditional-popular theatre, and the two categories certainly do not exclude each other. In a few cases, however, participatory theatre is not primarily a celebration of the hegemony, nor does it serve mainly for socializing the individual and subgroups into acceptable codes of behavior and belief systems or as a vehicle for such subgroups to reaffirm their respective social roles.

It can serve, alternatively, as a safety valve or as a conduit for complaints (the carnival being just such a medium), and it is often seen as a temporary breakdown of hegemonic relations and hierarchical structures. Yet even then participatory theatre is acceptable to the dominant social forces, not only because it serves as a temporary escape from intolerable conditions for the less-favored, but also because it is a means of fine-tuning the system to ensure its continued functioning without major disruptions. In any case the carnivals and the *mojiganga* (mumming) remain to this day two of the most important vehicles of popular dramatic participation, along with the Christmas *posadas* (a reenactment through carolling of the Holy Family's search for an inn); all three are of medieval or Renaissance origin; all three are forms in which different cultures have found a space for traditional expression and in which they have often merged.[5]

Three Cultures, Similar Stages

Although we often speak of "Native American culture" or "Mexican culture," we are conscious of referring to a plurality of cultures in various stages of historical development that existed when the Spanish and Portuguese settled in America. A similar situation holds true for the various cultures that were brought to America by the millions of enslaved Africans. Commonality can nevertheless be assumed in at least three categories:

(a) Similarities among different tribes and nations of America and Africa due to the stage of historical development; e.g., similar types of material culture, national consolidation, or stages in the growth of empire. The most common example of this is the role of dance dramas in the less-developed economies and social groups (hunter-gatherers of Africa and America), with remnants to be found in the peasant cultures of Europe of the late Middle Ages.

(b) Similarities between some of the cultural forms developed by American and African kingdoms, tribes, and groups, and some of those brought by the Iberians who conquered or enslaved them. An example is drama based on heroic legends or myths of creation, which can be found among the Aztecs, the Yoruba, and the Ife, and the *auto sacramental*, the mysteries, and the miracle plays among the Iberian promoters of Roman Catholic ideology.

(c) Similarities between the cultural forms of certain social classes in America, where miscegenation and consequent transculturation have occurred (but where the metropolitan culture remains dominant), and their counterparts in Spain and Portugal. These would be found primarily in secular forms that are mainly the realm of whites or mestizos, e.g., the *género chico* (short plays), which evolved from secular comedy of the sixteenth and seventeenth centuries, both in Spain and in America; and Native American or African-American comedy, which ranges from clowning and buffoonery to naturalistic social drama, often of moralizing intent. All of these would probably, in their origins, have formed part of festivals; the close connection between comic forms like the *entremés* and the religious *auto* and *loa* would appear to be a residual aspect of this original context.

It would be misleading to suggest that one can equate African cultures in America, which were largely fractured or syncretized by slavery, with Native American cultures, which had their home ground in which to persist. It would appear, however, that many dramatic forms, even highly evolved theatre and dance drama, were not entirely unknown either among transplanted Africans or certain Native American groups; similarly, the form and structure of some European drama were neither alienating nor totally alien to some of the Native American groups who saw it performed by the invaders.

Non-European Dramatic Forms

Various forms of dramatic performance were already in existence, and in many cases highly developed, in both Native American and African cultures, at the time of their first contacts with the Europeans. There is considerable historical evidence of the important role of both ritual drama and secular theatre in the sixteenth century in the Americas and in the early eighteenth century in Africa; that is, at the point when the slave trade became a massive enterprise, involving hundreds of thousands of Africans from numerous nations, and when the contact between Africans and Europeans (and in a few cases Native American) first became a factor in the formation of a distinctive American identity.

The marginal voices (primarily those of Native Americans and African-Americans) have, for the most part, been studied apart from Spanish-language dramatic literature and European-dominated theatrical presentations. We are including them in this chapter as an integral part of the complex body of performance arts in the Americas in which popular theatre can be found. We are also including them even though, because of the unequal balance of forces, one cannot say that genuine transculturation has been possible; we see Latin American popular culture as a mosaic of heritages in the process of being recognized, increasingly, as traditions of equal value.

The range and complexity of drama and theatre appear to correspond, both in Africa and in America, with the level of complexity of social and economic relations and with the size and level of development of a given civilization (e.g., the number of regions under its control or influence and the degree of centralization and integration of the cultural manifestations of those regions). Both ritual drama and some forms of secular drama (e.g., comedy) can be found in a majority of cultures, from the most isolated and least developed groups or tribes to the most powerful and developed empires. It is the levels of sophistication and complexity and the range of forms within each of the two categories that vary, according to the degree of development of the cultures that create them.

The literature on the drama and theatre that preceded contact with European domination is not identical for Africa and the Americas. The documentation on Africa is quite detailed and substantial for the period prior to the intensification of the slave trade, and it purports to deal with relatively autochthonous cultural creation. However, while the studies of Native American theatre describe aboriginal forms of performance that were established prior to any known contact with Europeans, the African studies deal with sub-Saharan cultures that had already had some contact, however minimal, with Europeans since the fifteenth century, and that had in all likelihood been influenced to some extent by North African and Arabic traders, certainly at least by the sixteenth century.

The correspondences and possible influences among Native American cultures prior to the conquest or shortly thereafter (through the forced transfer of large population groups) could be said to correspond roughly to the transculturation that began to occur among African-Americans. In many cases this occurred en route to the Americas or at least shortly after their arrival, as slaves from different nations, tribes, and social groups were thrown together in new socioeconomic configurations.[6]

Although one is faced with an oddly uneven documentation for pre-Hispanic American theatres and African-American theatres, the literature can be perfectly useful once the necessary historical corrections are made. They indicate that the African cultural forms imported to America were products of transculturation virtually at the point of arrival, while their Native American counterparts maintained some degree of autonomous identity as long as they remained within the geographic boundaries of their cultural group. The emergence of an

African-American theatre can therefore be seen not only as a direct or close equivalent to the pre-Hispanic Native American theatre, but also as an important building block of the emerging Latin American theatre in areas densely populated by African Americans.

As we categorize and describe the drama and theatre of African-American and Native American cultures, the reader should bear in mind the structural and evolutionary correspondences of the various categories in both of these broad cultural spheres. It should also be emphasized that in many instances we are citing Native American forms that suffered varying degrees of European influence and even transformation, but we include them if they are of pre-Columbian origin, or if they originated among the non-European communities during colonial or postcolonial times.

Native American Dramatic Forms

The pre-Hispanic theatre has persisted; of this there can be no doubt. What pre-Hispanic theatre is, and how it can be separated from post-conquest theatre and from folk drama, is another question. One of the best keys for the study of both the connections and the distinctions is provided by Gertrude Prokosch Kurath (1967), through the categories that she proposes for Mesoamerican dance drama. These categories, determined primarily by their place in ecological, ecclesiastical, and secular festivals, respectively, are very valuable for that region, because each of the festival categories is subdivided into: (1) aboriginal survivals (a) in the ecological calendar and (b) in the ecclesiastical calendar; (2) blended ritual dramas (a) introduced by the clergy during colonization and (b) created after the conquest; and (3) secular celebrations (Prokosch Kurath 1967:158).

A similar distinction between pre-Columbian dances (chiefly totemic and funeral rituals) and foreign dances or native creations that emerged after the conquest (including Spanish dances, the figures of the *diablillos* and the *negritos*, and the use of the Spaniard as an object of ridicule in the *sijlla*) is offered for Andean dance and dance drama by Pierre Verger (Verger 1945:12).

Both studies further classify the performances by content or meaning. Verger proposes the following categories: religious, totemic, warrior, guild dances, satyrical dances, regional dances, pantomime, agricultural, imported dances strictly of entertainment value, and mumming or itinerant dance and theatre, usually in carnival (Verger 1945:13). Prokosch Kurath's classification, elaborating on earlier studies of Mexico and Central America (e.g., Termer 1957) is based on a larger body of examples than Verger's.[7] Her analyses also have a greater wealth of detail, with particular attention to regional and subcultural variations in the role of animals and clowns; in the use of masks, props, and costumes; and in the dance steps.

Both these studies, as well as other historical and anthropological sources, emphasize the importance of acculturation and the survival or emergence of types of dramatic performance, virtually all of which are linked to both aboriginal pre-Christian and European Catholic roots. A number of other scholars, however, offer satisfactory evidence that indigenous, or Native American, theatre without foreign influences does exist to this day. The study of the indigenous theatre of Mexico has led some researchers to generalize about a similar persistence of uncontaminated indigenous theatres of other regions. We have not concerned ourselves with confirming or denying the specific facts regarding the existence of such widespread pre-Hispanic forms of performance, but we are sufficiently convinced of the validity of the criteria by which Latin American scholars judge whether a form or a piece is truly indigenous.

Miguel León Portilla (1959:13–36) divides pre-Columbian theatrical forms into four categories: (1) hymns in the form of a dialogue (probably the most ancient); (2) various forms of Nahuatl comic acting and entertainment; (3) representations of the great Nahuatl myths; and (4) themes related to family and society.

Estage Noel, Frischmann, and others are engaged in documenting the indigenous theatre, closely following certain fundamental criteria for distinguishing between authentic and syncretic contemporary theatre:

1. Preeminence of ritual, because of its continued connection to its origins in religion and magic. The preservation of cosmic balance remains one of the chief functions of drama.
2. The magical or quasi-magical nature of the performance: identi-

fication of mask/language/dance with a particular persona or character, hence the subsuming of the actor/dancer in the persona/character.

3. Importance of choreography, mime, color symbolism, numerology, and esoteric references to local mythology as vital elements and staging techniques. The overall structure is dependent on the persistence of these elements.

4. The nonrepresentational nature of drama, particularly in the presentation of historical actions. Linear plots and chronological differentiation between historical periods are replaced by symbolic mechanisms (masks, costume, color, language, etc.).

5. The use of comedy or other less-symbolic forms to confirm appropriate social patterns of behavior or to censor attitudes unacceptable to the community, including those of elders and judges. (Estage Noel 1988:5–7)

A sixth proposition, and the most original one, is that genuine indigenous theatre may sometimes resort to unorthodox forms, or assimilate European elements, "indigenizing" them, usually to camouflage their true nature. Estage Noel does not consider that such adaptations would necessarily make them *syncretic forms;* a similar argument, cited below, is offered for missionary theatre that disguised European forms with native elements to promote the Catholic dogma, while the core remained European and Catholic. This difficulty of categorization poses a particular problem to those of us who interpret acculturation or transculturation more liberally. For this reason we will treat this aspect further in chapter 2.

Although it can be assumed that in most cultures the production process was constructed and handed down orally, at least one documented case exists suggesting that performances were "scripted." The Mixtec codices include what at least one researcher has interpreted as pictographic codes of performance (Monaghan 1990). There is ample historical evidence of the training of professional actors and dancers in pre-Hispanic cultures, particularly in the more advanced civilizations (see Acuña 1978:16ff. for the Mayans, Lara 1957 for the Inca). At the community level throughout the hemisphere, the ceremonial buffoon seems to be fairly ubiquitous, probably as a counterpart to the shaman in his/her ritualistic drama (León Portilla 1959:25–29, Steward 1930). Prokosch Kurath (1952:239) includes "residual mimetic demonology" in this same category, along with the *Viejos* (old men, probably representing the ancestors), who occur from Mexico to Peru.[8]

The comic is present either in situational humor or in such figures as the Viejos and various types of *Gracejo*. Virtually every researcher has documented the uses of humor and comedy. Franz Termer (1957), for instance, catalogued at least six "dances with comedic content," which rely on slapstick (the Toro or Torito), mockery (of rival towns or of physical handicaps), clowning, and acrobatics (the *volador*). Conjuring and illusionism, though less widespread, were also fairly popular forms of entertainment. All evidence points to the existence of a broad range of skilled performers.

Agricultural and fertility rites, in which many if not most of the population participated, were probably the most common and widely practiced, according to all our sources. Many of the dramatic festivities associated with these rites involved some form of positive celebration, usually of a totem, and often included phallic comedy similar to that of the ancient Greeks.[9] Early chronicles (such as that of Fernández de Oviedo) recorded the ritual cult of the cacao god, in which natives wearing rich costumes and bird masks and painted in bright colors danced around a pole, on top of which sat the idol. The dance steps and chants were apparently quite varied and complex.

In Mexico and Central America, a pole or bare tree serves as the totemic centre of the widespread ritual of the *voladores*, or flyers. In these ritual acrobatics (similar to the modern circus act), several men attach themselves to the top of the pole by means of a rope tied around their torso, then whirl around the pole in different flying patterns.[10] Some historians believe that in pre-Hispanic times the volador ritual would occasionally involve human sacrifice, as one of the participants (a warrior or a priest) leapt from the top of the pole without a rope.

Agricultural rites range from the simplest offerings, such as pre-theatrical flagellation dances, to the varied and complex festivals of the Maya and the Nahua peoples.[11] Agricultural rituals could involve actual or symbolic sacrifices, as in the following passage, where there is barely a passing reference to the offering (opening) of the poet's heart. The Nahuas' *Atamalqualiztli* ("Meal of Water Tamales"), held every eight years and possibly related to the earth goddess's cycle, was one of the most complex festivities. We offer the following translation of León Portilla's summary of the sixteenth-century chronicle of Sahagún:

> Numerous characters appeared, dressed as animals, insects, birds, butterflies, street peddlars, and more abstract figures, such as "Sleep." After a chorus opened the festivities, affirming that "the poet's heart opens in the middle of the night, to surrender to flowers and song," a torchlight dance by the numerous costumed characters was held in the adorned square. Among those who appeared were the goddess Tlazolteotl and the corn god, Centeotl. Toward sunrise the chorus mentions the coming of the sun and Quetzalcoatl, who promises to assist the humans with their harvest:
>
> . . . .
>
> Our god is now singing:
> Listen to him.
> His redbreasts are singing!
> Can it be our dead man who is singing?
> Can he be the one who is going to be hunted?
>
> —I shall cool my flowers with the wind:
> The flower of human sustenance,
> The flower that smells like roasted corn
> Where the flowers stand tall.

In some cultures where human sacrifices were performed, the intended sacrificial victim assumed an acting role of unique significance. The prisoner or volunteer (who received favorable treatment, good food and entertainment, and a great deal of respect during the months that led up to his sacrifice) was coached in the dialogue and the ritual acts that he would perform as he was taken up to the place of sacrifice. This highly sophisticated rite (recorded mainly in the Aztec civilization) bears a structural correspondence to sacrificial rites in other cultures, the key being the grooming of the intended victim to make him more acceptable to the deities (León-Portilla 1959:18).

Proof of the existence of a similar rite among the Mayans has been seen by some scholars in the *Rabinal Achí* ("The Warrior of Rabinal"; Monterde 1955), a Guatemalan drama codified in the nineteenth century but generally considered to be pre-Hispanic (see Versenyi 1988:333, concerning the religious aspects of this drama). The protagonist of this play is a prisoner who recites repetitive challenges to his victors before he is executed; challenges and boasts were one form of ritual dialogue in which prisoners were expected to engage, to project their bravery and their caliber as warriors, thus proving the valor of their captors (Balmori 1955:600).[12]

Nahuatl poetry offers strong evidence that when the sacrificial victim was a child, as was usually the case for the ceremony of Tlaloc, the rain god, a chorus recited or sang both the child's role and that of the god being propitiated. Some of the sacred hymns of the Nahua people collected by Angel María Garibay (among the most beautiful pre-Hispanic poetry) appear to be dramatic recitations by the officiating priest, by the god Tlaloc, and by the sacrificial victim (see Garibay 1954). The following chorus (representing the people) speaks of repaying the debt of rain to the god:

CHORUS: Ah, in Mexico the god is being asked for a loan.
Where the paper banners fly
And along the four cardinal points
Human beings are standing.

and, later, the chorus (for the victim):

I shall go away forever:
It is time for his tears.
Ah, send me to the Place of Mystery:
At his command.
Ah, every four years
Among us is the rising up:
Unbeknownst, people without number
In the charnel house;
House of quetzal feathers,
The transformation takes place:
It is a thing of the Increaser of men.

The sacrificial theme is paramount in the theatre of the Americas, whether in its actual, "primitive" manifestation or in its increasingly sophisticated expressions. With the coming of the Europeans, the theme was taken up in the sacramental auto, which with its sacrificial substitution of Jesus Christ, was imported and adapted by Catholic missionaries from Mexico to Brazil. Indeed, as we shall see in the section on European dramatic forms, below, the sacraments, which linked humans to the Christian God, were central to a theatre whose primary intention was to bind Native Americans more closely to the Europeans.

African Dramatic Forms

The literature on African theatre includes a number of studies that shed some light on the historical origins of African-American dramatic forms. Most dramatic expression of African origin in the Americas is ritualistic in nature, and it is connected to shamanism, to festivals, or to both. This does not mean, however, that the experience of Africans who were brought to America over a period of more than four centuries did not include complex dramatic performance and an institutionalized theatre. We are inclined to deduce that whatever the forms African theatre was allowed to assume in its practitioners' new context, these forms were remnants of the varied cultural expression of kingdoms and nations that experienced social and economic changes similar to those of their American and European counterparts.

According to Ogunba (1978:3–6), theatre is an important component of the festivals that occupy much of the calendar of some African communities, and that are related to gods and goddesses, ancestors, spirits of nature, and other primal forces. Festivals are a central artistic institution, with cycles of performances addressing the history of the collectivity as well as religious matters. They usually become a display of all the artistic resources of a community. Annual reenactments respond in content as well as form to such changes as the replacement of an actor or dancer and in themselves come to represent renewal and growth.

Mahood (1966:23) calls these festivals *predrama*, an intermediate art form, something between religion and drama; this classification is confirmed by M. Echeuo, for whom "it seems subsumed in the ritual, not weaned and developed like Greek drama" (Echeuo 1975:25). Echeuo uses the terms *play*, *music*, and *performance* instead of *drama*. Notwithstanding these semantic distinctions, the theatre that these authors describe has a considerable amount in common with the Native American and European forms that we have chosen to call theatre or drama.

Festival drama in West Africa is organized into episodes that refer to historical events and legends. Stock characters are common comic figures. The overarching value is, however, a conceptual one; thus, dialogue is less important than the masks and costumes (Ogunba 1978:23). Supernatural figures, who constitute a majority of the protagonists of this drama, are masked; only the occasional human protagonist is unmasked. Much as with Native American drama, there is in West African drama a clear sanctification of the players' role by their costumes and masks, which identify them as "visitors from the land of spirits."

This depersonalization facilitated the connection that existed as late as the last century between the role of the professional Yoruba actor on tour and the role of medicine man that he sometimes assumed during the rainy season, when travel was impeded (Adedeji 1978:36). There is, moreover, a historical basis for this double profession: traveling theatre professionals derived their art from Olugbere, the first professional actor (late sixteenth century), who was a "ghost mummer" and also a medicine man. By the nineteenth century, they had also established cults and secret societies for their members, for protection against outside attacks and curses (a function assumed by similar societies in Cuba). The importance of the spiritual identity and agency of the actor was, apparently, increased over the centuries.

Guilds and family lineage played an important part in the specialization of the professional theatre of Western Africa, even after participation in the craft expanded, in the seventeenth century, to include grassroots participation from other lineages (Adedeji 1978:30–31). Troupes connected to different lineages specialized variously in poetry, dance, or sketches, for example, while mask-making guilds had a special role. Professional development was stimulated by annual competitions, held during the festivals. The Nigerian professional traveling theatres came under attack in the nineteenth century from Moslems in the north and Christian missionaries in the south, and they faded away around the time when the last slave shipments left for America.

The types of drama are similar to those found in Native American dramatic forms. They include: ritual reenactments of mythological subjects and the feats of legendary heroes; totemistic dramas involving animals as family symbols; and mimes (group and solo) and social sketches that analyze vices and morals and satirize strangers. Other forms, which can be grouped under the heading of "medicine theatre," include masques and exorcism cults that function as vehicles for psychological healing and social cohesion (Adedeji 1978:43).

The humanistic quality of Yoruba religion is reflected in the importance of the personality presented by the gods in the ritual dramas; the deities are not seen as abstractions. The supernatural characters of the performances rely on their worshippers for their continued existence, which only reinforces the importance of the actor's role in gaining and maintaining his spirit's following. This remains a strong element in African-American dramatic ritual (Beier 1960).[13]

An extremely important figure in the development of African and African-American cultures was the *griot*, whose storytelling techniques were the quintessence of one-person dramatic performance. In the Americas this storytelling tradition would appear to have been developed to a higher degree of complexity as a dramatic genre than any surviving European counterpart (chiefly through such elaborations as a more versatile use of the human voice and the addition of musical instruments and song).

The persistence of a number of these dramatic forms and, more especially, of the spirit of African drama in the emerging American theatre has not been quite as amply documented or studied as it has in the case of the Native American drama. As we shall see later, however, African-American dramatic forms offer a fairly consistent indication of ancestral connections.

European dramatic forms

Iberian theatre

Because the early stages of the conquest preceded the Golden Age of Spanish drama, the first explorers and settlers of Mexico and the Caribbean came with only late medieval drama in their cultural baggage. The first documented productions in America (1533, 1538–39) were held some time before the first known professional theatre companies were established in Spain and Portugal (the first *corrales de comedias*, or playhouses, were not opened until the 1570s), although the work of Lope de Rueda is roughly contemporary to the first missionary plays, and Gil Vicente, Torres Naharro, and Juan del Encina were already known. It was while the conquerors were consolidating their gains in some of the more remote parts of the continent that theatre was becoming one of the most important forms of cultural expression on the Iberian peninsula, and the enthusiasm with which the metropolis cultivated it soon spilled over into the Americas.

In Spain, as in England and France, the principal dramatic forms of the late Middle Ages evolved from pre-Christian fertility rites and carnivals (many of them absorbed into Christianity) and from the Catholic liturgy. The secular forms of popular dramatic representation and ritual may be seen as counterparts of African and Native American forms.[14] Miracles and mysteries (which evolved as sacramental autos) were first performed by priests and choirs of children before the altar and with simple staging (e.g., the choir loft as heaven). These recitations in Latin were apparently very popular, or else attendance was compulsory for the entire population; they were soon moved out of the sanctuary and into the public square or the largest courtyards adjacent to the church, to accomodate the number of spectators.

Other important forms that came out of the church include the "Shepherds' Play" (known as "Los Pastores" or *pastorela*), which came out of the *Officium Pastorum*, and its various versions ("The Three Kings," "The Journey of the Magi," and "Herod and the Star"). A lasting derivation is the itinerant Christmas drama, the "Posadas" ("The Search for an Inn"), which, like the "Pastores," is performed to this day in the U.S. Southwest and in Mexico.[15]

At least one important new dramatic form was already evolving at this time: the *loa* (derived from the *laudes*, one of the daily prayer services). The loa probably existed independently in Spain as early as the thirteenth century, usually as a monologue of praise to the Virgin Mary, to Christ, or to the saints. It first figured as part of a dramatic presentation only in 1551, and the first record of an American loa performance is in 1574 (Correa and Cannon 1961:19).

The oldest surviving dramatic text in the Iberian peninsula, and one which was transferred to the colonies, is the *Auto de los Reyes Magos*

("Three Kings"), which dates back to the late twelfth or early thirteenth century. The play shows an acute dramatic sense and the beginnings of character development, both in the individualization of the three magi and in Herod's anguished soliloquy. According to the Spanish literary historian, Menéndez y Pelayo, cited by Ballinger (1952), the latter could be a forerunner of the great Golden Age soliloquies. The "Three Kings" did survive, to be performed throughout the Americas as folk drama. In the 1950s it was collected and staged by Buenaventura and the Teatro Experimental de Cali (Rizk 1991) and revived in 1990 by Teatro La Fragua, the Jesuit missionary theatre of northern Honduras. After this auto there is an apparent gap, filled only by a "Dance of Death" (mid-fourteenth century) that was acted, danced, and probably sung by over thirty characters, and that was later codified by more than one playwright. In all likelihood the apparent gap could be due to a consolidation of talent in festivities for holidays such as Christmas, Easter, and Corpus Christi, when individual miracles or mysteries continued to be performed, with increasingly sophisticated staging and costuming.

Indications exist that from early times the stage consisted either of adjacent compartments (representing heaven, hell, the temple, Jerusalem, Bethlehem) or of a scaffolding on which the various loci were disposed simultaneously. Hell and heaven particularly were represented with great ingenuity and mechanical complexity; angels and saints moved between heaven and earth through systems of ropes and pulleys, while a monster's mouth served as the entrance to hell, which opened, shut, and belched flames and smoke (Chambers 1903).

In Spain, at least, naturalistic sets involved the use of real water and fire, animals and birds. This would also have been the case in America, where the setting and props consisted of both European and native elements. Professional directors were often contracted to produce dramatic festivals and ambitious plays, particularly during the most arduous festivities, such as Corpus Christi, which involved a considerable capital investment; the church or the town administration paid for the services and materials of carpenters, animal keepers, and actors alike. All social classes collaborated with the same degree of enthusiasm in the Corpus Christi festival: clergy and nobility, magistrates, and artisans.

All through the first century of the colonial period, the Corpus Christi festivities were the main common denominator of theatrical performances of all the population centers, and they provided a unifying participatory festival for practically all classes, just as they had in Spain and Portugal. Because the Corpus Christi procession contains the seeds of practically every Iberian dramatic form that came to America, it warrants our special attention as a paradigm of the festival.

Corpus Christi

The earliest Corpus Christi processions on record (although mandated by Pope Urban IV in 1264) were those held in Barcelona around 1320 and in Valencia around 1355. In its earliest manifestations, the feast of the Body of Christ was centered around processions whose tone was predominantly somber and tearful, as penitents prayed against plagues, floods, or droughts. Durán y Sanpere (1943) supports the theory of the secular/profane origin of the form the Corpus procession eventually took; he believes that its origins lie in popular or courtly ceremonies (possibly both).[16] By the late fourteenth century, the festivity had grown to include a variety of elements, but according to Durán y Sanpere, this is documented only in the sources dated about a century later, around the time when elements began to appear that broadened the popular base.

The Corpus festivities have generated some debate as to whether they can be considered theatrical presentations. In his contribution to the debate around the British Corpus, Withington (1930:575) emphasizes three elements that made it effective for medieval audiences: the anachronistic introduction of contemporary figures (to make the lesson more effective); the use of slapstick comedy; and the appeal to human emotions (through such episodes as Abraham's sacrifice of his son, Mary's suffering over her son's death, and the very terror of the Crucifixion).

Over the years the procession changed, as different elements came to predominate. From the first centuries, the *entremeses*, or interludes, were its key component genre; they included St. Michael and the demons, the Expulsion of Adam and Eve, and David and Goliath, all of which would later take root in America. Out of the entremeses, which provided much of the action, there emerged important and lasting dramatic figures and characters. *Tableaux vivants*, which were usually paraded on carriages or floats called *rocas*, were important because they did not involve dialogue and thus required less acting, thereby allowing for broader popular participation in the procession.

The paradigmatic character of the Corpus Christi procession as a festival of rituals can be analyzed in terms of its parts, as outlined by Falassi (1987). The rite of framing is provided by the procession of laypersons, sometimes followed by the religious, whose censers and prayers offer a rite of purification.[17] The procession ends with the parade of the nobility who assume, quite literally, the last word in the festival, after the ritual aspect is concluded.

The main body of the procession consists of ritual dramas (from Creation to the ultimate victory over death), and usually includes the ritual combat between Good and Evil (originally the "Cavallets i diables" in Catalonia, later "Moors and Christians"), the rite of exchange (the angel substituting a ram for Isaac in the auto of Abraham and Isaac, the journey of the magi to bring gifts to Jesus), and the rite of sacrifice (Abraham and Isaac, the Stations of the Cross, or the reenactment of the Crucifixion). The *gigantes* (giants) of Guatemala are residual representations of both supernatural beings of Mayan mythology (as represented in the *Popol Vuh*) and of Goliath; they often dance and have a semicomical, semi-intimidating function (Girard 1948:253–80).

The structure of the festivity has remained fairly constant over six centuries, as has the pattern of sponsorship. Guilds and *cofradías* (sodalities or church associations) were responsible for the production of specific floats and dramas, and the liturgical or theological importance of a particular float or drama (such as the Crucifixion or the Annunciation), as well as its position in the procession, were often an indicator of the relative prestige of its sponsors and organizers. One example often cited comes from Mexico, where in 1533 the gunsmiths occupied first place in the festivity, while in 1537 that position had gone to the silversmiths.

By 1425 the Corpus procession had come into its own as an ideological whole; its nine sections followed a logical sequence, from Genesis and Creation to King Alfonso the Great.[18] The *gigantes* (giants), *enanos* (dwarves), and *cabezones* (big heads) were among the earliest and the most popular figures to march or dance in the procession. The *diablos* (devils) played a prominent role from the earliest liturgical dramas, when (usually wearing animal heads) they darted in and out of the jaws of hell, according to Chambers; they tempted characters and audience alike or dragged sinners off to hell, acting all the while in a comical or obscene fashion.[19] The commonplace presentation of "devil" figures in blackface, both in Iberia and in the Americas, dates back to medieval Catholic theatre and religious ceremonies; according to Fernando Ortiz in his study of African-American theatre, these figures might have originated in imitation of pagan genii of fertility, or of Moors and Saracens (Ortiz 1951:361). A more recent study of the African-American theatre suggests that the black image may have entered the late medieval stage through the figures of Balthazar and Lucifer, but by the sixteenth century black figures, as demons, were associated with darkness and death (Hatch 1991: Introduction).[20]

If the dancers and other individual kinetic figures tested the frontiers of the "liminal" in the passing procession, the static environment took on a kind of mirror role for the festival. Ornamentation of the streets grew increasingly complex, until by the seventeenth century in Spain and in the major colonial cities, the decorations virtually competed with the procession. Baroque art found new expression in the circumstantial: arches of triumph, adornments hanging from balconies, and temporary additions to crossroads, streetcorners, and building facades turned parts of towns and cities into anachronistic sets that nevertheless were unlikely to jar the audience, since the telescoping of time was an intrinsic aspect of the pageants themselves. In at least one case (Mexico, 1580s), the arch erected by the viceroy for one such festivity celebrated Moctezuma and the Aztec civilization, thus constituting the first public acknowledgment of the indigenous line of origin of creole culture.

Participation in the festivities became increasingly important, until it was finally made mandatory in the mid-1590s. Corpus Christi organizers sought out the most talented actors, craftsmen, and, of course, playwrights and directors. The first documented theatre contest of the Americas was held in Mexico City, where Juan Pérez Ramírez was awarded the prize for the best sacramental play, on 18 May 1565. Between the presentation of the *Auto de Adán y Eva* in 1533, as an educational example for the Native Mexicans, and this first formal award to a local playwright, the Spanish theatre established itself in the colonies and simultaneously laid the foundations for an American theatre.

Theatre in the Americas

Conquistadores and missionaries brought with them at least three established forms: the auto (the Iberian version of the miracle play), the "Pastores" ("Shepherds' Play"), and the legendary-ritual drama "Moros y cristianos" ("Moors and Christians"). Within fifty years of the conquest of the mainland, at least three new forms were introduced, which gained great popularity: the *paso* (a short play) and its successor, the *entremés* (interlude), a secular genre; the loa (praise), fundamentally a religious genre but also used in tributes to secular figures and events; and the *coloquio* (dialogue), which one associates mainly with Renaissance humanism. By the late 1500s, of course, the *comedias* (dramas) of the prolific and talented Spanish and Portuguese playwrights were gaining popularity in the colonies.

An influential line along which the ritual contest evolved in Spanish and Latin American drama is the tradition that includes the "Conquest of Jerusalem" (one of the most spectacular productions of the early years of the Mexican missions); the dances of the conquest (e.g., "The Conquest of Guatemala"; see Bode et al. 1961); and ritual "building blocks" of the conquest plays: the "Moors and Christians" and "Los Doce Pares de Francia" ("The Twelve Peers of France," a dramatization of one of the Carolingian legends).[21] Brazilian versions of these forms include the "cheganças" or "Mouros e marujos" in the north and the "cavalhadas" in the south.

The forms of drama presented in the American colonies reflected not only the role that culture was required to play by each successive stage of conquest and colonization, but also, naturally, the development of metropolitan culture in its socioeconomic context. As conquest and tentative settlements gave way to the establishment of well-ordered cities and institutions, so too did the predominant theatre evolve from a missionary theatre of evangelization and occasional amateur performances at military outposts, through religious festivals, to humanistic college drama, courtly pageants, and traveling professional companies.

Scholars have usually emphasized the existence of two historical stages—conquest and colonization—with a corresponding evolution of cultural production. But in fact the theatre of the colonial period was divided by pioneer historians such as Arrom (1956) into three categories: evangelical or missionary theatre, school drama, and creole theatre (focusing chiefly on drama by native playwrights), with an emphasis on the religious nature of the first two and the secular nature of the last. In one of the most recent historical overviews of colonial theatre, Kathleen Shelly and Grínor Rojo (1982) stress the fact that religious drama was the fare for whites as well as nonwhites in the early centuries of Spanish and Portuguese rule. Its role for the nonindigenous population was primarily to revitalize religious sentiment and reaffirm ecclesiastical hegemony where it might be slipping or simply where it was considered most appropriate (e.g., among schoolboys), while its role for the indigenous population was to replace pre-Christian beliefs with the European ideology.[22]

The religious drama identified with missionary work flourished officially only until the 1550s in Mexico and Central America, probably into the 1560s in South America. It remained alive, however, for centuries after the church had withdrawn its official support, and it survives to this day, mainly in the more insulated communities of Native Americans and mestizos, where it is still commonly associated with local religious rituals and feasts.

Religious drama oriented toward the nonindigenous population was at first limited to medieval plays and other spectacles presented on religious holidays. These spectacles received a major boost from the theatre boom of the seventeenth century, when medieval and early Renaissance forms (the auto, the loa, the coloquio) were adopted by some of the most distinguished playwrights of the Golden Age, both in Spain (Calderón and Lope de Vega, among others) and in the Americas (Sor Juana Inés de la Cruz, González de Eslava, and several anonymous authors), and they flourished even outside the framework of religious holidays until the late 1600s.

College plays were written and performed by students and teachers. Most were on religious themes, although a fair number were also presented to honor a new viceroy or to celebrate the coronation of a new monarch. College plays with secular themes, however, are found mainly toward the end of the seventeenth century (see Descalzi 1968: chapter 2, García Soriano 1927).

Secular drama is known to have been performed by amateur players as early as the 1530s and quite possibly earlier. Among the most famous, or at least the most curious, are the musical and dramatic entertainment ordered by the conquistador Pizarro after his successful mutiny against Almagro, in Peru, and the presentation of dramas by Spanish soldiers, as a form of entertainment for their comrades, in what is now the U.S. Southwest, in the 1590s. Published plays were imported from Spain, and theatre companies toured and performed as early as 1597.

Fixed performance spaces (the *corral* between the late sixteenth and early eighteenth centuries, later the *coliseo*, or playhouse) were in demand mainly in the larger urban centers, while smaller communities tended to adapt existing public spaces for occasional productions. Court theatre as well as secular college drama developed in the eighteenth century, eclipsing religious drama, which remained relegated largely to feasts and holidays.

The first dramatic creations seen in the so-called New World were in the mold of what was most commonly seen in Iberian religious festivals: miracle plays, or autos, such as those presented throughout the mother countries, especially in the south. As they established their relationship with the indigenous peoples, the missionaries who accompanied the first expeditions used these biblical stories and dramatic reenactments of episodes from the crusades and the wars against the Moors as an important tool for proselytizing. Indeed, not only did this evangelical theatre prove to be the mainstay of the missionaries' work throughout the continent (as in Mexico, Central America, parts of Brazil and the Amazonian region, and various sections of the Andean region), but it was also the medium in which the first dramatic literature in this hemisphere was written.

2 • *The Emergence of an American Theatre*

Although the first plays to be performed in the Americas were either directly imported from Europe or modeled on European plays, and there are no works by native playwrights among the earliest performances, American elements are present practically from the outset, both in adaptations and in original works. Native Americans participated in the productions and the performances; local fauna and flora graced the sets, and many of the scripts were performed in aboriginal languages. Those first theatrical works served above all as instruments for the indoctrination and the resocialization of Native Americans under the rule of Spain and Portugal. They were in the main religious dramas and, as such, their structure and often their presentation bore a striking analogy to the drama of the peoples to whom they preached. The foundations of syncretism were laid in the first dramatic performances of the religious missionaries.

Evangelization

The Franciscans

The most complete documentation of missionary theatre exists only for certain areas of the continent where this dramatic form was used on the largest scale and to which the chronicles of the conquest have paid attention: Mesoamerica (Mexico and Guatemala) and Peru. The Franciscan friars were the first of the four major religious orders to come to America. They adopted the late medieval miracle play and the auto as a medium for converting the aborigines, because that allowed them to communicate basic tenets of the faith and of sacred history through mime and gesture, when the missionaries still had not mastered the local languages. It also facilitated "instant" conversions on a mass scale, and communicated to the largest possible audiences the church's condemnation of the "abominations" most common among local peoples, including polygamy, alcoholism, and idolatry. The Spaniards realized almost immediately, in fact, that these peoples responded extremely well to the presentations because theatrical expression was an important part of their own culture.

This favorable response was familiar to the Spaniards from the earliest journeys of exploration, when Columbus and his companions were spectators of the Arawak and Taino Indians' *areíto*, a form of dance drama or ritual dance common throughout the Caribbean. Indeed, the term *areíto* was used interchangeably with the Nahuatl *mitote* by chroniclers of Mexico to refer to the dance dramas and ritual dances of the inhabitants of the Aztec-dominated territories. Between 1519 and 1533, missionaries to Mesoamerica therefore had ample opportunity to develop their proselytizing strategies, which included: the study of Native American languages, cultures, and belief systems; the codification and translation of sacred texts; and the establishment of schools for the children of Indian chieftains. Less documentation exists as evidence of the missionaries' interest in the cultures of Caribbean tribes.

Whatever their preparation may have been for the Mexican experiment, the Franciscan missionaries understood the importance of theatrical forms among the resources in their campaign to win souls for the church. But the task of creating evangelical drama, like other tasks undertaken by missionaries in Mexico and in most places in America, was not assumed lightly. The handful of Franciscans who came to New Spain before 1528 became almost legendary figures because of their skill in learning not one but several local languages, and because of their intelligent, indeed shrewd, strategies of living among the natives in the proverbial poverty of their order, winning their respect and in many cases their love as well, and training Native Americans as catechists while they used them as translators and informants about every conceivable aspect of their cultures. The Franciscans also acquired considerable property and influence, especially among the local peoples, and less than a quarter century after the conquest of Mexico, they were being perceived as a potential threat by the colonial authorities, who soon limited the evangelical activities that the Franciscans pursued on a mass scale (Arróniz 1979).

The earliest reference to any form of dramatic performance involves the Corpus Christi festivities in the newly rebuilt Mexico City, in 1526. Autos as well as the processions and pantomime of the Corpus celebration were introduced quite possibly in the very first years after the conquest of the Aztec capital (Torres Rioseco 1945:15). The fusion of European and Native American performance arts began, in all probability, with the Christmas pageant in the mid- to late 1520s.

One man's ingenuity is credited with breaking through the local peoples' resistance to sermons and first penetrating their traditional forms of worship with Christian content. Noticing that dance and song were integral parts of their ceremonies of worship, Pedro de Gante (Peter of Ghent) composed songs for worship at the Nativity scene in the church of St. Francis, in Mexico (built on the razed site of Emperor Moctezuma's zoo).

It is said that when the chiefs of Texcoco, Tlatelolco, Chalco, and Huejotzingo heard Native Americans singing in their own language, they were greatly impressed and agreed to be baptized and to send their children to the school the Franciscans had built in that same convent—the first European school on the American continent (Arróniz 1979:32–33).

Two Franciscans who made crucial contributions to the rescue and preservation of Native American documents and traditions were also the authors and directors of the first two American plays. Father Andrés de Olmos was directly connected to the first staged production, in Tlatelolco. Fray Toribio de Benavente (known as "Motolinía," the aboriginal term for "poor man") appears to be connected to the second and third productions, in Tlaxcala. Andrés de Olmos arrived in New Spain in 1528, at the same time as his friend Archbishop Zumárraga (a Dominican who would later criticize the excesses of the popular theatre). A contemporary of Olmos and early historian of the church in Mexico called Olmos "one of the most perfect religious that New

Spain has had" (quoted in Arróniz 1979:38, n. 3). All sorts of legends arose about Olmos's powers as a healer and a survivor in the hostile wilderness, and he was held to be a unique promoter of the faith.

INDIGENOUS PARTICIPATION IN THE EVANGELICAL THEATRE

While he was working on his history of the Indians of New Spain, in 1533, Olmos presented a Spanish auto in Nahuatl translation at Tlatelolco, which was then on the outskirts of Mexico City; the performance was repeated in 1535, in Mexico. While it was not an original creation, the "Auto del Juicio Final" ("The Last Judgment") constitutes, as we shall see, the first consciously American production.

The theme of this auto was the sin of polygamy (which the Spaniards were trying to eradicate from local communities), and it was probably more of a religious text, a "sermon in dialogue form," than drama proper (Arróniz 1979:28). The impact of the various elements of machinery and devices, such as fires and trapdoors, on the local audience must have been tremendous, because they projected a brutal physicality (especially in the representation of hell) previously unknown to them in spiritual matters, primarily because the concepts of guilt or sin were alien to them. This auto on the Last Judgment was called an *ejemplo* (exemplum), in Nahuatl *nexcuitilli*, a term which was to be used quite frequently in the years of evangelization.

Bartolomé de Las Casas, the great defender of the human rights of Native Americans, was struck by the effectiveness and beauty of the 1535 performance he saw in Mexico, calling it almost indescribable, "never before seen by men" (Las Casas 1909:165). The following year, when he took up his duties in the region of Chiapas and Guatemala, he himself tried his hand at evangelical drama, which one could thus say was introduced into the Central American region by the Dominicans. The next milestones occur in 1538 and 1539, at Tlaxcala. The Tlaxcalans had, since the conquest, enjoyed the formal status of special allies of the Spaniards earned in their attack on the capital of Tlaxcala's Aztec enemies. They also included numerous converts, but a majority remained unbaptized. The dramatic performances of Tlaxcala, which to this day are considered to be logistical feats, are not attributed to a single author, but appear to be a result of the collective effort of the Franciscans operating in that area and of some of their brightest and most talented students. The most detailed account belongs to Fr. Toribio de Benavente, "Motolinía," and it is quite possible that this distinguished chronicler and missionary might have had a hand in the production, because of his close association with that mission.

If one is to judge by eyewitness accounts, the Tlaxcala productions were a tour de force on the scale of a film by D. W. Griffith or Cecil B. de Mille. In fact, according to Arróniz (1979:67), at least one of the plays is more like a film script. Both Tlaxcala performances were massive undertakings that involved the entire local population, drawing both on resources known in the European theatre and on the resources of the natives themselves. Although the plays were selected by the Spanish missionaries, and the technical aspects of the production reflected the European influence, all roles, including those of the Virgin Mary, the saints, and the Spaniards, were played by Native Americans.

The translators of the texts were also Native Americans, and there was ample room for improvisation and for the inclusion of native dance, clothing, and gesture. This has led commentators to believe that, with the exception of the Spanish director, most of the initiative that entered into the work came from the local people. The latter had an excellent ability for quick memorization, which both amazed the Europeans and facilitated such ventures of theirs as catechization and theatre. It was, no doubt, the Native Americans' facility with language and with memorization that enabled the friars to prepare a major dramatic production in less than a week, with the participation of hundreds of Tlaxcalans.

The procession of the Blessed Sacrament, in Tlaxcala in June 1538, was essentially a transplanted Corpus Christi festivity, similar to those of Seville and Valencia (Arróniz 1979:43). It consisted of tableaux vivants and ornate floats (*rocas* or *roques*, in Spain), with each group of silent figures representing a different biblical episode, but it also included some dialogue. (How the voices could be projected is hard to tell; there were thousands of spectators.) The carts and fixed sets were decorated with natural elements of the area: Mexican plants, flowers, animals, even reproductions of geological formations, together with the European reconstructions of biblical settings. Little or nothing is known about the details of earlier Corpus Christi festivities held in Mexico, but the account of Tlaxcala's demonstrates that by 1538, at least, the Corpus Christi ceremony was no longer a purely Spanish expression of popular participation.

The significance of Corpus Christi in 1538, however, lies not so much in its ornateness and in the great number of participants, but in the timing of what followed. The scope of the Corpus Christi ceremony was not in itself extraordinary, because the friars and their native assistants had had the better part of a year in which to prepare and, just like their counterparts in Spanish cities, albeit it to a lesser degree, they could count on the emerging fraternal orders (cofradías) and local guilds to take charge of the various tableaux. The unusual aspect of this festival was that immediately after its conclusion, the entire community was put to work on an even more ambitious production for the feast of St. John the Baptist.

It is not known whether some minor presentations had been planned beforehand. All we know now, still from the accounts of Mendieta (cited by Arróniz 1979) and Motolinía, is that the Franciscans suddenly decided to present four miracle plays, or autos, for 24 June, which gave them precisely four days in which to translate and rehearse them. They were not inconsequential sketches, but complete short plays; at least two of them were an hour long, and they involved dialogue, costumes, and action. The translations into Nahuatl were done on Friday and Saturday, which left two days for rehearsals and for the planning of additional details, such as the meals.

The "Annunciation of the Nativity of St. John the Baptist" featured a long improvisation by the actors playing the Angel and Zechariah, which exploited every comic possibility of the latter's deafness, to the delight of the audience. Three other plays followed: "The Annunciation of Our Lady," "The Visitation of Saint Elizabeth," and "The Nativity of St. John." The performance ended with a banquet at which Spaniards and Tlaxcalans sat down to celebrate together.

The feast of the Assumption (15 August) in Tlaxcala was illustrated in 1538 with the appropriate auto. "El Misterio de la Asunción" was performed entirely by Native Americans, and the Virgin Mary was carried heavenward on a movable platform, to the amazement of the audience. Father Las Casas, who had been invited by the Franciscans to celebrate the Mass at Tlaxcala, praised the play.

On Easter Wednesday in 1539, "The Fall of Adam and Eve" was performed. Motolinía called it "the best thing of its kind ever presented"

(Motolinía 1873:115). Certainly the Garden of Eden struck all eyewitnesses as a veritable earthly paradise, adorned as it was with plants and animals and filled with such details as a local young man disguised in a lion's skin, tearing apart and eating the carcass of a deer, while a live deer stood on a nearby hillock.

Motolinía suggests that the interaction of Adam and Eve around the temptation was largely improvised. The closing song, a charming *villancico*, has entered the traditional folk repertoire. Adam and Eve were led out of Eden by three angels each, singing "Circumdederunt me," to the accompaniment of organ music. According to both Las Casas and Motolinía, the audience wept as they witnessed such a vivid fall from grace.

The Corpus Christi celebration that year included four comedias (plays) that were even more involved productions than the first. The last three plays appear to have been fairly conventional in scope. "The Temptation of Christ by Lucifer" showed Lucifer disguised as a hermit, but with tail and horns in clear view, as he failed to persuade Jesus and was consigned to hellfire. Both the subject of temptation and its treatment, which were derived from medieval autos, were absorbed within the same century into loas whose main focus was the cult of Mary. "St. Francis Preaching to the Birds" was significant because it cast a Native American as the father of the mission's order, and showed live and stuffed creatures from the local fauna; approximately half the play was devoted to condemning drunkenness and witchcraft (Pazos 1951:173), and it included a harrowing scene of hell in which the damned appeared to be burned alive.

"The Sacrifice of Isaac" became part of the repertoire of the traditional popular drama of Mesoamerica and Mexico, and can be seen to this day in remote areas (Potter 1986). It was apparently selected for the appropriateness of its main theme (the divine command to abandon human sacrifice). The circumstances were, in fact, strikingly similar to those in which the Old Testament example was first applied to the Hebrews, and it was quite possibly the first time since its original use that the story of Abraham's sacrifice lent itself to such a literal interpretation. But the treatment of this medieval play also posed a particular problem to the missionaries, who were engaged in combatting sexual promiscuity as well. Therefore the presence of Hagar and of Abraham's natural son Ishmael had to be modified and their identity concealed. The resulting distortion is evident in the surviving versions of the play, where Ishmael appears as an envious onlooker and an ally of the Tempter.[1]

The *pièce de résistance* of the Tlaxcala festivities was "The Conquest of Jerusalem," which appears to be a combination of the "Moros y cristianos" ("Moors and Christians") genre, the "Danza de la conquista" (both of which have survived as the traditional popular drama), and late medieval reenactments of the crusades. It involved a cast of between eight and ten thousand. Pazos (1951:157) suggests that the Tlaxcala play might have been inspired in part by "The Conquest of Rhodes," staged earlier that same year in Mexico to celebrate the peace treaty signed by France and Spain in 1538.

"The Conquest of Jerusalem" was a carefully choreographed epic that involved: the conquest of the Holy City by the crusaders; its reconquest by the Turks; and the taking of Jerusalem anew by the Christians, this time with the help of their new allies from Tlaxcala. It is a masterpiece of anachronisms, but more significantly, it represents a deliberate attempt to identify the Tlaxcalans as the conquerors' genuine allies. An interesting detail of the play, which has led some (Arróniz 1979:83) to think that the Tlaxcalans had no small say in its creation (although Motolinía himself is supposed to have chosen the names of the main characters) and others to see in it a first glimmer of political theatre, is the fact that the actors who play the sultan and his men are dressed like Cortés and *his* men, that is, in sixteenth-century dress.[2] In a strange twist, the Tlaxcalans are rescuing Jerusalem for the True Faith, from infidels who might be identified with the conquerors of Mexico. St. Hippolyte (patron saint of the Indians) appears instead of Spain's patron, St. James, to carry the natives to victory. The sultan leads his men in accepting baptism in the Christian faith, at which point the local man who plays the pope is substituted by a real priest, who performs the sacrament for the literally thousands of local people who are both spectators and actors in this early American extravaganza.[3]

Nothing on record to this day indicates that this marvellous construction, a paradigm of ritual drama that merges historical periods, facts, myth and legend, and cultural expressions, has ever been attempted again, much less performed. The set was life-size, consisting of hills, woods, towers, and walls. There was simultaneous action on a three-dimensional set.[4] Hardly anything was left to the imagination, and the battle scenes were realistic. The text apparently included jibes at the soldiers from Cuba and Hispaniola, who are defeated because, explains Motolinía, they are incapable of calling on God as they should have—and as the heroic Mexican warriors did. (Pazos suggests that only a personal prejudice of Motolinía's would account for this satire of Spaniards from the Antilles.) Of course the invocation of the God of Christendom is central in this auto, as in every other one. Although it is not, technically speaking, an *auto sacramental*, "La conquista de Jerusalén" does have the essential element of the auto: the triumph of Christianity over the pagans.

The "Conquista" is considered to be a turning point in this type of mass theatre of evangelization. Arróniz (1979:81–82) believes that it was itself a statement in the debate concerning baptism by aspersion, by which the Franciscans baptized hundreds, even thousands of aboriginal people in a single day. The debate was being resolved by a papal bull of 1538, which vindicated the Franciscan practice while urging that it be restricted as much as possible to the severely ill or other urgent cases. Some church authorities in New Spain claimed, however, that their church was in fact a "new church," and that baptism by aspersion was acceptable because of the large numbers of its unbaptized followers. Arróniz further deduces that Brother Antonio de Ciudad Rodrigo, the provincial of the Franciscans and a member of the Ecclesiastic Board, transcribed the play in such detail because it was an answer to the order's rivals: a deliberate act in support of the sacrament of baptism as practiced by the Franciscans and possibly also a challenge to the colonial authorities, who were beginning to question the achievements of the order. In 1549 Archbishop Juan de Zumárraga decided to bar dramatic performances, dances, and other such activities from church premises, because he considered that native beliefs and customs were surviving in this way.

In 1555 Archbishop Alonso de Montúfar, a Dominican who did not look kindly on the Franciscans' work among adult Native Americans, banned all such performances from religious festivities where the Blessed Sacrament was present. Mass theatre nevertheless survived in remote areas, outside the reach of church authorities, a fact attested to by periodic bans issued by those authorities whenever they discovered another errant community, up to two hundred years later. But the fate of evangelical theatre was, by and large, linked to that of the Franciscan and Dominican orders, which were under increasing pressure from their rivals, the *encomenderos*. These landowners resented the criticism leveled against them by the mendicant friars for their mistreatment of the local people under their jurisdiction.

Still, missionary work survived. The Franciscans delegated much of their evangelical activity to aboriginal Catholics. They even handed over to them the administration of the College of Tlatelolco, between 1546 and 1566. During that same period, an increasing number of manuscripts were given to native disciples to translate, "observing the meaning rather than the letter" (Arróniz 1979:103), i.e., carrying out the task of ideological indoctrination in the language most appropriate to the target population.

Evangelical theatre proper continued into the seventeenth century, sometimes as the collective effort of Juan de Torquemada, fray Juan Bautista, fray Francisco Gamboa, and a plethora of native scribes, translators, and editors in the College of Tlatelolco, where the texts were also printed (Arróniz 1979:107).

The Dominicans

The first Dominican missionaries arrived in 1526; four of them died, four returned to Spain, and the remaining four were faced with the daunting task of evangelizing a territory that included part of Mexico and Guatemala. The first record of Dominican drama is Las Casas's introduction of songs in the native language, in 1537, before he witnessed the drama at Tlaxcala but after seeing the 1535 auto in Mexico City.

The local rulers, the conquistadores, laughed at Las Casas's peaceful educational efforts, preferring brute force to subdue the natives. Shelly and Rojo (1982) emphasize that Las Casas was the exception to the rule of allowing indigenous people only a minimal education and of restricting their active participation in colonial institutions. Las Casas's strategy was to use local people not only as informants but also as instruments. He selected four Christian aboriginal traders from Guatemala, who traveled several times a year to Zacapula and the Quiché. The priests taught them the songs and verses they had composed, and asked the natives to refine them and present them in their travels, as dialogues. Arróniz (1979:127) suggests that these catechists were employing a rudimentary kind of theatre.

In Oaxaca Andrés de Moguer built up the Dominican theatre over a period of about forty years. His work is known mainly because of the fatal events of 1586, when the balcony of the convent at Etla (near Oaxaca) collapsed during a performance, killing many local people and a friar. Moguer used the exempla with great success; his work and that of the other Dominicans received the support of a lay group, the cofradía of the Holy Rosary.

The documentation of missionary theatre for other regions of the Americas is much more fragmentary than it is for Mexico. Evidence exists, mainly through passing mention in chronicles and contemporary accounts, of similar evangelizing efforts by the Dominicans in Peru, but the most significant documented effort appears to have been that of the Jesuit order. Hence our emphasis for South America on the mission theatre of the Society of Jesus.

The Jesuits

The Society of Jesus was a singular latecomer among the missionary orders in the Americas. The order was founded in Spain in the 1530s; that is, after most of the continent had been conquered and apportioned among the existing religious orders. By the 1560s the extraordinarily dynamic Jesuits were in practically every corner not yet claimed by Franciscans, Dominicans, or Augustinians (the three most influential missionary groups of the time). The Society of Jesus had to overcome the strong objections of colonial administrators against the admission of foreign missionaries; it did eventually succeed in bringing in non-Spanish members of the order.

The Jesuits, who appreciated the educational value of drama, were quite given to having their students present dramatic performances, both in their remote missions and in their urban colleges. Native students recruited from the missions were taken to study in the cities, to return to their communities as lay missionaries or Jesuit brothers. One can safely assume that this was the manner in which the largely intellectual drama of the Jesuit colleges was brought into the sub-Amazonian missions. The organic link between these colleges and the forest missions was maintained until shortly before the order was expelled from its last bases in the Spanish colonies, in 1767.

The leading author of the Jesuit theatre in Brazil was probably José de Anchieta, whose work (from the 1560s to the early 1600s) is characterized by one scholar as a series of "mystifications along with demystifications and a whole series of theatrical heterodoxies, in the service of religious orthodoxy" (Pontes 1978:13). Anchieta's allegorical plays are on the cutting edge of grass-roots theatre, because their target audiences were primarily Native Americans; as prime exponents of evangelical or missionary theatre, they connect with the oral/nonliterate tradition, yet they must also be included among the earliest works of the Latin American literate theatre, because they were published under the playwright's name and did not enter the stream of folk drama. Moreover Anchieta's plays are also unique because they are bilingual (Portuguese-Guaraní) and occasionally multilingual (when Spanish or other foreign characters appear). Anchieta's contribution to the foundations of an American theatre was made on behalf of the Jesuit missions, yet his individual accomplishment ranks him among the most important playwrights of the colonial period.

Syncretism and Substitution

It would be impossible to survey here all the wealth of material that exists on the subject of Native American dramatic forms and folk drama, which, next to modern dramatic literature, have probably occupied most scholarly attention. Because our preferred focus is on the question of syncretism and the creation of a new American theatre, we have concluded that the field is far from having been covered. Much of the research published since the 1950s is thorough for specific regions, but a systematic study of Native American drama of the hemisphere remains to be done. This section deals with the types of grass-roots theatrical performance or folk drama that have evolved since the conquest, reflecting a synthesis of cultures.

We are also including postconquest Native American theatre, which has taken on some of the characteristics of folk drama even in its revivals of pre-Hispanic themes and dramatic forms. In this regard we acknowledge the distinction that Estage Noel (1988) defends, between contemporary Native American theatre and folk drama (theatre performed by or for non–Native Americans), and we have endeavored to classify these manifestations separately. Such distinctions are not always possible, however, particularly for festivals, where the Native American traditions and the more syncretic folk traditions coexist.

Syncretism and the Conquest

The philosophical emphasis in the standard dictionary definitions of the term *syncretism* bolsters the need to emphasize the ideological aspect of cultural production in areas where two or more civilizations meet. It is certainly not sufficient to examine coincidences or fusions of formal elements as if they were directly emblematic of the philosophy of a play or dance drama, but the structural connections that constitute the product do provide the key to that philosophy. The definition offered by Edmonson (1960:192), "the integration and [consequent secondary elaboration] of selected aspects of two or more historically distinct traditions," is sufficiently broad to take into account practically all the cultural productions with which we are dealing. In addition it is intrinsically, and quite explicitly, connected with belief systems; hence our ready acceptance of the term.

It is not always clear whether cultural productions and belief systems born out of the conflictive meeting of civilizations should be termed syncretic. The main objection to the use of the term is based on the nature of the power relationship between the cultures and on the outcome of the European venture with Africans and Americans (namely, the establishment of European hegemony and the destruction and replacement of economic and political systems and official ideology). It would be an idealization of these relationships to overemphasize the persistence of non-European beliefs and cultural forms as if they were always equal to those of the conquerors. The superimposition of one set of values over another is an undeniable premise in most cases, and one cannot dismiss out of hand the view that the main operational mechanism is substitution rather than fusion.

Nonetheless it should be sufficient to recognize the establishment of this new relationship without having to affirm also that the vanquished have surrendered every inch of ideological territory or that the victory was won without any concessions. Thus Frischmann (1991:3) marshalls convincing evidence that both the forms and the thematic content of the theatre of Yucatán are proof of the "strategic acculturation" adopted by the Maya in response to the violent imposition of the Catholic faith in the seventeenth century, a strategy by which they gained the breathing space in which to continue to exercise their traditions.

The Spanish and Portuguese empires were built by Christian nations which themselves had only recently emerged from a long period of complex relations with Islam and Judaism and which, like the rest of Europe, were still dealing with recently assimilated pagan cultures and beliefs. This gave them a flexibility and a strength that the more homogeneous native cultures had not had the time to evolve (Lévi-Strauss 1976:339ff., a theory partially anteceded in Iberian thought by Castro 1954). As Ingham (1986:181) points out, the civilization that came to America and brought Africans to America was itself a "blend of orthodox and pre-Christian culture." This heterodoxy would not be threatened so much as it would continue to be enriched by the new cultures it was assimilating in the New World.

The Inquisition, called into play for the most part to suppress the most openly identifiable cases of rebellion, resistance, or deviance, intervened periodically in the early stages of the conquest, as the Europeans sought to break down every aspect of aboriginal material culture that could facilitate the perpetuation of local value systems. Although individual clergy, acting directly or through aboriginal converts, did destroy records and symbols of the American civilizations, for the most part the church did not attempt to eradicate the cultural forms and human agents of those beliefs, but rather tried to harness them in the service of the new "True Religion." If and when it did attempt such destruction, its envoys were usually outnumbered and overwhelmed in the most remote regions. Rather than undertaking to erase the aboriginal cultures, the church contented itself with imposing its beliefs and most of its patterns of worship.

Parallels and symbolic analogies between the cultures of the two worlds became instruments both of European harnessing of the forces of cultural creation and of Native American retention of a strong measure of cultural identity while still satisfying their new rulers. One might even say that although Spain and Portugal "pacified" the local peoples through war and servitude, the latter in turn at least placated the Europeans by lending their cultural creations to the European religion and accepting primarily those European beliefs that had some correspondence with their own.

Of course they did so, for the most part, under the barrel of the gun. Even the most peaceable missionaries were able to accomplish what they did thanks to the implicit or explicit threat of armed intervention by their lay compatriots or by marshalling persuasive images of hell and damnation. Still this does not provide a complete answer to the receptiveness or at least the vulnerability of Native Americans to the European message.[5]

One explanation of this vulnerability is directly connected to dramatic expression. According to Versenyi (1988:331), the rigidity of the aboriginal systems is intrinsically expressed in the ritual repetitions that constitute the core of their performance rites. Such repetitions impeded the culture's flexibility to adapt and respond to the conquerors, who were better able to improvise. Versenyi's proposition when extended to the residual popular cultures can only lead us to conclude either (a) that their inflexibility served the Native American cultures well, because it allowed them to survive for so long; or else (b) that they developed the minimum amount of flexibility, in order to be able to assimilate those aspects of European civilization that enhanced and strengthened their own cultural expression.

Meanwhile the communication of basic tenets of Catholicism that had no counterpart in African or Native American belief systems (e.g., sin) demanded some inventiveness and flexibility on the part of the missionaries, and some concepts may well have been translated with license. The other factor was language. Often the minimal level of linguistic communication that existed between Europeans and Native Americans meant that subtleties were overlooked or dispensed with in the transmission of Catholic beliefs.[6] What was transmitted and accepted was often a gross simplification or a superficial correspondence. This in itself lends credence to the notion that the cultural conquest was not entirely a one-way affair.

A question that has become fashionable in the context of the quincentenary is: Who, in the final analysis, conquered whom? (see Versenyi 1989:226) The idea of a "mutual conquest" as transculturation is an acceptable compromise for some. Others, like us, are inclined to see this as a specious argument, given the overwhelming historical evidence of the systematic imposition of the conquerors' values and their socioeconomic systems.

Granted, after the initial violent subjugation had been accomplished, Native Americans enjoyed at least the theoretical protection of the crown, under special laws governing them during the colonial period. After independence such protection vanished. Aboriginal communities suffered disastrous losses of land, particularly with the ascendancy of the export economy, and migrations away from traditional lands resulted in the assimilation and cultural transformation of a high percentage of Native Americans.

The myth of three centuries of "peaceful coexistence" between whites and aboriginal peoples was, however, just that: a myth fostered by the exclusion of Native Americans from official history.[7] Most of the three hundred years of colonial rule consisted of periods of uneasy truces framed by uprisings and localized wars and often used by both whites and mestizos to extend their territorial control by means other than armed conflict; in this way they intensified the subjugation and marginalization of aboriginal peoples by economic and cultural means. Only remote communities that enjoyed the benign neglect of the church hierarchy and the civil authorities were somewhat predisposed toward cultural autonomy and survival, yet syncretism affected even some of the most isolated cultural areas.

The process by which an American theatre began to emerge as the expression of this syncretic culture can be traced through the evolution of several forms or genres, beginning with the missionary theatre and continuing with ritual dances, loas, and ritual dramas, to culminate in plays that have only been codified since the nineteenth century, but which are probably the direct descendants of much earlier popular creations.

Substitution as Subjugation or Resistance?

Substitution is especially prominent in the case of coinciding festivals, in selected ritualizations or performances, and in the case of individual characters or categories of characters. As a rule the timing and locus of performances are connected to their ritual or religious significance, while the substitution or interchangeability of characters is linked to structural analogies.

Most important festivals appear to fall into two categories: those in which the dates of the Catholic festivities coincided with preexisting Native American or African ritual periods, and those in which non-European rituals were moved to dates that the dominant classes imposed. The latter include holidays separate from the church calendar and often introduced after the end of colonial rule (e.g., Día del Campesino in Colombia, Día de la Tradición Popular in Argentina, etc.).

Among the most important of what one could term "joint," or coinciding, festivals are those held around the solstices and the harvest. For example, Corpus Christi and the feast of St. John the Baptist coincide, in various indigenous cultures, with celebrations around the summer solstice. In the Peruvian highlands, Corpus merged easily with Inti Raymi (also known as the Sun Easter), one of the holiest pre-Hispanic festivals. The festivities around the Epiphany coincided with the latter end of the winter solstice celebrations, and the participation of African-Americans in the 6 January festival (particularly in Cuba and Brazil) was consistent with African rituals around that period.

Fertility rites associated with spring, which no doubt contributed to the rich European festivities around carnival and Easter, coincided with the latter in some parts of the Americas; carnivals remain important festivals to this day. Like their European counterparts, the carnivals with predominant Native American and African-American content are primarily secular, and the syncretism found in them appears to be relatively free of imposed substitution.

Festivities such as those honoring the Virgin Mary and the saints were determined by the Catholic calendar, but the patron they honored was really more often than not a substitute for a pre-Christian patron. Numerous festivals have developed around the *patrona* (a manifestation of the Virgin who serves as a particular protector) throughout the Americas. They range from the worship of the Virgin of Guadalupe (generally acknowledged to be a substitute for the Nahua goddess Tonantzin) as the national protector of Mexico to that of the Virgin of *la Candelaria* (Candlemas), protector of miners in Bolivia. Festivities honoring local patron saints (who often correspond to pre-Christian deities, much as they did in Europe) may serve as a pretext for reenacting traditional dramas. Performers are sometimes contracted from other towns or villages, particularly if they have a particular skill or if they are the only known experts on a particular dance.

The festivals (particularly those of major saints or the Virgin Mary) usually attract people from other villages, and some (like the Copacabana festival on the shores of Lake Titicaca) have attracted tens of thousands of pilgrims. To such festivals not only spectators but performers come from other subcultures of the region, in greater numbers, of course, than to the smaller festivities for a local patron saint. One can safely say, therefore, that festivals were an important medium for the continuing cross-fertilization of the popular theatre and for the on-going process of syncretism.

Specific rites outside the religious festivals, such as the religious sacraments, can be identified with non-European rites of passage, and the festivities around such rites sometimes involve dramatic presentations. Official tolerance did not extend to non-Christian ritual dramas that could not be justified in syncretic terms, such as the "Dance of Tun Teleche" of the Maya (a genre, banned in the seventeenth century, to which the *Rabinal Achí* belongs) and most ritual performances associated with African secret societies in Cuba.

The syncretic characters are as intriguing in the folk drama of the Americas as some of their counterparts are in Europe. Tracing their genealogy is sometimes a difficult task, especially in those cases where the source character is equally well defined in two (or sometimes three) cultures of origin. The most difficult is the Diablo (Devil), which figures in practically every region of the continent and which we have discussed in chapter 1. It can be related to animal totems in different Native American rituals and to the characters of African drama. In the genealogy proposed by Ingham (1986:182), the European Devil is certainly fused with Tezcatlipoca, because of their common identification with death, wealth, the color black, and the coyote (see Robinson and Hill 1976). In Río Sucio, Colombia, there is a "Devil's Carnival," dating back over a century, in which Native American, African, and European elements have been happily united. In the manifestation that is closest to its European origins, the Devil plays a leading role (and a key speaking part) in the Guatemalan loas to the Virgin Mary.[8]

Myths and legends also are the subject of syncretic dramas. The Gigantes (Giants) of Mexico and Central America may be residual representations both of the supernatural beings known as the Twin Giants of Nahua mythology and of the Goliath of medieval processions. The Mesoamerican "Deer Dance," a totemic hunting ritual, was transformed during the colonial period into a type of loa, or drama of praise, to the Virgin Mary, with the animals turning from hunted beasts to worshippers.

Unlike aboriginal drama, folk drama is strongly influenced by the mestizos, whose economic status in the smaller communities and their donations to the festivities usually enhance their ideological influence. For the most part, the attitude toward authority in the dramas tends, therefore, to be noninimical.

Syncretic Ritual Drama

One occasionally finds records of folk drama or rituals that appear to be a perfect fusion of European Catholic and Native American elements. Such a ritual, the "Fiesta de Sumamao," was documented around 1940 in Santiago del Estero, in north central Argentina (Canal Feijóo 1943). This is a fairly complex dramatic ritual of a participatory nature, performed by Native Americans and mestizos; its structure is processional, and the object of worship is an image of Saint Stephen. The festivity is carried out on 26 December, St. Stephen's Day, and the pattern of much of the ritual is similar to the generic "Adoration of the Shepherds." Its component sections include rituals of primarily Spanish or indigenous origin as well as others in which the two elements are fused.

Included along with the praise of the saint are a show of respect to the donor (the owner of the *rancho*, who may have taken over the funding of the ceremony from the church), the payment of promises (chiefly through the procession and later a race into the forest), and the actual worshipping of the image (which is carried aloft by two women).[9] The ceremony includes the *quila*, a symbolic distribution of one's possessions (which appears to be an equivalent of the North American *potlatch*) and a sacrificial bloodletting rite before the totemic image. It also includes a classic pilgrimage situation, with participants moving on their knees toward the shrine. The unusual aspect of the bloodletting is that it is carried out immediately after the ritual of "correr a los indios" (chasing the Indians), in which men on horseback chase others on foot, whipping them. After this chase ends, and while the mass of pilgrims move penitentially on their knees, the character representing the authority (Don Suárez or Don Luna) slashes the runners' shins, with great skill and precision (according to some informants, to prevent cramps), as the runners kiss the trappings of the statue.

The setting includes arches made of boughs and the remnants of what must have been the totemic pole or tree, removed to make way for the structure in which the saint's statue is placed. The substitution appears obvious. What is not clearly obvious is the meaning of the chase: Is it perhaps a long-remembered reenactment of the arrival of the Europeans? At any rate the ceremony is definitely religious in nature, with a Christian focus but structured around a number of rituals that are clearly Native American. The integration of indigenous rites into the Catholic worship is analogous to ceremonies in regions where the indigenous and mestizo populations have a marked presence in pilgrimages and other similar rituals.

The "Fiesta de Sumamao" is an example of the complex combination of ritual and drama that has been found even in the most marginal of cultures. We thought it worth citing, even though it has virtually disappeared. Its practitioners include Native Americans and mestizos, and all geographic data indicate that their uneasy coexistence with the hegemonic culture in the heart of Argentina has resulted in its own unique form of syncretism, in which the Catholic European elements fuse with indigenous rites that echo those of other Native American cultures.

The Güegüence, Syncretism and Folk Drama

Just as the missionary theatre drew on the Native American talent for acting, dance, costuming, and music, so did the mestizo culture of the colonial period. One of the few known folk plays to have been documented (Brinton 1883) is an odd comedy, performed to this day in the context of the feast of the patron saint of Diriambá, Nicaragua. A fair amount has been written on "El Güegüence, o El Macho Ratón" ("The Old Man, or the Billygoat-Mouse"), particularly after the 1979 triumph of the Sandinistas, whose cultural policy promoted the documentation and retrieval of traditional culture. Some of the analysis is worth citing here.

The most interesting aspect of this play is perhaps the fact that it is considered to be a Native American play in Spanish. Brinton, its compiler, was the first to suggest that its lack of moral or religious purpose made it unlikely that it was introduced by priests, unlike virtually all folk drama of European origin. He also points out three elements of the "Güegüence" that defy the standard Spanish drama: (1) the heroine and the female characters have no speaking parts; (2) the action is continuous, with no prologue, scenes, or acts; and (3) the dialogue hinges on what Brinton, and many after him, found to be tiresome repetition, a Native American formula commonly found in Mesoamerican drama. Brinton also saw the main character (a comic old man) as the classic buffoon, and he considered the humor to be farily elementary, as it consists mainly of obscenities and of the Macho Ratón's central shtick, feigned deafness that leads to amusing verbal exchanges.

Sáenz (1988) accurately identifies the European elements of the play: its language is Spanish and its characters are dressed as whites or mestizos. Sáenz adds to Brinton's classification of the play's pre-Hispanic elements only one that we can accept as clearly indigenous: the personification of animals as characters. His other categories, in our opinion, could well be either Spanish or Native American, and in this play they certainly come across as mestizo: the characters dancing among the spectators, the performance in the streets and the church atrium, the trick of feigned deafness and the old man as protagonist, masked characters, and a festive ending or *mojiganga*, which closes the performance. All of these elements have been documented for medieval or Renaissance Iberian drama as well as for preconquest indigenous drama, while the play has been variously dated to the eighteenth and seventeenth centuries.[10] One element that has not been sufficiently emphasized in this regard is that the "Güegüence" is an urban play. Because its setting is clearly that of a town or city, it could not be considered a purely Native American play, and since it does not qualify as European, either, then it must have been a mestizo play. The "Güegüence" is quite unique, because it is fundamentally a satire of the corruption and the abuse of power by whites. The people can mock the pompous colonial authorities to their hearts' content through anthropomorphic characters who have the resources to evade punishment for their insolence.

The disrespect for authority and the contempt it shows for the arrogance of power through "defensive malice, intolerance of injustice and servility, irony, and wild imagination" (Sáenz 1988:11) make it a unique example of popular drama. Its role in the feasts of St. Sebastian appears to be similar to the role played by secular or secularized drama since before the conquest (in America as in Spain): that of comic relief, of participatory entertainment free of church control, and of a carnivalesque outlet for popular criticism of authority (see Rizk 1988).

The syncretism of the folk drama, whether it is ultimately an expression of a defeated people or of their will to resist, usually combines the ability of indigenous peoples to mask their beliefs and the reality of the marginalization of the underclass.

African-American Dramatic Forms

Little systematic documentation exists of black traditional theatre, aside from some for Cuba and Brazil and specific manifestations in Puerto Rico, the Dominican Republic, Peru, Venezuela, Ecuador, and Colombia, as well as the "danzas de negros" in parts of Peru and Bolivia. Among all the genres, Ortiz (1951:364) pays special attention to ritual dances of Cuban blacks that originated with Congo masked dancers and first appeared as the "Tata-nganga" ("Ganguleros") or "Nganga-nkisi" of the festival of the Epiphany (January 6), in which blacks were allowed to participate in colonial times. Another dramatic ritual dance is the "Kokoríkamo"; *koko* means "ghost" in Bantu and "ancestor" in Northwest Bantu.

Fear of the koko is holy terror; *kokoríkamo* is an extraordinary, awesome, or ineffable numinosity, a pretheological concept, according to Ortiz (1951:368–69), who goes so far as to speculate that the medieval European "Dance of Death" has African antecedents. Such ritual dances have both a religious and a social function, of "keeping alive the sense of mystery, of providing a catharsis for psychic tensions, and ensuring a stabilizing and cohesive tribal policy of all classes" (Ortiz 1951:373).

The Congos in Cuba used to celebrate the ancestors' ceremony ("Güiri") on 2 February, Candlemass (la Candelaria). The feast day of Santiago (St. James, identified with the African *orisha*, or spirit god, Ogún), 25 July, is of particular importance in three Caribbean towns and cities of which he is the patron saint: Santiago de Cuba, Santiago de los Caballeros (Dominican Republic), and Loíza (Puerto Rico). In each one of these locations, public celebrations include religious processions, carnivals, and ritual dances and mumming, which have their roots in Africa and Spain. The Puerto Rican dancers, who like their Cuban counterparts (the Diablitos), are costumed in grass skirts and masks and who shake noisemakers, are known as Vejigantes.

Much of the African drama that survives in the Americas is close to its original form and intent. We categorize it here as African-American rather than African: (a) because it represents, as a whole, a conglomerate of origins rather than a single culture; and (b) because most of the individual forms that did persist appear to have undergone some syncretism. Moreover, although its practitioners have usually identified themselves with specific African cultures or rites, and they have continued to practice their art and their rites in farily closed demographic environments, their context, and the context in which their drama exists, has been determined by their historical experience with slavery, white domination, and miscegenation, to the extent that some of the rites and dramatic traditions have come to be associated with Santería, Macumba, and other syncretic religious cultures.

Among the forms that have remained relatively pure are those perpetuated by religious sects like the Abakuá, in Cuba, whose liturgy of sacrifice Ortiz classifies as drama (1951:376–78). In this liturgy, as in other liturgies of African origin, the priests or initiates, when possessed, are "dressed to represent the mythical being that is in them temporarily and has reduced them to a mere physical vessel" (Ortiz 1951:343–44).

In addition to dramatic forms that survived in the context of their tradition of worship, Ortiz identifies others that have survived although the overall liturgical context has disappeared. The main example of this seems to be the Lucumí funeral dance of Egún, who personifies the dead person and the ancestors. The invocation to Egún is part of every Lucumí funeral rite. Although, as Ortiz notes, elements of these rites persisted despite the fact that no sect or brotherhood of Egungún was active in Cuba (Ortiz 1951:348), these ancestor-worship rites are one of the most solid links between African-American drama and its African predecessors (see chapter 1).

Besides the ceremonies of worship of the syncretic cults, there are those of secret societies (formed by former slaves in the nineteenth century as mutual-aid societies), such as the *ñáñigos*. The ñáñigo held night-long festivals (from which women and children were excluded); these festivals were structured into liturgical episodes, each with its prescribed dances (Ortiz 1951:360).[11]

An essential element of these festivals are the Íreme (Diablos), transculturations, according to Ortiz, of African ritual figures in Havana and neighboring ports. The role of the Íreme is to officiate at the ceremonies, with covered face but no mask, representing the invisible dead who become visible temporarily to be among the living. There are usually various characters, each with its particular costume and liturgical function (Ortiz 1951:361), but they are always directed by the priest and do not speak. They appear to be the counterparts of the West African characters described in chapter 1.

A feature of these festivals is the incorporation of the Diablitos (Little Devils), which were part of the ancient Corpus Christi processions in Spain, but which are identified primarily as African dramatic figures where the African-American presence is strongest. In the Americas the Diablito is dressed in traditional African or Native American costume and performs ritual dances or comic miming.

In transplanted African theatrical forms, as in early Spanish and Portuguese performances, there were no female players. According to Ortiz, female secret societies in Africa had female Devils, but apparently they do not appear in America, either in their counterpart secret societies or in most religious ceremonies.

In Santiago, Cuba, African-American participation in the festivities reflects the importance of the *cabildos*, the official or semiofficial bodies in which blacks of different origins were organized. There were the *cabildos de nación* (groupings by "nation," i.e., by African culture of origin), the *tajonas* (French-Haitian, established by slaves brought by immigrants from Haiti after 1791), and *congas* (which began in the nineteenth century and coalesced definitively in the mid-twentieth century). The white masters often participated in parades, and the queen of each cabildo was carried on a litter. *Comparsas* (mummers and ambulatory musicians) were accompanied mainly by African percussion.

The parades became, increasingly, an exhibition of music and dance, as the ritual dance dramas were diluted or simply vanished; elements of the dramas survive in the masks, the costumes, and some of the characters, reduced by the twentieth century to little more than folklore.

In Brazil the meeting of African cultures with Native American as well as European cultures resulted in the creation of syncretic rites that draw from all three dramatic traditions. A counterpart of the festival role of the cabildo can be seen in the samba schools of the modern-day carnival of Rio de Janeiro, with their elaborate costuming, choreography, and rhythms. Remnants of the dramatic function of the protagonists can be surmised from the representation of popular themes by each school, especially in the floats, the rather secular heirs of the religious tableaux vivants.

African-American influences, considerably more muted than in the spectacular Rio carnival, are present in the carnival comparsas of Peru, Bolivia, Uruguay, and to a lesser extent, in those of Argentina, as well as in the coastal cities of Colombia and Venezuela. The theatrical elements of these musicians and mummers include masks, costumes, derivations of African ritual dances, and choral and responsive singing (sometimes with mime, and often with a satirical or bawdy chronicle of contemporary events) that lend a strong dramatic component to the presentation. Most of these carnival festivities appear to be combinations of African and European (and occasionally of Native American and Chinese) elements.

SURVIVAL AND TRANSFORMATION

It seems quite significant that forms of non-Christian rites have survived to this day, especially in the context of the largely secular carnival, where the inversion ritual proper to the festival presumably serves as the permissive factor for the free expression of the marginal cultures. Moreover numerous religious dramas originating in missionary theatre or in non-European drama and ritual survive to this day, some transmuted by the superimposition of the hegemonic culture, others relatively intact. They are staged in public spaces, often closely connected to a shrine or other religious place, and are usually grass-roots participatory undertakings directed by religious authorities or led by civic leaders and conforming to prescribed patterns of ritual.

Secular festivities, on the other hand, are characterized by free-form participation, although they, too, are framed by their own conventions. Purely secular folk drama such as the "Güegüence" has (until recently at least) been performed customarily in the context of a major religious festivity. Lampooning of authorities commonly occurs in carnival parades, which are also showcases for the integration of traditional values (dance, costumes, music) with newly appropriated elements of the hegemonic culture (e.g., Hollywood characters). The assimilation of these elements is probably uncritical, and may indicate an ideological identification or simply an aesthetic appreciation (see Turner 1987).

Secular festivities commonly feature folkloric elements, some of which may have once been connected to non-Christian sacred rituals, but which are now decontextualized and reified. Traditional festivities, too, have in some cases been transformed into tourist attractions. What before the consolidation of the independent nation states (mainly Cuba and Brazil) could be a medium for the affirmation of cultural identity of marginal groups had become, less than half a century after independence, an avenue for marketing little more than the objectified shell of a religious culture.

The very process of the formation of nationality could be cited as one explanation for this folklorization. Moreover the commercialization of culture justifies its own tendency to devour or at least appropriate the more "marketable" elements of traditional popular culture. The commercialization of African-American and of Native American "folklore" is virtually simultaneous with the recognition of marginal cultural forms and the reduction of these forms to sanitized versions of the exotic Other. While not entirely deprived of their elements of mystery, of danger, or of the grotesque, they are all so decontextualized from their original intention that they may reinforce the interplay between fascination and rejection inherent in the viewing of the exotic (See Said 1979).[12]

Conclusions

Theatre and dramatic performance have been central to the cultural activity of the largely nonliterate populations of Latin American society since pre-Columbian times. Performance played a similar role, and included similar varieties, in the aboriginal cultures of America and in the cultures of origin of African-Americans. There were correspondences between the liturgical or religious drama of these cultural areas and the medieval Iberian theatre that was brought to America and became a cornerstone of traditional popular drama in this hemisphere.

The concept of syncretism was acceptable to us because of the ritual or religious nature of much of the nonliterate theatre and even the scripted theatre as adapted to nonliterate audiences and performers. The theatre of the conquest, evangelical drama, was primarily an ideological vehicle through which the friars engaged in a subtle contest with the aboriginal belief systems inherent in Native American rituals and dance dramas. The fusion of two or more cultures in a given region, which was contingent upon the degree of permanent contact between the groups, could therefore be seen as syncretism in the anthropological sense of the word. However, given the uneven nature of the encounter (even where the European culture is represented by a demographic minority), the weight of the military, political, and economic structures imposed on non-Europeans must qualify the use of the term, recognizing it only as a practical term without implying that the cultures had merged in harmony or even that the context was one of peaceful coexistence.

The festival of Sumamao offers an example of syncretic drama in which substitution and the coexistence of European Christian and Native American elements on the same plane appear to be essential to the structure. Ambiguity, too, is central: one can only speculate, now, whether the flagellation is a rite of submission introduced during the colonial or postcolonial period and retained through custom, or whether it is historical experience transmuted into symbolic action to vindicate the aboriginal blood rite under a protective disguise. The descriptive account of this festival demonstrates the inherent problem of studying the cultural production of extinct or near-extinct dramatic performances. But when the society itself becomes extinct or largely subsumed by mestizo or European culture, the possibility of interpreting and understanding the original significance of individual elements and of the ritual in its entirety is significantly diminished.

On the other hand, the strength and persistence of the "Güegüence" can be attributed to more than one contributing factor that enabled the sociopolitical environment of the play to function as a relatively stable community. The conservative character of the church-related festivities and the strong sense of identity and tradition in Diriambá contributed to keeping the play alive well into the twentieth century. In a community not yet shaken by modernization and economic change, religious festivals played a central role in the ritual restatement of its cultural identity. Under the cultural policies of the Sandinistas, artists and public officials cooperated in preserving, studying, and reviving popular traditions, and the national play of Nicaragua virtually enjoys the status of a national institution, supported by conflicting sectors of society.

The pervasive African dramatic forms of performance range from isolated symbolic elements in carnivals (elements often divorced from their representational roots) to the more complex structures of dance dramas in areas where African-Americans constitute a large sector of the population. The chief difference between the African-American and the other two main cultural groupings resides in the very nature of the condition of African-Americans as both subjugated and landless.

However widespread the early enslavement and later the economic enslavement of the aboriginal peoples may have been, however great the theft of their land, for over four hundred years they have not been legally enslaved nor have they, except for isolated groups, been taken far from their land, even those who have been stripped of the communal trusteeship of their territory. The loss by African-Americans of their economic base, their physical removal from their place of origin, and the forced integration of different original cultures into artificial demographic groupings (a process that the *cabildos de nación* may have slowed but could not prevent), are but three reasons why one could not expect African-American drama to develop in America as strongly as the medieval European drama or Native American forms. It should, however, be seen technically as the first theatre of exile in the Americas—reduced to its musical and dance components, but carrying still the clear echoes of the work of the traveling artists and healers and strong traces of the festival drama of their homeland.

The research for this book has included accounts of nonsurviving forms, of examples of unchanged aboriginal and medieval drama, and of forms that demonstrate various degrees of transculturation. The examples cited here are but a few of those that were found, and the materials surveyed should themselves be considered only the beginning of a necessary task: to continue to track down extinct and near-extinct forms, both as evidence of the continuity of popular theatre and because of the inherent value of historical preservation. These pages could therefore be read as a refusal to sound the death-knell of traditional popular theatre, but, on the contrary, to reaffirm its importance as a model of community-generated dramatic activity that continues today. How these varieties of popular theatre can be seen as part of a historical continuum, with the literate theatre and with the growing commercial popular/populist theatre will be the subject of part 2.

1. ENRIQUE BUENAVENTURA,
Colombia playwright and director.
Photograph, by Paul Lorgus, taken in 1972.

2. TEATRO EXPERIMENTAL DE CALI (TEC).
La orgía (The Orgy) by Enrique Buenaventura, performed at the Latin American Popular Theatre Festival, San Francisco, 1972. Photograph by Paul Lorgus.

3. GRUPO CULTURAL ZERO (MEXICO).
Carpa Zero (Mexico City, 1983).
Traditional Mexican vaudeville-style tent show with social commentary and political satire.
Photo by Donald Frischmann.

4. GRUPO ZUMBÓN (MEXICO).
Por qué el sapo no puede correr (Why the Toad Can't Run) (1983), Mayan traditional tale based on the Popul Vuh. Photo by Donald Frischmann.

5. CLETA (MEXICO).
La represión infantil (Repression of Children) (1983), a hard look at family relationships and the influence of mass media on children. Photo by Donald Frischmann.

6. GRUPO PUERPETCHE (MEXICO).
*Los hombres de los bosques (The Forest People) (1986),
a play about aboriginal peoples defending their ancestral
forests against exploitation by outsiders.
Photo by Donald Frischmann.*

7. GRUPO TEYOCOYANI (NICARAGUA).
Los ojos de Don Colacho (Don Colacho's Eyes)
(Managua, Nicaraguan Theatre Festival, 1984),
a play about land, traditions, and the counterrevolution.
Photo by Claudia Kaiser-Lenoir.

8. UNIÃO E OLHO VIVO (BRAZIL).
Bumba meu queixada (performed in 1980–81 in working-class neighborhoods of Sao Paulo). The social and political satire is presented in the framework of the Bumba, a traditional form whose origins go back to medieval Iberian drama. This play was first performed in 1979, in the suburb of O Sasco, where the workers of the important metallurgical industry were involved in frequent labor actions.
Photo by Leslie Damasceno.

9. GRUPO LA CANDELARIA (BOGOTA, COLOMBIA).
La Tras-Escena (Backstage) by Fernando Peñuela (1988), a contemporary allegory on conflict in Colombian society, using the theater as a referential framework.
Director Santiago García appears at the left.
Photo from the Dimensión Educativa files.

10. GRUPO TEATRO ESCAMBRAY (CUBA).
The cast of La emboscada (The Ambush) by Roberto Orihuela (Mountains of Escambray, Cuba, Festival Nacional de Teatro Nuevo, December 1978). Based on the documentary short stories of Jesús Díaz, this play deals with the counterrevolutionary war of the early sixties. Photo by Judith Weiss.

11. CABILDO DE SANTIAGO (CUBA).
De cómo el Apóstol Santiago puso los pies en la tierra
(How Saint James the Apostle Came Down to Earth)
(Santa Clara, Festival Nacional de Teatro Nuevo, December 1978).
A revisionist look at colonial Cuba, in which the patron saint of the city of Santiago joins the people's resistance against slavery and the arbitrary rule of a corrupt governor, and is duly punished.
Photo by Judith Weiss.

II

The Urban Theatre

3 • *Popular Forms, Characters, and Ideology*

In part I of this book, we elaborated on two concepts of "popular" theatre: traditional-popular, or residual, theatre and folk drama, including participatory theatre. Here we shall elaborate on the third and fourth uses of the term *popular*, which refer us (a) to popular artistic forms and social organization of the creative process and (b) to popular elements in mainstream or elite creations. Under the rubric of "popular forms" we include forms of artistic expression and genres that originate outside the dominant social sectors or are appropriated by them (e.g., farce, melodrama, entremés, sainete, musical comedy). By "popular types of social organization" we mean artistic organizations formed outside the mainstream, dominant culture; most often by small, independent entrepreneurs; and that appeal to popular tastes (such as circus, variety or vaudeville, radio theatre). Another common use of the term *popular* examined and evaluated here is that of "popular" elements within dramatic creations of the dominant sectors, such as characters and social types, language, and expressions of nonhegemonic value systems.

These categories apply to the three main currents of dramatic performance: scripted European and Creole drama, with a consciously literary identity; "nonliterate" European structures, as they continued in urban settings; and commercial theatres, which include scripted works and integrate theatrical works from the nonliterate structures. Overlapping and hybridization of these currents has not been uncommon, but the most consistent and complex of the fusions have occurred in the New Popular Theatre.

The first current consists of drama produced by and for the European and Creole classes ranges from class-identified productions (at courts and in colleges, and later in the bourgeois, petty bourgeois, and workers' theatres) to an elite "art theatre" or avant-garde in the twentieth century. This category must also include commercial productions of works that are part of the canon of Hispanic dramatic literature. (The latter, of course, include a majority of plays produced under contract for the Corpus Christi festivities in the colonial period and some plays produced for special occasions.)

The second current contains nonliterate European structures, which constituted themselves mainly in the eighteenth century out of marginal elements, and included the circus and the variety show and music hall. The circus has, since the early part of the nineteenth century, offered a locale for theatrical presentations (melodramas or comic sketches). Of course it also served as a home for the *commedia dell'arte* comic characters that did not get absorbed by the bourgeois theatre of the eighteenth century (Molière, Goldoni). It was in the circus that Pierrot, the Zannis, and others were able not only to thrive but also to reproduce themselves into thousands of individualized clowns, some of whom evolved into important comics of the Latin American commercial theatre and radio. The circus in Latin America has traditionally been a family-run and family-centered business, a model of small commercial entrepreneurs, artists, and impresarios often rolled into one.

The third current consists of commercial theatres, which produced scripted plays and musical comedies and introduced foreign touring companies. They were able, by the early twentieth century, to absorb elements of the circus and the variety show. In some respects the success of the commercial theatre as a popular-populist venture coincides in large measure with its reduction or banalization of the literate theatre and its partial absorption or integration of nonliterate or marginal theatre. It also coincides with the massification of art through such successful formulas as print advertising and the popularization of musical scores.

European Hegemony and the Power of the Lettered Classes

In outlining the development of the theatre in urban centers, we began from the conceptual framework suggested by Angel Rama's analysis of power and the written text (Rama 1984) and by Hernán Vidal's work on the social history of colonial literature (1985). In his posthumous essay on the "Literate City," Rama suggests that there exist both a geographic and a socioeconomic division between a primarily literate culture, dominated by successive elites or in the service of political forces (after independence, through journalists, legislators, and educators), and a predominantly oral, or illiterate, culture. Rama describes an encirclement of the literate minority by two rings of "linguistic and social enemies." The more immediate of these rings was the urban plebs, composed of an assortment of castes (foreigners; black and Indian freedmen; mulattoes, zambos, and mestizos; and poor Spaniards); the second ring, whose radius was far wider, included the suburban and rural settlements, farms, estates, indigenous villages, and villages established by runaway slaves. According to Rama, the written language functioned as a "defensive circle" to define the privileged identity of the propertied ruling class (1984:46).[1]

While Rama deals almost exclusively with the lettered classes, Hernán Vidal enters into greater detail concerning the socioeconomic tensions of the Latin American city. These constantly simmering tensions flared up in a variety of ways, from street crime to riots. Moreover the discontent came from the unemployed or underpaid classes of all races, not only the people of color, as the rulers insisted. This is a significant factor that is frequently overlooked; it should carry particular weight in the social history of the theatre.

As the urban centers grew, so did the dominant and intermediate classes of moderately or well-educated people. The church was the chief agent of this education; religious orders ran primary schools, secondary schools (or colleges), and universities. Between 1505 and 1725 universities were established in every major city, for a total of twenty-eight centers of higher education, including the University of San Carlos of Guatemala, San Marcos University in Lima, and the University of Córdoba, Argentina; these three are still leading universities in Latin America. Colleges and universities were, from the outset, places where plays were written and performed, and, along with the convents, they contributed to the formation of knowledgeable audiences.

In most of the colleges, the education of nonwhites was limited primarily to catechism and apprenticeships. Within three or four years of the establishment of the first schools in Mexico, in the late 1520s, pupils were being recruited from among the families of chieftains and higher castes of Native Americans. A small percentage of mestizo and mulatto pupils received advanced training, usually at seminaries in the Americas, and nonwhites were welcomed into religious orders, although there were restrictions on the highest rank to which they could aspire.

The educational system remained dominated by scholasticism until the eighteenth century, when the Bourbon dynasty supported the coming of the Age of Enlightenment to its American colonies, and a number of influential scholars and colonial administrators, including one or two viceroys, were active advocates of science and education. After the expulsion of the Jesuits, in the 1760s, many of their colleges were turned into centers of scientific study.

Through these colleges, through gazettes and pamphlets, and through discussions in masonic lodges, liberals and free-thinkers gradually managed to impose ideological models of the European Enlightenment. Ironically such models had been spawned in part from the idealization (by Voltaire, Rousseau, and others) of the "noble savages" of the Americas. These were the same "savages" whose reality was rejected, in the Americas, by most leaders of the Latin American Enlightenment, because it was plagued by superstition and ignorance, and because it considered them an irrational, dangerous, and barbaric fringe of their own society.

The illiteracy of these oral cultures was, no doubt, an important factor in the mistrust expressed toward them by the "enlightened" leaders of the emerging revolutions. The main reason for this mistrust was, however, rooted in the economic imperative of the landowning and mercantile classes that led the wars of independence. For this minority the aboriginal peoples (and, in the case of the coastal regions and the Caribbean, the African-Americans) posed a considerable threat to the Euro-American socioeconomic order, which was based mainly in the cities and the latifundia. Yet a small minority of whites would lend their literacy and their legal skills in the defense of Native Americans and, in some cases, of African-Americans.

The political independence of the new nation-states was a nominal freedom, if one considers the foreign debt under which some were born and which soon burdened the rest. Most Latin American nations fell into new spheres of influence and new relationships as economic colonies or satellites of Britain and the United States. Domestically none were spared violence, whether in the form of regional conflicts, of factional fighting between political parties, of civil war, or of border wars, some of which proved devastating (e.g., the war of the Triple Alliance against Paraguay; Mexico's war with the United States; the war among Chile, Peru and Bolivia; and the Chaco War). Even in periods of peace or undeclared conflict, the violence of poverty and displacement, of class oppression, and of foreign debt and economic pillage has rarely, if ever, been absent. It may be an invisible violence, but it is still a quintessential factor in the making and unmaking of the social contract and of the unavoidable contexts of cultural creation.

The city as designed by Spanish and Portuguese colonial rule was a microcosm of dependent relationships, a miniature metropolis, imitative of its mother cities in Europe. But it was also the bastion of European culture and of the power and authority of the lettered elites against the "barbaric" interior. We have examined the theatre and the dramatic traditions of those "barbaric" cultures; here we shall survey the almost exclusively European dramatic arts of the urban areas, dominated by the conventions of dramatic literature and economically determined by the interests of hegemonic classes or of classes rising to contest that hegemony.

Theatre and the Circles of Power

When we speak of the "lettered" classes, of those who control not simply the written word but, more importantly, the refined and arcane discourse of authority, we are referring to a small minority indeed (Rama 1984). Although the theatre is not necessarily a popular form of cultural creation, its collective character and its nature as a performance art led it to embrace systems of signs that are not restricted to the hegemonic classes, in order to include audiences outside the small, restricted groups of patrons and other authorities. This social inclusiveness is put into practice through the development of a range of artistic organizations and products, oriented to a corresponding variety of selected classes.

Although the model has proven to be open to popular input, the unstated objective of much of the theatre through much of its history could be considered antipopular; that is, it was inclined to please its sponsors or to provide entertainment while minimizing the risks of censorship or the wrath of the authorities. Thus even when urban theatre addressed the marginalized or the powerless, it was still primarily a theatre that curried favor to benefit the box office, or one that sought to draw the crowds to hear the hegemonic messages repeated in new ways. In fact one cannot say that the urban theatre spoke with any significant force for the powerless or the marginalized at any time, except when workers, and later peasants, took to the stage.[2]

Rama's figurative geography is, therefore, not simply a metaphor where the theatre is concerned. In other words the spatial symbolism of the city's "circles" is reproduced in the physical allocation of the theatre of the respective socioeconomic groups or demographic "rings." The separation began with the injunctions against the performance of certain types of drama *inside* the sanctuary of the churches; secular drama was periodically excluded from the sacred space because of its vulgar language and licentiousness—accusations that translate into the sexual and scatological elements associated with popular language and humor.

The viceroy's courts were themselves centers of artistic, musical, and dramatic activity. Many viceroys were patrons of the arts; they took a direct interest in the promotion of theatre and music, and they often surrounded themselves with European and American artists and scholars, who introduced the latest forms of cultural expression to America.[3] But what is more important, perhaps, in terms of the population at large, is the role of the rituals associated with the crown; like those of the church, they constituted an all-consuming center of social life. They served not only to maintain the constant fealty of the population, but also to remind the populace of the impregnable force of authority, through continual symbolic displays that included dramatic performances.

During the three hundred years of colonial rule, other institutions played roles that paralleled the influence of the crown (an influence that was directly felt only in centres where there was a viceroy). The main institutions were the municipal administration (in the cabildo, or town hall), the guilds, the church-affiliated associations such as cofradías, ethnic cofradías and cabildos, and the church itself. (The influence of each of these institutions fluctuated historically and differed from city to city.) The commissioning of plays for public or community events fostered acting and, to a somewhat lesser extent, dramaturgy. The independent commercial theatre in Latin America began with the earliest commissioned productions for Corpus Christi, and in many instances it was the public subsidies that allowed independent companies and playhouses to survive until they became viable as commercial ventures, backed by an increase in the urban population, specifically a mercantile class and ancillary sectors.

Lima stands out as an example of the fluctuations of the theatre's fortunes. During the first century of colonial rule, the theatre could not have found a more hospitable environment than in the new Peruvian capital—save, perhaps, for Mexico City or cities in Spain. Peru was the chief supplier of precious metals, and its capital was built in the context of a culture of ostentatious wealth, political intrigue, and a self-satisfied sense of relative autonomy. Few colonial cities were as enthusiastic about the theatre as Lima, which supported the most surprising level of dramatic activity for the better part of a century (between the 1580s and the 1680s), with a population of only 12,000 whites (Martin 1983:35).

At one point the authorities limited to two the number of companies resident in Lima, for fear of the negative moral influence of the artists on the general population (Lohmann Villena 1941). This limit irked the public as well as the artists who were drawn to Lima from Mexico and Spain. Just as it had flourished for the better part of a century, thanks to the relative economic stability of Peru, public dramatic activity suddenly declined as a result of a combination of factors. The trigger was the suspension of Corpus festivities for three years after the 1687 earthquake, which left the theatre companies less solvent, so that commercial theatre declined quite radically after 1699. The bourgeois theatre that arose in the late eighteenth century would be largely independent of official or other sponsorship or commissions, but it would not be entirely disconnected from its origins.

The Infrastructure of the Urban Theatre

The role of physical space and social organization can be seen as both neutral and active values in the survival and evolution of a popular theatre. Neutral, because popular elements are allowed to survive within them, in many cases, while dramatic activity continues to grow, to the benefit of Creole artists and writers as opposed to nonresidents of the Americas. Active, in that they are forerunners, part of the continuum, transformed apace with socioeconomic relations.

Theatrical forms contained in marginal performance media such as the circus, busker traditions, and variety shows owe their continued existence in part to the masses' need to confront the dominant culture, and also to the mobile or at least highly flexible nature of these forms of entertainment, as well as to their established ritual value within the community. Their roots lie in the "building blocks" of festivals (Falassi 1987), and their production space is the public space (temporarily appropriated and liminalized) or, in the case of the variety show, a privately owned space symbolically converted into a public and accessible space through moderate admission prices.

Organizational differences offer an alternative method for classifying the theatre. Scripted plays, comedies, and other full-length productions have for the most part been produced by groups under a managing director, who is usually also an actor. Marginal forms and structures such as the circus and the tent show and, to a lesser extent, vaudeville or variety shows, which are organized by an impresario, allow far more leeway for the actor's creativity and artistic autonomy.

Space and the Social Organization of the Theatre

The separation between outdoor (popular) and indoor (elite) performances became the established norm during most of the colonial period. Festivities that involved popular participation, especially those that celebrated the perpetuation of religious and royal hegemony, were held in public squares and streets in cities, towns, and villages. Although the main element of pageants was dance, this public celebration of power commonly included mime, dialogue, and a story line, giving the pageant a dramatic character similar to Native American or early European pageants. Indoor performances (in colleges, palaces, and eventually in playhouses and opera houses) almost without exception involved scripted works. The separation was sharpened soon after independence in a number of countries, where Native American and African-American performances (whether ritual or secular) were forbidden within town limits.

A common ground for city dwellers was provided by the use of the central square, or *plaza mayor*, for public festivities, and by "corrales," spaces occupied by the first impresarios for professional theatre productions.[4] By the end of the sixteenth century, most major urban centers in the colonies as well as in Spain had such spaces, where the main fare usually consisted of works by the most popular Spanish playwrights of the time. Thus the works of Lope de Vega, Tirso de Molina, and Calderón de la Barca drew both the literate minorities (such as courtiers, officers, lawyers) and the masses (such as tradesmen and artisans) and influenced the cultural productions of both groups. These scripted plays were, on the whole, of an extraordinary standard of dramatic and poetic achievement. They usually featured popular characters (the *Gracioso* or the *Bobo*—the Fool—and the Servants), high drama, and considerable violence and special effects.

Theatre companies were first able to acquire permanent locales through the long-term lease of land that belonged to a charitable institution or trust. The terms of the lease were, as a rule, that the company itself would make the space viable by erecting an appropriate structure on the leased land, with seating, galleries, etc., and that a considerable portion of the earnings derived through that space would devolve to the organization that owned the land. Thus a hospital, asylum, or other public-welfare institution that relied on charity (although it was run by religious) would benefit from the commercial venture; this enterprise was itself dependent, to a large extent, on public moneys derived through commissioned productions. The profit-nonprofit cycle was a fair arrangement, which protected more than one company from being closed down for the crime of lewdness; as a source of funding for the welfare institution, the theatre's fate was determined according to pragmatic criteria.

The corrales thus established were usually known by the name of the institution to which they were attached—sometimes quite literally, when they occupied a contiguous lot. Thus the Corral de San Andrés, built on land that belonged to San Andrés Hospital, in Lima, was the home of an important company headed by María del Castillo, from 1602 to her death in 1632. When she died the hospital trustees hired her nephew to continue as director of the corral, on which they had come to depend for operating funds. María del Castillo had emigrated from Spain to Mexico and then to Peru with her husband, a ne'er-do-well who became Lima's chief street paver. María del Castillo's relations with the cabildo soured over the years, but she continued to retain work for her company; in a way, the success and popularity of the company of San Andrés, guaranteed by the corral, protected it from any significant break with official Lima as long as the overall economic climate allowed.

The corrales are also the institutional forerunners of the playhouses that were built in the eighteenth and nineteenth centuries, first as a source of income for charity institutions such as hospitals and orphanages and later as independent enterprises serving the entertainment needs of the growing middle and upper sectors of urban society. By the early nineteenth century, the relatively primitive corrales had become marginal spaces or had disappeared, and they or equivalent locales were occupied by carpas (tent shows). The circus had entered the picture as the primary occupant of marginal sites (usually empty lots), and in Brazil, Mexico, and the U.S. Southwest, more than in most other areas, perhaps, the carpas brought itinerant theatre in patterns parallel to those of the circus.

Both the organizational and artistic structures of circuses and tent shows in Latin America are similar to those of their European and North American counterparts. An impresario serves as the motor and unifying force, and family members or other close associates trained by the director often provide internal stability and continuity. Individual artists may come and go, but specific roles and acts must be filled; hence, although stars may be drawing cards, it is often the particular acts that attract the same crowds and expand audiences. Paradoxically, therefore, what is in terms of physical space an essentially nomadic institution literally carries with it an organizational unity and continuity. This is practically the opposite of the permanent spaces that were built, beginning in the eighteenth century, as showcases of high culture, and which served both resident companies and also the more prestigious foreign artists on tour.

The American colonies acquired their opera houses and coliseums shortly after the construction of the first such structures in Europe. The Nuevo Coliseo of Lima, built at the height of the baroque period, with the latest in stage machinery and sets, was inaugurated in 1662 by the departing Viceroy Guzmán, who had made its construction possible.[5] Most coliseums, opera houses, and playhouses were built in the eighteenth century, under the enlightened monarchy of the Bourbons but largely by private capital, and by the time the wars of independence broke out, every main city had its principal theatre, which sometimes doubled as opera house. One of the most beautiful was built in Havana by Governor Tacón, at the height of Spain's brutally repressive rule of Cuba in the 1830s. It was originally named after Tacón, but it now bears the name of the playwright and poet Federico García Lorca.

Playhouses and opera houses joined the galaxy of structures that formed the symbolic core of power in the colonial city: the viceroy's or governor's palace, the cathedral, the bishop's or archbishop's palace, the main convents and their colleges, and the cabildo (town hall), which served as the only effective forum for the rising creole bourgeoisie. Each of these structures was the base of operations of a different power in the colony, balanced against the rest (or cooperating with them) in the complex system established by Spain or Portugal. Just beyond the edge of this core, usually not far from the commercial center of town, rose the new jewel boxes of elite culture, a kind of neutral zone where the various strata of the dominant classes would share operas, concerts, plays, variety shows, and even circus performances.

In addition to resident and touring companies, the coliseum presented circus acts and music hall acts or variety shows (sketches, songs, comedy). The coliseo of Mexico City, which also had a permanent company, has one of the earliest such programs on record (1788).[6] Clearly, then, the coliseo was important as a transitional or mediating space, which in some cases brought marginal forms under one roof, and in other cases introduced theatre to a broad audience. In this respect one could say that these playhouses were the institutional as well as the physical successors of the corrales.[7]

By the late nineteenth century, theatre houses were multiplying at a rate that reflected economic growth and its by-product: the rise of a middle class and of a working class with increased spending power and cultural aspirations. These groups of emerging political importance were not necessarily able to set their own standards or even to articulate independent cultural values in a society still dominated by the elite, but the repertoire often reflected their social and political aspirations or even their programs. The importance of independent impresarios grew with the increased opportunities for individual financial enterprise, with the commercialization of entertainment, and with the diminished importance of church censorship in determining artistic freedom.

The playhouses and opera houses soon became the venue for national touring companies and revues, many of which originated in the marginal spaces of the circus and the tent shows. It was not unusual, as recently as the 1920s if not later, for artists and directors to alternate between shows in urban theatre houses and tent shows that toured the interior and rural areas and eventually to move into radio theatre and the cinema.[8]

Radio eventually absorbed many artists of the "nomadic" theatre. Early radio theatre, however, was often produced by independent companies that were similar to the circuses and the tent shows in organizational structure and artistic training, and the shows were broadcast from small towns in the interior. The stories of these groups have been documented for Argentina in particular (Seibel 1985).

The allocation or appropriation of urban spaces replicates the demographic circles that Rama relates to power, authority, and the written word.[9] The six types of performance space described above are emblematic of this relationship, as the following summary should show.

The main public performance space in colonial times was the public square, or plaza, where commissioned productions were presented for religious festivities and civic occasions, which theatrical work was usually under the direct control of the authorities. The space was used equally by professional players and by popular performers (grouped mainly in religious and trade guilds and in ethnic cabildos or cofradías).

In contrast to the public square, the colleges and universities were the site of performances by students and teachers of the institution, and they thus represented a fairly controlled artistic environment as well as a restricted performance space, which could be opened or closed to the public, as its proprietors determined. The academic theatre space was useful for representing the specific political interests of the religious orders and eventually of students or political groups, in contrast to the public square, where the theatre was a vehicle for overarching and unifying ideological programs.

The early corral was both a quasi-independent and a quasi-permanent structure, usually attached to a public institution; it was administered and used exclusively by the company that held the lease on the property. Both because of the nature of the company's work (contracts or commissions for public events, plus commercial productions and box office) and because of the conditions attached to its existence (as a source of revenue for the public institution), the corral fulfilled an inherently dual function. Its permanence was contingent on the permanence of the company and its successors and on the administration of the public institution that it benefited. It was, in a sense, both an intermediary and a common space for theatregoers of most or all classes.

More stable structures, such as the coliseo and the opera house, are emblematic of permanence, although most of the performances were, in fact, by nonpermanent groups or foreign touring artists and companies. The solidity of the structure said more about the designs and self-image of the "lettered" classes who built them than about any organizational unity of the artistic presentations. Through these theatre houses, their funders and supporters could exercise their role as aesthetic arbiters (hence the importation of foreign artists and dramatic forms). On the other hand, the impresarios who gained access to some coliseums early on made them a kind of multipurpose space, with eminently popular acts and a variety of performers (Lohmann-Villena 1941: 511 and Rojas Garcidueñas 1935: 37–9).

Empty lots in the cities and on the edge of towns ("zero" spaces) became the habitual quarters for nomadic circuses and eventually for transient theatre and vaudeville shows (carpas). These marginal artistic structures, which evolved mainly after the political independence of Latin America, temporarily appropriated and converted nonspecific spaces, albeit in recognized and anticipated patterns. The impermanence or at least the vulnerability of the physical space to other uses belied the stability and relative permanence of its users: whatever the changes in personnel or in the detail of acts, both the circus and the tent shows had an organizational unity (single impresario or director) and continuity (family and close associates), as well as a relatively fixed internal artistic structure (e.g., types of acts, sequence).

The commercial theatre houses of the nineteenth and early twentieth century are the most closely related to the coliseos, both in physical design and in function. Initially many were mainly locales for foreign touring companies or, less commonly, for musical recitals or dramatic presentations by local artists, but by the late nineteenth century they provided the embryonic national theatres with growing middle-, lower middle-, and upper-class audiences. These buildings also housed musical comedy and revues, many of which were brought into the bourgeois environment by artists formed in traveling circuses and tent shows.

The various spaces are historically interconnected by a number of elements, which can be categorized as follows: (1) stable structures with a common use as venues for productions of scripted plays by professional artists (corrales, coliseos, and commercial playhouses); (2) nonspecific open spaces, temporarily but routinely allocated for theatrical performance (public squares and vacant lots used by circuses and tent shows); (3) spaces that permitted the artistic expression of marginalized social groups (public squares and vacant lots); (4) spaces owned by institutions (corrales, colleges); (5) spaces where performances were used primarily to promote or further a political program or for ideological propaganda (public squares, colleges); (6) spaces controlled by impresarios as commercial ventures (corrales, circuses and tent shows, commercial theatre houses).

Affiliation or Sponsorship

Although independent and commercial theatre has proved to be viable at various times, most theatrical production has, over the centuries, depended on organizational affiliation or sponsorship. Although in some cases it is difficult or impractical to distinguish between affiliation and sponsorship, such a distinction is valid for the most part. An affiliated theatre can be said to include the direct participation of members of religious cofradías and guilds, or of students and teachers of religious colleges and universities, in dramatic presentations for religious or civil festivities. Sponsorship involves the delegation or commissioning of the production and performance by individuals or organizations who offer payment, space, or in-kind rewards (the latter, of course, an instrument of psychological suasion).

THE CHURCH, THE GUILDS, THE COLLEGES

The cofradías' voluntary labor was oriented mainly toward maintaining the infrastructure of the churches, organizing religious activity, and providing charitable assistance. Beginning in the Middle Ages, these church-affiliated organizations, along with the trade guilds, were sponsors of important festivities. They were sometimes required by the colonial authorities to contribute whatever they could in the way of financial or artistic expression. Most specifically, ethnic cofradías and cabildos (of blacks, Indians, or mulattoes) were expected to bring out their typical dances for Corpus festivities, and these events offered the groups the opportunity to perform ritual dances in public.

Already in the mid-sixteenth century, guilds were expected to sponsor dramatic productions for the Corpus Christi festivities. Many guilds were directed by executive fiat to commission plays. In Chapter 2 we referred to the silversmiths' leading role in Mexico in the 1530s; it is worth citing that in Lima, in 1582, tavernkeepers and merchants contributed to the Corpus events by contracting with three writers for the production of three entremeses. In 1630, also in Lima, the birth of Prince Baltasar Carlos was celebrated with a series of plays sponsored or commissioned by various guilds: the candymakers (November 6), the *pulperos* (grocers or tavern-keepers; November 8 and 9), the blacksmiths (November 22), and the meat suppliers (December 10). Guilds were still sponsoring performances in the eighteenth century. In 1724, the tailors and grocers funded the production of a play by Agustín Salazar y Torres in honor of the Viceroy (Lohmann Villena 1941:376).

A different sector of the church was also actively involved with theatre: the religious orders, which operated for the most part with greater autonomy and authority than the cofradías, who were subordinate to church officials. We have already examined in some detail the evangelical activity of the religious orders as missionaries; it is equally important to recall the uses of dramatic performances in the colleges as well as in the outlying missions. Drama quickly became an attraction at the best religious colleges, and girls' as well as boys' schools would use the superiority of their drama education and their theatrical production as a recruiting device to gain an edge over their competitors. Public performances also gained some popular following, and were therefore quite useful to promote an order or to score political points.

The Jesuits in particular, with their great fondness for drama as an intellectual and artistic exercise, put their experience and artistic talent to practical use. As latecomers to the cities, where the territory was saturated with a variety of orders, each with its college, the Jesuits marshaled their best resources to compete. Drama for the Jesuit colleges was used not only as an excellent recruiting vehicle but also as a public relations tool. These colleges usually volunteered an original play (coloquio or auto) for important occasions (the consecration of a new bishop, the arrival of a new viceroy or administrator, the birth or coronation of royalty). Like their dramatic celebrations of newly beatified or canonized Jesuits, these incidental productions were customarily staged on college premises. On at least one occasion (Lima in 1595), however, the viceroy himself proposed that the Jesuits perform at the university, because the great popularity of their dramatic productions was bound to attract larger audiences than could be accomodated in the college.[10]

Although there is really little popular content or form in their presentations (and most of them were, in fact, little more than exercises in rhetoric and declamation), the schools and universities of the colonial period established themselves as centers of dramatic instruction and public performance. As such, they surfaced again in the twentieth century as important contributors to the national theatres of several countries. Thus the university theatres of Chile, Colombia, and Mexico, for instance, were not born in a historical vacuum in the mid-twentieth century, but rather were renewing one of the earliest institutional forms of dramatic production—especially in dramaturgy and performance.

PUBLIC SPONSORSHIP

During the wars of independence, dramatic performances were sometimes used to raise funds and to promote political causes.[11] The objective of these performances as ideological instruments was not very different from that of loas and similar dramas sponsored by the colonial authorities to celebrate the coronation of a new monarch or to record a successful defense against a foreign pirate attack. The point of both was to rally the audience to support an official program, in this case the emergence of the counter-hegemony of the Creole classes; the organizers of the cultural event were most commonly the members of a patriotic society, often a ladies' organization. The difference resided in the fact that many of these performances were also fund-raising events for the political and military activities of the group promoting the cultural event. Yet the concept of transferring the profits of a theatre performance to a worthy cause was not new, either, since box-office receipts had supported many a charitable institution during the colonial period.

In the early part of the twentieth century, in virtually every Latin American country, anarchist and socialist-workers' circles were active sponsors of cultural activities. Amateur theatre was one such activity affiliated to the workers' circles and clubs, which can be seen as key organizations in the promotion of a class-based theatre and a response to both the organization of the commercial theatre and the ruling-class ideology which that theatre tended to promote among workers and the lower-middle classes.

Public sponsorship of the theatre dates back to early colonial times, when the crown or the town hall (cabildo) commissioned performances. During the colonial period, a competitive market flourished in the theatre's most optimal environments, such as Lima and Mexico. It was not uncommon for the provision of plays for Corpus Christi to be opened for bids, and the lower bids would normally be awarded the contract.

After independence, particularly in the twentieth century, the municipalities and the state (national, provincial, or state government) gradually became involved in the sponsorship of cultural programs, including theatre. Governments have been most inclined to sponsor, subsidize, or initiate theatre either because of an influential internal progressive presence (usually in the ministry of education or another relevant government department), or because the government feels compelled to compete with radical political groups that are already sponsoring cultural activity. Both instances basically involve cooptation, but in any case the healthier circumstances have usually been those where the state has not assumed a monopoly on the support of cultural production, or when it has responded to pressure from progressive sectors to institute cultural programs.

The concept of popular theatre as a traveling extension program to bring elite drama (classics or modern works by established authors) to peripheral areas predominated wherever educational theatre programs were instituted, beginning in the 1920s (the widest-reaching being in Mexico). The value of such programs, which were promoted for the most part by ministries of education, lay in the development of new audiences for a national theatre and in the promotion of national dramaturgy (often underrepresented, nonetheless, in the repertoire of the extension theatre).

The Roots of the Commercial Theatre

The commercial-popular theatre is in a category of its own, although sponsorship and affiliation are a part of its origins. The earliest commercial theatre ventures relied on institutional funding for their survival, and financial viability of commercial theatres as quasi-independent ventures did not become the norm until the nineteenth and early twentieth centuries. Then theatre was enhanced by some sectors of the emerging mass media, only to be eclipsed later by others (cinema and television). Advertising in newspapers and magazines supplemented handbills and posters, while the mass production of sheet music and scripts, and later of recorded sound, contributed to the massification of isolated components of the theatre, and hence to the popular appeal of the commercial theatre.

Although one usually thinks of mass media in connection with the technological advances of the twentieth century that have saturated society (the recording industry, cinema, radio, the print media, television), the impact of mass culture could already be felt in the nineteenth century. The marketing of sheet music, scripts, and musical scores, popularized through advertising and mass distribution, could well have been a contributing factor in attracting spectators to the theatre, say, to hear a well-publicized artist perform a number already massified through that very sheet music, as well as piano rolls and the earliest recordings.

The virtual massification of theatre itself, through the variety show (*género chico*, *revista*, *variedades*, or *tandas*), can also be considered. The success of a given composition, plot, or staging concept generated imitations, which perpetuated themselves by moving from the realm of art into the lucrative repetition of a proven formula, often of a populist (i.e., opportunistic) nature. Thus while massification contributed to the financial success of the commercial theatre as part of a free-enterprise economy, it also initiated, on a more widespread level than had previously been possible, a spiral of imitation, trivialization, and reification of popular elements of the theatre and of components of popular entertainment.

Repertoire and the Inhibition of Creole Drama

As permanent settlements were established on the American continent, following the conquest of Mexico (in 1521) and of Peru (in 1535), the physical and ideological neutralization of the aboriginal peoples was yet to be completed. Around the time when this process was considered accomplished (most sources indicate the mid-seventeenth century for most areas), new types of cultural production were called for: on the one hand, a theatre that would reinforce the earlier evangelical work carried out among the indigenous population and move it to a more sophisticated level; and on the other hand, one that would reflect the state to which the arts had evolved in Spain and Portugal.

Every historical source confirms that of all the plays performed in the colonies, the number written in the Americas was minimal in relation to the number of scripts imported in bulk from Spain and Portugal. Moreover, less than a century after the conquest of Mexico, the colonies were welcoming increasing numbers of European touring companies and artists, whose commercial popularity, and probably also professional standards, tended to eclipse local artists. The preeminence of European dramas and the prestige of European professional companies were key factors in the overall development of the Latin American theatre, because they inhibited creole production, established aesthetic and production criteria that usually excluded consideration of a distinctive American culture, and competed unfairly with local talent. One can get an idea of the mechanism by which peninsular hegemony could be perpetuated if one recalls that hundreds of printed copies of Spanish or Portuguese scripts were shipped to cities and towns where the printing press was barely being established (if indeed there was any) and where censorship was an internal inhibiting factor.

The church censors (both the bishops and the Inquisition), as well as the civilian authorities, exercised a far closer scrutiny of new texts produced in the colonies than of those that had already been cleared in the mother country. Consequently the commercial risk of staging or publishing new works under the Damoclean sword of political and religious censorship was often avoided in favor of works that had already passed the test.

A complete compilation remains to be made of the public performances censured or closed during the three hundred years of colonial rule, but the picture that does emerge from the existing literature is one of a fluctuating, therefore unpredictable, severity. The church hierarchy intervened at various times and usually in different places, to ban the use of theatre in missionary work (permanently, by the late sixteenth century), to ban the secular theatre (periodically), to bar theatrical performances from the churches and to separate secular theatre from religious festivities (more or less permanently, by the late sixteenth century), and to restrict quite severely the rights of women in general and nuns in particular to act in any sort of performances (by the early seventeenth century).

The first universal ban on the inclusion of plays in the Corpus Christi festivities was that of 2 May 1598. The rationale was that the many secular "excesses" that permeated the dramatic presentations were an affront to the Body of Christ. The impact of this ban was felt as far as the Philippines; yet in Peru, apparently, players were not subjected to the full force of its implementation, thanks in no small measure to the prestige of the main companies that arrived from Spain (more than one of them part of Lope de Vega's circle) and to the positive disposition of the viceroy (Lohmann Villena 1941:54ff.). Regional bans by local authorities were felt periodically throughout the colonies, as in Lima in 1651, when the archbishop barred performances in the presence of the Blessed Sacrament.

The church eventually also banned the performance of religious dramas in corrales, where performers appeared to make a mockery of the faith by caricaturing holy figures and distorting events from Scripture with features introduced to cater to popular taste. Bible stories and the lives of the saints would sometimes be staged without the required ecclesiastical licence or approval. Ironically the groups that staged what the church considered to be travesties were usually the same companies that performed commissioned plays in the public square, with the utmost regard for modesty and morality. In their own space (the corral), they sometimes presented shows that verged on the obscene: women players bared their legs to the knee, and some were known to have appeared on stage as Venus, cloaked in a transparent veil that left nothing to the imagination (Lohmann Villena 1941).

Another important factor that cannot be overlooked is the absence of a sufficiently stable, prosperous, and autonomous local economy, which might have been inclined to seek and to promote a creole identity through the establishment of an appropriate dramatic repertoire. The mercantile classes and the entrepreneurial and enlightened elements of all literate sectors in the most prosperous colonies remained identified with Europe.[12] The theatre, reflecting this reality, provides only a few isolated indicators of the emergence of a creole identity. In a way the scarcity of a local repertoire, felt for so long and in most places, can be interpreted as an indicator of the restrictive nature of colonial society. Restrictions were imposed at first through the direct application of doctrinal controls and economic forces and, with the first stirrings of creole sentiment, through a simple shift to other, non-American cultural and intellectual models.

Dramatic Forms

The artistic structure of commercial-popular theatre in the nineteenth and twentieth centuries, like the folk drama of the backlands, can trace its origins to Spain and Portugal, often to the Renaissance and the late Middle Ages. Beyond the formal labels attached to them, genres can therefore constitute a valuable constant through which to trace the transformations and recognize the continuities of Latin American drama. A number of these genres are or appear to be connected in their evolution, establishing an underlying continuity through the substitutions that have occurred at various points.

It is important to note that there was frequently some integration of borderline types of entertainment and spectacle into the more commercial dominant theatre, as a way of guaranteeing its popularity. This is particularly true of musical drama and variety shows since the late eighteenth century, but it has also been a tradition since the sixteenth century, with the inclusion of a *sarao* (dance), of a peasant or black dance, or of a *fin de fiesta*, a closing act with popular songs, music, and dance.

The Loa

The loa is considered by some historians to be the most characteristic genre of Latin American theatre (Shelly and Rojo 1982:336). As we saw in Chapter 1, this dramatic form was first introduced in the mid-sixteenth century as an evolved liturgical genre devoted primarily to the worship of the Sacraments, of the Virgin Mary, and of the saints. By the late sixteenth century, a secular strain of the loa developed, while the popular religious strain took root in what we now refer to as folk drama. The loa of the urban centers was performed in royal festivities and pageants, in the court, in private homes, and by theatre companies.

Loas were prefixed to the autos of Lope de Vega and Calderón, and in Mexico, Sor Juana Inés de la Cruz too demonstrated her talent in composing loas. They are small plays on a similar theme or with a similar tone to that of the play to which they are attached; or they can be monologues of praise (to patrons or officials), anecdotes, or allegories. Sometimes a loa was organically connected to the play; sometimes an unrelated loa would be added by the printers to a published, full-length play.

The loa evolved along two parallel lines: as an expression of high culture, usually with a display of allegorical figures and ornate verse, and as a popular farce, relying increasingly on song, dance, and unsophisticated humor (Ticknor 1863, 2:529). It declined in the eighteenth century, along with its contemporary the entremés, to be replaced by the zarzuela and the sainete.

The Entremés

Like the loa, the entremés (or interlude) grew out of the early Renaissance; it faded in the eighteenth century, to be replaced by the sainete. Unlike the loa, however, it was always a form of secular, comic entertainment. As its name suggests, the entremés served as a light diversion between the acts of longer plays, but it also had a life of its own: the contributions of Cervantes, in Spain, and of Cristóbal de Llerena and Sor Juana, in America, which rank among the favorites in the canon of dramatic literature, are clear demonstrations of the vitality of the entremés as an autonomous genre.

This form was also the more authentically popular of the two genres, both because of its comic nature and because of its consistent preference for realistic characters and vernacular language. Unlike the loa, whose primary objective was to transmit ideological values, the entremés was intended solely for entertainment.

The Sainete

Like the entremés, the sainete was originally any short play inserted in longer works, strictly for entertainment; like the entremés, it too found an independent identity. Most critics agree that it is an artistic improvement over the entremés, particularly in its treatment of time, space, and characters, and in the greater importance it gave to set and scenery.

Ramón de la Cruz's sainetes of the late eighteenth century were comedies of manners and parades of picturesque types (mainly of the Madrid streets). Although they rarely included music and song, they still became wildly popular in Spain and Latin America, and authors in the late colonial period from Mexico to Argentina adopted them as models for what would effectively be the first national genres. It is generally agreed that the first American sainete was *El amor de la estanciera* ("The Country Girl's Love," an anonymous play attributed to Fr. Juan Baltasar Maciel, of the River Plate region, written between 1787 and 1792).

In Cuba a physician turned actor and playwright adapted the sainete made popular by Ramón de la Cruz. In a career that spanned fifty years, Francisco Covarrubias wrote, produced, and performed in over one hundred sainetes (all lost), in which the denizens of Madrid's lower-class neighborhoods were replaced by typical Havana residents, including blacks and Spanish storekeepers. These characters appear to have persisted after the death of Covarrubias (in 1850), to be incorporated into the comedy genre known as the *bufo cubano* less than two decades later.

The sainete's longevity is quite remarkable; it regained its extreme popularity toward the end of the nineteenth century. Between 1880 and 1890, 1,500 sainetes were written in Spain alone, and by then the spillover to the Americas was probably as abundant as it had been one hundred years previously, on the eve of the wars of independence. It is interesting that in Argentina the sainete, born for the first time in the 1790s, was reborn into even greater success (the *sainete criollo*) a century later, once again inspired by a recently imported Spanish model. Both incarnations are considered to be creole, or national, genres in Argentina.

The authors of sainetes prided themselves on their portrayals of social types and customs, occasionally introducing spicy notes into the plot. Light-hearted comedy dominates, however, in a genre that served a function similar to that of the género chico (an omnibus category of short sketches, musical numbers, etc.), which was not introduced, or at least not named, until the late nineteenth century.

Comedies

Alongside the short comic plays known variously as entremeses or sainetes, one must include the comic plays, many of which were written by authors better known for their tragedies and serious drama.[13] These full-length or nearly full-length comedies are akin to the shorter comedies of colonial authors, and they became, in turn, the most immediate models for the commercial-popular theatre, where full-length comedy flourished in the twentieth century. Thus in Cuba alone, two romantic playwrights known for their historical dramas and classical tragedies contributed to the growth of the genre: José Jacinto Milanés, with *El mirón cubano* ("The Cuban Spectator") and *Ojo a la finca* ("Look Out for the Farm"); and Joaquín Lorenzo Luaces, with *El becerro de oro* ("The Golden Calf"), *A tigre, zorra y bull-dog* ("Face a Tiger with a Fox and a Bulldog), and *El fantasma de Aravaca* ("The Ghost of Aravaca").

This genre and the sainete were the most inclined toward the portrayal of social customs (typical dress, manners, speech) and the folkloric representation of national identity. Influenced by romanticism and determined by the class affiliation of its creators (the creole landed aristocracy or emerging bourgeoisie), its portrayals of the popular classes and marginal social types verge not only on the folkloric but sometimes even on the exotic.

The Zarzuela and Other Musical Genres

The zarzuela, a musical drama, evolved in the eighteenth century into two distinct genres with several aspects in common. The zarzuela proper is a musical in three acts, a kind of operetta, and one of Spain's most important contributions to popular music. The *zarzuela chica*, or *zarzuela popular*, is a one-act musical that along with its cousin, the *sainete lírico* (as its name implies, a lyrical/musical version of the sainete), was the principal musical form to emerge in Spain in the late eighteenth century. Ramón de la Cruz is said to have produced the first zarzuelas chicas in 1768, as an antidote to foreign influences entering Spain through the Bourbon court. This is a significant historical fact, as he would later become known mainly as a pioneer of the sainete.

The sainete lírico, which became established in the nineteenth century, has its roots in the *jácara* (song with a picaresque theme), the *folla* (also a forerunner of the modern revue), and the *tonadilla* (whose plot—usually a love intrigue—is a pretext for music, song, dance, and jokes). These musical-comedy forms persisted in variety shows well into the twentieth century, most often transmuted into expressions of local culture.

The Género Chico

The género chico introduced the flexible structure of the variety show to audiences, impresarios, and performers alike. It was born in the period of political conflict during the revolution of 1868 in Spain, when the rudimentary stage of the *café concierto* began to fill the vacuum created by the impact of the troubles on the *teatro grande* (see Fernández Cid 1975:98).

Creations of the género chico, such as sketches, short musical numbers, comedy acts, and short melodramas, could be shuffled in various configurations for the variety theatre's several daily shows, or *teatro de secciones* (called tandas in Mexico). The shows each drew a different crowd, and by the turn of the century the audience of the variety theatre in most of Latin America was neatly divided by socioeconomic classes according to the time of day or night when they were able to (or chose to) attend (Bryan 1983, Frischmann 1987b, Pineda and Zelaya 1986).

Circus and Variety Shows

Revues and sketches, buskers on stage, musicians, dancers who popularized new rhythms and steps, and jugglers, acrobats, magicians, and clowns or comics—with some variation, these are the essence of both circus and variety show, which from traveling tent shows moved indoors, to create the equivalent of music hall or vaudeville. What the two types of artistic organization have in common is that they are a serial exhibition of mostly unrelated performances, brought together as a conglomerate of whatever is not theatre (Bost 1931).

Why, then, include these marginal performance media as theatre? First of all because individual performance styles were forged, and careers spawned, in the circus, where musicians and actors learned their craft. Second because, seen as institutions or autonomous cultural environments, they offer ritualistic commentary on their contextual culture (Bouissac 1976:5–9).

The circus in particular involves a series of what Bouissac terms "transgressive mirroring" of the "real world," which frees the audience temporarily from the constraints of their own environment. Ever since its earliest recorded manifestations—the buskers known by the Romans as *circulatores*, the medieval traveling troupes of acrobats, magicians, and animal trainers (Bouissac 1985:1–17)—the structure of the circus was perceived as threatening because of the subversion of roles and natural attributes on which much of its entertainment is based. Yet it can also be seen as a controlled subversion, a temporary escape, hence as not much of a threat to the wider society.

The subcodes of the circus are, in the main, nonspecific in relation to the national or regional cultures in which they function. This nonspecificity applies not only to the virtual exclusion of the spoken language as a system of communication, but also to the implicit references (direct, inverted, or transformed) to "all the fundamental categories through which we perceive our universe as a meaningful system" (Bouissac 1985:7). Such nonverbal discourse may include the apparent defiance of gravity by the trapeze artist, almost-human activities carried out by animals (walking erect, jumping through hoops, responding to commands), and incongruities of physical appearance and behavior of the clown.

Music-hall revues or variety shows and their counterparts, the tent shows, represent for some observers the coming together of fiercely independent performers interested in interpreting only themselves on stage; these institutions combine practically every performance element from the itinerant country fair (Amiel 1931:248). Like the circus, the music hall is a space in which individuals and independent small groups tend to present their own material or at least to organize it in their own unique way, while conforming in general terms to the code of their specific act as expected by their audience; if they violate that code, they tend to do so within certain limits.

The circus (a system of indirect, abstract, or symbolic acts that play with established codes of human culture) relies heavily in most of its acts on tension, surprise, and inversions or gross distortions of the expected. A conventional pantomime or sketch would probably stand out as the least transgressive act, while the clowns balance distancing effects and familiarity (down to the scatological and to routines based on Bergson's most basic definitions of humor). The revue, or variety show, is by comparison a less unconventional system of codes, and its popular appeal is based more on the familiar and the specific than on the unusual and the universal or symbolic.

Another difference lies in their relationship with the audience. The authors of Amiel's study (1931) of western European styles of performance point out that even if an identical act is transferred from the circus to the music hall (coliseum, *teatro de comedias*, or playhouse) as part of a variety show, it will enjoy a different physical relationship to the audience: a proscenium instead of an embracing arena, and a colder, more judging rapport than that which one finds in the circus, where wonder and a generally warmer acceptance are the norm (Amiel 1931:264).[14]

This observation would add an aesthetic dimension to the socioeconomic reasons for the continued existence of two parallel currents of similar artistic entertainment (circus and music hall, or variety show), after the variety spectacle of the urban playhouses had established itself as the entertainment of the middle classes and the working class. One might also add that the indoor spectacle became primarily a form of adult entertainment, while the circus became, increasingly, a space for families with children.

Variety theatre, heavily influenced by the género chico in the latter part of the nineteenth century, was also the logical venue for the political revue, which flourished in most countries as long as the authorities allowed it. Mexican revues under Porfirio Díaz were susceptible to sycophantic pro-Díaz routines, and after 1909 the playhouses became one more site where the Mexican revolution was fought out (see Bryan 1983, Maria y Campos 1956, and Merino Lanzilotti 1980). Brazil, meanwhile, had Arthur Azevedo producing his "Revista do ano" as a regular annual revue of political events.

Popular Voices and the Ideological Vehicles of Drama

In the theatre as well as in the dramatic literature of Latin America, theme, characters, and language are but three vehicles for the promotion of an ideology as part of the enforcement of hegemonic authority, or to promote an emerging counter-hegemony. The presence of marginal voices ordinarily serves one of two functions: these voices are either organically part of an artistic medium of popular appeal to marginal audiences (e.g., early farces and entremeses), or elements of popular (or populist) appeal embedded in an elite medium.

Our research has focused on the textual representation of these categories, first and foremost on the determining role of performance in supporting or subverting the textual surface of one or more of the three categories. This can be effected through nuanced or openly contradictory gest, or simply through the timing of the performance.[15]

A play on an exotic subject (e.g., José Martí's *Abdala*, 1869) could, because of its very theme and its presentation at the height of revolutionary fervor, be instantly perceived as relevant to the contemporary struggle for independence. On the other hand, many texts as we read them today are virtually pauperized of the irony, the topical innuendo, or outright mimicking that such performance elements as gesture, tone of voice, and timing could provide for comedy in its time and for its original audiences; such is the case with Juan del Valle y Caviedes's three satirical plays.[16]

Nor can one ignore the value attached to specific styles of dramaturgy and performance, such as oratory, by audiences of certain periods, or the passion projected by a determined type of dramatic monologue, which could move audiences in ways that we find exceedingly difficult to appreciate, based solely on the texts of certain nineteenth-century patriotic works (some plays, many dramatic monologues).

Ideological Values and the Politics of Nationality and of Class

The values transmitted or proposed by the content of Latin American drama do not include much radical questioning of the established order or of the order being proposed by an emerging counter-hegemony, and yet they sometimes, unwittingly, open the way for a more acutely critical theatre by pushing the limits or by creating the appropriate vehicles (such as characters or themes). Satire, which has been present virtually since the sixteenth century, has rarely offered a piercing challenge to the existing order, and yet by the time conditions were ripe for such challenges, artists had a formal tradition on which to draw.

Similarly the nationalist theatre (both comedy and serious drama) was, by and large, an instrument of the emerging creole ruling class and the holders of the legal power of the written word, but it has also become a precedent for modern-day readings of nationalism and imperialism. Indigenous people are first presented, in the romantic theatre, as idealized embodiments of the creole vision of an independent America, but with the growth of a social consciousness, the abstract precedent is transformed into a nativism concerned with contemporary conditions of injustice and with an analysis of what constitutes the modern nation. The comic figures of the Latin American theatre, significant conveyors of ideology, are often fraught with ambiguity regarding class, race and nationality; they too, in turn, are building blocks for successive visions of nationhood and American identity.

The Dawning of American Consciousness

Most scholars agree that the promotion of an American consciousness (let alone of nationalism) was virtually nonexistent in most Latin American drama until the outbreak of the wars of independence. There are, however, glimmers of such consciousness in some works before 1800. Among those most frequently and justifiably cited are two of the earliest plays (both Mexican, both allegorical) that make reference to the syncretic outcome of the spiritual conquest of America: *El desposorio espiritual entre el pastor Pedro y la Iglesia mexicana*, by Juan Pérez

Ramírez, and the loa for *El Divino Narciso*, by Sor Juana Inés de la Cruz.

The pastorela, or "Shepherds' Play," that Juan Pérez Ramírez composed in 1574 for an archbishop's ordination, celebrates the establishment of a Mexican church, or at least of the Catholic church in Mexico, with all that it entailed. (One should bear in mind that the Church had already been symbolically consecrated as a syncretic body more than thirty years earlier, when the Virgin of Guadalupe appeared at the site of worship of the Nahuat goddess Tonantzin, displacing her and becoming the new spiritual mother of all Mexicans.)[17]

In Sor Juana's loa, composed in the third quarter of the seventeenth century, America and its religion appear on stage as the dramatic equals of Europe and Christianity. Even though the latter is presented as the one true religion (and accepted as such by the Americans), the Native American is portrayed with great dignity and a high degree of spirituality and intelligence. Of course Sor Juana's own intellect was bound to prove the superiority of Catholicism through the test of a theological debate with its prospective convert, so that Christianity is only enhanced by its intellectual triumph (through rational persuasion) over a worthy opponent. Still, the resolution of the debate through what is quite clearly a rationalization of syncretism makes this a curious loa, particularly since the aboriginal people accept Christ as a version of *their* deity, that is, as the *true* "God of the Seeds".

The personae of America and the West (Occidente) close scene 3 swearing that a forcible conversion will never keep them from exercising their free will and worshipping their great "God of the Seeds" in their hearts. The persuasion occurs in scene 4, and finally, scene 5 ends with the same allegorical figures calling for the play ("The Divine Narcissus") to begin, so that they can see and know the God that will be given to them as nourishment, the "True God of the Seeds".

Another interesting aspect of this loa is the central role played in the debate by the contrasting approaches to knowledge. The aboriginal people expect to be given literal and material proofs of existence (a fair display of understanding, by Sor Juana, of the epistemological basis of what was commonly dismissed as idolatry). Religion patiently explains the basis of abstract belief and of Christian faith, tacitly acknowledging that it is an alien mode of thought to the Native Americans. For this alone the loa stands as a precious early contribution to intercultural respect and to recognizing the value of Native American spirituality.

Aboriginal Languages, Aboriginal Themes

The use of native languages and of Native Americans as characters and as actors in scripted plays dates back to Father José de Anchieta, who in 1586 wrote his *Festa de São Lourenço*, a trilingual play (in Portuguese, Latin, and Tupí) chronicling the early colonization of Brazil. In Cuzco the cleric Gabriel Centeno de Osma is credited as the author of the Quechua-language adaptation of a parable of spiritual vs. earthly riches: *Yauri Tito Inca o El pobre más rico* ("The Richest Poor Man"). Although the earliest extant manuscript is dated 1701, theatre historians cite performances among the aboriginal people between 1562 and 1600. This was originally an evangelical play, written with a missionary intent, yet both its protagonist and its original language validate (albeit for purely assimilationist purposes) the culture of the majority population of Peru, just as Anchieta's work addresses all three sectors (the nonliterate Portuguese and Creoles, the Native Americans, and the clergy) in their respective languages. Actors and audiences are united through an artistic creation that projects each culture to the others in a relatively equitative and sympathetic light.

The Native American emerges as a true protagonist about fifty years before the independence of Peru, in *Ollantay* and "The Tragedy of King Athahualpa." The origins of these two plays have never been successfully determined, but most historians now believe that they were codified in the mid-eighteenth century, before Tupac Amaru's uprising. In fact it is generally assumed that one or both were performed for Tupac Amaru during lulls in the fighting or shortly before he resorted to armed resistance.[18]

Ollantay appears to be based on a preconquest legend, embroidered with the addition of an unlikely romantic intrigue between the hero and a vestal virgin. It is precisely this embroidery as well as its happy ending, in which the forbidden relationship is forgiven (something inconceivable under the strict codes of the Incas), that betray the Spanish hand in its composition. One may assume that the anonymous author was a mestizo or a Native American who had received a European education and was well versed in Spanish drama.

"The Tragedy of King Athahualpa," on the other hand, is presumed to be a dramatic rendition of the final days of the last Inca, composed not long after the conquest. It glorifies aboriginal martyrs, and like *Ollantay*, it might have served as an effective mobilizing instrument for the rebellion that swept Peru in the 1760s. Both are rare works, because their transcription marks the entry into the literate sectors of a dramatization of history by its nonliterate protagonists. Their transcription is roughly contemporary with the earliest efforts by aboriginal peoples to reaffirm their land claims through the appropriated medium of the legal title.[19]

In the next important matrix of plays featuring the Native American, which appears during the nineteenth century, the protagonists are highly idealized representatives of a golden age, of a disappeared civilization. This small but influential core of *indianista* writers includes: José Fernández Madrid, a Colombian exiled in Cuba, whose tragedies *Atala* (1822) and *Guatimoc* (1825) present the colonial plight of America through the history of its earliest victims, the aboriginal people; the Cuban José María Heredia, who lived in Mexico for several years and wrote *Moctezuma o Los mexicanos* (1819) and *Xicotencatl o Los tlascaltecas* (1823); and the Dominican Javier Angulo Guridi, who lived in Cuba for a number of years and wrote *Iguaniona*, about a legendary chief in Santo Domingo. The idealization of the aboriginal past of Mexico persisted through the Benito Juárez years; one of its exponents in drama was Alfredo Chavero, in the 1870s, with *Netzahualcoyotl* and *Quetzalcoatl*.

With the rise of naturalism and realism in the late nineteenth and early twentieth centuries, the *indigenista* movement (significant throughout most of the continent through literature and cultural awareness) brings to the forefront the aboriginal roots of national culture and the aboriginal presence, often with a strong social and political perspective. One of its earliest expressions is a play that can be seen as a bridge between idealized indianismo and sociopolitical indigenismo: *Patria y libertad*, by José Martí. This work, which was inspired by the Cuban writer's sojourns in Guatemala and Mexico, unites anticolonial and proindependence themes with a vision of continental unity, with the Native Americans as the key to that future. Martí's unfinished play *Chac Mool* also uses a Native American theme to present the conflict between foreign rule and self-determination.

One of the strongest manifestations of the indigenista movement in the theatre is found in Paraguay where, particularly after the disastrous Chaco War of the 1930s, playwrights sought to affirm national culture through the use of Guaraní (the kitchen language understood by all but rejected by the upper classes). Thus the language of the majority found its space on stage in the twentieth century, mainly in antiwar plays and plays of social consciousness. Julio Correa carried out a particularly valuable task by gathering material from the oral tradition from around the country (much of it Native American or mestizo) and integrating it into his plays.

In the United States, the *Mitos* of Luis Valdez and the Teatro Campesino (early 1970s) could be seen as modern-day equivalents of the romantic nativist plays of Mexico. They project a similar desire to revive aboriginal myths and their legendary past as a spiritual foundation for a new nationhood. Valdez's *Mitos* present the dream of creating the nation of Aztlán in the former Mexican territories now held by the United States. Like his Mexican predecessors, Valdez was conjuring up a past that was historically disconnected from the present, often employing symbols of Mexican culture that were no longer a part of the conscious memory of Chicanos.[20]

The Marginal and the Underclass

Just as aboriginal peoples have been used to promote the vision of national identity or to affirm Americanism, so, too, has the creole been affirmed as a positive counterpoint to the foreigner; the creole character is most often identified with the underclass or marginal elements, where readily recognizable national characteristics could be found. There is a reason for including underclass characters in a study of popular elements, even though they are often used as symbolic instruments by competing hegemonic forces.

It is impossible to ignore the fact that the rise of creole consciousness, which led to the formation of the nation states, tended to reify or distort those symbolic instruments (peasants, farmers, Native Americans, blacks, or mulattoes) or, at the other extreme, manipulate them as relatively abstract notions, divorced from a reality that the emerging dominant classes probably despised.

However, even a hint that the concerns and the language of the marginal figures were being acknowledged was a potential building block for a broadened consciousness, and it could contribute to an eventual full-scale validation of the humanity of those figures, i.e., to their true voices. The growth of national and regional identity in Latin America, molded for the most part by the wealthy creole classes, did not necessarily profit the working classes (and it certainly ended up causing the aboriginal peoples greater hardship than colonial rule ever had), and yet the expression of that emerging Latin American identity contributed important functional elements to the national popular theatre.

Comic Characters: From the Circus to the Theatre

From the peninsular theatre of the seventeenth century came central comedy figures drawn from the marginal classes (including peasants and foreigners) and the underclass (servants, slaves). Their role in the plot could be central (the Gracioso or Bobo) or incidental (the Foreigner, the Country Bumpkin, the Black, the Physically Deformed). Marginal characters play a central role in groupings rather than as individuals, unlike the important figure of the Gracioso.

These figures served as foils for the "norm," which was represented by the main characters (except for specific genres such as the entremés, sainete, or bufo, where all protagonists may be from the popular classes). They stood for linguistic, physical, or cultural deviance or "otherness," sometimes feeding on popular prejudice even as they marked the presence of those elements in society. Collectively they correspond to comic types of other cultures, including the Greek, Roman, and medieval European, and they also bear a structural correspondence to Italian comedy. Latin American comedy eventually adopted these stock characters as central figures.

From the earliest days of the Luso-Hispanic theatre and its manifestations in the colonies, the popular classes (workers, servants, artisans, soldiers) have had a presence on the stage, as have such marginal groups as blacks, Indians, and others perceived as "foreign" to the accepted vision of a homogeneous nation (Jews, Moors or Turks, and, later on, the English, the French, the Italians, the Chinese). Each social type was accompanied in the theatrical space by its distinctive point of view and language, although these were often reduced to the barest scheme of the comical or the eccentric.

Drama published in Spain and Portugal in the sixteenth century already included comic figures (outsiders, foreigners, or marginal characters). Although these were for the most part residual characters from premodern dramatic forms and did not, therefore, constitute a major innovation, they were important elements linking preliterate to literate theatre, and they have survived (for the most part in excellent shape) to provide a common structural feature of commercial theatre to this day, just as they have survived in the theatre of oral cultures.

One might wish to draw a distinction between the "generic" foreigners, stereotypical characters built on observations of their external features and the reputation of their exaggerated national or cultural characteristics (e.g., the characters of the Cuban bufo), and the noteworthy exceptions (e.g., the Argentine character Cocoliche), who were drawn from real-life individuals. The bufo cubano and the figure of Cocoliche in their various stages of development represent significant contributions to the national theatres of Cuba and Argentina, respectively. They have in common, among other things, that they both express a form of public acceptance of the ethnic duality of their respective societies at a crucial period of nation building. Both the group of characters of the bufo and the single character of Cocoliche portray subjects of the underclass.

The Bufo Cubano

The bufo cubano was first introduced, between the end of the U.S. Civil War and the beginning of the first Cuban war of independence, by a small group of Spanish-Cuban actors impressed with the success of a touring minstrel show from the United States; by the touring Spanish group called the "Bufos madrileños," and by the Spanish revues known as género chico, which were just making their mark.[21] The actors, calling themselves "Los bufos cubanos," imitated the basic format of the minstrel show, with whites playing African-American characters in blackface and singing original songs with popular appeal.

In fact the main characters were comic archetypes with a national twist. Their forerunners are found (albeit in less vaudevillian style) in Spanish comedy of the Golden Age, while their more immediate antecedents probably lie in the lost sainetes of Covarrubias. At least one bufo type is derived from a character introduced to the Cuban stage in the comedies of Joaquín Lorenzo Luaces (1826–67): the *Catedrático*, a

Malaprop from the lower classes (usually black in the bufo), whose comicality lies in his pompous presumption to know the Spanish language.[22]

The "Bufos cubanos" gained instant popularity in Cuba, and other groups were soon established in Havana and other cities, although they were virtually out of circulation during most of the first war of independence (1868–78). During this period, however, bufo groups toured the Veracruz and Yucatán regions, introducing the new genre to Mexico.[23] Their emergence, in Cuba as in Mexico, coincided with the introduction of the género chico from Spain, where it became the rage in the late 1860s and immediately spread throughout Latin America.

The bufo benefited, no doubt, from the impact of this Spanish import. Because it was essentially a short variety show itself, it was easily integrated into the variety theatre in its second incarnation (after 1880), and bufo characters populated the famous Alhambra theatre revues and their successors in musical comedy.

The creators of the bufo were not Cuban patriots, although many of their spectators and some of the actors may have been. The content of the sketches could be satirical, but for the most part the scripts avoided political controversy and rarely expressed sympathy for anything stronger than political autonomy for Cuba within a Spanish commonwealth. After independence the bufos would take on notorious political corruption or social problems, usually in a superficial or tangential way. Their descendants in Mexico (particularly in the regional theatre of Yucatán) have maintained the strong actorial tradition to this day (Frischmann 1987a).

The ethnic characters of the bufo (the *Negrito*, or African-American; the *Gallego*, or Spaniard; the *Mulata;* and later the *Chino*, the Chinese man) were often coarse projections of social stereotypes, and like their prototypes in minstrelsy, they had an undeniably racist component that is not likely to have dispelled prejudice.[24] Still they were well liked by their audiences and were treated with patronizing affection masking the contempt. The bufo cubano as a national genre epitomizes precisely this contradiction and ambivalence, not only of its original creators, but of the Caribbean nations as a whole.

Cocoliche

While the playhouses, dependent for their overhead costs on the moneyed classes, hosted bufos who played with the "others" within their society, they also absorbed into their revues and plays characters born in the tent shows. Such characters sometimes managed to retain the autonomy of their class perspective in spite of the transition to the mainstream commercial-popular stage. One such persona, Cocoliche, stands out as the expression of a nation of immigrants that in the late nineteenth century was replacing traditional creole society in Argentina.

In the Argentina of the 1880s, Italian and Spanish immigrants introduced a new factor in the national equation, thanks to the government policy of encouraging massive immigration to populate the interior and to provide labor for the railroads, the large estates, and mushrooming industries. The most important circuses of the period belonged to the Podestá family, children of Italians who had immigrated some years before the officially sponsored wave. The Podestá brothers learned the trade from a traveling circus in Uruguay and started their own circus in Argentina in the 1870s; before the end of the century they had acquired several commercial theatre houses in Buenos Aires and had become leading impresarios and promoters of a national theatre in a field dominated until then by foreign companies, actors, and playwrights.

Among the new additions to the Podestá circus staff was a certain Celestino Petray, whose comic imitations of the speech of the Cocoliche brothers (Calabrian circus hands) caught the attention of Jerónimo Podestá. Podestá suggested that Petray develop his character; adopting his model's name for his new character (a rather unorthodox procedure), Petray introduced the new immigrant on the stage of the Argentine circus as a comically hopeless mangler of the Spanish language but nonetheless a sympathetic, hard-working, honest, and lovable new Argentine.

Cocoliche, who was quickly identified by actors and audiences alike as an appropriate incarnation of what had become the "other half" of Argentina, was widely imitated in comedies and dramas well into the twentieth century, and traces of him remain in contemporary popular comedy virtually as a generic term, not unlike the Gallego or the Negrito of Cuban comedy. In fact the metamorphoses, or rather the growth, of Cocoliche chronicles the growth of a mature Argentine theatre (Golluscio de Montoya 1980).

The first Cocoliche, the endearing immigrant type still touched, perhaps, by the sawdust of the circus, entered the playhouse at the turn of the century via the sainete. Nemesio Trejo and other masters of the sainete criollo introduced Cocoliche or similar characters to represent the new urban face of Buenos Aires, a city that had more than doubled in population thanks to European (largely Italian) immigration. With Trejo (a crime reporter, singer, and author of sainetes for twenty-five years), the political and social fabric of Buenos Aires was exposed, and his influence, along with that of Gregorio de Laferrere and others, edged the sainete in the direction of a more critical theatre. Around the time of the First World War, the *sainete criollo* had evolved into the *grotesco criollo*, a darker, more complex genre marked by naturalism, and Cocoliche thus lost much of his superficial innocence, as he was victimized by the machinations of corrupt political hacks and by economic conditions. Enrique Discépolo and his contemporaries exposed the underside of working-class Buenos Aires in their antibourgeois writings, making the grotesco criollo probably the most important new genre to emerge in Argentina in this century.[25]

In the half century or so after the first tours of the "Bufos cubanos," Latin American comic theatre bloomed with the influx of talented comedians and the spread of the variety show (revues, carpas, vaudeville). Much of the humor and the sketches are sexist and coarse, and their acting style tends to be broad and unsubtle. Yet this genre has revealed some truly brilliant acting (timing, delivery, improvisation, character creation), and serious actors have come out of apprenticeship with the more commercial-popular comedy forms. Nor can one say that all commercial-popular comedy is objectionable, because political and social satire has always had an important place in the revue and related media (including radio since the 1920s, and television since the 1950s).[26]

Even political satire, however, has either tended to be tame or else leads nowhere in terms of proposed action; it serves simply as a safety valve for society by providing audiences with a release mechanism. Its main weakness appears to lie in its superficiality, in its facile treatment of social relations—something for which the bufos, as they had evolved to become part of the Alhambra revues in Havana, were notorious. In this respect such a lack of penetrating criticism can be attributed to the genre itself, which is fundamentally a fast-moving entertainment. But the prevalence of this type of comedy in the commercial sphere can only be attributed, in turn, to the desire for a "safety" factor. The reluctance of producers or actors on the commercial stage to commit to any side and the tendency not to identify entirely with their characters without subjecting them to the implicit prejudice of the dominant classes could be seen as an expression of the commercial ethos.

Drama and Melodrama

The popular voice was heard throughout the nineteenth century and the early part of the twentieth century in a range of serious plays and melodramas. Rather than survey the field, we have chosen two contrasting plays. One explores the problems of identity in the newly independent Cuba (1905–15); the other is a glorification of a popular hero of the disappearing breed known as the *gaucho* in Argentina (circa 1880–90). The common point in these radically different plays is the strong value attached to the land as a lasting core of national self-identity.

In José Antonio Ramos's *Tembladera* (1916), a family struggles with the disgregating influences of foreign capital penetration, cultural attachments (Spain vs. the United States), and urban life. The family and its heritage are saved by the steadfastness and clear vision of the administrator of their estate, Joaquín Artigas, a veteran of the war of independence. This interesting resolution could be seen as a plea in favor of an emerging class committed to managing the country's resources. Ramos's contempt of the son who is still identified with Spain and who prefers to return there to live is as scathing as his criticism of the one who wants to find his answers in the United States. The characters who are not tired and dejected are presented as outright fools or confused individuals, yet Ramos is not unsympathetic to them; because, we suspect, he attributed considerable influence to the historical and economic transformations to which they were being subjected, transformations that seemed beyond their control. Ramos's almost idealized vision of retaining such control through a committed and efficient management of the land touches a sensitive chord in Cuba, as in most of Latin America. Therefore, although one cannot consider *Tembladera* a popular play, its attempt to analyze the meaning of nationality and the conditions that cause a class to decline sets it apart as one of a few groundbreaking dramas of ideas (Garzon Cespedes 1976 and 1981).

The other play (or cycle of plays) could not be more different. *Tembladera*, written as a stage play by one of the founders of the Cuban theatre society, portrays a disoriented society just emerging from a disastrous war followed by U.S. military occupation; its subject is the landed oligarchy in danger of collapse. *Juan Moreira*, on the other hand, is an adaptation of a feuilleton; its genesis around 1886 was purely a circus pantomime, and its theme is the victimization of the marginal class (that of the gaucho), the bearer of popular national tradition.

Even before the Italo-Argentine comic figure of Cocoliche became one of its main attractions, the Podestá circus had been the first company to introduce a pantomime with a national theme. *Juan Moreira*, based on the 1878 novel by Eduardo Gutiérrez that popularized the legendary outlaw figure as a victim of the law, was first presented as a vehicle for the display of equestrian skills, with much riding back and forth and around the ring of soldiers in hot pursuit of outlawed gauchos. The pantomime's success led to the introduction of a scripted version, closer to a conventional play, which became a staple with the Podestá company and spawned a unique genre, the gaucho dramas, most of which were mainly tragedies featuring unjustly persecuted gaucho heroes.[27]

The success of similar or even bloodier melodramas (known as *bambochatos* in Brazil), was the bane of serious playwrights in other South American countries. Despite its aesthetic weaknesses and its excessive reliance on melodrama, pathos, and violent action, the *gaucho* play must nevertheless be classified as a popular genre, because of its romantic emotional appeal. Moreover it is generally acknowledged to have been the catalyst for the popular acceptance of a national dramaturgy, opening the door for serious social playwrights. Among those for whom the low aesthetic standards of the gaucho dramas were intolerable, one must count Florencio Sánchez, author of sainetes in the first years of the century and later the creator of some of the most substantial conflict dramas on the themes of immigration and the land problem.

Political Drama

Drama with specifically political content can be distinguished from social drama (which focuses on general conditions affecting society or a class of people). Political drama, which concentrates specifically on political events or developments, has had a variety of expressions in Latin America, some of which we shall outline here. The subject of political theatre embraces a number of the categories we have already described, such as the sponsorship of patriotic drama during the wars of independence, from Argentina in 1817 to Cuba and Puerto Rico (in New York) in the 1870s; the use of native themes to further the philosophy of independence; or the organization of theatre groups by anarchist circles in the twentieth century. The dramatic literature that comes under this heading is, therefore, widely varied in content, although for the most part there is little deviation from the conventional forms of drama or comedy.

Among the first overtly political plays on record (dating back to the late sixteenth century), one must surely count the famous entremés of Cristóbal de Llerena, for which he was exiled from Santo Domingo because of its criticism of government corruption and excess taxation. In the same vein of sociopolitical satire, one can include nineteenth-century plays of Peru, Argentina, and Brazil. Manuel Ascencio Segura's *Sargento Canuto* (1838) satirized militarism; Juan Bautista Alberdi's *El gigante Amapolas* (1842) was a violent attack on the dictatorship of Juan Manuel de Rosas and a simultaneous jibe at a cowardly opposition; José de Alencar's *O demonio familiar* criticized the imperial court of Brazil; and his compatriot França Junior poked fun at the political process of the 1870s in *Caiú o ministerio*, *A republica modelo*, and *Como se fazia um deputado*.

Of all of these, Alberdi's play is probably the most original in its conception: the action revolves around a gigantic cloth puppet, the inanimate Giant Amapolas (Poppies), who intimidates every sector of the population through his silence. It is a common soldier who finally refuses to succumb to the generalized fear and who slays the giant. Alberdi shows little patience with the generals and other leaders, and whether consciously or not, he strikes a blow for the dignity of the common man while insulting one of the bloodiest and most active tyrants of the century by depicting him as a useless rag doll. Moreover Alberdi's use of the vernacular places *El gigante Amapolas* on a continuum with the early sainetes or the entremeses (Azor 1988:85).

Programmatic political drama in the twentieth century usually postulates a solution, which may be connected to party programs. In this respect many of these plays qualify as social dramas, but they are also putting forth a very clear message, and are usually inspired by a particular juncture in the political life of the country. Cases in point are offered by the Chilean workers' theatre, particularly the groups formed in the northern mining communities, to which the playwright Luis Recabarren contributed both materially and artistically. The repertoire of the early workers' theatre in Chile is one of the richest on record (Bravo Elizondo 1986). Anarchist and socialist cultural circles existed in practically every country before 1930 (see Golluscio de Montoya 1986 for Argentina). It is interesting to note that the anarchist leader of the Mexican Revolution, Ricardo Flores Magón, was the author of two plays on political and social themes (published in his complete works).

The melodramatic quality of many of these works contrasts with the sharp comic edge of the satires. Yet they too have a legitimate place as forms of popular theatre, even if they are weakly modeled on commercial-popular plays. It is almost impossible to question the popular appeal of the sentimental plots, the personal tragedies, and the righteous anger and other prominently displayed emotions that, after all, follow plot structures similar to the gaucho plays derived from *Juan Moreira*.

Conclusions

Conventional scripted drama, one of the two main currents from which the New Popular Theatre developed, has dominated Latin American urban theatre since early colonial times. It is closely connected to the lettered classes, who determined both the use of public spaces and the terms under which players (both professional companies and the ethnic and other groups associated with religious associations and guilds) were allowed or commissioned to perform. Sectors of the dominant classes also controlled the geographic enclaves in which the first commercial theatre locales (the corrales) were allowed to flourish, and they determined both the form and the function of the coliseos and other autonomous playhouse structures.

The coliseos, used primarily for the presentation of touring foreign artists and local companies, also served as mediating and transitional spaces between the bourgeois theatre identified with the high culture of the city and the variety shows often associated with traveling companies or circuses and hence with marginal artistic structures. The nineteenth century saw a multiplication of such spaces, with the growing popularity of variety shows, imported drama, and home-grown comedy, dramas, and melodramas.

The colleges and universities, administered and staffed by religious orders, were important centers of dramatic activity from the earliest days of colonization. Public performances were often instrumental in recruiting new students, in projecting the order's close allegiance to the authorities, and in establishing a competitive position for the college vis-à-vis those of other orders. Although most of its dramatic activity was not popular or in the public sphere, college theatre is of considerable historical importance today. The autonomy of the college drama programs as well as their pedagogic, artistic, and technical quality were traditions that the university theatre of the twentieth century resumed quite easily.

The affiliation of theatre companies with social-welfare institutions was effected through the leasing of land by the institutions to the companies, in exchange for box-office earnings. The same companies benefited primarily from official commissions of plays for public festivities, chiefly the Corpus Christi celebrations. This type of sponsorship, resumed by civil authorities after independence, is clearly one of the longest-lived organizational arrangements of the Latin American theatre, one which has both benefited and in some cases stymied the twentieth-century popular theatre.

Theatre has been affiliated with special interest groups since its inception in Spain and Portugal. Guilds and religious and ethnic associations were the main providers of dramatic material and of the personnel to present it for public festivities. During the wars of independence, patriotic societies used dramatic presentations to raise funds and to promote their programs. Beginning in the late nineteenth century, cultural circles born out of political groups (primarily the socialists and the anarchists) presented dramatic performances, often of original, partisan works. It is not impossible to categorize all these institutional connections as part of the same continuum of ideological (propaganda) work in symbiosis with artistic endeavors in need of funding.

Dramatic genres can be identified with various hegemonic cultural sectors. The loa in the urban theatre evolved as a secular genre, very much connected with college theatre, with tributes to dignitaries, and with scripted plays, often (although not always) on a religious subject. Unlike its rural counterpart, therefore, the loa does not persist as a form appropriated by the common people, and it vanished from the urban stage. The entremés survived from the Renaissance until the commercial theatre audience was well established; using a common language of entertainment, it was destined for the popular classes rather than the elites.

With the rise of an urban commercial stage, the sainete dominated the popular urban theatre, fed by two bursts of energy from Spain: the first, on the eve of the nineteenth century; the second, as the century came to a close. During that hundred-year period, the sainete laid the foundations for the growth of the national theatres of Cuba and Argentina, as well as that of other countries. In its second incarnation, it was supplemented by the género chico, which offered the artistic structure for the revue and reinvigorated the variety shows.

Marginal media like the circus and the carpas (tent shows) continued their nomadic activity into the twentieth century, bringing theatre and other performance arts to popular neighborhoods, but also into the playhouses. There artists and their acts were absorbed into the variety show or alternated between the playhouse and their circus or carpa tours.

The impresario became increasingly influential in shaping or otherwise influencing artistic material, as the commercial aspect of the theatre became more important. This is why we suggest that the artistic independence of the performer continues to distinguish the circus and carpa sketches, comedies, and melodramas (often original, improvised works) both from the scripted play (particularly in productions of stable companies) and from the larger variety shows and revues, as the latter become more conditioned by their dependence on the wealthier classes and by the profit motive.

In seeking to create a new popular theatre, Latin American artists of the 1950s and 1960s identified and absorbed two aspects of this marginal theatre: the alternative organization and control of production, hence of the artistic material; and the alternative codes that freed the artist from linear and textual systems. The styles and even the content of New Popular Theatre productions were sometimes adopted from the more commercial popular theatre of the cities, where such material persisted when the tent shows became rare.

Theatre has played a role in formulating the popular consciousness of nationalism, ethnicity, and class. One can find in early American plays an awareness of transculturation and the emergence of an American identity, but the concept of a distinct creole culture did not begin to assert itself until the preindependence period. Native themes appear periodically throughout the history of dramatic literature, with two prominent trends: the idealization of the pre-Hispanic past as a vehicle for formulating a national identity, and later, the recognition of Native Americans as oppressed members of contemporary society.

The comic theatre relies to this day on comedians who continue to create new personae for the classic Gracioso. The formats of the duo and the group of comic characters have survived through Iberian and Latin American theatre into the contemporary popular theatre, playing out archetypal relations, more often than not with minimalist humor. Because their strongest suit tends to be their use of language, foreigners and others who speak with the accent of a regional or ethnic dialect (Galicians, blacks, Native Americans) have been natural favorites. Marginal members of society thus appear on stage as the Other within national society, but also (where the purchasing power and political strength of the immigrant classes has grown) as idiosyncratic values that define the identity of the emerging nation. This tension between prejudice and national pride suggests an ambivalence of attitudes and identity in Latin American societies.

One cannot help noticing that most of these "others" are members of marginal groups or of the underclass, and much popular comedy is set among the popular classes. The popular melodrama of the nineteenth and twentieth centuries also spoke directly to those classes, both through its protagonists (often humble working folk or unjustly persecuted heroes) and through its direct language and situations charged with sentimental emotion.

The New Popular Theatre would often integrate these characters, or develop new ones based on them, altering their "otherness" to vindicate the working class and oppressed groups. Without losing their humor, Blacks, Native Americans, or street people would be cast as rebels or as exponents of everyday heroism. The popular character (linguistic difference, warts, and all) is sometimes transmuted into a less schematic role where, as in a palimpsest, the root character may still reveal itself.

As the overview in part 3 will show, the social and artistic history of the urban theatre branches quite logically into the New Popular Theatre, which learned its earliest lessons from a vibrant commercial theatre and from an amateur theatre affiliated either with universities or with political-cultural associations—all of these, in turn, the heirs of centuries of sustained patterns of organization and of barely metamorphosing artistic forms, themes, and characters.

III

Out of the Sixties

4 • *A New Theatre in Latin America*

The evolution of the Nuevo Teatro Popular (New Popular Theatre) cannot be separated from the social and political developments that boosted popular culture on an international scale in the 1960s and the 1970s. The Nuevo Teatro Popular was both a product and a crucible of the social and artistic history of the American continent and the Caribbean, which we shall survey briefly in this chapter. First, however, we shall describe the Nuevo Teatro Popular, identifying its objectives and the principal currents of the movement.[1] Following the overview of its historical contexts, we return to the specifics of our subject: the types of repertoire (as dramatic literature and subjects); of dramaturgy (individual vs. collective creation); of artistic forms; and of styles and processes of production, including the question of performance spaces and the relationship of the artists with their public. Here we also examine the vital role played by festivals and symposia in weaving the networks that constituted the New Popular Theatre movement.

What is the New Popular Theatre?

The prism for this history of the popular currents of the Latin American theatre is the movement that brought it all together: during the quarter century between the Cuban Revolution and the mid-1980s, a new theatre took shape, combining dormant forms and types of performance that had been marginalized for decades with classical European, pre-Columbian, African, and modern experimental theatre, from Brecht to psychodrama, along with current forms of commercial culture, such as soap operas.

The New Popular Theatre is characterized not only by a rich variety of expression, but also and more importantly perhaps, by the various forms of collective processes and nonhierarchical organizations through which it could maintain a close connection to its social context. It also developed consciously as an international cultural movement, a series of regional and hemispheric networks that have operated through tours, exchanges, and festivals.

There are two major and relatively autonomous tendencies within the Nuevo Teatro Popular: the grass-roots theatre, which is sometimes known as "theatre of popular participation" or "community theatre," and the artistic theatre, which is made up primarily of trained theatre professionals. The two tendencies have always intersected and interacted, with crossovers by artists between the two types. Professionals have worked as directors or consultants with nonprofessional, grass-roots projects and groups, while professional artistic groups have also included and trained nonprofessionals.

In describing the importance of the Nuevo Teatro Popular, we would venture to signal some similarities between this movement and the Modernismo movement, which toward the end of the nineteenth century transformed Latin American poetry: the contemporary networks of popular theatre, like the poetic circles of Rubén Darío's generation, have a spirit of cultural unity, a similar self-consciousness and sense of purpose, a similar bold energy in drawing from every available artistic influence to invent new expressions for Latin American cultural identity. Here the correspondences end with a major difference: the New Popular Theatre rejected the elitist aesthetic that characterized the Modernistas, and chose instead to explore every possible angle of popular cultural creation.

Defining Our Terms

The word *popular*, which is sufficiently inclusive for both the professional and the grass-roots theatre with which we are dealing in this book, is used here to refer to cultural products (and in most cases to processes) that, in their perspective or their practice, are connected to economically or socially marginalized sectors in a class- or caste-determined society, which is subordinated in turn to an external hegemonic power (Spain, Portugal, Britain, or the United States, according to the country and the historical period).

By the late seventies, the theatre that we will be examining in this chapter was being called "nuevo teatro" or "teatro nuevo" in some countries, but the term *popular* remained more widespread. To avoid confusion between these new expressions of popular theatre and other types (traditional, commercial populist, etc.) known commonly by the same name, we have adopted the term coined, as far as we were able to determine, in Mexico: *Nuevo Teatro Popular* ("New Popular Theatre").[2]

The Nuevo Teatro Popular is commonly considered a movement, and in many respects it has come to constitute a fairly developed network. The various tendencies within the Nuevo Teatro Popular do, after all, share a number of common immediate goals and even exchange material resources and staff; but most importantly, they tend to coincide in their analysis of art and society. The main objectives among virtually all groups and artists of this tendency are: to expose the mechanisms and dynamics determining general and specific social phenomena and the class character of economic relations, and to demystify the various strategies for manufacturing consensus among different social classes.[3]

The Nuevo Teatro Popular also was, and continues to be, part of the global explosion of popular culture. It is an important extension of the work begun by the politicized cultural workers and community activists of the sixties and seventies, who in many instances were either the very people who made the Nuevo Teatro Popular or those influenced by it.[4] Whether at the level of individual communities, as a national theatre, or as an international movement, the Nuevo Teatro Popular has gained widespread acceptance as a legitimate artistic response to the hegemonic system.

The critical as well as artistic rigor of its practitioners enabled them to distinguish their own propositions from what had earlier been labeled popular theatre (e.g., commercial variety shows), which can more accurately be labeled populist. More significantly, perhaps, it clarified the lines of commonality and divergence between traditional popular theatre, or people's theatre (e.g., indigenous drama), and a popular theatre that would integrate traditional forms and styles while questioning the validity of messages and themes shaped by an integrational propaganda aimed at reinforcing the existing hegemony.[5]

A Theatre of Its Contexts

The importance of the Nuevo Teatro Popular as a social phenomenon extends well beyond its specific stated objectives. Its evolution has paralleled the political and cultural changes of the continent and the particular demographics of exile. It grew into the first international theatre network rooted in a multifaceted approach to problems of class and national culture, with links to the popular theatres of other continents. It has influenced new generations of teachers and artistic communities. And it is based on popular elements found throughout the history of Latin American theatre; elements that become important markers in the social history of the Americas.

The individual groups and artists, as well as the movement or network as a whole, have played an important role in the cultural and political project that was being articulated by social scientists and artists alike, especially after the triumph of the revolution in Cuba. Moreover its artists have been committed to transforming the social stratification underlying the process of production and their own relationship to it and, consequently, also the internal structures of the theatre as institution and as community.

The Main Currents Within the New Popular Theatre

As stated earlier, most manifestations of the Nuevo Teatro Popular can be concentrated into one of two main currents, or tendencies: on one hand, the grass-roots theatre, a theatre of popular participation, or community theatre; and, on the other, the professional theatre, that is, one made up primarily of trained theatre workers and committed primarily to artistic creation. The two tendencies have historically been interconnected, although they also function along fairly autonomous lines.[6]

Differences over the appropriation of the term *popular* have revolved around the relative priority of the educational or political objective vis-à-vis the artistic. The current that espouses the former (*teatro coyuntural*) is sometimes accused of mechanically pursuing and promoting an instrumental theatre.[7] Theatre whose priority is the conscientization of its (nonprofessional) participants is often considered a form of paratheatre, yet artists and groups of undeniable talent have emerged out of workshops designed primarily for conscientization or community development.[8] There are numerous professional and semiprofessional groups throughout Latin America that owe their existence to such workshops, and professionals continue to become involved in community work with nonprofessionals. Thus although the more rigid extremes maintain fairly exclusive positions, a more versatile majority dominates the Nuevo Teatro Popular, alternating between professional and community work or simply occupying the intermediate space between artistic and social priorities.

The different tendencies have often come together in festivals and meetings (*encuentros*) that, as de facto institutions, represent the single most important common ground for the Nuevo Teatro Popular, allowing for the cross-fertilization of the theatres of different countries and regions. Small or large, festivals offer individual artists and groups and the movement as a whole three types of communal experience: formal presentations (performance), workshops (structured settings for professional development), and opportunities for informal contacts (nonstructured networking, dialogue, and sharing of concerns and artistic subjects). The encuentro (which usually combines workshops, round tables, formal presentations, and discussion) is a place where theory, method, and organizational matters are shared.

Popular theatre festivals and encuentros deserve close study because of their dialogical character and the ways in which they combine instructional, ludic, and ritual components of theatre work. It is partly within the framework of those events and through connections with them that the history of the New Theatre has been made.[9]

Not all grass-roots popular theatre can automatically be counted as Nuevo Teatro Popular. Despite the fact that both movements are oriented toward specific constituencies and seek to include them in their creative process, much popular theatre fails to meet one or more criteria of the Nuevo Teatro. For instance, one cannot include grass-roots theatre that does not engage the subject matter from an analytical angle, or one that does not exercise a significant measure of independence from state or other structures with regard to artistic decisions, selection of subjects, and development of material—or even one that is strictly instrumental.

Having stated this, however, we are faced with the dilemma of any hard and fast exclusionary tendency: how not to exclude representatives of different currents in an arbitrary and simplistic fashion. For example one can neither pigeonhole nor ignore those groups or artists whose personal situation leads them to work within the context of grass-roots development programs (thus precluding them from following through on critical analyses of the underlying conditions). Nor can one discount the value of groups formed in grass-roots development programs, because they serve as a potential radicalizing force in their communities and also, in some cases, as contributors to the professional theatre, even though many of them have not severed ties with sponsoring institutions. Nor does simple exclusion solve the problem of where to place groups and artists that move in and out of mainstream theatre, even oscillating sometimes between conventional or commercial theatre (with the concomitant dissolution of a strong popular, independent line) and a genuine commitment to national, independent, and popular theatre. Finally we have been unable to exclude what is known as teatro coyuntural (circumstantial theatre) and its related expression, the ritual drama invented by social movements.

We must state such caveats precisely because the Nuevo Teatro is not a monolithic movement, but a network of groups and local and regional organizations that, in addition to their diversity of subjects and styles, also display an uneven development along three main continuums: the historical, the geographic, and the social. There is a way out of both of the above conundrums, and it lies in the identification of the two related aspects of the Nuevo Teatro Popular that constitute its key features: its insertion into the process of social change and its significant contribution to revolutionary art.[10]

As an art form it is particularly appropriate for revolutionary times and for the more recent movements of cultural affirmation and resistance, not only because of its ideological character, but also because of its physical mobility and its capacity for broad outreach. As an adjunct of political movements or social activism, it has continued to spread and in many cases has gone beyond its initial educational or agitational function, becoming a medium of collective expression and a vehicle of empowerment for countless marginalized and disenfranchised groups. The key element in the polarization between professional and nonprofessional, and between commercial/artistic and grass-roots theatre can be more readily elucidated by examining how each one connects with the praxis of social change.

History and Politics: The Necessary Contexts

Over the past four decades, a vast number of artists and intellectuals have been political activists or at least, in keeping with the Latin American tradition, have involved themselves actively in debating theories about their societies (theories that are often impossible to separate from praxis). Detachment is not the rule but the exception, and committed individuals are influenced by the events of their age, either because they are directly involved in student, labor, or human-rights activity, or because, in the dualistic view of the dominant sectors of the hemisphere, they can almost invariably be suspected of partisan sympathies or outright subversion. The political environment as we describe it below corresponds to the gestation period of the New Popular Theatre, immediately after the Second World War.

The Postwar Period in Latin America

Two major external factors contributed to the emergence of Latin America into a more significant place on the world stage after World War II: the political independence of the majority of the remaining colonies (in Asia, Africa, and the Middle East) and the organization of these former colonies into the nonaligned nations (in the fifties and sixties, when the concept of the third world became common currency); and U.S. hegemony in this hemisphere, which became more clearly defined in political, economic, and military terms after 1948, with the Doctrine of Hemispheric Security.

Internally the Latin American peoples had, in the years leading up to World War II, already begun to recognize their own potential as agents of history. This was due to such factors as industrialization, urban growth, and the rise of trade unions, which led to the political education and organization of workers and peasants, to the rise of populist political leaders, and to the spread of alternative definitions of socioeconomic justice and of democracy.

Eventually the growth of agribusiness and the failure of infrastructural reform programs (beginning in the 1950s) led to the land-tenure crises of various countries (Colombia, Mexico, Brazil, Guatemala, El Salvador, and the Dominican Republic, to name some of the most serious instances).[11] These crises resulted, in turn, in the urban explosion of most of the continent and in the formation of armed self-defense groups, some of which grew into today's guerrilla movements.

The immediate historical context of the subject of this chapter can be divided, in general terms, into two periods. The first (1945/1948–60), one of relatively undisputed control by the United States, began with the formation of the hemispheric security alliances and ended with the triumph of the Cuban Revolution and a shift in U.S. strategy under President Kennedy. The second period (1960–85) was marked by a succession of experiments in contestatory politics, in armed struggle against economic imperialism and internal exploitation, and in counter-insurgency and psychological operations, which were the standard response against the "subversion" of the established order. This period, therefore, also includes the decades in which military regimes ruled a majority of the Latin American nations, and it ends around the mid-eighties, with the return to civilian, elected government in most of the hemisphere and with the neutralization of most unified social opposition and insurgent movements, i.e., the end of counter-hegemonic options modeled on the Cuban Revolution.

The United States and Latin America

A key factor in the postwar period has been the evolution of the alliance between the United States and sectors of the local oligarchies, the armed forces, and the middle class, including some labor leaders. In Central America, Mexico, and the Caribbean, this alliance had defined power relationship since the 1800s. In the hemisphere as a whole, particularly in South America, the cooperation evolved in two stages after the Second World War, marked by the key dates of 1948 and 1960. The reorganization of the Pan American Union into the Organization of American States, in 1948, was accompanied by the signing of the Inter-American Defense Treaty, by virtue of which the United States undertook the training of virtually the entire officer corps of every Latin American army and police force.

The years 1959–61 mark the beginning of a new stage in U.S.–Latin American relations, in response to the Cuban "problem." The nationalizations and land reform by the revolutionary government of Cuba in 1959–60 and the birth of armed movements in several other countries led the Kennedy administration to formulate a new Latin American policy that combined moderate reform proposals with increased, and more sophisticated, counterinsurgency training and support.

By the 1960s the United States had established much closer ties with the police and the armed forces of nations whose history was independent of the United States (unlike those of most Central American and Caribbean nations). Training and assistance programs mushroomed in response to the perceived influence of the Cuban Revolution. The Kennedy-Johnson years saw the active and direct involvement of U.S. personnel (special advisors, the Green Berets, CIA, FBI, and AID). Hand in hand with the Alliance for Progress, Latin America experienced the implementation of the "national security" doctrine, which shifted the primary function of the armed forces from defending the borders of their nation states to that of an aggressive domestic role in the war on insurgency and eventually on all "subversion," in an ever-widening definition of the term. Between 1964 and 1983, "national security" states were preeminent in Latin America.

Over the past forty years, there have been several cases of direct U.S. involvement, including the CIA-sponsored overthrow of reformist president Arbenz of Guatemala (1954), the Bay of Pigs invasion to overthrow Fidel Castro (1961), the military occupation of the Dominican Republic (1965, this time under the cover of a joint mission by the Organization of American States) to reverse the constitutional coup that supported president Bosch, and the invasion of Panama (1989). Evidence also exists of logistical and tactical support for the 1973 coup in Chile.[12] U.S. military advisors have been in the field throughout Central America (1966–68, 1982–present) and in Bolivia (1966–67), and the United States, through various agencies, is thought to have aided the military coups in Brazil (1964) and Uruguay (1971), as well as the training and supervision of police personnel in at least half the Latin American republics.[13]

Labor unions became a vehicle for the anticommunist project in Latin America in the 1950s, under U.S. sponsorship. The ORIT (Inter-American Regional Organization of Workers) and then the American Institute for Free Labor Development (AIFLD) recruited, funded, and trained labor leaders and subsidized trade unions whose philosophy and tactics differed radically from the established unions, many of which had been founded by Communist militants. The new unions preached cooperation with management along with a fierce anticommunism couched in nationalist (i.e., anti-Soviet, anti-Cuban) terms; in Latin America over the past four decades, as in North America and Europe in the postwar years, the more militant trade unions have been sabotaged, destroyed, or drained. The Honduras national strike of 1954 was lost partly because of the compromises reached by ORIT-funded unions, and Chilean affiliates worked to undermine the economy under Allende in 1972–73, just as Brazilian affiliates had worked against Goulart in 1964 and Salvadorean affiliates would serve to create an initial power base for the "moderate" Duarte in 1983.

Because our history includes the Latino theatre movement of the United States, we should also recall the climate that led to the formation of that movement, pioneered by the Teatro Campesino (1965). Against a background of increased involvement in Southeast Asia, the blockade of Cuba, and insurgency throughout the hemisphere, the United States was living through a decade of domestic upheavals that began with the civil rights movement, then continued with the ghetto riots, Native American protests, the farmworkers' movement led by César Chávez, antiwar demonstrations and student riots, prison rebellions, and the cultural movements of virtually every minority.

The Chicano and Puerto Rican movements were particularly strong on college campuses. The most radical wing of the Chicano movement contemplated restoring the U.S. Southwest to Mexican-American rule, as the Nation of Aztlán, while the Puerto Rican independence movement grew in force in the United States as well as in Puerto Rico. Out of these political movements emerged Latino writers, theatre workers, and researchers who have contributed to the establishment of the Hispanic arts, theatre, and literature in the United States. The women's movement and the gay-rights movement of the seventies are also reflected in the dramaturgy of Latino writers.

Cuba and Latin America

Cuba, meanwhile, had compensated in some way for its expulsion from the O.A.S. in 1963 and for the U.S. blockade, by becoming more integrated into COMECON (CAME), the Eastern bloc economic community, while it also rose to a prominent position in the nonaligned movement.[14] This international status, as much as its earlier identification with the Soviet bloc, served to guarantee the legitimacy of the revolutionary government and, in some ways, its security from U.S. attacks. Cuba has also had the support of many of Latin America's leading artists and intellectuals, who took up the anti-imperialist banner all the more fervently because they saw an attack against Cuba as an attack against the future hope of their own societies.

The artistic and intellectual climate of the first postwar period had been characterized by a certain anomie: individual writers and artists at odds with the system lived out a forced or self-imposed exile, suffered persecution, or explored apolitical or broad historical subjects in search of an elusive identity. All this they did, for the most part, alone or in the context of personal friendships, many of them in France, Britain, the United States, or Eastern Europe, or in a less-hostile Latin American country.

With the triumph of its revolution in 1959, Cuba offered itself as a Spanish-speaking haven where such people could meet and share experiences, creativity, and prospects, and the intellectual and artistic processes of the hemisphere could become, if not collective, at least increasingly collaborative and certainly more open to the processes of other continents. It is quite logical, therefore, to speak of two contemporary periods in the postwar Americas: before 1959 and after 1959, decades lived practically as the converse of each other, by the same generations of artists, intellectuals, scholars, and political activists.

It is not an exaggeration to say that the triumph of the Cuban Revolution was the first pivotal event of the century in Latin America since the Mexican Revolution of 1910–20.[15] Its impact on the culture and the political history of the hemisphere can be summarized in a few key points:

1. After 1959 revolutionaries from virtually every country traveled to Cuba to seek training, support, medical treatment, political endorsement, or simply a place of temporary exile. The government's policy of not turning away fellow revolutionaries could not always be distinguished from a willingness to support their armed insurrection. This provided the reason for the expulsion of Cuba from the Organization of American States, in 1964, and for the support of the U.S. blockade by most countries in the region.
2. Cuba became a refuge for dissident and exiled intellectuals and artists. The Cuban government sponsored conferences, festivals, exhibitions, competitions, and influential intellectual reviews. The cultural institution Casa de las Américas remains an important international meeting place where guest artists and writers from different countries find a stable environment in which to engage in dialogue with their counterparts. Over the years many of those who returned to their country of origin did so with a clearer commitment to radical social transformation.
3. The example of a successful revolution that not only effected radical social and economic changes but also was able to resist the hemispheric superpower, coupled with internal pressure arising from existing conditions, spurred radicals all the way from the United States to Argentina to undertake a similar struggle. With or without material aid from Cuba, guerrilla movements grew in the countryside and in many cities of Latin America. It was against this background that intellectuals and artists, including theatre workers, applied their skills increasingly toward creating critical materials and developing a methodology of creation and organizational structures that would best reflect the processes of change.[16]

Populist Roots of the Revolutionary Movements

Between the 1930s and the first postwar period, Latin America experienced a form of government that marked a transition from the dictatorships (Ubico of Guatemala, Machado of Cuba) to a "third way." A few charismatic individuals, at various times and in various countries, offered a brand of populism that combined nationalism and a type of social-welfare state as an alternative to Communism. Although most intellectuals and artists mistrusted them, they did gain a popular following that progressives were eventually hard-put to reject. This individual leadership, which often tends to be markedly demagogic, has played an important role in forging radical political movements or at least in organizing a nation around a nationalist ideology and reformist social programs, and certainly in galvanizing young activists.

The populist rule of Hipólito Irigoyen in Argentina in the 1920s and 1930s, Lázaro Cárdenas's presidency in Mexico, and Getulio Vargas's in Brazil in the 1930s, are fairly representative of this activist period in three quite different societies. Social justice and economic sovereignty were the benchmarks of these regimes, on which the Peróns' project in Argentina (1947–55) was probably modeled.[17] Internationally, Perón's proposition that peripheral nations adopt a "third way," unaligned with either the East or the West, places him as one of the earliest advocates of a nonaligned movement.

Perón's successful nationalist-socialist programs, combined with an effective mass organization that reached into the remotest communities, appear to have found a derivation in Colombia in the mid-fifties. President Rojas Pinilla made an unsuccessful attempt, in 1956–57, to capitalize on populism in order to retain power against the wishes of the two traditional parties (which had originally placed him in the presidency to suppress the peasant insurgency). After his ouster Rojas Pinilla built a fairly large populist organization and tried to return to power in the 1970 election campaign, which, according to most sources, he lost through fraud. It was directly as a result of this frustrated populist victory that the "19th of April" ("M-19") guerrilla movement was formed, which attracted Rojas Pinilla followers and disaffected members of left-wing parties.

Similarly, inside Argentina, Perón's departure in 1955 did not mark the end of his mass movement, and throughout the sixties and early seventies Peronists from the left and right wings of the party battled each other and a succession of governments opposed to Perón's return. The "dirty war" of 1974–83 was waged in large measure against left-wing Peronist youth.

Two populist leaders who might have been elected president in the late forties but died tragically on the eve of a key election are widely considered to have been catalysts for radical events in modern history. The first, Jorge Eliecer Gaitán, was murdered on the eve of the 1948 election in Colombia. His death sparked major riots that in turn led to widespread repression throughout the country. Liberal party supporters formed armed self-defence groups, which were eventually ordered to disband by the party leadership. Many refused, and some of the self-defense groups joined to form the first Marxist guerrilla movement, the FARC (Colombian Revolutionary Armed Forces).[18]

Parallel with the events around Gaitán's death, another real-life drama was to be played out in Cuba: Eddy Chibás, a popular leader whose personal and political appeal was quite similar to Gaitán's, committed suicide, in what was interpreted as an expression of frustration with the corruption and decay of his country's political system. One of Chibás's closest followers was a law student named Fidel Castro, who had recently witnessed the events in Bogotá.[19]

The death of this leader led to a temporary pause in Fidel Castro's political work, but in response to Fulgencio Batista's 1952 coup, he joined other students and workers to stage an attack on the main barracks of Santiago, in 1953, which was put down with considerable loss of life. The student movement later played a significant role in the 26th of July Movement, which Fidel Castro led to victory in 1959.

Young Revolutionaries and Grass-Roots Resistance Movements

The Argentine, Cuban, and Colombian examples are among the most revealing, not only of the impact of populist leadership, but more importantly, perhaps, of the role of youth activism. Student militancy increased throughout Latin America after the triumph of the Cuban Revolution, whose young leaders inspired their contemporaries throughout the continent. Students and teachers have played a vital role in practically every social and insurgency movement: they were active in the 1960s' guerrilla movements of Peru, Venezuela, Bolivia, Brazil, Uruguay, Argentina, Colombia, Ecuador, and Central America; in the 1970's, young students and workers were the main supporters of Allende in Chile, the radical activists in Mexico, the combatants of the Sandinista movement in Nicaragua, of the FMLN in El Salvador, of the UNRG in Guatemala, and of both present-day guerrilla movements of Peru.

Violent repression has coincided, in the past two decades in particular, with the emergence of mass organizations around sectoral interests (aboriginal peoples, slum dwellers, religious workers, peasants, students, teachers, workers in different sectors from heavy industry to housekeeping) and around specific issues (the disappeared, land reform, the national dialogue between warring parties, torture, hunger) and demands (schools, electricity, land claims, health care).

In the 1960s, many Latin Americans expected revolution to sweep through the hemisphere, to break established patterns of domination, to allow the emergence of cultures that had been suppressed, marginalized, or simply co-opted or distorted by the hegemonic sectors, and to promote the formation of a new, revolutionary culture. However, this conviction as to the immediacy of the process and the imminent victory of the revolutionary forces was unduly optimistic. Social change has not taken the single, uncomplicated path nor the short time that many expected it to take, and the sacrifice has been enormous.[20] Change is, nevertheless, becoming evident throughout the continent; unevenly and often in perplexing and unexpected ways, it is presenting new forms that spring from grass-roots movements such as peasant and indigenous organizations, labor unions, Christian base communities, women's organizations, and human-rights groups.[21]

Migration

Of course most of these problems were not new; what was new was the emergence of groups and organizations that focused on them. And while new mechanisms of resistance were being formed within each Latin American nation and often across borders, large numbers of Latin Americans were leaving their countries of birth for political reasons. The militarization of the Southern Cone and the revolutions in Central America and elsewhere in the sixties and seventies spawned communities of Latin American exiles and refugees who migrated in unprecedented numbers. As a result there has been a new cross-influence among artists and academics from different nations, among whom there had previously been little significant interaction.

Progressive artists and intellectuals gathered not only in Havana, Eastern Europe, or Paris, but also, increasingly, in Mexico and Venezuela, the U.S., Spain, and other Western European countries, where they became models for new generations of students and artists interested in Latin America. They have contributed a Latin American perspective to the study of third-world problems and European cultures.[22]

In addition to the Cuban Revolution and the economic and political upheavals, the enormous flux of refugees, exiles, and displaced artists and intellectuals has also been a key determining factor in the emergence of the Nuevo Teatro, for a number of reasons. The practitioners of a committed theatre often found new homes—some temporary, some permanent—in countries where they would never have dreamed of living; old prejudices had to be erased or at least set aside, and new perspectives on their own continent had to be learned. Bolivar's old dream of forging a continental consciousness came a step closer to being realized.

A second factor was the role that many of these exiles and refugees played in the artistic life of their new countries of residence, both as participants and as founders of new groups. Because of their international connections, they were also in a position to facilitate festivals and exchanges. This important and positive consequence of the state terror and social change that gripped virtually every corner of the hemisphere is examined in some detail below.[23]

Popular Theatre and Grass-roots Development

Theatre as an intrinsic component of development projects, from Chilean and Peruvian slums to Mexican villages, has become the nucleus of diversified educational, cultural, and organizational drives; and the projects themselves were initiated in many cases by cultural workers trained in the methods of educator Paulo Freire and theatre director Augusto Boal. By 1991 grass-roots theatre organizations had been formed in at least sixteen countries, mainly around community- and adult-education programs represented by CREAL (a Latin American adult- and community-education organization).

The insertion of the artist into the community is now a feature of most grass-roots cultural processes. Of course this is not entirely a historical novelty. The cultural policies of elected civilian governments and left-wing parties in different countries have at various times provided significant openings for fairly broad-based work in popular culture.[24] It is, however, the first time in the history of the hemisphere that so many democratic options coexist in society and that so many diverse and dynamic expressions of popular culture exist in competition with the cultural policies of hegemonic sectors.[25]

The institutional relationship between the Nuevo Teatro Popular and social movements today differs in at least one respect from the relationship that it enjoyed in its earlier years: the social movements of the past decade have been developing their own potential as autonomous creators of culture, and in most instances there no longer is a perceived need for a cultural, artistic, or intellectual "vanguard."[26]

Ironically one of the objectives of revolutionary artists and intellectuals of the sixties has in fact been achieved, partly as a result of the vacuum created by the repression of the past decade. Massive repression removed most of the self-appointed "cultural leaders," through death or exile, and the reemerging social movements learned to fill the vacuum, in many cases with versatile, nonindividual initiatives. In this context theatre is historically important as a linchpin of a rising counter-hegemony.

The Birth of the New Popular Theatre

Although it is quite impossible to indicate precisely when the Nuevo Teatro Popular was born (in fact it was really a multiple and repeated birth that took place over the better part of a decade), one might attempt to identify its immediate forerunners.[27] There are connections to certain movements that preceded it, such as *teatro independiente* (i.e., the independent, noncommercial theatre) in the Southern Cone and, throughout the continent, the university theatre and workers' theatre. The Nuevo Teatro Popular also has other historical connections, including the circus and radio theatre in Argentina and traveling tent shows in Mexico and the southwestern United States, carnivals in Brazil and the Caribbean, and Native American rituals in Central America and the Andean highlands. It might be useful, therefore, to identify the possible influences that were at work in the Latin American theatre of the fifties and sixties, out of which some of the main artists and groups of the New Theatre emerged.

Of all the possible unifying influences, one name invariably recurs: Bertolt Brecht. His impact, both direct and indirect, can be traced through a surprising variety of connections.[28] The first sources, and seemingly the most obvious, are the writings of Brecht himself, who had become widely known in Latin America at least by the time of his death (1956). By the late fifties, productions of Brecht's plays were being staged in the main Latin American cities, and his writings on the theatre were available in translation (in Spanish, English, or French). In the early sixties, theatre practitioners from the German Democratic Republic were offering seminars on Brecht in Cuba.

Other lines of influence, or correspondence, prove to be more interesting, however, because of the vitality of their practical experience, which was quite different from the quasi-academic or textual approaches to Brecht-as-Gospel. We have identified at least three such lines of indirect influence or correspondence.

1. Europe: It is certain that in the 1950s, at least one of the pioneers of a new theatre, Enrique Buenaventura, had first-hand knowledge of three of the most dynamic exponents of Brechtian theatre: the Berliner Ensemble, Giorgio Strehler's Piccolo Teatro di Milano, and Jean Vilar's T.N.P., in France. Santiago García studied for several months at the Berliner Ensemble. The role of Enrique Buenaventura, Santiago García, and Carlos José Reyes in building the New Popular Theatre cannot be sufficiently stressed, because in addition to their successful contributions to their national dramaturgy and to restructuring the means of production, they also laid the basis for Latin American theatre theory, which has, until very recently, been all too sparse.
2. North America: A decade or so later, Mexican and Chicano theatre workers were able to study the technique of the San Francisco Mime Troupe and its offshoot, the Teatro Campesino. A number of groups from various countries became familiar with the Teatro Campesino at festivals, including those at Nancy and Caracas.
3. Latin America: When Mexican theatre artists made their "pilgrimage" (their own word) to the Manizales festivals in the early seventies, they were coming to learn from the masters (Buenaventura, García, Boal, del Cioppo). What they got and took back to Mexico to link up with Teatro Campesino method, was probably a reworking of original methods, because the Colombian pioneers were, in a way, recycling the South American experience.

One must not forget Buenaventura's exposure in the 1950s to the grass-roots extension work of the Fray Mocho Theatre of Argentina and to Chilean university theatre, and the apprenticeship of Santiago García (founder of La Candelaria) and Fausto García (founder of the Theatre School of Bogotá) with Seki Sano, the Japanese-Mexican director who had been invited by the Colombian government to teach in Bogotá and who was expelled less than a year later for his Communist leanings. (Seki Sano also taught several important Mexican *teatristas populares*, including Felipe Santander; Rodolfo Valencia, a director of development theatre projects; and María Luisa Martínez Medrano, who is linked with Teatro Conasupo and the Laboratorio de Teatro Campesino e Indígena.)

Between the mid-sixties and the eighties, groups like the TEC and La Candelaria, Teatro Arena and Opinião, El Galpón, Teatro Escambray, the Grupo Octubre, Libre Teatro Libre, and the CLETA affiliates became models for literally hundreds of new groups, mainly through seminars, workshops, tours, and festivals. Each of them had been exposed to Brechtian ideas of theatre through different sources, and while none of them can be singly credited with "inventing" the Nuevo Teatro, altogether they constituted a network of pioneers.

The most significant original contribution of these artists came, however, from their own roots, through traditional popular culture and the rediscovery of the theatrical traditions of their own societies. Much of this tradition was integrated into the New Popular Theatre in such ways that the effect could be interpreted as Brechtian. It is certainly not difficult to see some correspondence between the use of a traditional storyteller or a musical ensemble as epic narrators, and the device that is so often considered one of Brecht's main contributions to the modern stage.[29] The recurrence of Brechtian or quasi- or neo-Brechtian elements is such that one might well ask oneself how relevant it is to be looking for Brecht at all.

The Emergence of a Common Strand

Just as the nomenclature itself did not gel until the late seventies, well into the maturing of the movement, it is impossible to state that it was born with the founding of a particular group or the publication of a particular statement. There was no clear-cut historical break from earlier developments, but rather a gradual emergence of increasing numbers of groups whose stated objectives and methods appeared to coincide.

In the mid- to late fifties, groups were beginning to search for alternatives to the canon of Western theatre. Many artists were proposing a critical reexamination of their own societies and engaging their audiences in an ongoing dialogue (marking, in the words of playwright Carlos José Reyes, a change of ownership; cited in Garzon Céspedes 1978). In some countries, where the influence and organization of the Communist party was strongest (e.g., Brazil, Uruguay, Chile) the program of the progressive theatre coincided with the cultural project of the Left, e.g., the *centros de cultura popular* and community cultural centers.

It was these national networks most closely identified with the organized Left that codified their objectives in such manifestos as the statement of principles issued in 1962 by the Uruguayan Federation of Independent Theatres. This document expresses the philosophy and goals that we found to be common to most Nuevo Teatro work. While the wording, the scope, and the nuances of the manifestos and programs of the various national theatre movements might differ slightly, the fundamentals are basically the same (Galpón 1973).[30]

The authors of the statement still consider that they belong to the teatro independiente, which is neither grass-roots theatre nor even the same as the workers' theatre of earlier militant artists, but rather a movement of noncommercial theatre groups and artists whose main objective was to "raise" the artistic appreciation of the "masses." Still the Uruguayan statements attest to the links between the teatro independiente and what was to become the Nuevo Teatro Popular.

Another important forerunner was the university theatre, which provided both the technical training and the historical precedent for theatre activists in the sixties and seventies. In virtually every country (e.g., in Colombia and Argentina in the sixties and in Nicaragua and Mexico in the mid-seventies, as described in the examples in chapter 5), many of the groups involved in the Nuevo Teatro Popular were founded by a student, a teacher, or a graduate of a fine arts or drama program of the university. A number of universities also have their theatre ensembles, often of professional calibre, such as the ICTUS in Chile and the theatre of the INBA (National Institute of Fine Arts) in Mexico—groups which, although they can be classified for the most part as experimental theatre, have also promoted theatre of commitment.

A groundbreaking manifestation of this in the Mexican experience was the Teatro Trashumante, founded by students in 1965 in Atlixco, Puebla. Its eight groups presented 340 performances in Mexico City alone in its first eighteen months of existence. Works were selected on their literary and didactic merit. Mariano Leyva, founder of Mascarones, worked as one of many directors of this project. Within six years thirty-seven groups had been formed (Nájera 1971). These are but isolated examples, which multiplied throughout the continent.

Structures of the New Popular Theatre

Of the hundreds of groups that make up the movement known as Nuevo Teatro Popular, relatively few were constituted by trained professionals; but these include the artistic groups who made the most outstanding contribution as teachers and theoreticians. In studying the organization, the repertoire, and the artistic methods of the Nuevo Teatro Popular, we limited ourselves to key representative groups from different countries, which are mainly professional (i.e., composed of full-time artists) or have at least developed an important professional component. It was logical, however, to include also some groups formed at the grass-roots level, because of the professional standards they achieved and because of their contribution to the theatre movement.[31]

We have chosen three areas where theatre of commitment has combined with artistic theatre, and which illustrate ways in which the new popular theatre developed in opposition to commercialism, antipopular elements, and hierarchical structures: organization, repertoire, and space.

The Organization

As social organizations, Nuevo Teatro Popular groups have tended to conform to a nonhierarchical internal structure. As political or quasi-political organizations, they are usually democratic and egalitarian, and discussion and decision-making are conducted according to "scientific methods."[32] Members of this type of cultural organization are encouraged to diversify their areas of expertise while continuing to study and perfect their strongest skills, although such special skills and talents are usually recognized and given their due.

External relations conform to similar patterns, whether in connection with other organizations (from community groups to the state) or with the groups' audiences and constituencies. The notion of a theatre of context and of commitment comes to life as these groups explore in varying degrees the complex relationship of the theatre to the *polis*. Thus the spectacle or performance becomes important not only in relation to space and to the organization of the production, but also in relation to the events surrounding each performance, to the life experiences of every successive audience, and to the transformations of text and artists' lives that occur between performances and between productions. This duality becomes particularly obvious, of course, at junctures when the artists are most involved in the events of the times.

Most of the prominent groups have been forged by strong artistic directors. Outstanding examples include El Galpón (Atahualpa del Cioppo, Uruguay); the Teatro Experimental de Cali (Enrique Buenaventura) and the Teatro la Candelaria (Santiago García), both of Colombia; Teatro Arena (Augusto Boal, Brazil); Grupo Octubre (Norman Briski) and Libre Teatro Libre (María Escudero), both of Argentina; Nixtayolero (Alan Bolt, Nicaragua); Teatro Escambray (Sergio Corrieri) and Cubana de Acero (Albio Paz, who left the Escambray group after five years), both of Cuba; Contigo América (Blas Braidot, Mexico, formerly of El Galpón); and União e Olho Vivo (César Vieira, Brazil). The problem of hierarchy and of defining roles must appear to be paradoxical; if we are to judge from the above list, we can only conclude that despite the general rejection of the "star" principle, the nonhierarchical collective is most successful when the group is most closely identified with a strong founder and director. At least this certainly seems to be the case with all the groups we have mentioned. Yet all these groups have succeeded in developing a successful internal process and sharing of responsibilities, which would indicate that the director's role must also be that of a skillful coordinator and facilitator.

The professional development of artists in the Nuevo Teatro Popular varies considerably, from that of young actors and technicians trained in grass-roots development workshops to the experience of older theatre workers with over a quarter century in professional companies, radio, television, cinema, and university theatre. Most members of established groups received their training either in university or fine-arts programs, or in professional workshops and training within groups.

Relationships with other organizations may be local, regional, national, or international, a scope determined by various voluntary and involuntary factors (e.g., forced exile). Groups are most frequently connected to other groups through individual members and through alliances and organizations, although one occasionally finds a more-established organization entering into an advisory or cooperative relationship with a younger or sometimes a nonprofessional group. Individual cooperation and exchange is quite common: distinguished directors, especially, are in great demand to work with groups other than their own; actors sometimes cross over between groups and companies; and playwrights associated with one or more groups in particular may see their works produced by other groups.

Relations between groups (at the local, national, and international levels) are usually of a serial nature—members leave to form a new group or to join an existing one, often bringing with them the methods, perspectives, and philosophy of their former associates—and these departures are not always unfriendly, by any means, so that each individual would be likely to serve as a bridge between groups, regions, or even countries. Cuba presents an interesting case study of this situation with the multiplier effect of the Teatro Escambray, from which four members left, over a period of five years, to establish three grass-roots theatre groups: La Yaya, Teatro de Participación Popular, and Cubana de Acero. In Mexico, Mascarones offshoots include the Grupo Cultural Zero, Los Enanos de Tapanco, and independent theatre workers such as José Manuel Galván (who has acted and directed in Mexico, California, the U.S. Southwest, and Washington, D.C.).

Exile, particularly from the Southern Cone, has been a significant cause of such cross-fertilization. A partial list (in which groups formed in Europe should be included) serves to illustrate the scope of this movement (Pianca 1991). Chile's theatre workers have distinguished themselves throughout the diaspora: playwright Jorge Díaz, radicalized by the overthrow of Allende, formed the Compañía Chilena de Teatro, in Spain (1978), and published a newsletter on theatre in exile; Sergio Liddid Céspedes, instead of rejoining El Aleph in Paris after the group was released from prison, went to work with the Teatro Popular Chileno, in Britain; the Compañía de los Cuatro, of Venezuela, made up of four distinguished Chilean actors, won state subsidies and several local awards; in Costa Rica, award-winning playwright Alejandro Sieveking and Bélgica Castro formed the Teatro del Angel, which acquired its own playhouse.

Artists of the New Popular Theatre of Argentina who survived the neofascist onslaught of the seventies contributed also to the development of popular theatre abroad. The group Libre Teatro Libre went to Mexico; there they added new actors, then moved to Spain and dissolved. But the individual members scattered to form other groups, such as the Teatro delle Radici (Cristina Castrillo), or to work as freelance teachers and artists (María Escudero, who has played an important role in the New Popular Theatre of Ecuador). The Latino theatre of New York gained the experience of Norman Briski, who formed a new community-based group and, after the election of Alfonsín, returned to Argentina to face charges connected to his earlier political activism and to carry out some of the new projects of the popular theatre.

Some groups could only grow and survive in exile. Sol de Río 32, from El Salvador, established itself in Mexico, and Teatro Vivo, of Guatemala, distinguished itself first in Mexico and then in Paris. The Uruguayan group El Galpón offers a study in courage and endurance. When they were banned, in 1976, and forced into exile after suffering arrest, torture, and the confiscation of all their property, the group moved to Mexico, where they continued to perform and to teach. Between 1976 and 1983 (shortly before they returned to Uruguay), they accumulated an impressive record of tours, performances, workshops, and individual participation in conferences and seminars. They presented close to 1,800 shows in Mexico and 250 abroad, reaching over 600,000 spectators, with a repertoire of twenty-four titles; they received four prestigious awards in Mexico and six abroad, including the Ollantay prize twice (1976 and 1980).[33] Two of its members, Blas Braidot and Raquel Seoane, remained in Mexico with the group that they had formed there, Contigo América, choosing to integrate themselves into the historical process of Mexico.

Alliances among theatre groups or between theatre groups and other cultural organizations may be ad hoc or of a more permanent nature. They are galvanized by specific issues, such as a political crisis, the organization of a cultural event (e.g., a theatre festival), or the need for action around some civic or cultural issue (such as the funding of new facilities). They also take the form of federations, associations, or corporations, united as a rule by a common philosophy (empowerment of the community, art to serve the community, critical reflection of reality, advocacy of social change) and by common objectives (promotion of popular theatre regionally and nationwide; protection, through high visibility, against hostile political currents; national and international exchange, tours, festivals and seminars; and enhanced lobbying for funding and infrastructural support).

Among the best-known ad hoc alliances of recent years is the Teatro Abierto movement of Argentina (1981–85; see the fifth case study in chapter 5), which brought together over one hundred playwrights, actors, and groups. The chartered associations with the highest profile and the strongest track record have included the Colombian Theatre Corporation and Mexico's CLETA. During the particularly violent period of the eighties, the Colombian federation navigated through some of the most perilous waters (the Scylla of overt government or paramilitary hostility and the Charybdis of the resurgence of commercial theatre).[34]

Although the Nuevo Teatro Popular is fundamentally an independent theatre, i.e., autonomous and not directly sponsored by any single agent but the community, the rules of sponsorship, support, affiliation, and alliances appear to be quite fluid and to exclude only two types of relationship: an official, exclusive identification with one or two agents, and support or sponsorship that results in some form of interference with the artistic integrity of the group's work. Regarding associations with political parties or movements, it would seem that whenever a director or the leading figures of a group are known militants with a specific party affiliation, the group's cultural activities tended to support the cultural program of that party and artists played a vital role in formulating the cultural policy of political organizations. We have not developed a detailed study of the repertory of such groups to analyze the connection between their thematic priorities or approaches to a given problem and the corresponding party policies of the moment, but the artistic integrity of most of those groups (Grupo Escambray, La Candelaria, El Galpón) is so firmly established that one would be hard pressed to attribute a direct prescriptive role to their political party in the choice and treatment of artistic subjects.

The relationship between groups and the state varies according to at least two factors: the openness of the society (the degrees of tolerance exercised by the different levels of government and the degree of popular participation each one allows) and the extent of a group's radical propositions vis-à-vis the government.

In 1976 El Galpón stood convicted under the state security laws of serving as an agent of subversion and as a front for the outlawed Communist Party, and all their assets were confiscated. At the same time, in Argentina, the term *subversion* officially became a terrifyingly elastic term used as grounds for arrest, disappearance, or death, and community cultural workers could be shot or tortured for organizing a cooperative or printing a list of disappeared persons, while an actor could be tortured to death for advocating armed resistance to the dictatorship. In Mexico, however, theatre workers committed to community empowerment and social change negotiated an agreement with the government of President Echeverría that guaranteed noninterference in the state-subsidized community program of the Conasupo theatre brigades; although theatre workers sometimes encountered violence from local police or vigilantes in response to the subject matter of their plays or to their grass-roots activism, the state's displeasure was usually shown only through a total lack of cooperation by the authorities.

The difference appears to be due to the type of regime and state apparatus that artists confront. Police states tend to have a unified policy, whereas the policy and strategy of civilian elected governments may be different at the municipal, provincial/state, and federal levels. Mexico, for instance, still has an official commitment to the goals of popular education and culture put forth by the revolution in the 1920s, but the degree of local or state support that a theatre group or network receives may vary considerably from what the federal government affords it.

In the gray area represented by states of siege in electoral democracies, on the other hand, we find an uneasy peace between theatre and state institutions. Uruguayan, Chilean, and Brazilian theatre workers just before and immediately after the military coups continued to perform until they were physically prevented from doing so; in Brazil, after the first eight years of *mano dura* (heavy hand), the arts began to find loopholes.

Even after the return to civilian government, artists have had reason to feel uneasy (Pianca 1991). Among the most publicized cases are the death threats issued by a Chilean underground group calling itself "Comando Trizano" against theatre artists that it called "Marxist diehards" (Pianca 1991:9), and the assassination in Guatemala of a leading member of the theatre group working with the Coca Cola strikers (Levenson 1989).

Colombia, which has been in a state of siege for almost all of the past forty years, abounds with anecdotes, such as those of La Candelaria and the T.E.C., who tell of performing *Guadalupe, años sin cuenta* and *Soldados* in militarized rural areas or marginal neighborhoods. Armed soldiers surrounded the audience, so that the actors in their role as soldiers were playing directly to the military—who often relaxed their guard and joined in the audience's enjoyment of the play.

In addition to the differences between "national-security" states and functional electoral democracies, there is a third type of state, represented by Cuba: a single-party system in a workers' state. State subsidy and certainly state approval are necessary at some level (whether nationally through the Ministry of Culture or locally through Poder Popular, the administrative structures introduced in 1975). In Cuba amateur theatre, community-development, or grass-roots, theatre, and the Teatro Nuevo (New Popular Theatre) have enjoyed official support from the outset; and it could hardly be otherwise, as the groups had to work within the framework of their community, with the Party, with the unions, and with mass organizations (the Women's Federation, the Committees for the Defense of the Revolution, etc.).

Theatre in Cuba has enjoyed a fair degree of artistic freedom but, one might add, most groups have tended to air concerns that do not conflict with overarching official priorities. The theatre collective has the status of a workplace like any other. In other societies, the Cuban model may function at a community level, but it would be difficult for groups to achieve or even perhaps to desire the type of relationship that Cuban groups enjoy with the state apparatus.

In Latin America, then, the polarity is a given, between the cooperation of theatre and state organizations that one sees in Cuba and the natural enmity of popular theatre toward the right-wing state. In between those poles, the range of possibilities will vary according to the particular needs of the group (and the government) and according to the correlation of forces at any given moment.

The autonomy or independence of a New Popular Theatre group may appear to be jeopardized at specific junctures because of its alignment with a partisan group for a production or series of productions or for a mobilization or political action. There are indeed some groups that are derived from a given constituency or else work in such close connection with a specific sector that they are in fact an extension of it; one case in point would be the Cubana de Acero group, based at the large metallurgical plant of the same name, in Havana. Still, such groups are a minority in the movement, because most groups, including grass-roots community groups, tend to have a broad or multiple base (e.g., cooperative members, miners, and women; or the various subgroups in an urban neighborhood). One example of this is the Grupo Zopilote, which is affiliated with a Popular Arts School and the Union of Neighbors and Victims of the 1985 earthquake, in Colonia Roma, Mexico.

Any identification with outside organizations also tends to be, by and large, a multiple one, and it varies according to the scope of a given group. Groups that have a broad program, including workshops, arts projects, community organizing, and performance, would be the most likely to work simultaneously with a variety of grass-roots and other organizations (such as church or union) and possibly with government or nongovernmental organizations. CLETA and other networks in Mexico (e.g., Conasupo, the community-development organization, which was terminated in 1976; the TECOM, or National Association of Community Theatre; and the popular theatre groups of INEA, the national institute for adult education) fall into this category. Some groups are connected to nongovernmental organizations through national or international funding schemes. OXFAM, Inter

Pares, and the Canadian International Development Agency (which usually channels funds through OXFAM and other nongovernmental organizations) are but two foreign sources that fund theatre through development projects. In addition to the Nicaraguan Theatre Foundation (discussed below), funded in part by Swedish and Canadian sources, the Grupo Zopilote's Escuela de Arte Popular received funds from Switzerland for three years following the 1985 earthquake. These theatre projects in some cases develop such autonomous activity as professional touring, but they are still a rare exception. There is a great deal of room for expansion of this type of cultural-development activity in the future.

The clearest relationship of the Nuevo Teatro Popular is with its audience, which is both an assembly of spectators and a constituency. Audiences are not there merely to be played to, or talked at, but to be engaged in a dialogue that goes well beyond the limits of a single performance. The group establishes the basis for the dialogue by reaching out to learn about the community and understand it. A considerable majority of groups conduct research among their audiences (and their main objective is certainly not to market their product); this research is discussed more closely below.

We referred earlier to the "constituencies" of the New Popular Theatre. One could say that there is a single broad constituency: the mass of dispossessed, displaced, and disenfranchised people, along with the discriminated minorities and the select few among the intelligentsia and the bourgeoisie who can identify with the majority. This view of a "broad audience," unfortunately, projects either the narrow radical vision of the "masses" or the blindness of the ruling sectors to any differentiation among the marginalized or the vanquished.

Therein lies the significance of the work carried out by most New Popular Theatre groups with a diversity of audiences and of the special attention they give to cultivating their dialogue with identifiable constituencies. In the rural areas of the continent, Indians (of various nations, tribes, and regions), fishermen, peasants (both agricultural workers and small farmers), artisans, miners, and blacks; in the urban areas, industrial workers, laborers, artisans, students, service-sector workers, residents of marginal sections and slums, and the middle classes; and everywhere, women and children: all have either been the constituency with which some theatre group has come to work, or they have generated their own theatre, through the agency of a theatre worker.

To develop its relationship with its social and political environment, the group or its individual members often participate in various types of cultural activity with other organizations. They will also explore a range of themes that reflect on that social context, from child abuse and the oppression of women to the analysis of a community's economic woes in the context of global monetarism.

Repertoire

The concept of a national theatre has evolved radically since the early 1950s and goes beyond simple questions of theme or language. The generally accepted definition that we find time and again in the New Popular Theatre includes four criteria: it must project the point of view of a cultural identity (hence, it allows little or no room for impartiality or detachment); it is historically determined; it is bound to class struggle; and it is linked to an internationalist consciousness. It is an important assumption that historical and class analysis lend a sharper focus to the critical examination of what is meant by cultural and national identity.

The texts of the New Popular Theatre can stand up to a number of generalizations. First, they include a wide range of subjects, with the content of a considerable proportion of the works being either social or historical, and with national culture being an important underlying question. Second, they include both works by a single playwright and collective creations, and they include original materials and classical or other previously performed works. Third, the range of styles of production and performance and of forms or genres is very broad, especially in the movement viewed as a whole.

SUBJECT MATTER

Taking its cue from the activist generation of historians and social scientists, the theatre of the last quarter of the twentieth century has been aggressively involved in offering its audiences tools to enable them to question certain values and to develop a critical understanding; it is also active in retrieving or reconstructing those elements of national culture that help validate the emerging consensus or strengthen the identity of the marginalized and the dispossessed. The theatre has thus been involved in a process of retrieval, validation or recodification, celebration, and dissemination of national culture.

The official versions of history had to be dissected and alternative versions retrieved and presented. Although many productions did not display a thoughtful, sophisticated analysis, and there were many flaws and weaknesses in the criticism, such flaws would be found primarily in the works of inexperienced groups or in hastily assembled productions. In the case of the groups with the highest degree of artistic competence, even simplistic analysis or two-dimensional renderings could be cleverly (and often intelligently) presented in quality productions (e.g., Cubana de Acero's *Huelga*).

Throughout the movement as a whole, practically the entire span of American history has been shown. The past of aboriginal societies is seen through a revival of pre-Columbian epic dramas and dance dramas about legendary Native American heroes. The conquest and colonization figure most often as parts of a historical overview while the institution of slavery and the enslavement of aboriginal peoples and the poor, heroes and heroines of the war of independence, U.S. hegemony, and recent history are routinely inserted in the theatre.

In a majority of the plays that treat the various periods of Latin American history, the protagonists very often transcend their well-established position of victims (a role to which they tended to be confined in social or political drama of the earlier part of the century). More significantly they figure as witnesses and as agents of the historical circumstance and the future of their community. In the absence of a collective protagonist (an uncommon device because of its difficulty of representation), individual subjects will frequently typify the collectivity; legendary or historical figures considered to be positive models are sometimes decanted from demiurge status to their everyday humanity, although not necessarily stripped of their exemplary virtues, while figures with negative values (the United States, the Capitalist Entrepreneur, the Police, the Dictator) are frequently typified in the simplest agit-prop style, stylized or caricatured.[35]

Unlike historical themes, myth, legend, and oral tradition have sometimes become contentious subjects because of the way in which the group (or director) chose to present them. In general the New Popular Theatre has tended to present myths and legends in revisionist readings that explore their connection to history and material culture. But this generalization is only valid in the case of works that follow a materialist view of history. Groups that present a myth or a legend with little or no historical analysis have been criticized for doing "folklore" or even of proposing escapism and superstition (see Luis Valdez's *Mitos*); more recently, "anthropological" or "anthropocosmic" theatre (Eugenio Barba) has been suspected of similar opportunistic distraction from the community's most pressing concerns.

Perhaps the real question that one should ask is not how "correct" or acceptable any of these treatments of myth and legend are in global terms, but rather what important function they can serve in their communities. Thus one can obviously see no problem with the revival of the *Chan Wech* ("The Little Armadillo") by a Native American group in Mexico in the past decade, because of its underlying social message, or at least because the modern production's stress on the analysis of economic disparity and injustice does not conflict with its artistic integrity as traditional-popular drama. The "myths" presented by Teatro Campesino in the early seventies were criticized because they appeared to idealize what were seen as instruments of the old hegemony (the Virgin of Guadalupe and Quetzalcóatl).

It would be quite conceivable for a Brazilian group whose first priority is the validation of African culture to present an African myth without the reelaboration to which it would be subjected in a society like Cuba, where myths have been examined for the most part in the context of slavery and of the manipulation of myth for social control.[36] The Cabildo de Santiago (Cuba), in *Cefe y la muerte* ("Cefe and Death"), strives precisely for that integration of traditional values with a critical vision of present-day conditions that the Mexicans seek with their Mayan legends.[37]

Contemporary issues are probably the single most abundant source of material. General themes include economic conditions of workers and peasants; political problems (from dictatorship and the disappeared to the counterrevolution); social problems, including the condition of women, children, and students; and the role of the church. Productions have ranged from agit-prop and "rapid response" theatre around crises to well-developed plays that respond to such crises with a critical analysis of their broader context. Thus reactions to the killing of a university student in Córdoba (Argentina), in 1969, gave rise both to ephemeral street theatre and to Libre Teatro Libre's *Asesinato de X.* "Rapid response" theatre fulfills a social function first, with a rawness that fits the immediacy of the work, but it is the polished text or the model provided by a good production that remains as documentation.

The type of response to a given social problem, too, may vary from production to production, reflecting different filters on the same subject matter. La Candelaria's *Golpe de suerte* (1980) is a hard-hitting critique of drug trafficking and its impact on social values and individual lives; eight years later, they produced *El paso*, which presented the climate of fear and confusion that gripped Colombia, without referring specifically to the causes, which include the production and marketing of drugs.

THE QUESTION OF DRAMATURGY

The playwright's name under a play's title usually warrants further investigation. Because of the collective process that carries a production from research to "post mortem," individual authorship is often the equivalent of editing or writing down drafts and the final text based on group input. And in the case of preexisting authored scripts, the director's hand and the group's decisions will influence the shape of the production. Thus two factors stand out in the study of a text of the New Popular Theatre: the history of its creation and the intention and the process of its production.

Although the movement has been characterized by the extensive work of its groups in collective creation, most groups also produce scripted works by individual authors. The production determines the final form that such a text will take, and in some cases the text is really a *pretext* for an original production that also involves considerable input from all group members. A preexisting script is usually taken to the stage with little modification as a quick production, and examples of this do abound, from medieval farces to contemporary Latin American plays. One can deduce from surveying the context of such productions that they served such functions as introducing the group to a new community or audience or presenting a showcase production for a tour or festival. Implicit in an unmodified text, moreover, is an assumption of the universality of a given subject or genre.

All too often collective creation would be equated with original texts, in the mind of the novice, but this is only partially an accurate understanding. The collective process involves much more, of course, and it is often a vehicle in the appropriation and modification of classical texts. The process can consist of adapting a classic to convey part of a political agenda (e.g., *Oedipus Rex* presented by Buenaventura on the steps of the capitol in Bogotá in the late fifties, recalling Rojas Pinilla's repressive regime), or simply of reworking prose and poetry into avant-garde montages (*Opera bufa* of the TEC, *El buscón* of La Candelaria) or choral poems (the pre-Columbian texts presented by Mascarones in a period that corresponded to a politicization of consciousness around Mexico's Native American past).

Collective creation does, of course, contribute its great share of new texts. Some, as we indicated above, are credited to a single author and others to the entire group, as an actual collective work. Often it is only the product, the end result, that differs, because the process in both types of original works is very similar. Most groups carry out research prior to undertaking a production, both to determine the priorities among issues of general concern or the level of interest in different topics and to establish how best to develop the production, what artistic methods are most suited to it, and what elements of communication can be adopted from different sectors of the community. Virtually all groups encourage audience feedback, in discussions after each show and through surveys and interviews afterwards.

The research may be conducted in a variety of ways. Some groups work with specialized research teams (such as social-science students or social workers) or develop their own skills in these areas. Many groups are participant observers in the communities in which they spend most of their time and often live; this way the interviewing becomes more informal and encourages a more spontaneous input into the production (e.g., approaches to character development or different points of view on a problem).

What is researched in an established or potential audience? One important objective for most groups is to find alternatives to the "official story" (i.e., the official, documented account of a historical event, or a documented analysis of a social issue), through oral history, informal conversation, and questionnaires. Another objective, which is part of the groups' work in cultural retrieval and preservation, is the accumulation of lore, including legends and customs, also through oral history techniques. A third objective is the determination of the community's priorities and the points of view that inform them. A fourth is the character of the community as expressed in verbal and nonverbal expression (the study of idiomatic language, pronunciation, tone, and physical gestures and body language in general).

With this knowledge and understanding, a group is more likely to transcend both the paternalism evident in less-informed productions and in much of the earlier extension or educational theatre and the populism that characterizes some theatre that, while calling itself "popular," indulges in stereotyping and demagoguery.

Another important feature of collective creations is that the text undergoes changes as they are required, based on new research, changing circumstances, or audience criticism. The transformation of text through successive versions often parallels the evolution of the ideology of counter-hegemony. One excellent and often-quoted model of this process is Buenaventura's dramatization of Tomás de Carrasquilla's colonial tale, *En la diestra de Dios Padre*, whose five versions (between 1960 and 1985) reflect changing perspectives on the church and the influence of liberation theology.

The main contribution of collective creation does not lie only in the creation of a new text or even a new production, but rather in the complex process itself, which (1) serves as an educational experience for the group members, in relation both to a historical or social question and to their relationship with the community or audience; (2) builds links with research institutions or scholars, on the one hand, and community organizations, on the other; (3) equalizes task sharing within the organization and empowers all members with critical skills; and (4) contributes to the development of repertoire and styles of production and performance that contribute to the cultural strength of a specific sector of its society and to the development of a national theatre.

ECLECTICISM OF STYLE AND VARIETY OF FORMS

Although most groups and artists have a marked preference for specific styles or theatrical forms or genres, none limits itself entirely to less than two or three. In general, every style or form is adapted to the objectives of a given production. As we assigned broad categories to the repertoire of the New Popular Theatre, however, we gave primary consideration to the form itself, with some examples of its various uses. The general categories include the following: traditional or residual popular forms, popular commercial forms, European influences (both classical and modern), and participatory theatre as developed by Augusto Boal.

The traditional or residual forms may have liturgical, ritual, or carnavalesque associations, and they include Native American and African dance drama, medieval Spanish miracle plays, choral drama, pantomime and pageantry, and storytelling. When presented in their unmodified versions, they are virtually indistinguishable from folk drama; their primary use is one of retrieval and validation of traditional culture, often in areas where it is disappearing, or where the impact of alien forms such as those of mass culture cries out for a reaffirmation of traditional values. Most groups, however, have critically appropriated traditional popular forms and made them vehicles for the revisionist reading of myths, legends, history, and the very structures of the rituals. Clowning can be included in this category when the clown or comic figure can be clearly identified with the buffoon of traditional cultures, but it is the circus clown of European ancestry that one finds most commonly today. Still the clown, along with other circus figures, can be linked not simply to the circus, which is a fairly modern institution, but to medieval itinerant players, jugglers, acrobats, and musicians, or to equivalent traditional popular figures in Native American and African cultures.

The popular theatre today will also appropriate the style and structures of what can be considered virtual institutions of popular commercial entertainment, from the circus to the music hall or variety shows, from melodrama and farcical comedy to the radio theatre. The original organizations were headed by impresarios, but their internal structure was often cooperative or even, as in the case of family circuses, collective. This and the fact that they were all, in one way or another, marginal, made them as attractive to the contemporary artist as they had been for decades, even centuries, to the general public. What spoke to the New Popular Theatre was most specifically their humor (or pathos), their energy and vitality, and the sense of continuity built into their character types, formulas, and organizational structure. The fact that much of the commercial popular theatre lived on primarily in the mass media (radio, cinema, and television), made it doubly attractive to theatre groups who were competing with the media or who were at least measured by the media's standards in the eyes of a popular audience.

Classical European forms still used in the New Popular Theatre include Aristotelian drama, usually in its modified Shakespearean–Spanish Golden Age versions, or as nineteenth-century naturalistic drama. Most groups shy away from this form when developing new material, but the structure persists sometimes, in plays with linear constructions and simple plot development. The use of Brechtian techniques, in purely derivative ways or with modifications, is quite prevalent in full-length dramas, but despite the use of a narrator or music for "distancing" and of an open ending to be resolved in a discussion with the audience, many of these are not, strictly speaking, epic dramas.

Other modern European influences besides Brecht and Piscator include multimedia montages, the theatre of cruelty and the theatre of the absurd, and such forms as the tribunal or forum. Multimedia presentations are of little value for groups that operate on limited budgets and for traveling productions (especially those that go to locales with limited resources, including electricity). Like colonial pageants, they become viable with the material contribution of different sectors of the community, in a fixed locale, and as part of a larger project such as a festivity, a celebration, or a festival.

The theatre of cruelty and the theatre of the absurd take on new dimensions in the Latin American sociopolitical context. One of the best examples of this was the 1981 Teatro Abierto cycle of short plays that, outside the fresh experience of widespread political terror, disappearances, torture, and death, could belong with little difficulty to the modern European canon. In the real context of the moment and of the recent past, however, it would be absurd to attempt to connect them to a purely existential bourgeois anguish or abstract terror, except in the degree to which the Argentine experience of the 1970s had become so ingrained in the consciousness as well as the unconscious of artists and progressive people that its most effective expression would be found in the highly decanted essence best conveyed by those European genres. (Continuing censorship and fear of repression were also probable factors for this artistic choice.) A similar interpretation holds for the pattern that emerged in Colombia in the late 1980s, against a backdrop of moral and psychological disintegration of the society, coupled with the spread of paramilitary violence linked to the drug traffic and to political extremists. Here too it would make sense to connect the "absurd" and the "cruel" to more than just an alienated trend.

These productions, to which (in the shorthand of theatre criticism) we most often affix the labels of their European counterparts, are powerful indictments and often judgments of some of the most terrible realities to afflict the soul of their societies. They are in a way a last resort for the expression of generalized states of mind produced by very real terrors that sometimes defy specific naming or naturalistic rendering. Occasionally events and personalities whose impact, however great, is emotionally "manageable" are handled in what might be seen as the converse of the "absurd" and as a somewhat rational cousin of the theatre of cruelty: the tribunal. Peter Weiss's trial format has appealed to Latin American groups because it allows spectators to share an immediate process, that is, one that is not mediated by reconstruction or reenactment. When events are retold, they are mediated by a Brechtian kind of dialectical process—the use of logic and reason by the prosecution and the defense to convince judges or jurors.

Finally we return to participatory theatre and its categories as described by Augusto Boal. Its most immediate origins lie in improvisational theatre of the postwar period, in the psychodrama developed in New York in the 1950s, and possibly in the role-playing games introduced by social workers in Chicago and other North American cities in the 1930s. Its main function is the empowerment of the participants by means of an integrated approach to raising consciousness, using dramatic exercises both as expressions of emotion and mental attitudes and as a physical basis for transforming those attitudes. Boal extended the framework of psychodrama from the individual to the social and the political, based on a philosophy of popular empowerment that coincides with Paulo Freire's theories of education.

Some of Boal's exercises or quasi-performances involve trained actors, while others involve both the trained actor and participants from the audience. "Performances" may involve ten different variations on reading the newspaper in ways that highlight a number of critical issues; they may range from exposing distortions of the news to developing the reader's skills in connecting the economic and political causes of news events. They may also involve "invisible theatre," in which actors provoke a generalized discussion of pressing issues in public places. Much of Boal's theatre is an internal community process, however, and its techniques cover the gamut from simple role playing to creating physical "images" or having the actors act out such roles on the audience's instructions. More complex role playing might analyze photo romances or soap operas, repressive social patterns, or the meaning of myths and legends. Boal also favored the trial format for analyzing issues.

During his years in Paris, and through his workshops in New York, Boal developed new strategies for working within postindustrial society. This method, which Boal calls the "cop in the head," harks back to psychodrama, and it focuses on the individual's internalization of oppression (Boal 1990). Unlike traditional psychodrama, however, it is not intended as an integrative "cure," but as a deepened process of critical analysis, addressing the societal rather than the individual sources of alienation. The "cop in the head" workshops, perfected in France, Canada, and the United States, appear to be equally effective in the Brazilian cities, where Boal has resumed his work since 1987 (Schutzman 1990, Taussig and Schechner 1990).

The Ideologized Space

The physical spaces used by the New Popular Theatre for production and performance reflect the geographic and demographic scope of the movement. There is hardly a kind of place that has not been appropriated (temporarily or permanently) by popular theatre groups and artists for their work, and few types of spaces that they have not constructed. Historical precedents exist, as we saw in earlier chapters, for the expropriation or appropriation of space; with the Nuevo Teatro Popular, it becomes possible to catalogue and categorize an even broader range. What stands out in most cases is the ideologizing of space, either in the more theoretical sense, as we see in the conflicts over the rights to use specific locales, or in the more specific, concrete sense of charging existing spaces or new ones with the ideology of the emerging popular culture.

The ideological conflict is engaged most radically in cases where the margin of freedom enjoyed by the artists is restricted by the authorities, either directly or indirectly (through the refusal of permits, the forced evacuation of the space, or the censorship of a production). Yet because in a majority of cases the space is occupied through unilateral appropriation or through pressure brought to bear on the authorities either by the artists or through a supportive community, there is often some conflict, whether stated or unstated.

Temporary Transformation of Existing Spaces

The existing spaces most commonly used for performances by groups of the New Popular Theatre are probably the public squares or plazas and parks, streets, and workplaces. The latter would include factories, fields (Teatro Campesino's performances for the United Farmworkers in California and Nicaraguan groups performing for agricultural coops and peasants), schools and universities, and (in Cuba and Nicaragua) army barracks and camps. Many of these performances are by invitation, and some bookings reflect an ongoing connection to the specific constituencies.

With the thawing of the old tensions between the church and progressive activists, the popular theatre has returned to what can be considered one of its original sources. Small theatre groups sometimes spring from Christian base communities, to perform in the church or under the auspices of the local religious. At the same time, groups not directly connected with religious institutions now perform in spaces controlled by those institutions: either in the church structures themselves, or in outdoor ceremonies such as religious feasts or processions, which constitute a temporary extension of "sacred space".

One example is provided by the "Tandas Culturales de Tlaltenango," an annual popular arts festival of a progressive nature, organized from 1975 to the mid-1980s by a priest associated with the local church. The Tandas were part of the annual fair held on the December feast day of the Virgin Mary, and they were co-organized by Mascarones (López

Bucio 1983). Other examples include the work of Jesuit theatre worker Jack Warner with Teatro La Fragua, in Honduras (a young-people's group that tours with religious plays and performs as part of the religious services), and the very secular group Pregones, which in New York City has found a permanent home in St. Ann's Episcopal Church, in the Bronx.

Theatre artists work in markets, both in the fixed permanent structures and in the temporary market place set up by farmers and tradespeople in squares and streets; the latter represents a penetration of a space temporarily appropriated by a larger group. Itinerant and "rapid-response" performers have acted on the back of trucks in Patagonia and Brazil, while community-based groups routinely rehearse and perform in vacant lots or in the inner courtyards of tenement houses in Buenos Aires, San Juan, Santo Domingo, Havana, and New York City.

Appropriation or penetration of segments of carnival festivities are less likely to meet opposition because of the inclusive, open nature of the carnival space. Thus the "murgas" of Montevideo and Buenos Aires, the *samba* schools of Rio, or the *caymán* (alligator) dances of the Caribbean coast of Colombia might, for instance, offer a relatively safe place for protest theatre. A related case involves Brazilian artists who, during the military dictatorship, tagged the spatial configuration of their work as "public entertainment." They thus qualified for a different category of permit, which freed them from "prior censorship of the text" and from censorship of performance, and they even qualified for public funding.

Disputed Control of Existing Spaces

The category of "temporary appropriation" applies also to prisons and concentration camps, where inmates have carried out some of the fiercest struggles for the right to perform. This struggle, with all its predictable setbacks, could result in officially tolerated productions in Chilean prison camps or, in the least favorable of its outcomes, in the secret amateur presentations of music, drama, and dance performance in the women's prison of Buenos Aires (often in the showers).[38] These venues are obviously the most vulnerable to the whims of the authorities and to dangers of physical reprisal against the performers.

The history of the New Popular Theatre includes a wide range of disputes over the temporary or permanent use of spaces. Teatro Campesino did not always perform in public squares with official permission, nor did artists at Brazilian football matches protest the dictatorship *after* submitting their plans to the censors; there are numerous instances of the penetration or temporary appropriation of public spaces in direct confrontation with the authorities.

Among the most famous confrontations over the access to or control of theatre venues, there are the cases of the Manizales Festival, in Colombia, and the Foro Isabelino and the Casa del Lago, in Mexico City. In both cases radical young artists, opposed to official sponsorship or subsidies by government institutions, occupied the spaces by force, after being barred or after excluding themselves from the programmed activities.

Theatre groups in search of a home sometimes join the squatter community, occupying abandoned sheds, movie theatres, or other structures. The occupation may be intended as a temporary one, until the group finds other resources, or it could be sufficiently attractive to justify a fight for permanent occupancy. The Chilean exile group El Aleph squatted in an empty factory building in France until they were forcibly evicted by the police; the authorities then tore down the structure.

The dispute over control of an existing space has extended to the artists' influence in a school or university, as in the cases of the School of Fine Arts in Cali, Colombia, under Enrique Buenaventura (forced to leave the directorship of the school in 1969 after staging *La Trampa*, a work about the dictatorship of Ubico in Guatemala, which was interpreted as a criticism of the government) or the UNAM (National Autonomous University of Mexico), where politically radical artists participated in but soon split from what they considered to be an establishment-controlled institution.

Creating New Spaces

The purchase or leasing of a building or other type of permanent space independently controlled by a theatre group has been an important element of the infrastructure of the New Popular Theatre. Some groups merely work in their space, while others use it also as living quarters. The space could be a preexisting structure (as in the case of Latino groups in the United States or in most Latin American cities, from

Santiago de Cuba to Santiago de Chile, which lease or own spaces in the city), or it can be built by the group itself, as has been the case of the base camps of Teatro Escambray, in the hills of Cumanayagua, Villa Clara province (Cuba) and of the Nicaraguan groups Nixtayolero and Teyocoyani, on agricultural cooperatives in Matagalpa and León, respectively.

A permanent base implies a commitment to the surrounding community. A group's involvement can range from ongoing or ad hoc activities with citizen's pressure groups and self-help organizations to its total integration with the economic and social infrastructure, which normally includes participation in the community's productive sectors.

Losses

The material setbacks involved in the loss of a space have been both minor and major, temporary and permanent. The kind of destruction or confiscation of property carried out in a cultural center in a Chilean neighborhood or in a French city (the case of El Aleph) could be irreversible, especially if carried out by force. In cases where widespread public sympathy for the group has inhibited an overt assault on the space, arson has worked; for example, the Teatro Picadero (of Teatro Abierto), was destroyed in a mysterious blaze.

On the other hand, in one of the most celebrated legal cases against a group under a police state (El Galpón), the group's rights were protected in the long run by a community boycott of attempts to hand the space over to other companies, and El Galpón reestablished itself in its old space on its return to Uruguay, in 1984.

The Role of Festivals and Symposia

The history of the New Popular Theatre can be traced by the one phenomenon that enables us to look at it as a movement, a network of networks: the theatre festival and related seminars or meetings (see Frischman 1990 and Pianca 1990). It was at the Festival of Nations, in France, that many Latin American theatre artists discovered Brecht and one another in the late fifties, and at the Nancy Festival (First Festival of University Theatre, 1964), Latin American groups participated and began their dialogue. The concept of grass-roots theatre became a reality through the first festivals and conferences of amateur theatre (e.g., in Cuba in 1960, in Chile in 1968). Cuba took the initiative in this hemisphere in the promotion of international meetings, beginning with its first Festival of Latin American Theatre (1964), with works presented by Cuban groups and individual representatives from fifteen countries; in 1968, for the first time, the international theatre festival drew groups and productions from different countries. Also in Havana, in December 1967, over one thousand theatre workers met for a week to study the role of theatre in society.

In 1969 the Colombian Theatre Corporation was formed, with two of the strongest exponents of the New Popular Theatre at its core: the T.E.C. (Teatro Experimental de Cali) and La Candelaria. In 1971 TENAZ (Teatro Nacional de Aztlán) was founded, with membership from Mexico and the U.S. Southwest; they have organized sixteen festivals since then. In 1973 CLETA was formed in Mexico. These have been perhaps the three foremost justifications for the existence of a network and a movement, because of their national impact, their high international profile, and the organizational strengths they brought to individual groups and to the joint planning of Latin American events. They have also been instrumental in the planning of major festivals for twenty years.

Just as these important organizations have been involved in endless disputes, at different times, with the more conservative establishment and with the more radical cultural workers, festivals have been both an autonomous and a disputed space. The very first Manizales Festival (Colombia, 1968) opened less than one week after the massacre of Tlatelolco in Mexico City, and in the context of a state of siege that had troops around the university in Bogotá. Although most of the productions were not very political, the discussions were, and set the terms of an ongoing debate for future gatherings: the discourse became more sharply defined and participation increased.

By 1973 Manizales had attracted over eighty groups from all over the continent, in the Fifth Latin American Theatre Festival and First International Theatre Showcase. Acrimonious disputes continued to break out when the more radical political groups accused organizers and some of their fellow participants of trying to enshrine Manizales as an institution aligned with the establishment. The vibrant atmosphere created by the four thousand participants in 1974 would not be repeated, as the dispute over control of the ideological space practically blew Manizales apart.

During that same period, Quito, Caracas, and Puerto Rico had also organized what were supposed to be annual festivals (and which only Caracas has sustained into the eighties), and the 1969 Nancy Festival introduced Luis Valdez's Teatro Campesino to the world, fresh from the 1968 Radical Theatre Festival in California. In 1974 Chicano and Mexican popular theatre groups met in Mexico, in the first Latin American–Fifth Chicano Theatre Festival, with high-sounding declarations of Latin American unity and cultural identity. That, however, was the year when the TENAZ Chicano movement began to split along what to some observers were clearly ideological lines, with one of its pioneers, Luis Valdez, moving into the revival of *mito* (myth)—his spiritual phase.

The 1974 Mexico meeting disappointed its participants partly because of the high political expectations it had fostered and partly because of the power struggle between followers of the PCM (Mexican Communist Party) and the PST (Revolutionary Workers' Party), with the Chicanos caught in the middle. And then the 1975 Manizales festival failed to take place. Caracas was turning into an international showcase, with far less emphasis on the popular theatre, dialogue, or workshops for Latin American groups; by 1978 it would become the host of the Festival of Nations, and by 1980, of the 5th World Theatre Festival. What had begun to feel and act like a movement of popular theatre was on shaky ground.

In fact a number of producers and festival organizers were moving in the direction of larger commercial ventures, institutionalized in large measure through guaranteed box-office returns and with corporate and state support. None of the established festivals excluded groups or productions for ideological reasons; on the contrary, they have continued to do what the Nancy Festival undertook: to present the most progressive artistic groups.

The exclusion of nonprofessional groups and artists was simply a clear indicator that these were not Popular Theatre Festivals. Still they function as important showcases for those professional groups (La Candelaria, Yuyachkani, El Galpón, Teatro Vivo) that maintain their grass-roots connections. The annual festivals of Manizales (Colombia) and Córdoba (Argentina) in the late eighties became part of this circuit, which includes the Caracas Festival (itself modeled on Nancy) and the New York Latino Festival (see below). In the late eighties, the city of Bogotá also began to sponsor an impressive international theatre festival.

They were joined by other festivals outside Latin America. The Festival Internacional de Teatro de Expressão Iberica (FITEI), in Oporto, Portugal (begun in the mid-seventies as a Luso-Hispanic showcase and now expanded to include representatives from Angola and Mozambique), the summer Festival de Théâtre des Amériques, of Montreal (initiated by Marie-Hélène Falcon, who modeled it after the recast New York Latino Festival that she attended in 1982), and the autumn Festival de Teatro Iberoamericano of Cádiz (inaugurated in 1986) are proof of the international success of a theatre movement that owes much of its dynamism to its roots in the popular theatre. All continue to be important points of convergence.

Continuing the line of popular theatre, the biennial TENAZ (Teatro Nacional de Aztlán) festivals have included groups and artists representing the East Coast association of New Popular Theatre, COLAT (Corporación Latinoamericana de Teatros), which in 1990 cosponsored the festival in conjunction with ATINT (the Association of Theatre Workers and Researchers), who co-organized the symposia.

In 1976 in the United States, Teatro Cuatro, a community-based group from New York, presented the first Festival of Latin American Popular Theatre (which was in effect the second Latino Theatre Festival), once more separate from the TENAZ Festival. The founder-director of Teatro Cuatro, Argentine expatriate Oscar Ciccone, and his wife, the Salvadorean artist Cecilia Vega, directed the organization of three subsequent popular-theatre festivals in New York (1978, 1980, and 1982).

The first festivals were sponsored by the Museo del Barrio and by Teatro Cuatro. Beginning in 1980 the New York Shakespeare Public Theatre became involved. Perhaps as a consequence of its own momentum of energetic growth, the last festival exceeded its financial capability, and it was bailed out by Joseph Papp, who became its sole sponsor and producer. By 1984 it had dissolved into the Latino Theatre Festival and eventually the Joseph Papp Latino Festival, expanded to include cinema and music. Ciccone and Vega continued to direct the festival as members of Papp's organization.

In 1978 Cuba held its first national festival of New Popular Theatre, with about fifteen groups participating. The fact that the Ministry of Culture was giving its clear support to the grass-roots and community-oriented theatre did not go unnoticed outside Cuba, and gave a boost to what loose movement there was. During the eighties Cuba hosted two international symposia, or encuentros, of Latin American theatre workers, with an emphasis on the New Popular Theatre. Nicaragua offered an alternate venue for one of the seminars, in 1983, and initiated its own international popular theatre festivals. Out of the Cuban and Nicaraguan experiences, the Latin American Theatre School was established. Under the direction of Osvaldo Dragún, it began its annual one-month workshops in 1989. The workshops, which are held in a different country every year, are directed by Latin American and other professionals of international acclaim and long-standing reputation in the popular theatre (see Epstein 1990).

Meanwhile there are also theatre festivals that bring together grass-roots and community theatre groups within different countries.[39] Organizations of theatre for community development and theatre for adult education are often linked to amateur theatre, and as the last decade of the century begins, many of these groups, representing a majority of the Latin American population, are participating in biennial festivals of community theatres organized by federations of adult- and community-education associations.

A summary does little justice to the significance of all these festivals. They have provided the space where groups can share their work, not only in performance but also in critical sessions, workshops, and informal discussion; in fact, they are often the only place where some of the younger groups could be exposed to the work of the more experienced artists and where significant political and artistic discussions can take place. They serve as a forum where the role of theatre is debated along with political and artistic differences, where any line of development can be engaged, and where sound theories of the Latin American stage can evolve.

The history of the festivals parallels, and often mirrors, the uneven course of the popular theatre of the past quarter century: the ideological splits, the periodic breaks by some groups or artists away from activism and toward artistic theatre, the ways in which artists have related to their communities, and the efforts to create a new and original idiom that was not merely an extension of its forerunners. Their history also highlights the disparity of training and intellectual education among the artists, which can lead to repetitive debates about the same issues regarding art and society. And, of course, there is the crisscrossing of references: national theatres crossing borders through the links established by groups and individuals. The unchartable intertextuality of the New Popular Theatre can almost be charted through the festivals and seminars, the very gatherings that have kept the movement alive and its parts multiplying.

5 • *Faces of the New Popular Theatre*

The following case studies illustrate the range of theatre that can be included under the rubric of Nuevo Teatro Popular. Through them we would like to demonstrate the levels of artistic as well as political sophistication, the experience of social and historical adaptation, and the various degrees of instrumentality that coexist under this rather large umbrella. They also illustrate a richly varied intertextuality of artistic and social praxis that, while affirming the historical rootedness both of art and of social action, also allows the New Popular Theatre to leap with ease across restricted space, historical time, and myth.

Teatro Escambray, Theatre in Search of a Context

Nine years after the triumph of the Cuban Revolution, a group of theatre professionals moved out of Havana to bring their artistic work closer to the areas of the country where the revolution was carrying out its most significant socioeconomic transformations. Over the next fifteen years, they were pioneers in the development of community-based theatre and in the training of new theatre professionals and of grass-roots theatre groups.

Teatro Escambray's roots were in the avant-garde theatre, in the political theatre, in the independent theatre movement, and, ultimately, in the twentieth-century European and North American professional theatre. How they transferred their training, their method, and their technical skills to the central mountains of Cuba to contribute to the accelerated development of that region was acknowledged as a model throughout the developing world. How they built audiences, integrated themselves into their communities, contributed to their cultural growth, and branched out throughout the country, both in professional and in grass-roots theatre activity, makes Teatro Escambray a highly successful model of integrational propaganda.

In the mid-sixties the professional theatre in Cuba was an urban and quite sophisticated and diversified institution. Experimental, avant-garde, political, and musical theatre, as well as classical drama coexisted on a solid professional base carved out of decades of collective experience in Havana and training abroad, out of a relatively strong film and radio industry, and out of a post-war flourishing of small independent theatres, most of which continued right through the revolution of the late fifties and into the new era after 1959. There had also been a people's theatre and workers' theatre, particularly in the 1930s and 1940s (with Paco Alfonso as one of its leading figures); among the Spanish exiles to arrive in Cuba in the 1940s, there was at least one (Rubia Barcia) who had worked directly with Lorca's grass-roots theatre, La Barraca.

Parallel to the urban professional theatre, the amateur or community-theatre movement (*teatro de aficionados*) began to grow apace with government support after 1960, but the two remained quite separate. In 1968 as a result of weeks of meetings and reflections on the role of the artist in the revolution, a number of theatre professionals from Havana decided that it no longer meant very much to them to be performing scripted plays for the same audiences in the same traditional spaces, or to be experimenting with an avant-garde (Grotowski) better suited to European audiences.

They began a radical process of consultation and cooperation with political organizations and social scientists, to identify a region of the country where they would be most effective as an artistic vehicle for the revolution. Within a few months, in early 1969, they agreed on the Escambray, which lies roughly in the center of the island. The Escambray included some of the most problematic populations and was one of the main targets of state-planned economic modernization. It was also in this region that a fierce counterrevolutionary war had been fought between 1960 and 1965.

The men and women of the Teatro Escambray were facing a series of daunting challenges: to move from the sophisticated intellectual environment of Havana to one of the most backward areas of the countryside (backward both politically and socioeconomically); to establish a base camp for the rainy season and a touring schedule for the rest of the year; to identify the most important issues on which to develop a repertoire; and, throughout all this, to work on gaining the confidence and support of the population of dozens of small villages and of isolated settlements over hundreds of square miles.

This was not the first professional group to establish itself outside the playhouse, among the grass roots. The Conjunto Dramático de Oriente had been established, some years earlier, in the city of Santiago, by graduates of the local university and local community artists. Their success could be explained in part by the fact that most of the group was from that area; that they had a fairly limited target audience to cultivate, one which was largely working-class, black or mulatto, and overwhelmingly supportive of the revolution; and finally, that they worked with deeply rooted forms of collective popular entertainment, such as the *relaciones*, a type of mumming that relied heavily on music, dance, and audience participation. The situation of Teatro Escambray was quite different.

Not only were their target audiences dispersed in different communities, but a considerable number of them were involved in the collectivization of dairy farming; many had been resettled in new communities as a result of the war of the early sixties and as part of the central government's plan to bring basic services to the entire population (small towns and villages being far more viable than small plots of land widely scattered around the hills). Much of the region was still recovering from the trauma of the counterrevolutionary war, which had been cruel and intense, dividing families and leaving numerous dead, exiles, and political prisoners. Now radical social and economic programs were being introduced that challenged the deeply rooted conservative values of the traditional small farmers and peasants—from their attachment to private landholdings to their attitudes toward women. Once Teatro

Escambray had committed itself to creating popular theatre for these communities, it had to work closely with grass-roots organizations and the Party in developing its materials and cultivating audiences.

The group's first rainy-season base was at the regional teacher-training college of Tope de Collantes, where they established a useful working relationship with young people who would be based in the same communities as the group. From the college they launched their tours, which began with medieval farces, children's theatre workshops, and dramatic storytelling (drawing largely on the traditional art of the storyteller, who was probably the main traditional vehicle of entertainment in the Escambray, and the closest that population came to the theatre arts).

Their base camp, La Macagua, was built at Cumanayagua, a fairly central spot. There they developed their repertoire of full-length plays, which dealt with such topics as collectivization, the role of women, and the proselytizing activities of the Jehovah's Witnesses.[1] Within less than five years, the group was the main showcase of revolutionary theatre in Cuba, one of the preferred sites for internships by young artists, social-science researchers, writers, and even critics, and for a time, a preferred ambassador on tours and at international festivals.[2] The group has also worked in Angola, primarily with Cuban troops. In the mid-seventies they set up their "Frente Infantil" (children's division), and in the early eighties they began to work intensively with adolescent youths, an involvement that yielded works that for the first time moved into a more radical questioning of the status quo and were less inclined to promote an official line (e.g., *Los novios* ("Boyfriend, Girlfriend").

There are a number of reasons, apart from its high profile as an excellent professional ensemble and as a paradigm of Cuban revolutionary art, why Teatro Escambray merits its place in the New Popular Theatre movement; two historical reasons stand out. First it represents a link between a heterogenous prerevolutionary professional theatre (commercial and independent, avant-garde, classical and experimental) and a more homogeneous theatre linked directly to the grass roots. Second it stands roughly at the midpoint in the development of the movement.

The group, under the direction of theatre, film, and television actor Sergio Corrieri, brought together artists from at least five different groups in Havana, and it soon began to add new talent from the National Arts School and from the University of Las Villas (chief among these one of the group's most successful authors and actors, Roberto Orihuela). It also produced important offshoots, as individual members moved on to found other groups with different constituencies (the first three being Teatro de Participación Popular, La Yaya, and Cubana de Acero). Because of its outstanding position as a professional group, it attracted bright and promising interns who would eventually join other groups or the Ministry of Culture.

Although it brought professional theatre in Cuba into a new relationship with its constituencies and with the state apparatus, however, it was a new experience only because its context (a socialist society) was new for Latin America. The use of theatre as a vehicle for ideological education had been promoted in the 1920s as a policy of the Mexican Revolution, and extension work by professionals in rural areas had been done in republican Spain as well as in various Latin American countries. The main difference lay in the willingness of the Escambray's artists to move into those rural communities and become a permanent part of them.

But this too had been attempted by left-wing artists in Brazil in the 1950s and in other countries in the 1960s. The main difference between them and the Escambray was that the Cubans were favored by their quasi-official status, as well as by the fact that they were not the ones primarily involved in promoting political messages or programs (something that the Brazilian popular-culture brigades had arrogated unto themselves), but were working in close connection with officials and community representatives, who developed policy.

Their internal organization was not entirely new, either. El Galpón of Uruguay and the TEC and La Candelaria of Colombia were already well established as independent collectives. Teatro Escambray adopted the structure and also explored collective creation, following a process common to similar groups (employing surveys and intensive research, discussion with audiences, revision of texts, etc.). Enrique Buenaventura's work on collective creation was already known in Cuba when Teatro Escambray was formed, as was the work of Argentine collectives such as Libre Teatro Libre and Octubre. In this regard also, then, Teatro Escambray stands as a promoter in Cuba of a movement that had already begun to snowball throughout the developing world. Nationally it was recognized as a pioneer, internationally, as a paradigm of what the New Popular Theatre could be and do in a socialist society.

But Teatro Escambray can also be said to have revived traditions that were no longer part of the modern artist's experience, and that in Cuba had been so most recently only in the music hall. At least one aspect of their work involved in teaching and training new theatre workers connects them with the tradition of the theatre guilds of Europe (and also, coincidentally, of West Africa). Neither of these historical connections were consciously made by the group's founders, and there is little in the background of the individuals involved that might suggest it, since none of the artists were, before the revolution and even in most cases before they moved out of the city, involved to any significant extent in cultural extension work.

The successful social organization and artistic production of Teatro Escambray would, therefore, provide a strong argument in support of the proposition that popular theatre will independently evolve and adopt systems that bear considerable similarity to those of other historical periods and different cultural areas where the chief task of the artist was also to entertain, to socialize, and to give voice to the collective identity of the community.

Axial Theatre

Grass-roots theatre can serve one or two main functions: community development and/or artistic creation. Some types of popular theatre are not intended as an activity to be enjoyed for its own sake; they fall, rather, into the category of instrumental theatre. Theatre in the context of community development and adult education places, on the whole, less of a priority on the aesthetic. For most people involved in it (as in psychodrama), it remains a vehicle for conflict resolution, for role playing in preparation for community action, or for leadership training. It might be presented as entertainment, and it can be a group's (or an individual artist's) first step toward developing artistic sophistication, but its primary objective is educational or related to training in areas quite apart from the arts. Although the product is sometimes presented to outside audiences (e.g., government representatives), development-related theatre or educational theatre in the context of the community is primarily a vehicle of internal empowerment.

The Nicaraguan model is particularly appropriate to this study, and it has been cited fairly extensively in the literature on popular education and on grass-roots development (see Kidd 1982). Its genesis is virtually inseparable from the popular insurrection against Somoza and especially from the organizational tactics employed by the FSLN among peasants and rural laborers, and its growth is closely tied to the growth of the organizations that were born out of the 1977–79 insurrection or soon after the triumph of the FSLN.[3]

Between 1980 and 1983, the National Theatre Festival grew from 39 works to 576, from 13,000 spectators to 139,000. These statistics offer proof not only of an effective organization, but also of the theatre's success in connecting with Nicaragua's rich traditional popular culture. Before 1979 the theatre did not occupy an important place in elite culture or among the bourgeoisie, although the Rubén Darío Theatre was quite a landmark of Managua until the 1972 earthquake. Moreover, unlike the New Popular Theatre of certain other countries, which is historically connected to the bourgeois theatre (because practitioners of the Popular Theatre often came out of the commercial or the avant-garde theatre), the theatre of the Nicaraguan Revolution is almost entirely rooted in popular tradition and material culture. It also tends to reflect the culture of the majority of the population, which is either rural or village based.

Traditional theatre in Nicaragua, as in the rest of Mesoamerica, has been connected for centuries with rituals that combined dance, music, and drama, mainly around agrarian and religious cycles. The *Güegüence*, a bilingual (Spanish-Nahuatl) dance drama and the oldest mestizo play on record in the Americas, is still performed every year in Diriambá. The origins of Nicaraguan national theatre are evident in some of its other important exponents: the ritual dance drama of the *Toro venado* (the Deer Bull) of Masaya, which appears to be related to similar dance dramas on animal themes found in Mexico and Guatemala; the *Gigantona* (Giantess), a large papier-mâché figure who dances her way through many fiestas around the country, and who has her roots in carnival parades and Corpus Christi festivities in medieval Spain; and the *Palo de Mayo* (Maypole), a central ritual of the Atlantic

Coast, derived from the British West Indians who settled that region. Masks are of paramount importance in traditional drama and popular festivities, and are inherited from both the indigenous cultures and the Spanish settlers.

The New Popular Theatre was bound to integrate elements from such a rich heritage, and in order to study them carefully and thoroughly, the cultural workers of the revolution resorted to live informants and teachers from the villages. This was being done as early as the mid-1970s, as the FSLN intensified its activity and widened organizational efforts throughout Nicaragua. The Teatro Estudio Universitario (TEU), a university group formed in the seventies, had served as a preparatory stage for the political cultural work of many Sandinista cadres. Like the poetry magazines and literary circles of the time, the theatre was a space for the affirmation of national identity—a reaction and a challenge to the cultural preferences of Nicaragua's vehemently pro-U.S. political elite. It was quite logical that, like the poets and historians opposed to Somoza, the theatre workers involved in the Sandinista movement should look to the national heritage for their artistic resources. The founder of the TEU, Alan Bolt, and other Sandinistas including Jaime Wheelock (who would become minister of agrarian reform) set out, during the late seventies, to learn about this heritage and to organize rural dwellers and train them in basic dramatic techniques as a means of gaining self-confidence and presenting grievances before landowners and employers.

Thus when the Sandinistas triumphed, in July 1979, the foundation had already been laid for the establishment of theatre collectives. Then the literacy campaign of 1980, the Movimiento de Expresión Campesina Artística y Teatral (MECATE, a branch of the Farmworkers' Association), and the Association of Cultural Workers (ASTC) all favored the establishment and spread of grass-roots theatre. Much of it came to be directed by what one could consider to be professional theatre workers (university graduates or artists trained in other groups).

Workshops led to the formation of theatre collectives, which contributed in turn to the mobilization of large segments of the population: peasants, workers, students, soldiers, women, and children's groups. Their function was largely pedagogical, i.e., to use techniques of sociodrama as mechanisms for learning and reflection. Their success was based on the ease with which the theatre workers could enter a particular constituency or community and on the ease with which this popular theatre could challenge, subvert, and redefine its own traditional role.

One eloquent example of the thrust of this theatre movement is the fact that one of the two main groups, Teyocoyani, was formed with several young people who had just learned to read and write in the literacy campaign. Theatre for them, as for the communities in which they worked, was not part of a folklore renaissance, nor were they interested in what is still referred to as folk drama. Traditional culture, including important elements of traditional popular theatre, was rescued and revitalized as an important expression of national identity; rather than glorify the past, it articulates a contemporary world view.

Audiences identify through the iconography and the verbal and physical codes of the plays. One finds local linguistic variants, proverbs, masks, music, and religious customs and beliefs combining to make a work intelligible to its audience. For example when they undertook to explore the dilemma of an uncommitted peasant caught between the Sandinistas and the counterrevolution (*Juan y su mundo*, *Los ojos de Don Colacho*), they combined dream sequences, dance battles gracefully choreographed, masks, the witch doctor (or popular healer), traditional gestures such as saluting the Four Winds before entering a body of water, and comic stereotypes. The resolution was left open, although ultimately the *contras* were represented as the aggressors and the only threat to the peasant's livelihood.

Most of the works produced by Teyocoyani and Nixtayolero (the other main theatre collective) have as their common denominator an exploration of attitudes (individual and collective) and of the historical and social factors that condition them. The objective was not to persuade or to offer solutions. Alan Bolt put it quite simply: "Developing a critical consciousness doesn't mean making people think the way we do. People aren't stupid" (see Bolt 1983).

Just as its themes and the system of signs it employs reflected the overall concerns and approaches favored by a majority of Nicaraguans, so too did the organization of the Nicaraguan popular theatre. The groups were financed by the Nicaraguan Theatre Foundation, which was jointly funded by the government, by nongovernmental organizations (e.g., Inter Pares of Canada), and by a portion of the independent revenues of the groups.

In the first year after the triumph of the Sandinista Revolution, Nixtayolero and Teyocoyani, the first groups associated with the foundation, joined agricultural cooperatives or state farms known as Uniones de Producción Estatal (which provided subsistence and some added income), and they also contracted their services to community groups in their respective regions to organize workshops in sociodrama and the arts. Nixtayolero was founded by Alan Bolt, in Matagalpa; Teyocoyani was established, in León, by a team that included a Cuban, an Argentine, and several Nicaraguans associated with the ASTC (it appears to have no single founding director on record).[4]

The roots of other similar groups lie in the literacy campaign of 1980, in which thousands of youths participated, close to seventy of them in theatre brigades. The theatre brigades continued beyond the literacy campaign, through the various periods of agricultural and military mobilization. Most of them, including Teyocoyani, served as artists on the front lines of the Contra War, in a total of sixteen regional cultural brigades. The average age of these theatre workers was between seventeen and twenty; few of them were over twenty-five years of age.

The groups also served as consultants to the government, informing and sensitizing technical personnel about aspects of the local culture that could be relevant to the projects at hand (e.g., local history, community attitudes regarding discussion and decision making, planting in certain phases of the moon). Much of this information would have been gathered as part of the groups' research into customs, traditions, and forms of expression in the various communities where they compiled material for their works.

For most theatre groups, the goal of economic self-sufficiency, or at least of a limited dependence on government support, has also guaranteed a very productive relationship with their communities, because the services and in some cases the new infrastructures developed by the groups (e.g., a bamboo-furniture factory) benefit their cooperative and one or more of their other constituencies (such as miners, peasants, laborers).

Teyocoyani and Nixtayolero have also served as models of artistic accomplishment for the satellite theatre groups of the foundation. The caliber of their full-scale productions has been recognized in international tours and festivals and set an internal standard within the Nicaraguan theatre movement. Another important aspect of these productions is their organic connection with the groups' ongoing work with community development and Nicaragua's cultural heritage. Thus even if one of these productions may at first seem to be a far cry from the everyday work of the groups in planting crops and managing livestock on cooperatives, in open rehearsals on street corners, and in nutrition or leadership-training workshops, both the codes and the information of the plays originate in such extratheatrical contexts.

It is no more extraordinary for theatre to propose a return to Native American spirituality than it is to hear its defence of a Christianity inspired by liberation theology. In the theatre as in other aspects of life in Nicaragua (at least as part of the official policy between 1979 and 1990), these values are connected to a profound concern with ecology and human society. If the arrogance of a local official threatened that delicate fabric, the theatre could become a forum in which to expose it, just as, during the early stages of the revolution, theatre had served to expose the abuse of landowners. (In at least one case, the Sandinista official who was so challenged resigned.) If the empowerment of the common people was threatened—whether by the Catholic hierarchy, irresponsible gossip, personal grudges, environmental damage, prejudices against women or homosexuals, or virtually anything else—the theatre proved to be an effective channel through which to resolve the threats. Through images and action that merge the imaginary and the real, through discussions on stage and off, and through changes of behavior and attitude encouraged by these discussions, the theatre provided a means of confronting all of them.

The activity of the New Popular Theatre in Nicaragua can be termed "axial," because its methods as well as its primary objectives lie roughly along a 180° angle. They range from the purely instrumental role of theatre in workshops, where it serves an important though ancillary function, to the full-length performances for audiences outside the group's radius of ongoing activity. For a foreign audience, or even at a Managua gathering, these performances may be, first and foremost, original artistic creations rooted in the semiology of Nicaraguan culture, and only secondarily the product of a process of articulating social or political issues of current concern.

In between these poles one can find a range of variations. For example the same production that for an audience in Managua, Montreal, or Stockholm was an interesting expression of Nicaraguan culture and a work critical of the Sandinistas, back in León or Matagalpa represents a very immediate experience of community values, traditions, and local problems, not at all critical of the revolution. Similarly it is not unusual for participants in a workshop on the uses of sociodrama to become interested in theatre as an art form, and thus become involved in a community group when they return home. Nor are a group's rehearsals simply an internal matter; it is common for one of the locals who are looking on to correct an actor's pronunciation or gestures, or to demonstrate the "right way" to do a certain dance or song, as his or her grandparents knew it. Practically the entire production, from the initial research to polishing the finished product, is therefore a dialogical process.

CLETA and the Second Mexican Revolution

Fifteen years ago the events of 1968 were still an immediate memory in the Mexican student movement.[5] Despite the deaths at Tlatelolco and the continuing repression of dissent, the radical student movement had been unleashed for good; certain sectors, at least, would not give up the ghost.[6] In the late sixties, groups formed at the university and at the National Institute of the Arts (INBA) had initiated extension programs in various working-class communities, while they also challenged the academic status quo, introducing radical propositions to the educational system and a revolutionary repertoire to academic venues.

One of the short-lived but influential groups formed at this time was the Frente de Arte Revolucionario Organizado (FARO, Organized Front for Revolutionary Art), devoted to popular street theatre. In 1973 an organization of radical students was formed under the acronym CLETA (Centro Libre de Experimentación Teatral y Artística). The first fifteen years of CLETA's existence were marked by violent confrontations with academe and by at least one major internal split. CLETA still survives, although barely. It is a unique organized network because of its diversified artistic work, its effectiveness in community organizing, and its uncompromising politics, which are often dogmatic and sectarian.

CLETA's main task has been the deconstruction of the institutions with which theatre has been traditionally associated: academic centers (the university, high schools, and colleges of fine arts), cultural organizations, and theatre groups. Their main vehicle has been the deautonomization (and deatomization) of institutions and the breakup and reassembling of their own organizational structures, by direct action if necessary. One of the best known examples of this was the case that led to the formation of CLETA: the taking of the Foro Isabelino, an off-campus space that independent groups effectively wrested from the academic authorities on 21 January 1973.

The movement arose not out of the groups' work with popular sectors of the population but rather, in the words of one of its founders, Luis Cisneros, "out of a split between the petty bourgeoisie and the liberal bourgeoisie" (see F. Campbell 1983). From its very inception, it was given to heavy doses of analysis of process, one example being its categorization of CLETA members into those involved full time with art, students who also did art, and people for whom CLETA was a vehicle for personal or political growth. This tendency toward analysis and self-criticism often makes them appear to be purists, and groups that disagreed would resign in protest or be forced to resign. (The main area of dispute was the question of accepting state subsidies or collaborating with the government in any way.)

One of CLETA's policies from the outset was to establish international links, usually by participating in theatre festivals and meetings. The main object of this was to ensure either the safety afforded organizations with an international reputation or at least the solidarity of foreign theatre workers, in the event of repressive actions against CLETA by the state.

In 1974, after the expulsion of the group Mascarones, CLETA devoted two years to building bases in the high school.[7] In their evaluation, CLETA's internal critics called this the "populist" phase, because the *cletos* went out into streets, schools, and neighborhoods without clearly defined plans; they were in search of "the people," while at the same time arrogating a vanguard role in the community workshops they set up as part of their own "proletarianization." Their work with the marginal classes did, however, result in their artistic enrichment because of the contribution of the neighborhood dwellers, and it led CLETA to realize the need for workshops in technical theatre training.

In May 1976, as part of a series of terrorist actions against CLETA, cofounder Luis Cisneros was kidnapped and held for two months. (He refused to discuss the details of his abduction because he was under a death threat.) CLETA entered a particularly divisive phase (1976–79), characterized by government efforts to co-opt CLETA members into "cooperative" grass-roots projects such as their Youth Education Resources Council (CREA), and culminating in the first CLETA congress. Eroded by debt and weakened by political division and government harassment, CLETA decentralized, keeping a small staff in the Mexico City center while groups developed in other states.

The Mexico City groups soon became solvent, but their space in the Foro Isabelino was literally wrecked by the authorities because of the artists' support for striking university workers in 1977. At the same time, the Chihuahua group hosted the fourth national encuentro, and groups from the capital fell out with the organizer, who had become too closely aligned with the PCM (Mexican Communist Party). The fifth meeting, in Guerrero in 1978, was the scene of conflict between those who favored closer ties with parties like the PCM and the PRT (Revolutionary Workers' Party), and those who shied away from partisan alliances. The 1979 meeting resulted in a compromise to save the organization: CLETA was defined as an artistic front, and each group would work independently along the lines it chose. One result, as CLETA recognized in a later assessment, was a ferocious war of "practical" examples of the correctness of each group's artistic and political position (CLETA 1983).

Between 1979 and 1982, CLETA was declared officially dead at various times by various groups, and at times it seemed that its demise was indeed at hand. Four of the founding groups and pillars of the organization (Zopilotes, Zumbón, Saltimbanqui, and Tecolotes) resigned. The Tecolotes, at least, gradually worked out an individual compromise with the university and the government; they ended up criticizing their own earlier positions and opting to work with official cultural organizations, thus deepening the rift between them and the few groups with whom they maintained some connection (e.g., the Chidos).

In 1982 the Tecolotes, who controlled the Foro Isabelino, reached a "nonaggression" pact with the more militant Chidos. The documentation from this period is most interesting because its "live and let live" message belies a maturing, a pragmatic acknowledgment that the state will always be in conflict with the radical left, and that individuals will always be susceptible to such "compromises" as teaching or working in state-sponsored cultural programs.

After the resignation of the Tecolotes, CLETA entered a period of intense activity and reconstruction. The number of CLETA centers in Mexico City rose to five, and CLETA has sponsored numerous music, poetry, plastic arts, and theatre festivals throughout the country. It still defines itself as a cultural organization, and it continues its work in slums, working-class areas, indigenous communities, and schools and colleges; but it also continues with strikes and demonstrations. According to its brochures, it works in three areas: art, propaganda, and proletarian education, to "compile information pertaining to customs, history, scientific knowledge, and activities of daily life" (Frischmann 1990:164–165).

CLETA recognizes two main classes: the bourgeoisie and all its allies, from financiers to bourgeois intellectuals; and the working classes, the producers who sell their labor. The organization also states its independence of all political parties, and welcomes the participation of workers, students, and "cultural workers," who are defined as "workers who choose to make culture their profession."

In reading CLETA's history, one is immediately struck by the intense commitment, the energy, and the capacity for critical analysis and for organization that its members bring to it. The importance of CLETA as a theatre movement also lies in the fact that its resources are multiplied through other forms of cultural expression, including the printed text (poetry, newsletters, theatre scripts), and through constant work with grass-roots sectors and with students and independent artists. Among the objectives of the CLETA collectives is the reappropriation of mass media, through the publication of comic books and broadsides in community workshops to present the grass-roots perspective. Theatre can thrive because its mass-media context is not strictly competitive, but rather a supportive one.

The dramatic forms preferred by CLETA theatre workers include those of long-standing popular appeal: the comic sketch, the comic monologue, the street-vendor act (snake-oil salesmen, magicians, etc.), and the vaudeville-style dialogue (inherited from the circus and the traveling carpas). Most CLETA performances lend themselves to street corners and plazas, and they tend to avoid the heavy-handed aspects of agit-prop through their intelligent use of comedy and humor and their interaction with the public.

CLETA's contribution to performance and cultural creation has been the preservation of traditional popular forms (some of them really adaptations of populist forms, such as certain types of comic sketch and dialogue) and the polishing of agit-prop. Its more unique contribution, however, may well be its history as an organization and the process whereby it deconstructed organizational problems to reconstitute itself and to maintain its rhythm of growth as a community-oriented network.

União e Olho Vivo, Community Theatre in the Police State

Teatro União e Olho Vivo, of São Paulo, directed by César Vieira, is a prime example of the nonprofessional theatre (teatro amador) that flourished in Brazil's large cities in the 1970s, a movement that can best be categorized as a fusion between urban professional theatre and the rural popular theatre of the periphery (chiefly the Northeast). In describing the contexts of União e Olho Vivo, certain categories need to be clarified first. The term *nonprofessional* carries a particular weight in Brazil, since it does not necessarily refer to untrained artists, but rather to actors, directors, and groups who are working outside the Equity system. The status of nonprofessionals may be one of choice, determined by the impossibility of achieving the levels of funding required by Equity production. In the seventies it could also be one of necessity, determined by the political nature of the artists' work in the context of heavy censorship and political repression. The economic impact of this arbitrary repression was, in some respects, more damaging than imprisonment, because professional work was subject to arbitrary censorship, to last-minute authorizations for performances or denials of such permits, to the closing of theatres, or the cutting of lines or even of performers. Groups and individual artists, therefore, had little or no power to guarantee a performance as it had been announced, and the financial and psychological toll could be devastating.

Partly for this reason, but also in some cases motivated by their own anticommercial principles, practitioners of the teatro amador also rejected the tyranny of the box office and the imposition of firm production dates that could curtail the satisfactory development of a piece. This, coupled with a refusal to work under commercial producers or impresarios, left such groups and artists to carve out their own space on the margins of commercial theatre.

The "center-periphery" polarity, in turn, is neither neat nor simple in the context of the working-class inhabitants of São Paulo or Rio de Janeiro. Because many of them have migrated from the rural periphery, cultural production geared to an urban working-class audience must therefore integrate or otherwise take into account both their world view and their cultural values.

A theatre that sought to engage in an organic relationship with its audiences, therefore, had to make intelligent artistic and financial choices in order to survive and to be successful. The options available to the different groups, as well as the governing principles of each (e.g., a willingness to perform for middle-class audiences in order to raise their income), resulted in a nonmonolithic movement or constellation of independent grass-roots theatres.

The marginal spaces in Rio and São Paulo were similar to those of CLETA's groups in Mexico: a community center in a working-class suburb, or a small theatre that belonged to labor groups or small-business associations in a blue- or white-collar neighborhood, or simply the streets. Because most groups were also active in grass-roots organizations, because they also received some support from government agencies, and because they formed networks that functioned as lobby groups, state and municipal buildings (auditoriums and theatres) also became available.

In the early eighties, there were about twenty groups in Rio and another twenty in São Paulo. In São Paulo especially, the group members often had close working relationships with industrial workers, in order to establish closer ties to their constituency. Their artistic work was readily accepted, in the tradition of the workers' theatre that Italian anarchists had brought to Brazil decades earlier.

All these precarious existences unfolded along an uneven continuum that reflected the alternation between cultural openings and the more repressive periods of the military regime. The historical roots of teatro amador are not only in the workers' theatre but also, and more directly, in the politically conscious avant-garde theatre of the early sixties (Teatro Arena) and in the political-cultural work of the organized left (mainly through the Centro Popular de Cultura, or CPC, of the National Union of Students). Some of the individuals who joined the teatro amador had worked in the rural periphery during the administration of President Goulart; others had worked with the artistic avant-garde or with political theatre in the cities.

A good many of the teatro amador activists had been imprisoned and even tortured after the military coup of 1964. Although the first years after that coup were hellish for artists and intellectuals, some members of the disbanded CPC still managed to stage "Show Opinião" (Opinion Show), from which the tradition of the musical review with political content evolved. In December 1968 the military regime intensified the repression, suspending habeas corpus and unleashing the worst period of torture and censorship. Theatre was singled out because of its political nature, because it encouraged contacts with the audience and among the members of the audience, and because it was so highly mobile and often took the form of "guerrilla" or "lightning" theatre.

In 1970 many theatre practitioners went into exile, while others continued to work in the nonpolitical commercial theatre, under the close scrutiny of the censors. Of the rest, some staged what were called "works of cultural aggression" as acts of protest, while others presented hermetic allegories and sometimes incomprehensibly metaphorical plays in pocket theatres, to minimize the financial risk.

In 1972 the emerging teatro amador organized its first festival, which became critical to the development of the movement. These festivals provided the opportunity for theatre workers to share techniques, survival mechanisms, and analysis, and it was out of the first festival that a national federation (FENATA) was formed, which in 1977 became a confederation (CONFENATA). CONFENATA acted as a lobbying coalition and as an exchange medium for festivals, publications, and conferences.

In 1974 the government announced a policy of détente, and the Ministry of Education and Culture formulated a cultural policy detailing support for national and popular culture. The teatro amador benefited from this policy as a national-popular movement. Censorship remained in force, but now it was rarely applied to nonprofessional groups; there was an added incentive for political artists to join the nonprofessional movement.

Just prior to the political opening of 1979, protests against censorship increased. Guerrilla theatre, which had not been seen much since the early months after the 1964 coup, once again became a widespread form of resistance. Ad hoc groups performed in streets and public squares, seeking to mobilize the public in support of the restoration of civil rights. Participants often integrated into their work in the teatro amador techniques they had developed for these actions.

União e Olho Vivo was founded in 1971, with the stated aim of "debating the ground rules for the beginning of a popular theatre." By "popular," the group clearly stated that it meant a theatre linked by its themes to the immediate interests of the people, using resources of the traditional popular theatre, and addressing a popular audience.

Its members included students, typists, teachers, lawyers, salespersons, and bank employees. They devoted two or three evenings a week and weekends to the theatre, and in accordance with a policy of international solidarity, they spent their one month's annual vacation on tour abroad, usually in socialist countries (Cuba, Angola, Nicaragua).

Once their connections to grass-roots and community groups were well established, they regularly received invitations to perform in spaces provided by their hosts (theatre, school, square), charging the equivalent of a bus fare as admission. The group's performances for middle-class audiences helped subsidize its work in the poorer neighborhoods.

Their performance style owed a great deal to carnivals and circuses. The group would sing and dance its way into the performance space; amusement park games would often provide the background against which the actors played the roles of the traditional "Bumba meu boi," often through pantomime.

União e Olho Vivo appropriated popular tradition, making it the centerpiece of its artistic and political work. The traditional product evolved simultaneously with the political relationship of the audience with its own reality, and elements would be modified or new ones added to respond to the deepening critical perceptions of the participating spectators. Play and the dualistic relations (good vs. evil) of the traditional theatre thus became a vehicle for political theatre.

Some groups did not transcend the dualistic view of social and political reality, common in traditional forms (from African rituals and Iberian festive rites like the "Bumba meu boi" or the "Moors and Christians" to the modern revue). Others, such as União e Olho Vivo, cleverly avoided the pitfall of clearcut answers and a superficial satire that promoted neither dialogue nor critical reflexion. Such works would have been patronizing and populist at best, if not outright reactionary.

The ludic element provided the means to avoid the trap of simplistic answers to complex problems. The dualistic formula would be central to the creation of a mental or physical space within which to manipulate the simplifications. Manipulation and distancing were achieved through play, which often included the audience in the performance space. One example of this was the introduction of wooden dolls representing celebrities (e.g., Pelé, Roberto Carlos) whose attitudes ran contrary to the needs of the community. The spectators were encouraged to engage these puppets in a debate on important issues (and to pelt them with balls). The purpose of this exercise was to explore the complex relationship of the people with their popular heroes, a relationship that defies a purely didactic treatment.

Incidental Theatre and Ritual Drama

This fourth case study falls into the category of "public empowerment," which takes at least two forms: incidental theatre (often "invisible") and ritual drama. The invisible theatre is played out by members of the community who sometimes cannot be distinguished from their audience or, at least, from other members of the community, and who may dramatize events from the life of their community in a way that will attract attention to the problem. The acting may or may not be confrontational, but if it is, it may or may not confront the authorities directly. It is usually the work of individuals or groups of individuals who act on behalf of the collectivity and enjoy its support and whatever protection it may afford through solidarity.

The Chilean women who claimed that the anonymous bodies found in rivers or garbage dumps were those of their own brothers or sons, husbands, or daughters, were acting (in both senses of the word) the part of relatives, often in complicity with their neighbors; the lie was also a symbolic role they acted out, one which enabled them to challenge the dehumanization of the regime. By taking as their husband, brother, or child an outsider and often an unknown person, they reclaimed the dead as a part of the community and restored their human dignity.

The young people who used traditional masks to cover their faces during the Nicaraguan insurrection were appropriating, for a very practical purpose, a popular art form whose origins lay in Native American ritual drama. Their figures on the barricades, not unlike the masked goalie at an ice-hockey game, gave them an essentialist aesthetic air as they went about confronting the National Guard and trying to keep their faces hidden from later reprisals. Now a similar effect can be seen in demonstrations everywhere, most often in smaller towns and on university campuses, albeit it with scarves and handkerchiefs.

Neither of these types of action are theatre as we understand it, and only the former is theatre as representation/acting; they are simply dramatic actions that use elements of the theatre, and the theatricality is incidental, although it is often what makes the action effective. They are not invisible theatre in the sense that Augusto Boal proposed it, i.e., actors blended into a crowd suddenly acting out.[8] The two examples that we cite illustrate a type of theatre that plays with/on invisibility even as its actors detach themselves temporarily from the collectivity through a series of deliberate gestures (the quasi-passive resistance of the "widows" as they faced the authorities to claim the bodies, the active resistance of masked Sandinistas as they threw their molotov cocktails at Somoza's tanks or ran across open squares with a gun as a precious trophy). We are referring to the verbal invisibility of the lie of feigned kinship and to the plastic invisibility of the covered face: the first, to counter the anonymity of the dead and to resist the enemy; the second, to challenge the soldiers' ability to identify the insurgent's face. In the end they both serve to reinforce the unity of the popular resistance, and they are both incidental to the struggle.

The other type of theatre of public empowerment deliberately employs visibility. It is drama in its most primeval form, as pure ritual of mimesis, symbolic reenactment, or invocation.[9] It is the vehicle of human-rights groups and political demonstrators who hold up to the nation an image of itself, as a mirror "cracked" in more ways than one (if one recalls that its exponents are often dismissed as mad). Two examples come readily to mind: the Chilean relatives of the disappeared and the Mothers and Grandmothers of the Plaza de Mayo.

In the early 1980s, a group of Chilean women, cheered by the example of the Mothers of the Disappeared, across the border in Argentina, began a series of unique actions of civil disobedience to draw attention to their "disappeared" or imprisoned relatives. They would chain themselves to public buildings and national monuments, and the police would then have to cut the chains or spring the padlocks before dragging the demonstrators off to jail. As political protests they were rather unusual, because in addition to being acts of nonviolent civil disobedience, they had the element of guerrilla theatre: the demonstrators remained chained, often chanting their slogans, long enough for spectators to gather and for popular solidarity to express itself. By attaching themselves to historical structures (the Cathedral) or symbols of national values (the Supreme Court or the monument to a national hero), they drew attention not only to their own plight but also to the larger problem of the betrayal of the nation's history and its highest civic values. This gave the actions their dimension of tragedy in a wider context of nationhood-as-community.

The agitational-propaganda value of such creative activism places it in the category known in Spanish and Portuguese as teatro coyuntural (which we translate freely as "incidental" or "occasional" theatre); it is not instrumental in the same way as theatre in community development. Despite their being primarily vehicles invented by desperate relatives to express their grief, their grievances, and their demands, these actions of the dispossessed have an important aesthetic dimension. Their codes are at once political and artistic, and they serve as a mirror to the artistic community.[10]

The Chilean women enacted a quasi-ritual drama whose venue and style of presentation shifted constantly (from monument to monument in public protests; from riverbank to dumpsite to riverbank, claiming as their own the anonymous victims of the dictatorship). The Mothers of the Plaza de Mayo, on the other hand, adopted a simple and predictable ritual, whose minimal codes are observed as faithfully as a weekly religious service: the assembling of individuals of their own free will every Thursday afternoon from two to four, the adoption of a symbolic distinguishing and unifying "mark" (the white kerchief), and the carrying of photographs as virtual icons, plus, gradually, the introduction of plain slogans or chants (e.g., "They took them alive, we want them back alive").[11]

The Mothers have had a major impact on both the political and artistic life of Argentina. They were the only overt opposition left at the height of military and police repression of dissent, and they gained worldwide admiration as models of political and civic courage and became magnets for increasing numbers of protesters opposing the military regime.

The artistic community, which had been largely destroyed by deaths, disappearances, and exile, began to regroup in 1980–81. Theatre workers formed Teatro Abierto (Open Theatre), a loose collective dedicated to rebuilding the independent theatre through productions that reflected a commitment to social and political change. Playwright and director Osvaldo Dragún recalls the earliest meetings, which were veiled in secrecy and where fear and a feeling of powerlessness predominated at first.[12]

Someone suggested that the group should explore the strength of the circle, which the Mothers were demonstrating in their weekly confrontation with fear and marginalization. The artists sat and talked and did their exercises in a circle, and they concluded that the Mothers' formula was indeed an empowering one. They also began to explore their own historical connection to the aboriginal cultures, which had vanished from that part of the country and remained suppressed in much of Argentina; the Native American circle of empowerment and community around the bonfire (where dreams were recounted, wars planned, and problems solved) was handed down to modern Argentina through the gaucho's social custom of drinking *mate* tea in a circle, from a common gourd. Suddenly, sitting around drinking mate, the Teatro Abierto nucleus (Marxists, Peronists, Jews, Christians, and atheists) was finding courage and power through a symbol that served as a psychic bond to a national identity (the gaucho and, indirectly, the disappeared Indians of the *pampas*) and to the political body (the Mothers of the Plaza).

Performances, in turn, became public assemblies: successful productions served as a motive for large rallies and demonstrations. Teatro Abierto brought the subject of the disappeared to the stage for the first time, with Ricardo Halac's *Lejana tierra prometida*. After the restoration of civilian rule, Teatro Abierto workers went off to the provinces to search out the indigenous cultural remnants of Argentina, thus returning to (and broadening the scope of) the extension work of the independent theatre as professionals in community outreach.[13]

The example of the Mothers illustrates the cyclical or dialectical relationship between political and cultural/artistic forces and their codes. It also illustrates the growing connection between cultural work and community action, as well as the broadened definitions of political work that have now become more acceptable.[14] And because the Mothers engage a dialogue of symbolic reaffirmation, they demonstrate the permeability of the line that separates public ritual from ritual drama, even to this day.

The New Popular Theatre in Historical Perspective

The evolution of the Nuevo Teatro Popular has been determined to a great extent by its social and historical contexts. In the sixties and seventies, radical political activity by artists, students, and intellectuals, or simply the profound mistrust with which repressive regimes view culture and grass-roots activism, resulted in wholesale persecution (censorship, jail, and assassination) and in the creation of large communities of exiles, many of whom have played important roles in the development of the theatre in their host countries. A positive effect of this has been the extension and strengthening of international ties among both professional and nonprofessional theatre workers.

The unique type of popular theatre that emerged in the 1960s throughout the Americas grew into a self-conscious movement, as part of the social and political project for the radical transformation of society. In its search for new forms of expression and more importantly, perhaps, new relations of production, the Nuevo Teatro Popular would incorporate popular traditions as well as different currents of the modern theatre and of other cultural idioms.

The Nuevo Teatro Popular is unquestionably a counter-hegemonic movement. It has defined itself as such both literally and indirectly. Its groups have exchanged artists and have been active in festivals, workshops, and encuentros throughout the hemisphere since the earliest efforts to create new national theatres, to restructure the organization of dramatic production, and to expand the boundaries of theatrical creation into new geographic areas and new constituencies, always challenging the norms, the formulas, and the frameworks proposed by the dominant sectors.

Although it is possible to distinguish, in the broadest terms, the professional current from the nonprofessional, both have been essential for the movement. Beyond that there has been frequent interaction between professionals and untrained practitioners, between artists whose primary objective is the artistic process and a polished product and those whose work lies in social action or community development. The professional artists are also teachers, and their groups have served as models for emerging artists and groups, only a handful of which may become professional.

The grass-roots theatre gained strength in the mid-eighties, through popular-education networks and through the resolve of artists and educators who worked with, and often within, social organizations (such as community groups, churches, unions, women's associations, Native American groups) as resource persons rather than leaders. Meanwhile the professional artists and groups have earned a distinguished place on the international theatre scene and in some cases entered the mainstream without surrendering their critical vision.

This new theatre has been both a composite of artistic and traditional theatre and a reformulation of popular theatre as it had been handed down for centuries. The practitioners of the Nuevo Teatro Popular adopted artistic genres as well as other forms of popular culture (e.g., language, music, material culture), and they have also worked successfully to appropriate elements of mass culture. As we have seen in the previous chapters, expressions of identity by and for the popular classes were not, in themselves, anything new: they had been a significant presence in Latin American theatre since pre-Columbian times. Moreover it was only in the nineteenth century that strong popular elements appeared to fade away from officially sanctioned theatre, although they continued to thrive in what came to be considered marginal forms, especially those connected to the circus, the carnival, and the variety show. On the other hand, the Nuevo Teatro Popular was also tapping indirectly into European popular theatre through an artistic theatre that originated wholly or partially in popular traditions (the Brechtian theatre and the Italian and Spanish comic styles).

As one examines the social organization of the New Popular Theatre, its methods and its forms of artistic expression, the overall pattern becomes clearer in all its rich variety. A strong social and historical consciousness led to the formation of hundreds of groups and thousands of artists in twenty nations, as well as in the Hispanic communities of the United States. The Nuevo Teatro Popular has been a medium through which various strata, including the theatre community itself, could define their collective identity and explore their options for survival and for growth. The key, then, lies in the ability to keep that social and historical consciousness alive and active and free not only from prescriptive dogma, but also from destructive winds that want to cut Latin America from its historical moorings and set its people adrift in unfamiliar tides.

Notes

INTRODUCTION: CHARTING OUR COURSE

1. Much of Losada's and Rama's work was done abroad. Their sociohistorical research has been continued, since their death, by their students: Rama's, mainly by individuals; Losada's, in a collective project at AELSAL (Free University of Berlin), a social history of Latin American literature.

2. This type of theatre includes the *bufo cubano*, the Argentine *sainete criollo* and *gaucho* dramas, and widespread variety shows and musical comedy.

3. For practical purposes, we would prefer the labels *populist*, *commercial popular*, or *impresario* theatre.

4. Much of the work done by Alejandro Losada and his students, between the model that he first proposed in 1975 and the last work before his death in 1985, is devoted to expanding and refining this proposition. Losada (1983) includes a valuable bibliography covering the period 1800–1980. See also Belic (1972) and Goic (1975).

5. Among the most relevant works on European drama, we would include Chambers (1903), Crawford (1911), Hardison (1965), and Lázaro Carreter (1965). For ritual, play, and popular entertainment, see Bakhtin (1968), Bouissac (1985), Bristol (1985), Schechner and Schumann (1976), Schechter (1985), and Turner (1980, 1985).

6. The term *populist* is perhaps not applied quite as frequently as it should be to art and most specifically to the Latin American theatre. We opted for this categorization as the more appropriate in the case of the decontextualized assimilation and manipulation of elements of popular or people's culture for the promotion of values alien or inimical to the interests of their original creators.

7. The sociological approach to the question of cultural policy proves quite useful for demonstrating the organic connection between paradigms and their

historical and economic context. We would not wish to suggest that such paradigms were deliberate designs, but rather that they were the projection or extension of social and economic policy. Of the six paradigms described by García Canclini (1987:22–53; our translation), two ("heritage-oriented traditionalism" and "neoconservative privatization") would probably be the most instrumental in the reification, distortion, and weakening of popular cultures; two paradigms ("liberal patronage" and "populist state initiatives"), while they might not be directly harmful, do not guarantee popular initiative and control; "cultural democratization" promotes "egalitarian access to high culture." Only participatory democracy would seem to offer genuine guarantees to the agents of popular culture (through "the pluralistic development of the culture of different groups, promoted by progressive parties and independent political movements").

8. Beatriz Seibel's companion volumes (1985a and 1985b) give detailed accounts of this environment in Argentina. María y Campos (1939) describes its evolution in Mexico, while Kanellos (1987) extends his study to the southwestern United States.

9. See, for example, Bakhtin (1968), Bastide (1959), Bristol (1985), Cortázar (1949), Fox Lockert (1990), and Zapata Olivella (1978).

10. See Bonfill Batalla (1983), García Canclini (1984, 1987), Margulis (1983), and Mattelart (1973).

1. Frames of Reference

1. Although the nonliterate and the oral cultures are in some cases the same, we would like to emphasize the fine distinction between oral societies, which had no writing, and the nonliterate sectors of societies where writing was a differentiating instrument of power. The relationship between written and oral cultures has only recently become a central focus for the historiographer of literature and the arts, serving as a means for reevaluating the importance of the marginalized cultures. Because of the connections that they establish with the dramatic tradition of those groups, the works of Rolena Adorno (1982) on colonial discourse and indigenous literature, Angel Rama (1984) on the historical role of the "Literate City" (Ciudad Letrada), Hernán Vidal (1985) on colonial culture, and Nathan Wachtel (1976) and Martin Lienhart (1989) on Native American responses to the culture of domination have proven extremely valuable in establishing a framework for our study. We have also found Paul Connerton's (1989) recent study of the embodiment of historical memory in performance very relevant to this concern with the transmission of nonliterate practices.

2. Folk culture refers, essentially, to culturally *mestizo* or peasant societies that are most commonly marginal to the dominant national culture and have continued to create or recreate syncretic dramatic forms since the colonial period. Among the better known one can include the dance dramas of the U.S. Southwest, ritual battles of the jaguars in various Mexican communities, the annual reeanactment of the *Güegüence* in Nicaragua, the *Bumba meu Boi* in Brazil, the *Diabladas* of Oruro in Bolivia, and the *Moros y cristianos* in its various forms throughout Central America.

3. Poets and dramatists in Spain and Portugal, as in Elizabethan England, often integrated the popular idiom and even a popular world view into their works. The fact that this was done consciously is illustrated by Lope de Vega's *Arte nuevo de hacer comedias*, which advocates (albeit for commercial reasons) the inclusion of popular characters and language on the Spanish stage.

4. We would readily accept the term *class struggle*, with the extended meaning of the word *class* to include all groups (classes of people) with a defined identity: women, peasants, students, Native Americans, African-Americans, laborers, and industrial workers, among others. We chose *popular struggle* instead, in the understanding of its inclusiveness of all classes in need of redress, rather than use a term that might emphasize the individual groups actively involved in that larger movement against economic injustice and social disarticulation.

5. Examples of the valuable research that is currently being done on the subject can be found in widely differing publications, e.g., Espinosa Domínguez (1988) and Fox Lockert (1990).

6. In certain cases (e.g., Cuba), however, some African cultures of origin managed to retain their identity, or regained it after a short period of dispersal in the New World; Fernando Ortiz, one of the leading students of Afro-Caribbean culture, has documented categories of dance and theatre by nations of origin (1951).

7. This may be because of the richer variety found in Mesoamerica than in the Andean region, but more likely because of the different objectives of the two authors. Verger speaks of the existence of over two hundred *dances* in the Andean region; that is, he includes simple dances of entertainment, but he does not provide an exhaustive classification of rituals, which Prokosch Kurath and others have done.

8. Old men and old women also figure in European drama. It would be inaccurate to attribute specific provenance to these characters, which serve, rather, to demonstrate the possibility of coincidence in distinct origins.

9. References to the comic-ritual use of the phallus are found in Antolínez (1946) for Amazonian natives in northwestern Brazil; and Verger (1945) for Andean dance drama; Steward (1930), regarding the natives of the U.S. South-

west, California, and Mesoamerica and Balmori (1955) for the Aztecs. In this context Balmori also cites the Nicaraguan classic mestizo drama, the *Güegüense* (which we shall be discussing in detail further on). One might safely say that such devices are fairly universal in early dramatic representation.

10. Barbra Dahlgren (1954:285) sees this ritual as part of a complex of ceremonies that include the "piercing," which corresponds to the North American Sundance ceremony.

11. Two South American examples are: the gathering feasts of the Amazonian Arawaks, cited in Antolínez (1946:118), and the *sursur waylla* of Peru, cited in Verger (1945:17–18). The piercing ceremonies of Mesoamerican and North American peoples may be analogous to flagellation. Because flagellation rituals were a part of European religious processions, one would have to consider very closely the provenance of any such rituals in Native American groups that have coexisted with Europeans and practiced popular rites of Catholicism for centuries.

12. The Incas engaged in similar practices, and at least one Amazonian tribe was known to observe complex rituals integrating prisoners into the community as a preparation for their sacrifice. The chief self-declared eyewitness of the dramatic dialogue in which the captured warrior and his executioners engaged is the seventeenth-century French explorer Jean de Léry. Carneiro (1946), who summarizes the experiences that Léry claimed to have had among Amazonian cannibals, doubts the absolute veracity of Léry's testimony in the absence of other eye-witnesses. More recent studies (Sanday 1986, Batalha 1992) confirm the existence of ritual anthropophagy.

13. This is certainly not unique to African drama. For example, as late as the 1940's, descendants of the Chibchas in the Andean region of Venezuela continued to perform their drama as a way of keeping alive both their god (Chen, the father of light) and the spirit of death (Antolínez 1946:118).

14. Such forms include carnivals to expel death and winter, clowns, animal masks, *diablos, muertes* (personifications of death), maypoles and flowered arches, processions, and such symbolic dramas as "Moors and Christians" (Prokosch Kurath 1952:239).

15. Robe (1954) provides a convincing picture of the theatricality of "Los Pastores" and places it in the larger framework of the other folk dramas.

16. Durán y Sanpere cites an 18th century text, *Explication des cérémonies de la fête Dieu d'Aix en Provence*, according to which the Corpus, a pageant of Aix, "originated in a wish by René d'Anjou to perpetuate the knightly pomp of his small court in the great eucharistic following; it was he, apparently, who initiated the pageant, with profane games and farces whose presence would otherwise be difficult to explain" (Durán y Sanpere 1943:10). The same student of the Spanish Corpus Christi stresses the connection between specific

elements of the procession and certain courtly festivities, such as dances and tournaments, the *ball de bastons*, and the game of *cavallets i diables*, which is far removed from religious liturgy. The popular procession could be an echo of the noblemen's tournaments.

17. Falassi (1987) refers to the opening of the festival as "valorization" and to its closing as "devalorization," rites of framing the special values of the festival.

18. The program is of great interest to theatre scholars because of the allegorical figures, settings of rocas (floats), and themes of dramas included in the procession over a century before the first Corpus festivities were held in the Americas. We summarize it as follows:

A) Genesis and Patriarchs, including hell, accompanied by a *comparsa* (mummers) of angels and devils fighting with swords; ending with twelve tribes and twelve angels.
B) Prophesies: Life of Jesus; group of Jews; Herod and the Innocents; twelve angels singing to the Host.
C) St. Ann's Collegiate; St. Joachim; St. Ann, St. Elizabeth; Constantine and St. Helen and exaltation of the Cross; accompanied by doctors and knights and other saints.
D) Mercedary fathers: fourteen virgins; Calvary of Jesus alone, with cross; good and bad thieves (with angel and devil, respectively); Longinus, Joseph of Arimathea, Nicodemus, angels, sepulchre.
E) Founders and Doctors of the Church.
F) Martyrs.
G) Apostles, followed by dancing animals (mainly allegorical, such as eagle, representing John).
H) Musician angels with candles.
I) King Alfonso the Great carrying the Host.

19. Not only the excesses of the devils, but the very content of some of the performances (presumably the most popular ones) occasionally grew too daring for the authorities, who periodically restricted the festivities as a result of such scandalous deportment.

20. According to Ingham (1986:32), the Devil also evolved later into two figures: the Clown and the Villain.

21. Most historians and anthropologists consulted for this study (e.g., Bataillon 1949, Ricard 1958) have dealt with the ubiquitous "Moors and Christians." Its structural and thematic relative, "The Twelve Peers" ("Los Doce Pares"), about the knights of Charlemagne, has been studied most extensively by Nicaraguan scholars interested in its tradition in the region around Niqui-

nohomo. This drama also persists, as a sung or recited version and as street theatre, from New Mexico and Puerto Rico to Chile and Argentina (see Mejía Sánchez and Durand 1982). The source of this drama is considered to be a Spanish translation of a history of Emperor Charlemagne (Seville, 1521), which would place it as a latecomer to the family of "Moors and Christians" and "The Conquest."

22. Shelly and Rojo propose a diachronic categorization whose method of dating the distinctive periods fine-tunes Arrom's without invalidating it. Surveys of repertoires and performances between 1550 and 1800 tend to confirm this periodization. There was, in fact, a two-tiered system of religious and secular drama, with the religious drama in turn serving a double function and secular drama restricted largely to the European population.

2. The Emergence of an American Theatre

1. A valid question can also be raised by this biblical story in the Spanish context: What possible influence on its popular retelling could be attributed to the Moslem influence in Spain (which probably persisted in the marginal population of recent converts)? In the Arabic-Islamic version, Ishmael, not Isaac, is Abraham's prospective sacrifice.

2. Arróniz and Pazos both find this strange, because it could easily be seen as offensive. Pazos's explanation is that the mass of indigenous spectators were not concerned with such subtleties, but simply with the spectacle and the basic message. A simpler explanation could lie in the politics of the moment: Because Hernán Cortés was under investigation by the crown for corruption and abuse of power, the missionaries chose to distance themselves from him (Versenyi 1988). Or one could speculate that the local participants were given sufficiently free rein in the production to enable them to construct the reenactment according to their own analogical view of history. Bricker (1982:129–54) analyzes the carnival of San Juan Chamula (Chiapas) as a paradigm of this tendency to treat analogous events from different historical periods as contemporary, and to work with the "basic units of mythic and ritualistic structure, e.g., hero, villain, setting, battle, [etc.]" rather than with a strict individuation. In this context one can conclude that "The Conquest of Jerusalem" is the first known example of American-European syncretism in the theatre. At the same time, it is important to recognize that in medieval drama a similar analogous ritualization was fairly common, such as in the Corpus dramas; thus the missionaries would not have found what the Tlaxcalans did with the conquest either outrageous or particularly strained.

3. It is not clear whether there was much spoken dialogue and, if so, whether

some individual parts might not have been recited chorally by a group of actors. Otherwise, as Arróniz (1979:42–44) points out, it is difficult to see how a single voice could have been heard in such a wide-open space by so many spectators. Pazos (1951:171) states that it was entirely pantomimed, with no dialogue, and that its theatricality was based entirely on plot and movement, but he later contradicts himself by quoting content that could only be expressed verbally. In any case, there is a record of the text, in the letter of Fr. Antonio de Ciudad Rodrigo transcribed by Motolinía (*Historia de los Indios*, p. 89, note 21).

4. This production demonstrates the sophistication of the missionaries in state-of-the-art staging; see Shoemaker (1935).

5. Todorov (1984) analyzes the differences in attitudes toward the conquered, including the first mestizo responses to the conquest; Adorno (1982), Lienhart (1989), and Seed (1991) emphasize the latter.

6. Among the most recent contributions to the question of translation and assimilation, see Seed (1991), on the first encounter between the Inca emperor and a Spanish missionary.

7. Valuable bibliographical and historical references can be found in Rappaport (1991).

8. The Spanish element in the Guatemalan *loas* documented by Correa and Cannon (1961) is very dominant. Alonso (1924) studied the "Loa de San Pascual" presented in Castejón de las Armas (Zaragoza), a loa that other Spanish villages dedicate to their corresponding saints. This loa has several central elements common to the Latin American folk drama: the Devil's intervention, popular characters (shepherds, a deaf man, a fool), and the struggle of Moors and Christians.

9. The men race on foot into the forest, in the direction of a mythical sacred space, but they go only as far as they had pledged to the saint.

10. On the subject of the Viejo as a character of Native American or mixed origins, at the other end of the continent, in the Andean highlands, Rubio Zapata (1988:33–35) documents the dance of the Macho Tusuq, figures of old men attired much like the Macho Ratón (layers of colored clothing, rags, feathered hat, and European mask, with paste-on mustache) and with some of his buffoon characteristics. On the subject of deafness, the same routine elicited similar hilarity when it was used by the local man playing Zechariah in the missionary production of the "Nativity of St. John the Baptist" in 1539.

11. These secret societies and their dramatic rituals were variously linked to: slave flights and conspiracies; the Puerto Rican independence campaigns; nineteenth-century conspiracies against Spain in Cuba, which included the Maceo brothers; and twentieth-century politics, especially the 1912 rebellion waged mainly by blacks against the government. Mummers were banned by

the captain-general at critical moments of revolutionary activity, for fear that they would be used to disturb the peace or serve as a base for conspirators (Ortiz 1951:27).

12. The marketing of Latin American folklore is also part of a historical continuum. The Hispanic element is "folklorized" in North America much as Spain was "folklorized" by French, English, and Russian artists and writers in the nineteenth century.

3. Popular Forms, Characters, and Ideology

1. Rama appears to be following Lewis Mumford's analysis of colonial urban structure as a series of carefully laid-out circles of power; cited in Vidal (1985:141).

2. We do not include students in the same category as workers and peasants, because their primary class identification remains a socioeconomic one; however great the repression against student activity may be, the university remains a relatively privileged place (or at least one protected by autonomy or by international connections).

3. Hernán Vidal prefers to emphasize, as a motive for the promotion of the arts, the ostentatiousness of the upper levels of society and their virtual need, strictly in terms of competition and jockeying for power, to flaunt their wealth and acquisitions (Vidal 1985:104).

4. We use the terms *impresario* and *director* loosely, as the head of the company was normally an actor (male or female) who took on the role of manager and director. In the sixteenth century, the term *autor* (literally, the author of a production) was used for the director.

5. This viceroy's popularity made him the logical choice for the local population, which was upset both at his transfer and at the appointment of a new ruler with a weak military record; his opening of the theatre served as an open snub of the incoming viceroy (Lohmann Villena 1941:254).

6. One particular history of the clown, María y Campos (1939), establishes clear connections between the circus and the theatre.

7. The coliseos were built to include, rather than exclude, the popular classes. While the boxes were exclusively for the upper classes, the orchestra or pit was where servants, coachmen, and the like would sit, on benches rather than seats, and the dirt floors were usually bare. The Coliseo Ramírez, of Bogotá, offers one documented example (Cordobés Moure 1978:58).

8. An interesting example of this is found in the individual experience of Enrique Buenaventura, who worked in Argentina in the early fifties both with the *teatro independiente* group Fray Mocho and with the Carpa Mesa Nicholls.

The Colombian artist traveled as far as Venezuela with the Mesa Nicholls company, whose theatre (mainly broad melodramas and comedy) was largely improvised (see Rizk 1991).

9. The "circles" are not absolutely symmetrical, of course. In the core of most Latin American cities, residences of the wealthy, the middle classes, and the poor can be found within a radius of a few blocks. In the past thirty years, vacant lots have become less common as squatters migrating from rural areas crowd into the cities.

10. This particular case could also have been connected to the crown's interest in forcing a reconciliation between the Jesuits and other orders.

11. Such was the case throughout Spanish America between 1809 and 1824, approximately, and among Cuban and Puerto Rican exiled nationalists beginning in the late 1860s.

12. By the late eighteenth century, creole interest in England and France grew, although the cultural ties with Spain were rarely, if ever, in danger of being severed. A survey of the repertoire of Chilean theatres in the eighteenth and nineteenth centuries seems to confirm this: apart from the hiatus of the war of independence, there appears to have been no effective rejection of Spanish drama. The Spanish Romantics (Larra, Hartzenbusch, García Gutiérrez) were staged in Santiago and Valparaíso alongside Andrés Bello's translations and productions of Victor Hugo.

13. The term *comedia* in Spanish and Portuguese is closely linked to its Latin meaning; that is, it refers to a play that is not on a serious theme, unlike the *drama* (play) or the *tragedia* (tragedy). Over the past two centuries it has taken on the additional meaning of a comic play.

14. The term *music hall* does not become common until the twentieth century, and even then it does not replace the term *variedades*.

15. We do bear in mind, as indicated in earlier chapters, that what we now have to work with is often half, or less, of the original product. We have even less regarding the process of its creation, with what could be relevant information concerning the circumstances surrounding the source, the elaboration, or the adoption of the work.

16. *Entremés del Amor Alcalde* ("Interlude of Love, the Mayor"), *Baile del Amor Médico* ("Dance of Love, the Physician"), and *Baile del Amor Tahur* ("Dance of Love, the Cardsharp").

17. For a critical view of the phenomenon of the "appearances" of the Virgin of Guadalupe, see Lafaye (1977).

18. For an extensive listing of Native American resistance movements throughout the Americas from 1510 to 1941, see Edmonson 1960:186–88.

19. *Ollantay* first appears in the Paz codex in 1735 (Azor 1988).

20. For a complete study of the evolution of Valdez's work, see Flores 1990.

21. The indirect link between the bufo cubano and the circus as an early venue for variety shows appears to lie in minstrelsy. The earliest documented minstrel shows date back to the 1820s, when distinguished North American artists known as "buffos" sang such songs as "Massa George Washington and Massa Lafayette" and "Coal Black Rose" (some, like George Dixon, accompanying themselves on the banjo). These performers would sometimes appear as virtuoso acts in the circus. Their name (buffo) suggests an identification with the immensely popular opera rather than with comic acting. What had been an isolated circus act became a performance genre when the Virginia Minstrels were formed, in 1843 (see Greenwood 1970).

22. The *Negro catedrático* appears as the *Jíbaro catedrático* (a peasant Malaprop) in Puerto Rican theatre of the period, particularly in the works of Alejandro Tapia y Rivera (1826–82). It should be noted here that we have been unable to find any reference, in histories of the Latin American theatre, to Mrs. Malaprop of the English stage, nor have we been able, so far, to identify any concrete link that may suggest an influence.

23. At least two recent studies deal with the influence of the bufo cubano on the development of Yucatán regional theatre: Frischmann (1987c) and F. Muñoz (1987).

24. Stereotypes were by no means exclusive to Cuban popular comedy. F. Muñoz (1987) and Frischmann (1987a), for example, both discuss the Arab merchant and the Chinaman, ethnic character types developed in Yucatán. Other theatres, too, exploited stereotypes for easy laughs.

25. The grotesco criollo emerged in the 1920s, fusing the Italian *grottesco* theatre of the early twentieth century with Argentine comedy and melodrama of popular origins (see Kaiser-Lenoir 1977).

26. The history of the Mexican *patiño* (straight man) parallels the development of the Cocoliche. Born in the circus, where ringmaster Carlos Patiño engaged in humorous dialogues and sketches with the great British-Mexican clown Ricardo Bell, the Patiño soon became a fixture in the género chico. Cantinflas introduced the routine as a subgenre in the revue theatre, and his character later gained worldwide acclaim through the cinema (María y Campos 1956:403).

27. Only one, Martiniano P. Leguizamón's *Calandria* ("The Last of the Line," 1896), had a happy ending.

4. A New Theatre in Latin America

1. As we indicated elsewhere, the term *nuevo teatro* (new theatre) was not common currency everywhere, while *teatro popular* was; we use the latter term

to distinguish the popular theatre that was part of the movement for social and political change in the fifties, sixties, and seventies, from other theatres that have been considered popular. The differences our research collective has had to acknowledge and integrate into this history are perhaps best illustrated in studies of four of the leading theatre communities: Cuba (Boudet 1983), Colombia (Rizk 1987), Brazil (Damasceno 1988), and Mexico (Frischmann 1991), together with an overview of Latin American popular theatre from 1959 to 1989 (Pianca 1990).

2. Throughout its most active years, the movement was referred to simply as "teatro popular." The theatre festivals that were organized as meeting places for like-minded groups and artists were almost invariably called *festivales de teatro popular*. In 1978 Cuba's Ministry of Culture sponsored the first festival of its kind under the title of "teatro nuevo" (new theatre), used into the early eighties in Cuba (Boudet 1983). The term *nuevo teatro* was coined or at least first widely circulated by Enrique Buenaventura, the leading authority on and of the movement, in the late seventies (Rizk 1987).

The hybrid term *nuevo teatro popular*, which appears to have first become common currency in Mexico (Frischmann 1991), seemed to us to be the most adequate, because it could not be identified with uses of the term *popular* that were not sufficiently precise. Further on we stress this distinction, pointing out why we do not see *popular* as interchangeable with *mass culture*, or with *populist* tendencies in the theatre. The addition of the word *nuevo* (new) further distinguishes the subject of our study from any single component, such as workers' theatre or traditional drama, to which the term *popular* is also applied.

3. While the nature of this hegemony differs in the various Latin American societies, just as it must differ from the hegemonic structures described by European theoreticians in Europe, we are generally in agreement with the analysis provided by Williams (1988) and (in its specific application to Mexico and Latin America) by García Canclini (1984). Although the concept of hegemony and the creation of consensus applies generally to most cultures, particularly because it transcends mechanistic approaches and allows for multiple correlations between base and superstructure, we nevertheless cannot reject dependency theory out of hand, or even some of the earlier models for the analysis of colonialism, especially in the case of societies (usually those in which there is little participation in the political process) where the breakdown of existing cultural forms has been achieved with little or no regard for the subtleties of consensus.

4. The same philosophy of popular culture and popular education that informs the New Popular Theatre has even found a fruitful environment in international organizations (including UNESCO) and in third-world government agencies, which have adopted some of its methods and operating principles.

5. We have adopted the concept of "integrational propaganda," as one of the key defining categories of the ideological function of the theatre, from Szanto (1978).

6. Professional and nonprofessional groups often sustain each other. The nonprofessional groups go under different names; they are called amateur (*amador*) in Brazil, but they differ from their counterparts in the Cuban amateur theatre movement, which although related to *teatro de comunidades* or *teatro comunidad* ("grass-roots theatre"), is closer to what is commonly known as community theatre or amateur theatre in North America.

7. In Latin America the main polarity is represented by Augusto Boal vs. Enrique Buenaventura. Luzuriaga (1990) is the most complete recent study of Latin American theories of the theatre.

8. The term *conscientization* was popularized by Paulo Freire, whose *Pedagogy of the Oppressed* directly influenced literacy methods, grass-roots theatre (as practiced by Augusto Boal), and techniques of community organization.

9. See especially Pianca (1990), where the study of festivals is accompanied by valuable documentation.

10. It is not easy to avoid this type of terminology when many of the artists with whom we deal in our study have defined their work in these very terms. "Revolutionary" implies both an instrumental art and a medium radically transformed by the committed artist. In the 1960s it was often applied quite indiscriminately to the social role of the artist as well as to cultural creation that responded to and reflected the social and historical changes that determined it.

11. The crises in El Salvador, Guatemala, and certain regions of the larger nations had a longer history. The expansion of landholdings for export crops at the expense of indigenous communal lands and small farmers dates back to the economic liberalism of the second half of the nineteenth century.

12. See the report of the Church Committee of the U.S. Congress (1975). Our main sources for the analysis of events over the past two decades include the NACLA *Report on the Americas*, the LASA *Forum*, and the *Economist for Latin America*.

13. This training took place at the International Police Academy, in Washington, D.C. (closed in 1976). Information on Brazil, Uruguay, and the Dominican Republic is provided by Agee (1970). Lieuwen (1964) is an authoritative work, with insights reflecting a U.S. perspective, as are Beaulac (1980) and O'Donnell (1986).

14. Mexico and Canada never interrupted diplomatic and trade relations with Cuba.

15. While recognizing the domestic significance of the Bolivian revolution

of 1952, one would be hard pressed to cast it in the same mold as either the Mexican or the Cuban revolutions, because of its limited international impact and also because of the short-lived nature of many of its gains.

16. Against this overview of the broad political framework, periodization is helpful for understanding both what specific countries or regions have in common and what distinguishes them.

17. After Eva Perón's death, in 1952, Juan Perón pursued a policy less oriented toward a working-class base and designed more to attract the white-collar sector, but his ouster in 1955 did not mean the end of the mass movement, and it even made its mark outside Argentina.

18. At the height of guerrilla insurgency in Colombia, through the 1970s, the FARC was probably the largest of the rebel groups.

19. Fidel Castro was a delegate to an international student conference timed as a protest against the inaugural meeting of the Organization of American States. He had planned to meet Gaitán, who was the object of great admiration among progressive youth, but Gaitán was murdered a few minutes before Fidel Castro reached his office, and the latter was caught up in the ensuing riots.

20. Estimates indicate that between 500,000 and 750,000 civilians were killed or "disappeared" in counterinsurgency operations, in civil wars, by death squads, or in demonstrations between 1948 and 1988. In the same period, economic, social, and political upheavals have created between four and six million exiles or refugees, an indeterminate number of "economic" emigrants, and up to forty million internally displaced persons; these figures include a conservative estimate of people fleeing violence and famine in the Brazilian northeast, the Peruvian highlands, and the Colombian and Mexican farmlands. The demographic shift has been almost catastrophic, with urban and suburban populations now equaling or exceeding those of the rural regions in Mexico, Argentina, and other nations, where half a century ago the relative population of the cities was no higher than 25 percent in most cases.

21. One of the earliest and clearest analyses of this trend is given by Kidd (1980:10–14).

22. The phenomenon bears some historical resemblance to the renewed exchange between Spain and the Americas brought about by the exile of a million persons after the Spanish Civil War.

23. For first-person accounts of the displacements, see Pianca (1991).

24. These have ranged from the populist extension theatre projects implemented by the Mexican Revolution (under the guidance of José Vasconcelos) and by Getulio Vargas in Brazil, to the work of the CPCs (Committees of Popular Culture) in Brazil under Goulart and the Centers of Popular Culture in Nicaragua after the triumph of the revolution, to the policy of the Alfonsín

government that has favored cultural extension. For a detailed study of cultural policy, see García Canclini (1987).

25. García Canclini (1987:27) describes six paradigms of cultural policy.

26. The movement of relatives of the disappeared in Chile and Peru pioneered the marketing of "story quilts," or *arpilleras*, and, as is seen below, these same groups have also invented or rediscovered new forms of protest theatre.

27. Some members of our research team have tended to emphasize the period of consolidation of the movement between 1963–65 and 1973–75 as the main focal point. We all agree that the politically committed and collectively oriented New Theatre was already well represented, by the mid-1950s, by the work of the Teatro de Arena in Sao Paulo (founded in 1954 by Jose Renato), especially in its play-writing seminars of 1957 and 1958, and by El Galpón in Uruguay and the later years of the *teatro independiente* in the Southern Cone. What matters most about this movement is its dynamism and the sharing of influences that has occurred over a period of approximately thirty years. The mid-sixties mark the establishment of an international and self-conscious movement, but it should be stressed that the first stirrings of this new popular theatre were registered in Brazil (e.g., with the work of Hermilo Borba filho, in Pernambuco) and in isolated pockets of other countries in the 1950s, and also that there is no firmly drawn line (of rejection or denial) separating the Nuevo Teatro Popular from most of its immediate forerunners.

28. We say "indirectly" because many of the pioneers were doing what might be called Brechtian acting and staging before they were exposed to the Brecht-Piscator ideas of the stage. This was the experience communicated by the founding members of two of the most long-standing groups, El Galpón and La Candelaria, at the symposium on "Brecht in the Americas," cosponsored by the International Brecht Society and ATINT in August 1984 (see the 1986 Communications *Yearbook of the International Brecht Society*).

29. Some playwrights were told they were writing "Brechtian" plays although they claim that they had not read Brecht. Members of El Galpón joked about such experiences in the 1950's, at the symposium on Brecht in the Americas (Brecht 1986). Felipe Santander responded to similar comments about his play *El extensionista* in an interview in *Conjunto* 57 (1983), p. 24.

30. We quote the stated objectives verbatim, because of their documentary significance:

> 1. INDEPENDENCE from commercial control, from restrictive involvement by the state, from any antipopular interest; from any expression that is an obstacle to spreading culture, which is understood to be an ingredient of individual and collective liberation.

2. ART THEATRE: To seek, through an ongoing relationship with the people, to be culturally, technically, and institutionally suited to the real level of development of the masses and to their historical function, maintaining a strict standard of excellence and a demanding artistic line.
3. NATIONAL THEATRE: To act as ferment for the community, promoting the values that favor historical development, paying attention to the needs of the people's action, through national themes and a language of national roots and purpose, and Latin American in scope.
4. POPULAR THEATRE: To further the popularization of theatre, in the understanding that an instrument of culture is the expression of a country, insofar as it is part of the people's heritage.
5. DEMOCRATIC INTERNAL ORGANIZATION: It must be expressed in its institutional system, by which we mean the voluntary grouping of democratically organized persons, who are working in the collective interest, without personal or individual privilege.
6. CULTURAL EXCHANGE: To be active in the exchange between the peoples of different countries, mainly spreading the authentic values of our culture internationally.
7. MILITANCE: The Independent Theatres are dynamic organizations that must fit into the process of the human situation in the community, and of the community itself; in that sense, they will create in their members the consciousness of men of their country and of their time; and the movement, as an organization, will struggle for freedom, for science, and for culture.

31. A surprising number of groups have remained in existence for over a decade or even a quarter century, despite the economic and political difficulties that face this type of theatre. For the purposes of this study, we have managed to compile fairly thorough information on at least twenty-five groups founded between 1949 and 1979; the majority were founded between 1963 and 1978.

32. This terminology is commonly used by different sources. In English it might be more acceptably rendered as "rigorous" or "following social-science methodology"; or it can be interpreted more specifically as signifying a method of analysis most compatible with scientific socialism, i.e., Marxism.

33. The Ollantay Prize was established by the Federation of Theatre Festivals of America, and is now awarded by CELCIT (the leading federation of Latin American theatre critics, researchers, and producers) and the Ateneo of Caracas. It is given to the most outstanding individuals or institutions of Latin American theatre and represents a kind of "lifetime achievement award."

34. Anonymous tracts attributed to right-wing paramilitary groups and distributed throughout Colombia, in 1987, accused Patricia Ariza, the director of

the Colombian Theatre Corporation, and all theatre artists affiliated with the Left of being agents of the guerrilla movement; these people were targeted as "cultural aggressors" against the state and as dangerous subversives. Yet this is the same Colombian theatre federation whose members have enjoyed official subsidies, with no strings attached, from governments that are far from sympathetic to the Left, but which remain committed at least to a public show of pluralism.

35. A survey of over one hundred plays produced by the New Popular Theatre (including twenty selected for their prominence and the rest on a random basis) revealed this generalization.

36. We cite Brazil as the one country where African-American theatre has been particularly active. The Teatro Experimental do Negro (Black Experimental Theatre), cofounded in 1944 by sociologist and playwright Abdias do Nascimento, created theatre space for black actors and playwrights promoting Afro-Portuguese culture and challenging the racism of the dominant culture in Brazil. They did deconstruct traditional myths from a radical contemporary perspective, but their primary concern was racism.

37. The studies of Mexican indigenous theatre have been more numerous than those of the black theatre (with the exception of Brazil's). For a good introduction to indigenous theatre, see Meyer Pape (1980).

38. Judith Weiss interview with Alicia Partnoy, 10 February 1987, and Pianca 1991.

39. Brazil, Chile, Cuba, Colombia, and Mexico are probably the largest networks, reflecting the population base and the number of grass-roots development programs and social organizations.

5. Faces of the New Popular Theatre

1. The Witnesses became particularly active in the region around the mid-sixties. They gained hundreds of converts by playing on the conservative instincts of the small farmer, and they antagonized the government by fostering conscientious objection to military service, by having children and adults refuse to salute the flag, and by refusing innoculations and blood transfusions. The official line, propagated in at least three of Teatro Escambray's main plays, was that the Witnesses were at best opportunistic and at worst agents of U.S. imperialism, because they preyed on weak and doubting individuals, exploited their psychological vulnerability at a time of radical social transformation, and divided the population against itself and against the state.

2. Critics in Cuba often spend time with various groups, to familiarize

themselves with the process, which is, of course, at least as important as the finished product. The internships to which we refer are usually held by graduating students of the National Arts School (ENA) or, after 1980, of the Higher Institute of the Arts (ISA); social-science researchers and arts students from various universities also spend periods of residency with these groups.

3. The main sources in English include: Brooks (1983), Martin (1987), Morton (1983), and Weiss (1989). Our sources in Spanish include: Bolt (1980), Kaiser-Lenoir (1989), Pianca (1991), Rizk (1989), and Rojas (1982).

4. Julio Saldaña, director of the theatre division of the A.S.T.C. and director of the National Theatre Workshop, interviewed by Marina Pianca, 1986 (Pianca 1991).

5. This history of CLETA was excerpted from the manuscript of Frischmann (1991).

6. A massacre by government forces of hundreds of demonstrators took place at Tlatelolco square, also known as the "Plaza de las Tres Culturas." Students were active in the leadership of the strikes and demonstrations around that period.

7. Mascarones favored a political line that stressed anti-fascism and anti-imperialism and thus allowed strategic alliances with the Mexican government; this would have justified accepting some funding from the state. The controversy exploded over the way in which funding was obtained for the fifth Festival of Chicano and Mexican Theatre in Mexico City in 1974. Mascarones accepted funding from sympathetic government officials for food, buses, etc. and was thus accused of having sold out to the government.

8. One important clarification, provided by Boal himself, concerns the difference between guerrilla theatre and "invisible theatre." Boal stresses that guerrilla theatre is clearly a "theatrical" experience because it plays to spectators who remain passive, whereas with "invisible theatre," "the theatrical rituals are abolished; only the theatre exists, without its old, worn-out patterns" (Boal 1979:147).

9. After completing this section, and in response to questions regarding its place as theatre, the authors read Jay Cantor's essays on Patty Hearst and Hamlet (Cantor 1981). In "History as Theatre," Cantor, with acknowledgments to Freud and Jan Kott, analyzes the dramatic values of terrorism (both by the state and by individuals or political groups) as sacrificial action (the sacrifice of the part to protect the whole) carried out publicly. Cantor also quotes Sorel, who equates the representative role of the parlamentarian with that of the terrorist. The authors would suggest that in the case of the relatives of the disappeared, there is a similar representation. Unlike the makers of the sacrifice, however, these actors bring a reply to the sacrifice, denouncing

the rupture and the violation of the minimal human dignity (habeas corpus beyond the strictly legal sense of the term) allowable to a prisoner or a dead person.

10. On the social, political, and artistic aspects of the popular culture of the Chilean *población*, see Cesareo (1987).

11. Like their Chilean counterparts, they assemble in front of two of the country's main centers of power, Government House and the National Cathedral, and in front of the Cabildo (town hall), which was the scene of the first popular demonstration for Argentine independence, in 1810. For a feminist reading of the Mothers' movement, see Rossi 1989).

12. Most of this information was gathered in informal conversation with Osvaldo Dragún in Washington, D.C., in May 1986.

13. One of the pioneering groups in this type of work had been the Fray Mocho group, where Teatro Abierto leader Osvaldo Dragún began his theatre career, in the early fifties.

14. These include the establishment of organized networks and institutions for the moral and economic support of the families of detainees and victims of violence. The influential role of women in these grass-roots movements could be a reason why the parameters of traditional political work have been broadened. This benefits the position of women in popular culture. Their gender-identified products gain more perceived value, and their role as theatre workers is enhanced as they are freed from the male hegemony of traditional relations of production.

Bibliography

Acuña, René

1975 *Introducción al estudio del Rabinal Achí.* Mexico City: Universidad Nacional Autónoma.

1978 *Farsas y representaciones escénicas de los mayas antiguos.* Mexico City: Universidad Nacional Autónoma.

1979 *El teatro popular en Hispanoamérica. Una bibliografía anotada.* Mexico City: Universidad Nacional Autónoma.

Adame Hernández, Domingo

1985 "El teatro rural patrocinado por el estado." *Escénica* 2:5–13.

Adedeji, Joel

1978 "Alarinjo: The Traditional Yoruba Travelling Theatre." Pp. 27–51 in *Theatre in Africa*, ed. by Oyin Ogunba and Abiola Irele (Ibadan: Ibadan University Press).

Adorno, Rolena

1982 *From Oral to Written Expression: Native Andean Chronicles of the Early Colonial Period.* Syracuse, N.Y.: Syracuse University Press.

Adorno, Theodore, and Max Horkheimer

1984 *Dialectic of Enlightenment.* Cambridge: Harvard University Press.

Agee, Phillip

1975 *Inside the Company: C.I.A. Diary.* Harmondsworth, England: Penguin Books.

Aguilar, Alonso M., et al.

1985 "Cultura, historia y luchas del pueblo mexicano." *Política Cultural Mexicana* 20:76–103.

Almeida Naveda, Eduardo

1989 "The Contemporary Theatre of Ecuador." Unpublished manuscript, in author's possession.

Alonso, Damaso
1924 "Representaciones populares." *Revue Hispanique* 137:187–88.
Alvarez Lejarza, Emilio
1883 "El Güegüense o Macho-Ratón." [Managua].
Amiel, Denys, ed.
1931 *Les spectacles à travers les âges*. Paris: Editions du Cygne. In particular, see: Henri Lyonnet, "Les cirques," pp. 199–246, and Legrand-Chabrier, "Le music-hall," pp. 247–88.
Antolínez, Gilberto
1946 "El teatro, institución de los Muku y Jirajara." *Revista Nacional de Cultura* (Caracas) 7/56:113–29.
Arellano, Jorge Eduardo
1988 "A propósito de 'El Güegüense' en Diriambá: Las Fiestas de San Sebastián." *Ventana* (Managua), 23 January 1988.
Arrom, José Juan
1946 "Documentos relativos al teatro colonial de Venezuela." *Universidad de la Habana* XXI–XXII, 64–69:80–101.
1956 *Teatro Hispanoamericano: Epoca colonial*. Havana: Anuario Bibliográfico Cubano.
Arróniz, Othon
1979 *Teatro de evangelización en Nueva España*. Mexico City: Universidad Nacional Autónoma.
Azor, Ileana
1988 *Origen y presencia del teatro en nuestra América*. Havana: Editorial Letras Cubanas.
Bakhtin, Michael
1968 *Rabelais and His World*. Trans. by Helene Iswolsky. Cambridge, Mass.: MIT Press.
Ballinger, Rex Edward
1952 *Los orígenes del teatro español y sus primeras manifestaciones en la Nueva España*. Mexico City: Universidad Nacional Autónoma.
Balmori, Clemente H.
1955 "Teatro aborigen americano." *Estudios Americanos* IX, 45:580–601.
Barrera Vázquez, Alfredo
1965 "El teatro y la danza entre los antiguos mayas de Yucatán." Intro. to *El libro de los Cantares de Dzitbalché*. Mexico City: Instituto Nacional de Antropología e Historia.
Bartra, Roger
1989 "Culture and Political Power in Mexico." *Latin American Perspectives* 16/2:61–69.

Bastide, Roger
1959 *Sociologia do folclore brasileiro*. São Paulo: Ediciones Anhembi.
Bataillon, Marcel
1949 "Para un inventario de las fiestas de moros y cristianos: Otro toque de atención." *Mar del Sur* (Lima) 3/8:1–8.
Batalha Viveiros de Castro, Eduardo
1992 *From the Enemy's Point of View: Humanity and Divinity in an Amazonian Society*. Translated by Catherine V. Howard. Chicago: University of Chicago Press.
Bayle, Constantino I.
1947 "Notas acerca del teatro religioso en la América colonial." *Razón y Fe* (Madrid), 47/590:221–34; 47/591:335–48.
Beaulac, Willard L.
1980 *The Fractured Continent: Latin America in Close-up*. Stanford: Hoover Institution.
Beier, Uli
1960 "A Year of Sacred Festivals in one Yoruba Town." *Nigeria Magazine* (A Special Production; Lagos).
Belic, Oldric
1972 La periodización y sus problemas. *Problemas de Literatura* I,2.
Bergson, Henri
1969 *Le rire, essai sur la signification du comique*. Paris: PUF.
Blasier, Cole
1985 *The Hovering Giant: U.S. Responses to Revolutionary Change in Latin America, 1910–1985*. Rev. ed. Pittsburgh: Pittsburgh University Press.
Boal, Augusto
1979 *Theatre of the Oppressed*. New York: Urizen Books.
1990 "The Cop in the Head: Three Hypotheses." *TDR* 34:335–42.
Bode, Barbara
1961 "The Dance of the Conquest of Guatemala." Pp. 205–92 in *The Native Theatre in Middle America*, by Gustavo Correa, Calvin Cannon, W.A. Hunter, and Barbara Bode. New Orleans: Tulane University, Middle America Research Institute. Publication 27.
Bolt, Alan
1980 "El teatro estudiantil universitario." *Conjunto* 45:5–13.
1983 "Manifiesto del teatro comunitario." Managua.
Bonfill Batalla, Guillermo
1982 "Lo propio y lo ajeno: una aproximación al problema del control cultural." Pp. 79–86 in *La cultura popular*, ed. by Adolfo Colombres. Mexico City: Premia/SEP.

Borges Pérez, F.
1942 *Historia del teatro en Costa Rica*. San José: Imprenta Española.
Bosch, Mariano G.
1929 *Los orígenes del teatro nacional argentino y la época de Pablo Podestá*. Buenos Aires: L.J. Rosso.
Boudet, Rosa Ileana
1980 "Sobre arte popular, un libro útil y polemico." *Conjunto* 46:103–4.
1983 *Teatro Nuevo: Una respuesta*. Havana: Editorial Letras Cubanas.
Bouissac, Paul
1985 *Circus and Culture: A Semiotic Approach*. Washington, D.C.: University Press of America.
Bravo Elizondo, Pedro
1981 Intro. to Sergio Arrau, *Digo que Norte-Sur corre la tierra*. Lima: Lluvia.
1986 *Cultura y teatro obreros en Chile, 1900–1930*. Madrid: Ediciones Michay.
1989 *Antecedentes del Nuevo Teatro en Chile*. Unpublished manuscript, in author's possession.
Brecht, Bertolt
1964 "A Short Organum for the Theatre," pp. 179–205; and "Appendices to a Short Organum . . . ," pp. 276–81 in *Brecht on Theatre*, ed. by John Willett. New York: Hill and Wang.
Brecht Society
1986 *Communications (Brecht Yearbook)*, 1986. Special issue on "Brecht in the Americas," ed. by Maria Lima. Proceedings of the symposium on Brecht in the Americas, organized by the Asociación de Trabajadores e Investigadores del Nuevo Teatro, Joseph Papp Latino Festival, New York, 1984.
Bricker, Victoria Reifler
1973 *Ritual Humor in Highland Chiapas*. Austin: University of Texas Press.
1982 *The Indian Christ, The Indian King: The Historical Substrate of Maya Myth and Ritual*. Austin: University of Texas Press.
1985 *Supplement to the Handbook of Middle American Indians*, vol. 3, *Literatures*. Austin: University of Texas Press.
Brinton, Daniel G.
1883 *The Güegüence*. Philadelphia: Library of Aboriginal American Literature, 3.
Bristol, Michael
1985 *Carnival and Theatre*. New York: Methuen.
Britto García, Luis
1980 "Problemas y soluciones del teatro popular." *Conjunto* 46:4–11.

Brookes, Chris
1983 Brookes, Chris. *Now We Know the Difference*. Vancouver, B.C.: N.C. Press.
Bryan, Susan E.
1983 "Teatro popular y sociedad durante el porfiriato." *Historia mexicana* 129:130–69.
Buenaventura, Enrique
1979 "Teatro e identidad cultural." Cali: T.E.C.
1981 "El debate del teatro nacional." *Conjunto* 47:14–23.
1988a "Texto verbal y textos no verbales." Pp. 52–54 in *Inventario del teatro iberoamericano*, vol. 1, ed. by Carlos Espinosa Domínguez. Madrid: Ministerio de Cultura, Centro de Documentación Teatral.
1988b "Un movimiento con conciencia histórica." Pp. 305–6 in *Inventario del teatro iberoamericano*, vol. 1, ed. by Carlos Espinosa Domínguez. Madrid: Ministerio de Cultura, Centro de Documentación Teatral.
Caballero, Attilio J.
1988a "Semana Santa en Nicaragua: Rito, tradición y contemporaneidad." *Conjunto* 77:92–96.
Campa, Arthur L.
1960 "El origen y la naturaleza del drama folklórico." *Folklore Americas* XX, 2:13–48.
Campbell, Federico
1983 "A 10 años de CLETA, dos líneas: Trabajar o no con el Estado." *Proceso* 370 (5 Dec. 1983):58–59.
Campbell, Margaret
1958 *The Development of the National Theatre in Chile*. Gainesville: University of Florida Press.
Canal Feijóo, Bernardo
1943 *La expresión popular dramática*. Tucumán: Universidad Nacional de Tucumán.
Cantes, Juan
1920 "El teatro de la Ranchería, o casa de comedias." *Revista argentina de ciencias políticas* 20:115–17; 145–53.
Cantor, Jay
1981 "History as Theatre." Pp. 61–92 in *The Space Between: Literature and Politics*. Baltimore: Johns Hopkins University Press.
Carella, Tulio
1957 *El sainete criollo*. Buenos Aires: Hachette.
Carew, Jan
1988 "Columbus and the Origins of Racism in the Americas." *Race and Class*. Part one 29(4):1–19; part two 30(1):33–57.

Carneiro, José Fernando

1946 *A antropofagia entre os indigenas do Brasil.* Ministerio da Educaçao e Saúde. Coleçao Brasileira de Divulgaçao. Serie II. Etnografía. No. 2.

Carvalho Neto, Pablo de

1964 *Diccionario de folklore ecuatoriano.* Quito: Casa de la Cultura.

Casa de las Américas. [Editors]

1992 "La Casa de las Américas ante el Quinto Centenario." *Casa de las Américas* 184:3–13.

Castagnino, Raul

1944 *Contribución documental a la historia del teatro en Buenos Aires durante la epoca de Rosas (1830–1852).* Buenos Aires: Comisión Nacional de Cultura, Instituto Nacional de Estudios de Teatro.

1958 *El circo criollo.* Buenos Aires: Colección Lajouane de Folklore Argentino, vol. 4.

1963 *Sociología del teatro argentino.* Buenos Aires: Editorial Nova.

1981 *Circo, teatro gauchesco y tango.* Buenos Aires: Instituto Nacional de Estudios de Teatro.

Castaneda, Carlos

1932 "The First American Play." *The Catholic World* 134:429–37.

Castro, Américo

1954 *La realidad histórica de España.* Mexico City: Porrúa. (Rev. ed. of *España en su historia.* Buenos Aires: Losada, 1948.)

Cervera Andrade, Alejandro

1947 *El teatro regional de Yucatán (1900–1947).* Mérida.

Cervera Espejo, Alberto

1983 Cervera Espejo, Alberto. *El teatro indígena viviente.* Mérida: Fondo Editorial de Yucatán.

Cesareo, Mario

1987 "Estética y constitución de sujetos en la cultura poblacional chilena. Pp. 121–69 in *Poética de la población marginal,* vol. 2, ed. by James Romano. Minneapolis: Prisma Institute.

Chambers, Edmund Kerchever

1903 *The Mediaeval Stage.* Oxford: The Clarendon Press.

Chang-Rodríguez, Raquel

1982 *Violencia y subversión en la prosa colonial hispanoamericana, siglos XVI y XVII.* Madrid: José Porrúa Turanzas.

Chinchilla Aguilar, Ernesto

1963 *La Danza del Sacrificio y otros estudios.* Guatemala: Ministerio de Cultura.

Cid Pérez, José, and Dolores Martí de Cid

1964 *Teatro indio precolombino.* Madrid: Aguilar.

CLETA
1983 "A discusión," 4a parte, *El Chido* 59 (Feb. 1983):8.
Colombres, Adolfo, ed.
1982 *La cultura popular*. Mexico City: SEP.
Connerton, Paul
1989 *How Societies Remember*. New York: Cambridge University Press.
Cordobés Moure, J. M.
1978 *Reminiscencias de Santa Fe y Bogotá*. Bogotá: Colcultura.
Cortázar, Augusto Raúl
1949 *El carnaval en el folklore calchaquí*. Buenos Aires: Editorial Sudamérica.
Crawford, J. P. W.
1911 "The Pastor and the Bobo in the Spanish Religious Drama of the XVI Century." *Romanic Review* II.
1922 *Spanish Drama before Lope de Vega*. Philadelphia: Extra Series, Romanic Languages no. 7.
Crow, John A.
1939 "El drama revolucionario mexicano." *Revista Hispánica Moderna* 5:21–31.
Dahlgren, Barbara
1954 "La mixteca: su cultura e historia prehispánicas." *Colección Cultura Mexicana* (Mexico City) 11.
Damasceno, Leslie
1988 "Brazilian Theatre." Pp. 338–48 in *Dictionary of Brazilian Literature*, ed. by Irwin Stern. New York: Greenwood Press.
1990 *Cultural Space and Theatrical Conventions in the Work of Oduvaldo Viana Filho*. Unpublished manuscript, in author's possession, Princeton, New Jersey.
Dauster, Frank
1973 *Historia del teatro hispanoamericano, siglos XIX y XX*. México: De Andrea.
Davila, Arturo V.
1961 "La pastoral del Obispo Arizmendi sobre las comedias." *Revista del Instituto de Cultura Puertorriqueña*, 4/12:27–32.
Deleito y Piñuela, José
1949 *Origen y apogeo del "género chico"*. Madrid: Revista de Occidente.
De Los Ríos, Edda
1989 "Popular Theatre in Paraguay" Unpublished manuscript, in author's possession.
Del Saz, Agustín
1967 *Teatro social hispanoamericano*. Barcelona: Editorial Labor.

Descalzi, Ricardo
1968 *Historia crítica del teatro ecuatoriano*. Quito: Casa de la Cultura Ecuatoriana.
Díaz Araujo, María G. González de
1982 *La vida teatral en Buenos Aires desde 1713 hasta 1896*. [Mendoza]: Ediciones Culturales Argentinas.
Díaz Roque, José
1979 "José Antonio Ramos: Su teatro y su ideología." *Islas* (Universidad Central de Las Villas, Santa Clara) 63:93–150.
Durán y Sanpere, A.
1943 *La fiesta del corpus*. Barcelona: Ediciones Aymá.
Echeuo, M. J.
1975 "Dramatic Limits of Igbo Ritual." *Research in African Literature* 4(1):25.
Eckdahl-Ravicz, Marilyn
1970 *Early Colonial Religious Drama in Mexico: From Tzompantli to Golgotha*. Washington, D.C.: Catholic University of America Press.
Edmonson, Munro
1960 "Nativism, Syncretism and Anthropological Science." Pp. 181–203 in *Nativism and Syncretism*, ed. by Munro Edmonson et al. New Orleans: Tulane University Press, Middle American Research Institute Publication 19.
1986 *Heaven Born Merida and Its Destiny; The Book of Chilam Balam of Chumayel*. Austin: University of Texas Press.
Englekirk, John E.
1957a "The Source and Dating of New Mexican Spanish Folk Plays." *Western Folklore*, 16(4):232–55.
1957b "El teatro folklórico hispanoamericano." *Folklore Americas* 7(1):1–35.
Epstein, Susan
1990 "Open Doors for the International Theatre School of Latin America and the Caribbean." *TDR* 34(3):162–76.
Espinosa Domínguez, Carlos, ed.
1988 *Inventario del teatro iberoamericano*. Madrid: Ministerio de Cultura, Centro de Documentación Teatral.
Estage Noel, Cayuqui
1982 "Danza dialogada huave *Olmalndiuk* (y texto en zapoteco)." *Tlalocan* (Mexico City: Universidad Nacional Autónoma) 9:229–48.
1988 "Indigenous Theater: What it is, what it isn't, what it seems to be and what it should be." Unpublished manuscript, in author's possession.

1989 "True Theater in Native Dance." *The Christian Science Monitor* (14 March):16–17.

Falassi, Alessandro

1987 "Festival: Definition and Morphology." Pp. 1–10 in *Time Out of Time. Essays on the Festival*, edited by Alessandro Falassi. Albuquerque: University of New Mexico Press.

Fernández Cid, Antonio

1975 *Cien años de teatro musical en España, 1875–1975*. Madrid: Real Musical Editores.

Fernández Moreno, César, ed.

1972 *América Latina en su literatura*. Mexico City: UNESCO and Siglo XXI.

Fiori, Lavinia

1990 "Reflexiones para una antropología teatral en Colombia." *Actuemos* (Bogotá) 7/26:39–56.

Flores, Arturo

1990 *El Teatro Campesino de Luis Valdez*. Madrid: Editorial Pliegos.

Fox Lockert, Lucía, ed.

1990 *Expresiones colectivas en el teatro y en los espectáculos populares*. East Lansing, Michigan: Imprenta La Nueva Crónica. (Sociedad de Investigaciones Socio-Literarias de Hispanoamérica, Antología Anual II).

Franco, Jean

1982 "What's in a Name? Popular Culture Theories and Their Limitations." *Studies in Latin American Popular Culture* 5/(1):5–14.

Freire, Paulo.

1973 *Education for Critical Consciousness*. New York: Seabury Press.

1981 *Literacy and Revolution, the Pedagogy of Paulo Freire*. Edited by Robert Mackie. New York: Continuum.

1985 *The Politics of Education: Culture, Power and Liberation*. Translated by Donald Macedo. South Hadley, Massachusetts: Bergin and Garvey.

Frischmann, Donald H.

1987a " 'Cholo' habla del Teatro Regional." *Novedades de Yucatán* (Mérida) Sunday Cultural Supplement (15 March):1, (21 March):6–7.

1987b "México 1987: Avance del género de revista y del teatro popular." *Diógenes (Anuario Crítico del Teatro Latinoamericano)* 3:77–90.

1987c "Mito, carnaval e identidad étnica: La funcionalidad social y política del nuevo teatro indígena de México." Paper presented at the Pacific Coast Council of Latin American Studies, in author's possession.

1989 "The Age-Old Tradition of Mexico's Popular Theatre." *Theatre Research International* 14(2):111–21.

1990 *El nuevo teatro popular en México*. Mexico City: Instituto Nacional de Bellas Artes.

1991 "Active Ethnicity: Nativism, Otherness, and Indian Theatre in Mexico." *Gestos* 6(11):113–26.

Galeano, Eduardo

1971 *Open Veins of Latin America*. New York: Monthly Review Press.

Galich, Manuel

1981 "Teatro e ideología en América Latina." *Conjunto* 47:24–32.

Galpón, Grupo Cultural el

1973 *Manifiesto del teatro independiente del Uruguay*. Montevideo: Grupo Cultural el Galpón.

Gans, Herbert J.

1974 *Popular Culture and High Culture*. New York: Basic Books.

García, Santiago

1981 "Ubicación de la ideología en el proceso creativo." *Conjunto* 47:5–13.

1988 "La urgencia de una nueva dramaturgia." Pp. 55–58 in *Inventario del teatro iberoamericano*, vol. 1, ed. by Carlos Espinosa Domínguez. Madrid: Ministerio de Cultura, Centro de Documentación Teatral.

García Canclini, Néstor

1977 *Arte popular y sociedad en América Latina*. Mexico City: Grijalbo.

1984 *Las culturas populares en el capitalismo*. México City: SEP.

1987 *Políticas culturales en América Latina*. Mexico City: Grijalbo.

García Soriano, J.

1927 *El teatro de colegio en España. Noticia y examen de alguna de sus obras*. Madrid: Biblioteca de Autores Españoles 14:235–77.

Garibay, Angel María

1954 *Historia de la literatura náhuatl*. 2 vols. Mexico City: Editorial Porrúa.

Garzón Céspedes, Francisco

1976 Intro. to José Antonio Ramos, *Teatro*. Havana: Editorial Arte y Literatura.

1978 *El teatro latinoamericano de creación colectiva*. Havana: Casa de las Américas.

1981 "José Antonio Ramos: Una línea ascendente de rebeldía." *Latin American Theatre Review* 14(2):5–10.

Girard, Rafael

1948 *Esoterismo del Popol Vuh*. Mexico City: Editores Mexicanos Unidos.

Gisbert de Mesa, Teresa

1962 *Teatro virreinal en Bolivia*. La Paz: Dirección Nacional de Informaciones de la Presidencia de la República.

Goic, Cedomil

1975 "La périodisation dans l'histoire de la litterature hispano-américaine." *Etudes Littéraires* 8(2–3):269–84.

Goldmann, Lucien

1976 *Cultural Creation in Modern Society*. Intro. by William Mayrl. Trans. by Bart Grahl. Bibliography and appendices comp. by Ileana Rodríguez and Marc Zimmerman. Saint Louis: Telos Press.

Golluscio de Montoya, Eva

1980 "Le 'cocoliche': Une convention du théatre populaire du Río de la Plata." *Cahiers du Monde Hispanique et Luso-Brésilien (Caravelle)* 35:11–30.

1986 "Círculos anarquistas y circuitos contra-culturales en la Argentina del 900." *Contre-cultures, utopies et dissidences en Amérique Latine. Caravelle* 46:49–64.

Gontard, Denis

1977 "An Example of 'Popular' Itinerant Theatre: Gémier's National Travelling Theatre (1911–12)." Pp. 123–32 in *Western Popular Theatre*, ed. by David Mayer and Kenneth Richards. London: Methuen.

González, Hernán

1979 "Teatro ritual americano: 'El Cautivo Cristiano.'" *Cuadernos Hispanoamericanos* 347:442–51.

González Cajiao, Fernando

1986 *Historia del teatro en Colombia*. Bogotá: Instituto Colombiano de Cultura.

González Stephan, Beatriz

1987 *La historiografía literaria del liberalismo hispanoamericano del siglo XIX*. Havana: Casa de las Américas.

Goodlad, J., Sr.

1971 *A Sociology of Popular Drama*. London: Heinemann.

Gramsci, Antonio

1957 *The Modern Prince and Other Writings*. Trans. by Louis Marks. New York: International Publishers.

1971 *Selections from the Prison Notebooks*. Quentin Hoare and Geoffrey Newell Smith, eds. New York: International Publishers.

1977 *Selections from Political Writings, 1921–1926*. New York: International Publishers.

Granja, Agustín de la.

1988 "El entremés y la fiesta del Corpus." *Criticón* 42:139–53.

Greenwood, Isaac J.

1970 *The Circus: Its Origin and Growth Prior to 1835*. New York: Benjamin Franklin.

Guerra, Jairo

1990 "Hacia una teoría del teatro popular." *Actuemos*, 7/26:63–69.

Hardison, O. B., Jr.

1965 *Christian Rite and Christian Drama in the Middle Ages: Essays in the Origin and Early History of Modern Drama*. Baltimore: Johns Hopkins University Press.

Hatch, James V., ed.

1991 *The Roots of African American Drama*. Detroit: Wayne State University Press.

Heckel, I.

1947 "Los sainetes de Sor Juana Inés de la Cruz." *Revista Iberoamericana* XIII, 25:135–40.

Hendrix, W. S.

1924 *Some Native Comic Types in the Early Spanish Drama*. Columbus, Ohio: The Heizer Printing Co.

Hessel, Lothar, and Georges Raeder

1972 *O teatro jesuitico no Brasil*. Porto Alegre: Editora da Universidade Federal de Rio Grande do Sul.

Horcasitas, Fernando

1974 *El teatro náhuatl: Epocas novohispanas y moderna*. Mexico City: Universidad Nacional Autónoma.

Icaza, Francisco A. de

1921 "Cristóbal de Llerena y los orígenes del teatro en la América española." *Revista de Filología Española* VIII, 2:121–30.

Ingham, John M.

1986 *Mary, Michael and Lucifer: Folk Catholicism in Central Mexico*. Austin: University of Texas Press.

Jaye, Barbara H., and William P. Mitchell.

1988 "The Only Game in Town: The Latin American Fiesta System and the York Feast of Corpus Christi." *Fifteenth-Century Studies* 13(213):485–503.

Johnson, Harvey Leroy

1941 "Notas relativas a los corrales de la ciudad de México, 1641–1826." *Revista Iberoamericana* (Mexico City) 3:133–38.

1951 "Nuevos datos sobre el teatro en la ciudad de Guatemala (1789–1820)." *Revista Iberoamericana* XVI, 32:345–86.

Jones, Willis Knapp

1966 *Behind Spanish American Footlights*. Austin: University of Texas Press.

Kaiser-Lenoir, Claudia

1977 *El grotesco criollo: Estilo teatral de una época*. Havana: Casa de las Américas. (Premio Casa)

1989a "Arte y práctica social: El nuevo teatro de Nicaragua." *Conjunto* 78:75–8.

1989b "Nicaragua: Theatre in a New Society." *Theatre Research International* 14(2):122–30.

1989c "El *Nuevo Teatro* y la tradición dramática popular en Argentina." *Alba de América* (Westminster, California) VII, 12–13:87–96.

Kanellos, Nicholas

1987 *Mexican-American Theatre: Legacy and Reality*. Pittsburgh: Latin American Review Press.

1990 *A History of Hispanic Theatre in the United States*. Austin: University of Texas Press.

Kidd, Ross

1980 "People's Theatre, Conscientisation, and Struggle." *Media Development (Journal of the World Association for Christian Communication)* 27(3):10–14.

1982 *Popular Performing Arts, Non-Formal Education and Social Change in the Third World*. The Hague: CESO.

1984 *From People's Theatre for Revolution to Popular Theatre for Reconstruction: Diary of a Zimbabwean Workshop*. The Hague–Toronto: CESO-OISE.

Lacosta, Francisco C.

1965 "El teatro misionero en la América Hispana." *Cuadernos Americanos* CXLII, 5:171–78.

Lafaye, Jacques

1977 *Quetzalcóatl y Guadalupe*. Mexico City: Fondo de Cultura Económica.

Lara, Jesús

1957 Intro. to *Tragedia del fin de Atahuallpa*. Cochabamba: Imprenta Universitaria.

1972 "El teatro en el Tawantinsuyo." *Memorias*, XV Congreso del Instituto Internacional de Literatura Iberoamericana, Lima, 1971. Lima: Universidad Mayor de San Marcos.

Las Casas, Bartolomé de

1909 *Apologética historia de Indias*. Madrid: Bailly, Bailliere, e hijos.

Lázaro Carreter, F.

1965 *Teatro medieval*. Second ed. Valencia: Editorial Castalia.

Leal, Rine

1970 "Ramos dramaturgo o la república municipal y espesa." *Islas* (Universidad Central de Las Villas, Santa Clara) 36:73–91.

1975a *La selva oscura*. Havana: Editorial Letras Cubanas. (vol. 1, 1975; vol. 2, 1982)

1975b Intro. to *Teatro bufo, Siglo XIX*. 2 vols. Havana: Editorial Arte y Literatura.

1978 Intro. to *Teatro mambí*. Havana: Editorial Letras Cubanas.

Leis, Raúl Alberto

1979 "The Popular Theatre and Development in Latin America." *Educational Broadcasting International* 12(1):10–13.

León Portilla, Miguel

1959 "Teatro náhuatl prehispánico." *La Palabra y el Hombre* (Mexico City) 9:13–35.

1972 *Religión de los nicaraos*. Mexico City: UNAM. Instituto de Investigaciones Históricas. Serie de Cultura Náhuatl, 12.

Leonard, Irving A.

1935 "A shipment of *comedias* to the Indies." *Hispanic Review* II, 1 (1934):39–45.

1940 "El teatro en Lima, 1790–1793." *Hispanic Review* 8:93–112.

1951a "The 1790 Theatre Season of the Mexico City Coliseo." *Hispanic Review* 19(2):104–21.

1951b "The Theatre Season of 1791–92 in Mexico City." *Hispanic American Historical Review* 31(2):349–64.

Lester, Geoffrey

1986 "Holy Week Processions in Seville." *Medieval English Theatre* 8(2):103–31.

Levenson, Deborah

1989 "The Murder of an Actor and a Theater." *NACLA Report on the Americas* 23,3:4–5.

Lévi-Strauss, Claude

1976 *Structural Anthropology*. Trans. by Monique Layton. Vol. 2. New York: Basic Books.

Lienhart, Martin

1989 *La voz y su huella. Escritura y conflicto étnico-social en América Latina, 1492–1988*. Havana: Casa de las Américas. (Premio Ensayo)

Lieuwen, Edwin

1964 *Generals versus Presidents: Neo-Militarism in Latin America*. New York: Praeger.

1966 *The U.S. and the Challenge to Security in Latin America*. Columbus: Ohio University Press.

Lohmann Villena, Guillermo

1941 *Historia del arte dramático en Lima durante el Virreinato*. Lima: Imprenta Americana.

López Bucio, Baltasar (Presbítero).

1983 *Tandas culturales de Tlaltenango*. Cuernavaca: El Santuario de Tlaltenango.

Losada, Alejandro

1975 Losada, Alejandro. "Los sistemas literarios como instituciones sociales en América Latina." *Revista de Crítica Literaria Latinoamericana* 1(1):39–60.

1983 "Articulación, periodización y diferenciación de los procesos literarios en América Latina." *Revista de Crítica Literaria Latinoamericana* 9/17:7–37.

Luzuriaga, Gerardo

1990 *Introducción a las teorías latinoamericanas del teatro.* Puebla: Universidad Autónoma de Puebla.

Lyday, Leon

1970 "The Colombian Theatre before 1800." *Latin American Theatre Review* 4(1):35–50.

McGrath, John

1979 "The Theory and Practice of Political Theatre." *Theatre Quarterly* 9/35:43–54.

1981 *A Good Night Out: Popular Theatre—Audience, Class and Form.* London: Eyre Methuen.

Magaña Esquivel, Antonio

1961 *Medio siglo de teatro mexicano (1900–1961).* Mexico City: Instituto Nacional de Bellas Artes.

1972 "Los teatros en México hasta el siglo XIX." *Revista Inter-Americana de Bibliografía* 22:242–56.

1977 "La política en el teatro mexicano." *Revista Ibero-Americana de Bibliografía* 27:125–34.

Mahood, M.

1966 "Drama in Newborn States." *Présence Africaine* XXI, 60:23.

Marchetti, Victor, and John D. Marks

1974 *The CIA and the Cult of Intelligence.* New York: Knopf.

Margulis, Mario

1982 "La cultura popular." Pp. 41–65 in *La cultura popular*, ed. by Adolfo Colombres. Mexico City: Premia/SEP.

Marial, José

1984 *Teatro y país (Desde 1810 a Teatro Abierto, 1983).* Buenos Aires: Ediciones Agon.

María y Campos, Armando de

1939 *Los payasos, poetas del pueblo.* Mexico City: Ediciones Botas.

1956 *El teatro de género chico en la Revolución Mexicana.* Mexico City: Instituto Nacional de Estudios Históricos de la Revolución Mexicana.

Marqués, René

1966 "Nacionalismo vs. universalismo." *Cuadernos Americanos* XXV, 146:215–30.

Martin, Luis

1983 *Daughters of the Conquistadores: Women of the Viceroyalty of Peru*. Albuquerque: University of New Mexico Press.

Martin, Randy

1987 "Country and City: Theatre in Revolution." *The Drama Review* 31/4 (116):58–76.

Martín Barbero, Jesús

1987 *De los medios a las mediaciones: comunicación, cultura y hegemonía*. México City: Ediciones G. Gili.

Mattelart, Armando

1983 *Transnationals and the Third World: The Struggle for Culture*. Translated by David Buxton. South Hadley, Massachusetts: Bergin and Harvey.

Mejía Sánchez, Ernesto, and J. Durand

1982 "Teatro popular nicaragüense: Los Doce Pares de Francia en Niquinohomo." *Anuario de Letras* (Mexico City) 20:287–332.

Meléndez, Carlos

1976 "Apuntes sobre el teatro culterano colonial en el reino de Guatemala." *Revista del Pensamiento Centroamericano* 2/18:82–89.

Merino Lanzilotti, Ignacio

1967 "El teatro de revista política en México; Estudio de tres obras de Pablo Prida y Carlos M. Ortega." M.A. Thesis, UNAM, Mexico City.

1980 "La tradición fársica en México: Carpa y revista política." *La Cabra* (Mexico City) III, 27:i–xx.

Meyer Pape, Germán

1980 "Entre leyendas y despojos: Un movimiento de teatro indígena." *La Cabra* (Mexico City) III, 16–17:6–9.

Michalski, Jan

1971 *O Palco Amordaçado: 15 anos de Censura Teatral no Brasil*. Rio de Janeiro: Avenir.

Millán, José Agustín

1851 *Biografía de don Francisco Covarrubias*. Havana: Imprenta del Faro.

Monaghan, John

1990 "Performance and the Structure of the Mixtec Codices." *Ancient Mesoamerica* I, 1:133–40.

Monleón, José

1978 *Teatro y revolución*. Caracas: Ateneo de Caracas.

Monsiváis, Carlos

1985 "Notas acerca de la cultura obrera." *Universidad* (Mexico City) 25–26:14–17.

1985a "De las relaciones entre 'alta cultura' y 'cultura popular'. *Texto Crítico* 11(33):46–61.

Monterde, Francisco

1955 Intro. to *Teatro indígena prehispánico (Rabinal Achí)*. Mexico City: Ediciones de la Universidad Nacional Autónoma.

Montes Huidobro, Matías

1988 "Lenguaje, dinero, pan y sexo en el bufo cubano." *Cuadernos Hispanoamericanos*, 451–52:241–53.

Moraña, Mabel

1984 *Literatura y cultura nacional en Hispanoamérica (1910–1940)*. Minneapolis: Institute for the Study of Ideologies and Literatures.

Morton, Carlos

1984 "The Nicaraguan Drama: Theatre of Testimony." *Latin American Theatre Review* 17(2):89–92.

Motolinía (Fray Toribio de Benavente)

1914 *Historia de los Indios*. Barcelona, Herederos de J. Gili.

Muñoz, Fernando

1987 *El teatro regional de Yucatán*. Mexico City: Grupo Editorial Gaceta.

Muñoz, Matilde

1946 *Historia de la zarzuela y el género chico*. Madrid: Tauro.

Nájera, Luz María

1971 "Entrevista con Alejandro Bichir, coordinador de Extensión Teatral del Departamento de Teatro del INBA." *La Cabra* (Mexico City) I, 17–18:2–6.

Nicholl, Allardyce

1931 *Mask, Mimes and Miracles*. New York: Harcourt, Brace.

Obregón, Osvaldo

1986 "Teatro e identidad cultural." Pp. 121–30 in *Identidad cultural de Iberoamérica en su literatura*, ed. by Saúl Yurkievich. Madrid: Editorial Alhambra.

1982 "El 'clásico universitario' chileno: Un caso singular de teatro de masas." *Revista Canadiense de Estudios Hispánicos* 7(1):67–80.

O'Donnell, Guillermo, Philippe C. Schmitter, and Lawrence Whitehead, eds.

1986 *Transitions from Authoritarian Rule*. Baltimore: Johns Hopkins University Press.

Ogunba, Oyin

1978 "Traditional African Festival Drama." Pp. 3–28 in *Theatre in Africa*, by Oyin Ogunba and Abiola Irele. Ibadan: Ibadan University Press.

Ogunba, Oyin, and Abiola Irele

1978 *Theatre in Africa*. Ibadan: Ibadan University Press.

Olavarría y Ferrari, Enrique

1961 *Reseña histórica del teatro en México*. Mexico City: Porrúa. 5 vols.

Ordaz, Luis

1979 *El teatro. Desde Caseros hasta el zarzuelismo criollo*. Buenos Aires: Centro Editor de América Latina.

Ortiz, Fernando

1921 *Los cabildos afrocubanos*. Havana, "La Universal".

1951 *Los bailes y el teatro de los negros en el folklore de Cuba*. Prólogo por Alfonso Reyes. Havana: Ministero de Educación, Dirección de Cultura.

Oyarzun, Kemy

1989 *Introduction* to "Cultural Production and the Struggle for Hegemony," special issue of *Latin American Perspectives*, 16(2):3–11. Newbury Park, California: Sage.

Pané, Fray Ramón

1974 *Relación de las antigüedades de los indios* [1498]. Ed. by Juan José Arrom. Mexico City: Siglo XXI.

Parker, Alexander A.

1935 "Notes on the Religious Drama in Medieval Spain and the Origins of the 'Auto Sacramental.'" *Modern Language Review* 30:170–82.

1939 "La introducción del gracioso en Lope de Vega." *Hispanic Review* VII, 1:1–21.

Pasquariello, Anthony

1951 *The Entremés, Sainete and Loa in the Colonial Theatre of Spanish America*. Ph. Dissertation, University of Michigan, Ann Arbor.

1970 "The Evolution of the *Loa* in Spanish America." *Latin American Theatre Review* 3(2):5–19.

Pazos, Manuel R.

1951 "El teatro franciscano en Méjico, durante el siglo XVI." *Archivo Ibero-Americano*, 42:129–89.

Pereira Salas, Eugenio

1974 *Historia del teatro en Chile: Desde sus orígenes hasta la muerte de Juan Casacubierta. 1849*. Santiago: Ediciones de la Universidad de Chile.

Petras, James

1991 "The Retreat of the Intellectuals." *Socialism and Democracy* 12:43–81.

Pianca, Marina

1989 "Postcolonial discourse in Latin American Theatre." *Theatre Journal* (Johns Hopkins University Press) 41(4):515–23.

1990 *El teatro de Nuestra América: Un proyecto continental (1959–1989)*. Minneapolis: Institute for the Study of Ideologies and Literatures.

1991 *Testimonios de teatro latinoamericano*. Buenos Aires: Grupo Editor Latinoamericano.

Piga, Domingo

1978 "El teatro popular: consideraciones históricas." Pp. 3–23 in *Popular Theatre for Social Change in Latin America*, ed. by Gerardo Luzuriaga. Los Angeles: UCLA Latin American Center.

Pignataro, Jorge

1967 *El teatro independiente uruguayo [1937–1967]*. Montevideo: Arca.

Pineda, Miguel Angel, and Leslie Zelaya, eds.

1986 "El teatro de revista en México (1870–1944)." Mexico City: CITRU (unpublished manuscript, 1986).

Pla, Josefina

1967 *El teatro en el Paraguay*. Asunción: Diálogo.

1990 *Cuatro siglos de teatro en el Paraguay: El teatro paraguayo desde sus orígenes hasta hoy (1544–1988)*. Asunción: Universidad Católica "Nuestra Señora de la Asunción," Departamento de Teatro. Vol. 1.

Pontes, Joel

1978 *Teatro de Anchieta*. Rio de Janeiro: Ministerio de Educaçao e Cultura/ FUNARTE.

Potter, Robert

1986 "Abraham and Human Sacrifice: The Exfoliation of Medieval Drama in Aztec Mexico." *New Theatre Quarterly* 2(8):306–12.

Prokosch Kurath, Gertrude

1952 "Dance Acculturation." Pp. 233–242 in *Heritage of Conquest: The Ethnology of Middle America*, edited by Sol Tax. Glencoe: Viking Seminar on Middle America.

1967 "Drama, Dance, and Music." Pp. 158–90 in vol. 6 of *Handbook of Middle American Indians*, ed. by Robert Wauchope. Austin: University of Texas Press.

Quackenbush, Louis H.

1971 "The Latin American *Auto*: Themes and Forms." Ph.D. Dissertation, University of Illinois.

Race and Class

1992 "The Curse of Columbus." Special issue of *Race and Class, A Journal for Black and Third World Liberation* 33:3.

Rama, Angel

1974 "El área cultural andina (hispanismo, mesticismo, indigenismo)." *Cuadernos Americanos* 33(197):136–73.

1974 "Sistema literario y sistema social en Hispanoamérica." Pp. 81–108 in *Literatura y praxis social en América Latina*, ed. by Fernando Alegría et al. Caracas: Monte Avila.

1984 *La ciudad letrada*. Hanover, N.H.: Ediciones del Norte.

Ramos Tinhorão, José

1966 *Musica popular—Um tema em debate*. Rio de Janeiro: Ediciones Saga.

Rappaport, Joanne

1991 *The Politics of Memory: Native Historical Interpretation in the Colombian Andes*. New York: Cambridge University Press.

Rela, Walter

1988 *El teatro jesuítico en Brasil, Paraguay, Argentina. Siglos XVI–XVIII*. Montevideo: Universidad Católica del Uruguay.

Reyes, Carlos José, and Maida Watson Espener, eds.

1978 *Materiales para una historia del teatro en Colombia*. Bogotá: Colcultura.

Ricard, Robert

1938 "Notes pour un inventaire des fêtes de "moros y cristianos" en Espagne." *Bulletin Hispanique* 40:311–12.

1958 "Otra contribución al estudio de las fiestas de 'moros y cristianos'." *Miscellanea Paul Rivet* (Mexico City) 2:871–76.

Rivera Achá, Alfredo

1988 "Popular Theatre in Bolivia" Unpublished manuscript, in author's possession.

Rizk, Beatriz

1987 *El nuevo teatro latinoamericano: Una lectura histórica*. Minneapolis: Prisma Institute.

1988 "La Revolución y el teatro en Nicaragua." *Diógenes* 4:159–68.

1989 "The Colombian New Theatre and Bertolt Brecht: A Dialectical Approach." *Theatre Research International* 14(2):131–41.

1991 *Buenaventura: La dramaturgia de la creación colectiva*. Mexico City: Escenología.

Robe, Stanley

1954 *Coloquios de Pastores from Jalisco, Mexico*. Berkeley and Los Angeles: University of California Folklore Studies no. 4.

Robinson, Gail, and Douglas Hill

1976 *Coyote, the Trickster: Legends of the North American Indians*. New York: Crane Russak.

Robreño, Eduardo

1961 *Historia del teatro popular urbano*. Havana: Oficina del Historiador de la Ciudad de la Habana (Cuadernos de Historia Habanera, 74).

1979 Introduction. *Teatro Alhambra*. Havana: Editorial Letras Cubanas.

1985 *Como lo pienso lo digo*. Havana: Ediciones Unión.

Robreño, Gustavo

1984 "Cuba a través de La Alhambra." *Bohemia* (Havana) 71:161–62.

Rodríguez, Ana María
1984 *Samba negra, espoliaçao branca*. São Paulo: Editora Hucitec.
Rojas Garcidueñas, José
1935 *El teatro de Nueva España en el Siglo XVI*. Mexico City: Imprenta de Luis Alvárez.
Rojas, Marta
1982 *El aula verde*. Havana: Ediciones Unión.
Rojo, Grínor
1972 *Los orígenes del teatro hispanoamericano contemporáneo*. Valparaiso: Ediciones Universitarias de Valparaiso.
1985 *Muerte y resurrección del teatro chileno, 1973–1983*. Madrid: Ediciones Michay.
Romano, James, ed.
1987 *Poética de la población marginal*. Minneapolis: Prisma Institute. 3 vols.
Rossi, Laura
1989 "¿Cómo pensar a las Madres de la Plaza de Mayo?" *Nuevo Texto Crítico* II, 4:145–53.
Rubio Zapata, Miguel
1988 "Diablos en Puno: De máscaras y danzantes peruanos." Pp. 33–35 in *Inventario del teatro ibero-americano*, vol. 1, ed. by Carlos Espinosa Domínguez. Madrid: Ministerio de Cultura, Centro de Documentación Teatral.
Sáenz, Faustino
1988 "Revalorización de nuestra Comedia Maestra." *Ventana* (Managua) 23 January:7.
Said, Edward
1979 *Orientalism*. New York: Vintage Books.
Sanday, Peggy Reeves.
1986 *Divine Hunger: Cannibalism as a Cultural System*. New York: Cambridge University Press.
Santa, Jairo
1990 "El teatro popular en Colombia. Un teatro comprometido." *Actuemos* (Bogotá) 7(2):4–10.
Schechner, Richard, and Mady Schumann
1976 *Ritual, Play and Performance*. New York: Seabury Press.
Schechter, Joel
1985 *Durov's Pig: Clowns, Politics and Theatre*. New York: Theatre Communications Group.
Schilling, Hildburg
1965 *Teatro profano en la Nueva España (fines del siglo XVI a mediados del XVIII)*. Mexico City: Imprenta Universitaria.

Schutzman, Mady

1990 "Activism, Therapy, or Nostalgia? Theatre of the Oppressed in New York City." *TDR* 34(4):162–76.

Seed, Patricia

1991 " 'Failing to Marvel': Atahualpa's Encounter with the Word." *Latin American Research Review* 26(1):7–32.

Seibel, Beatriz

1985 *Los artistas trashumantes*. Buenos Aires: Ediciones de la Pluma.

1985A *El teatro bárbaro del interior*. Buenos Aires: Ediciones de la Pluma.

1989 "Teatralidad popular en Argentina: Coexistencia de múltiples manifestaciones." *Latin American Theatre Review* 23(1):27–36.

Shelly, Kathleen, and Grínor Rojo

1982 "El teatro hispanoamericano colonial." Pp. 319–52 in vol. 1, *Epoca Colonial*, of *Historia de la literatura hispanoamericana*, ed. by Luis Iñigo Madrigal. Madrid: Ediciones Cátedra.

Shoemaker, William Hutchinson

1935 *The Multiple Stage in Spain during the Fifteenth and Sixteenth Centuries*. Princeton, N.J.: Princeton University Press (reissued by Greenwood Press, 1973).

Sten, María

1982 *Vida y muerte del teatro náhuatl*. Xalapa: Biblioteca de la Universidad Veracruzana.

Steward, Julian H.

1930 "The Ceremonial Buffoon of the American Indian." *Papers of the Michigan Academy of Science, Arts and Letters*, 14(4):187–207.

Suárez Radillo, Carlos Miguel

1981 *El teatro barroco hispanoamericano*. Madrid: Porrúa.

Subirá, José

1933 *La tonadilla escénica, sus obras y sus autores*. Barcelona: Labor.

Szanto, George

1971 "The Dramatic Process." *Bucknell Review*, 19(3):3–30.

1978 *Theatre as Propaganda*. Austin: University of Texas Press.

Taussig, Michael, and Richard Schechner

1990 "Boal in Britain, France, the U.S.A.: An Interview." *TDR* 34(3):50–65.

Termer, Franz

1957 Etnología y etnografía de Guatemala. Guatemala: Ministerio de Educación Pública.

Ticknor, George

1863 *History of Spanish Literature*. Boston: Ticknor and Fields.

Todorov, Tzvetan
1984 *The Conquest of America*. Trans. by Richard Howard. New York: Harper Colophon Books.
Torres Rioseco, Arturo
1945 *Ensayos sobre literatura latinoamericana*. Los Angeles: University of California Press.
Trenti-Rocamora, José Luis
1947 *El teatro en la América colonial*. Buenos Aires: Editorial Huarpes.
Turner, Victor
1969 *The Ritual Process: Structure and Anti-Structure*. Chicago: Aldine.
1980 "Social Dramas and Stories about Them." *Critical Inquiry* 7(1):141–68.
1985 *On the Edge of the Bush: Anthropology as Experience*. Tucson: University of Arizona Press.
1987 "Carnival, Ritual and Play in Rio de Janeiro." Pp. 76–90 in *Time Out of Time*, edited by Alessandro Falassi. Albuquerque: University of New Mexico Press.
United States Congress. Senate. Select Committee to Study Governmental Operations with Respect to Intelligence Activities. Frank Church, Committee Chairman.
1975 *Alleged Assassination Plots Involving Foreign Leaders: An Interim Report*. Washington: U.S. Government Printing Office.
Université de Provence
1991 *Le Théâtre Latino-Américain: Tradition et Innovation*. (Actes du colloque international réalisé à Aix-en-Provence du 7 au 9 décembre 1989). Aix-en-Provence: Publications de l'Université de Provence.
Valencia, Antonio
1962 *El género chico*. Madrid: Taurus.
Verger, Pierre
1945 *Fiestas y danzas en el Cuzco y en los Andes*. Buenos Aires, Editorial Sudamericana.
Versenyi, Adam
1988 "Searching for El Dorado: Performance and Ritual in Early Latin America." *New Theatre Quarterly* IV, 16:330–34.
1989 "Getting under the Aztec Skin: Evangelical Theatre in the New World." *New Theatre Quarterly* V, 9:217–26.
Vidal, Hernán
1985 *Socio-historia de la literatura colonial hispanoamericana: Tres lecturas orgánicas*. Minneapolis: Institute for the Study of Ideologies and Literatures.

Villegas, Juan
1988 *Ideología y discurso crítico sobre el teatro de España y América Latina*. Minneapolis: Prisma Institute.
Wachtel, Nathan
1973 *Sociedad e ideología*. Lima: Instituto de Estudios Peruanos.
1976 *Los vencidos*. Mexico City: Siglo XXI.
Watson Espener, Maida
1976 "Enrique Buenaventura's Theory of the Committed Theatre." *Latin American Theatre Review* 1976 9/(2):43–48.
Weber de Kurlat, Frida
1963 "Sobre el negro como tipo cómico en el teatro español del siglo XVI." *Romance Philology* 17(2):380–91.
Weiss, Judith A.
1989a "Teyocoyani and the Nicaraguan Theatre." *Latin American Theatre Review* 23(1):71–78.
1989b "Traditional Popular Culture and the Cuban 'Nuevo Teatro': Teatro Escambray and the Cabildo de Santiago." *Theatre Research International* 14(2):142–52.
Wiide, Maritza
1988 "Las Diabladas de Oruro." Pp. 30–32 in *Inventario del teatro iberoamericano*, vol. 1, ed. by Carlos Espinosa Domínguez. Madrid: Ministerio de Cultura, Centro de Documentación Teatral.
Williams, Raymond
1980 *Problems in Materialism and Culture*. London: Verso.
1988 "The Uses of Cultural Theory." *New Left Review* 158:19–31.
Withington, Robert
1930 "The Corpus Christi Plays as Drama." *Studies in Philology* 27:573–82.
Yúdice, George, Juan Flores, and Jean Franco, editors.
1992 *On Edge: The Crisis of Contemporary Latin American Culture*. Minnesota: University of Minnesota Press.
Zapata Olivella, Manuel
1978 "Comparsas y teatro callejero en los carnavales colombianos." Pp. 278–82 in *Materiales para una historia del teatro en Colombia*, ed. by Carlos José Reyes and Maida Watson Espener. Bogotá: Colcultura.

Index